ONE TASTE OF LOVE

Ryn's heat surrounded her and took away all the chill as he moved his mouth gently over her neck. He sucked, he licked, he moved strands of red windblown hair out of the way so he had before and beneath him a wide expanse of unobstructed skin.

Juliet did not stop shivering, but the tremble changed as he continued on and on. Ryn used his tongue, his lips, and even his teeth, in a gentle way. Physical sensations she had never imagined danced through her body. After a moment she no longer attempted to pull away or fight, but instead found herself leaning toward the mouth that tasted her . . .

P9-BVH-319

the Moon Witch

LINDA WINSTEAD JONES

BERKLEY SENSATION, NEW YORK

THE BERKLEY PUBLISHING GROUP
Published by the Penguin Group
Penguin Group (USA) Inc.
375 Hudson Street, New York, New York 10014, USA
Penguin Group (Canada), 10 Alcorn Avenue, Toronto, Ontario M4V 3B2, Canada
(a division of Pearson Penguin Canada Inc.)
Penguin Books Ltd., 80 Strand, London WC2R 0RL, England
Penguin Group Ireland, 25 St. Stephen's Green, Dublin 2, Ireland (a division of Penguin Books Ltd.)
Penguin Group (Australia), 250 Camberwell Road, Camberwell, Victoria 3124, Australia
(a division of Pearson Australia Group Pty. Ltd.)
Penguin Books India Pvt. Ltd., 11 Community Centre, Panchsheel Park, New Delhi—110 017, India
Penguin Group (NZ), Cnr. Airborne and Rosedale Roads, Albany, Auckland 1310, New Zealand
(a division of Pearson New Zealand Ltd.)
Penguin Books (South Africa) (Pty.) Ltd., 24 Sturdee Avenue, Rosebank, Johannesburg 2196,
South Africa

Penguin Books Ltd., Registered Offices: 80 Strand, London WC2R 0RL, England

This is a work of fiction. Names, characters, places, and incidents either are the product of the author's imagination or are used fictitiously, and any resemblance to actual persons, living or dead, business establishments, events, or locales is entirely coincidental.

THE MOON WITCH

A Berkley Sensation Book / published by arrangement with the author

PRINTING HISTORY
Berkley Sensation edition / May 2005

Copyright © 2005 by Linda Winstead Jones.
Cover art by Bruce Emmett.
Cover design by Lesley Worrell.
Interior text design by Stacy Irwin.

For information address: The Berkley Publishing Group,
a division of Penguin Group (USA) Inc.,
375 Hudson Street, New York, New York 10014.

ISBN: 0-425-20129-5

BERKLEY® SENSATION
Berkley Sensation Books are published by The Berkley Publishing Group,
a division of Penguin Group (USA) Inc.,
375 Hudson Street, New York, New York 10014.
BERKLEY SENSATION and the "B" design are trademarks belonging to Penguin Group (USA) Inc.

PRINTED IN THE UNITED STATES OF AMERICA

10 9 8 7 6 5 4 3 2 1

The Fyne Curse

For more than three hundred years, the Fyne witches lived under the cloud of the curse that robbed them of any chance at true love. The men they dared to love either died before the age of thirty, or else woke one morning to see something repulsive in the woman they had come to call their own. Death or desertion always followed love, for those descendants of the Fyne witch who'd rejected the affections of a powerful wizard. Still the line survived, as the women of the Fyne House either braved the curse or settled for a loveless match, in order that the bloodline might endure.

In the 366th Year of the Reign of the Beckyts, Sophie Fyne defied the curse, falling in love with the rebel soldier Kane Varden and giving him a daughter. She opposed not only the curse, but the command of Emperor Sebestyen, the ruler of Columbyana who wished to use Sophie for revenge. In facing the emperor, she brought his most feared prophesy down upon him.

Seventeen years earlier, the wizard Thayne foretold that the touch of the sun on Sebestyen's face would signal the end of his rule and his life. With her newly found powers, Sophie called the sun into the Imperial Palace.

In the autumn of the 366th Year of the Reign of the Beckyts, Sophie and her rebel married. She carried their second child within her—a daughter who magnified her powers a hundredfold—as they escaped from the Imperial Palace and joined the rebel army intent on displacing Sebestyen from the throne.

And Kane turned twenty-nine.

On Fyne Mountain the other Fyne witches, Juliet and Isadora, await news of their sister, unaware that Sebestyen has decided to harness their power for himself.

I

Fyne Mountain

JULIET SQUIRMED IN HER BED, AWAKE LONG PAST THE hour when she normally fell asleep. The back of her neck prickled. She reached beneath her loose braid and rubbed vigorously, but still the sensation did not entirely subside. Something was wrong; she just couldn't determine exactly what that something was.

For the past three days she'd been unusually restless, pacing when she should be sitting, and snapping at Isadora over the smallest disagreements. That just wasn't like her. For the past three nights when she'd gone to bed, she'd tossed and turned for a long while, unable to get comfortable. When sleep did come, it was filled with vivid and odd dreams she could not decipher. In some of the dreams there was heat and blood. Her heart pounded hard and fast, and a sea of faces swarmed too closely around her. She could never tell when or where she was, and when she woke, she remembered none of the faces.

In addition to the dreams that made no sense, she'd been having an old nightmare for the past two weeks. It had been months since she'd had that dream from which she always woke in a cold sweat, the nightmare that had made her swear years ago that she would never lie with a man.

Her psychic ability was all but useless where her own life was concerned. Juliet could see the past and the future of a complete stranger, but she never knew what tomorrow would bring for her. She hadn't even been able to find her favorite hairclip when it had come up missing. Still, she knew in her heart that the nightmare was more than a fear. It was a premonition. And for the past fourteen nights she had suffered with that nightmare every night.

The dream always started pleasantly enough. The sensation of being taken into a man's embrace was nice. That closeness warmed her to the depths of her soul and caused her insides to do strange things. At the pit of her being she burned and fluttered, and in the shelter of the surprisingly strong arms she realized that there was something wonderful waiting for her and the man who held her.

But that realization of something good to come soon changed, and pain came without warning. It came with agony and blood. The arms that had held her so tenderly changed, a man held her down so that she could not move, and claws tore her flesh. She always saw the claws and knew what was coming, but she couldn't scream, not even as they ripped into her body.

Lying in bed, afraid of the nightmare that might or might not come again tonight, Juliet turned her thoughts to another subject of concern: her younger sister. Her ability to see what would come for her sisters was often no more clear than the window into her own life, but she knew in her heart that Sophie was safe. She didn't know where Sophie and her daughter Ariana slept on this night, but she knew without doubt that no danger threatened them at the moment.

The premonition that Sophie would never see this cabin again remained strong. Perhaps the youngest Fyne sister had still not forgiven her elder sisters for interfering where they should not, and perhaps she never would. But she was not in danger. No, Sophie was not the reason for this wave of anxiety that disturbed the night.

Juliet threw back the covers, lit the candle at her bedside, and walked to the window. On this cloudless night a softly shining half moon added a touch of light to the land surrounding her mountainside home. She lifted the lace curtain to peer outside. Her fingers brushed against the icy glass, and her toes quickly grew cold. Months had passed since Sophie's departure. It had been warm when Sophie and her rebel had ridden away in search of their daughter. Now the leaves on the trees beyond the barn had turned to vibrant reds and golds, with a few bright blue leaves mixed amongst them. Some of those leaves had died and fallen to the ground. When the sun shone down, the days were comfortable enough, with just a touch of a chill in the air. But the nights were cold as winter approached, time passing normally even though Juliet was certain nothing would ever be normal again.

Again her neck prickled, and she reached around to once again rub at the odd warning sign. It was downright frustrating to have a gift that could be used to help others, but was all but useless where her own life was concerned. Not that she wanted to know every detail of what the future held for her, of course, but still . . . when she had strange dreams she could not remember well, and that unsettling nightmare plagued her, and this odd sensation at the back of her neck disturbed her sleep, she did wish she could see a glimpse.

Of course, it was possible such a glimpse would not soothe her at all, but would only make matters worse.

Juliet's head snapped around sharply, drawn to the autumn trees. It was too dark in the mountain forest for her to see anything at all, and yet she was almost certain that something out there moved. Something that did not belong. A man.

Juliet let the curtain drop and flutter into place, then turned and ran on bare feet to the hallway. "Isadora!" she shouted. Outside the cabin she heard the rustle of boots in the dirt and the whisper of male voices that seemed to assault her from all sides. The footsteps and the whispers sounded in her head, not her ears, and yet they were real. Very, very real.

Isadora, rumpled with sleep and wearing a plain white nightgown, stumbled into the hallway still more asleep than awake. "What's wrong?" she asked, a touch of annoyance in her voice. She likely suspected that a startling vision of some sort, or perhaps a frightening dream, had disturbed her gentler sister.

"Men," Juliet said. "They're coming."

Isadora came instantly awake.

Juliet halted while she was still several feet away from her sister, her heart heavy with the knowledge that her understanding of the warning had come too late. "They're here."

The front door splintered open with a resounding crack, windows throughout the house shattered, and men dressed in green invaded the Fyne home in a thundering loud swarm. They shouted threatening words and screamed ear-splitting war cries, and carried torches that lit their way and swords that gleamed in the firelight.

There were so many of them. Five, ten . . . twenty. And they were dressed the same, with only a few minor variations here and there. Emerald green trousers and tunics, some plain, some with the markings of their rank or awards for services rendered to the emperor. Soldiers. The men who burst into the Fyne cabin through the front door and the windows surrounded the sisters almost instantly after breaking into the cabin.

Isadora spun and reached for the nearest soldier, surprising the man who wielded his sword in a threatening manner and gripped a dagger with a slim blade as if he were ready to make use of it. The eldest Fyne sister stretched forward sharply, her hand graceful but quick, and laid two fingers over the man's heart.

"Ishna foreg. Ackla foresh," Isadora whispered in a gruff voice, the deadly spell spoken in the ancient tongue of the wizards that Lucinda Fyne had taught her daughters. The soldier's reaction was immediate. He dropped his weapons, his eyes rolled up in his head, and he sank to the floor. Dead.

Isadora wasted no time in snatching up the man's sword. She swung it wildly, and those soldiers closest to her stepped quickly back. "Get out," she said, "before I stop the heart of every man in this room the way I stopped this pig's small heart."

For a moment all was still in the hallway and beyond. The soldiers were afraid of Isadora, and with good reason.

Behind her, Juliet heard the steady clip of boot heels on the floor. Soldiers stepped aside as the new arrival made his way to the hallway, but she did not turn to look. Her eyes were riveted to Isadora and the soldiers around her. Someone whispered to the man who continued to move forward, ordering him to stop before the dark witch killed every man in the room with a word.

But he did not stop. Juliet turned her head in time to see the burly man brush past the soldiers at the end of the hallway. His head was turned, the features lost in deep shadows away from the firelight cast by blazing torches.

"If the dark witch could kill us all with a word, why aren't we dead yet?" he asked.

"I don't care to deal with the cleaning that would come after," Isadora answered sharply. "Take your man, be grateful there is only one dead, and go."

The man stopped directly behind Juliet. When she made a move to join Isadora, he grabbed her upper arm and held on tight. Memories of the night Ariana had been kidnapped flashed through Juliet's mind, so clearly it was almost as if that night were happening again now.

"I don't believe it." He drew a knife from the scabbard at his waist as he pulled Juliet up against his large, solid body. One swift move and the tip of the knife touched her throat. She could not so much as breathe without feeling the sharpness of the blade.

"Drop the sword, or I kill her."

"You'll kill us anyway," Isadora argued. She tightened her grip on the sword's hilt, even though a momentary flash of fear in her eyes gave away her uncertainty. "I plan to take a few of you with me."

The man who held Juliet glanced down at the dead soldier. "We're not here to kill you, though as always I will do what I must."

For years Isadora's protective spell had kept men like this away from the mountain. There had been no violence here, not until the night Ariana had been kidnapped. Juliet shuddered. That tingling began at the back of her neck again. This time it ran down her spine. That gruff voice. The rough hands. She turned her head slightly, feeling the increased pressure of the blade, and looked into the face of the man who held her.

It was him—the man who had kidnapped her infant niece.

"You!"

The large, decidedly ugly man smiled. "The name's Bors, and yes, I have been here before, as I'm sure you remember. How's your head, Red?"

On his last visit to this cabin he had rendered her unconscious with a blow to the head. She never would've allowed him to take Ariana otherwise.

"Do you plan to kidnap us, too?"

"Yes. The Emperor Sebestyen requests the pleasure of your company."

In a rage Isadora stepped forward, her sword pointed directly at the man who held Juliet. The rash move was a costly one. While her attention was on Bors, a soldier to the rear moved bravely forward and raised his sword. Juliet cried out but it was too late. The young soldier lifted the sword high, brought it down swiftly, and slammed the heavy hilt into Isadora's head. She crumpled to the floor beside the man she'd killed.

The soldiers who had been frightened of Isadora moments earlier were not at all afraid of the unconscious woman on the floor. Isadora didn't look particularly frightening in her nightgown, with a dark braid falling down her back and her hands limp. One of the soldiers, a friend of the fallen man perhaps, moved forward and shifted his sword so that the sharp tip touched the back of Isadora's neck. His intention was to kill, unlike the soldier who had hit Isadora on the head to stop her.

Bors growled and then barked. "The witch is to be delivered to the emperor alive, as ordered."

"She has murdered an emperor's man," the soldier argued. After a moment, he grudgingly shifted the threatening blade to one side.

Again all was still for a moment, and then a soldier who had been standing well behind Isadora stepped forward. "There are other ways to make the women pay." His observation was met with titters of laughter and a few nodding heads. The man who had spoken winked at Juliet and grabbed his crotch in a vile manner.

"I suppose you can do with them as you wish," Bors said casually.

A chill ran up and down Juliet's spine. Was this why the nightmare had returned? Had it been yet another warning deciphered too late? She had always feared joining with a man, thanks to the dream, and had shunned all thoughts of marriage for that reason. Her sisters thought her refusal to marry was her answer to the curse which promised that the women of the Fyne House would never know a true and lasting love. She had heard of too many Fyne women burying the men they loved before their time, and she had seen Isadora suffer, thanks to the curse. Isadora had buried her beloved husband before his thirtieth birthday, as many of their ancestors before them had done.

In truth there was much more to Juliet's decision to remain chaste.

Pain, and blood, and the inability to move . . .

Some of the men were smiling, but not all were amused or pleased by the crude soldier's suggestion. Perhaps the soldiers who had invaded the cabin weren't all evil. Juliet sensed that some were doing what they considered to be their duty by serving the emperor, while only a few truly enjoyed hurting people.

Juliet attempted to pull forward as the young soldier who had suggested making the women pay made a move toward Isadora, who still lay unconscious on the floor.

"However . . ." Bors began. Again, he commanded the soldiers' full attention as he yanked Juliet back into place. "I wouldn't touch that one." He nodded toward Isadora. "She killed Hynd with a few words, and from what I hear of her, it might not be wise to touch her. The villagers at the foot of the mountain are all afraid of that one."

The soldier gave Bors's words serious consideration. "What about the redhead? She hasn't hurt anyone. She seems right meek, in fact. I don't think she'd put up much of a fight. Not for long, in any case."

Bors shrugged, as if he didn't care.

Juliet lifted her chin and gathered every ounce of strength she had locked inside her. "I assume the emperor asked for us because he has some use for the powers we possess."

"I assume," Bors answered. "He does not confide in me, you understand. I was hired for this job because I've been here before and this cabin is unusually hard to find."

"I doubt the emperor would send you so far to fetch two women who could not help him in some way. The journey from Arthes to Fyne Mountain is a long and not entirely easy one."

"True enough."

Juliet didn't lie. Normally. But the idea of these men touching her caused a fear well beyond any she had ever known. "If a man abuses me, I will lose my gift of sight." It was a common notion that seers had to remain virginal, and the notion might even be true in some cases. It might even be true in her own case, but she did not think so. Her grandmother, the first Ariana Fyne, had had the gift of sight herself, and her psychic ability had survived not only years of an unhappy but true marriage with a man she had never loved, but the birth of Lucinda Fyne, her only daughter.

With the touch of a hand and a bit of concentration, Juliet could see into a person's mind, into their future, into their past. Even now, with all that was happening around her, she could see into the mind of her captor. Bors was a greedy man, but did not see himself as such. He thought himself ambitious, clever, and powerful. His death would be ugly and painful and it would come soon, but it would not come today. He loved his wife and his children, in his own selfish way, but did not treat them well. He thought love a weakness, and so he denied it.

He had been kind to Ariana on the long trip to Arthes, protecting the baby from the carelessness of Galvin Farrell, but his kindness had been motivated by greed. He'd realized that a dead child would be worth nothing.

In a sharp flash that momentarily wiped away the night's reality, Juliet knew that Galvin Farrell, the man who had orchestrated Ariana's kidnapping in a failed attempt to force Sophie to become his wife, was dead.

At times the psychic events Juliet had experienced all her life were gentle, but often they were so intense they almost blinded her. She could control the ability to an extent by the lifting of her hand away from the subject of the premonition, or by forcing her mind elsewhere. If she did not touch, she often could not feel. There were times when breaking the connection was not enough to end the event. Often the images and sensations continued for a while.

If such a gentle touch triggered visions and premonitions that caused her head to pound and wiped out all reality, what would happen if a man were actually inside her? If she were literally joined with a man, would she be bombarded with images and sensations? In her nightmare the pain was so great it literally blinded her. The pain she experienced in the dream was not the simple discomfort of a virgin's first encounter, but a shattering agony that threatened to tear her in two. What if the pain didn't stop? Ever?

Isadora groaned and lifted her head.

"Bind her," Bors said quickly, nodding to the soldiers nearest Isadora. They hesitated, but not for long. "Tightly," he instructed.

The soldiers hauled Isadora to her feet and quickly tied her hands with a rough length of rope. She did not look fearsome, in her white nightgown and bare feet and that girlish braid. But her eyes were dark and dangerous. There was hate in those eyes. Pure, hot, hate.

She was going to fight, and if she did, she would die here.

Juliet locked her eyes to her sister's. "Don't," she whispered. "It's time."

Isadora had never accepted the fact that some things in life were inescapable. "Time for what?"

"It's time for us to leave this place."

The eldest Fyne sister did not embrace such truths easily. She never had.

"If you fight, we will die," Juliet said quickly. "And Sophie still needs us."

The mention of her youngest sister's name made Isadora go still.

Bors shifted his knife away from Juliet's throat. The small cut stung and Juliet suspected there was a spot of blood there.

"You will, of course, allow us to dress appropriately and pack a small bag of our belongings." There were things she wanted to take with her when she left this place. She could smell the smoke, as if the fire that was to come had already been lit. Best not to tell Isadora just yet that the soldiers planned to burn the cabin and everything in it.

"You have five minutes." Bors gave Juliet a little shove that sent her toward her sister. "Only because you talked some sense into your sister and saved me from explaining to the emperor how two women took out a number of his soldiers." He glanced at the man on the hallway floor. "One I can justify. More might cost me my head."

"Untie her hands," Juliet said, nodding to her sister.

Bors narrowed one eye. "I doubt that's wise."

"I cannot dress her and myself in five minutes if her hands are bound behind her back, and if she travels in her nightshift, she'll freeze. You did say the emperor would prefer to have us alive, did you not?"

Bors nodded his head, and a wary soldier released Isadora's hands.

Juliet did not waste time, but grabbed Isadora's arm and dragged her into the closest bedroom. Cold air rushed through the broken window of Isadora's bedchamber, making the plain curtains there dance gently. Juliet tried to close the bedroom door, but a soldier caught it and shook his head slowly. They would not remain unguarded.

Isadora spoke in the language their mother had taught them, a precious and sacred language the soldiers would not understand.

"I can kill them."

"Not tonight." Juliet threw open Isadora's wardrobe and grabbed a black dress made of a soft, warm fabric. She tossed the frock to her sister, grabbed a pair of boots, and headed for the door. *"Come."*

They brushed past the soldier in the doorway, who took great care not to touch Isadora, and past the other young men who had gathered in the hall. Each and every one stepped out of the way, eyeing Isadora with a mixture of hate and suspicion. She had killed one of their own with a touch and a few words they did not understand, and the idea of escorting her to the palace untouched and unpunished didn't sit well with them.

But they did not wish to risk touching her themselves.

The sisters ran into the room where Juliet had, just minutes earlier, been trying desperately to get to sleep. The window where she'd stood and looked out on the cold landscape was broken. Cold air rushed in, and the lace curtains fluttered. She went directly to the wardrobe and threw open the doors.

Warmth was her first priority, comfort the second. She laid her hands on a dark green gown with a full skirt and slightly puffed long sleeves and pulled it from the wardrobe. Everything else would be left behind.

They pulled the frocks on over their nightshifts, since the soldier who had been ordered to guard them once again stood in the doorway and watched insolently. Sitting on the side of the unmade bed, they pulled on thick socks and their boots. Isadora's tall boots were black, as was almost everything she'd worn since her husband's death, and Juliet's were a warm brown. As with the dresses, the footwear had been chosen with comfort and warmth in mind. They did not don their best and prettiest shoes, but instead chose sturdy walking boots.

The minutes ticked past, and Juliet didn't expect Bors was the type of man to give them more time if they needed it. What does one take when leaving home for the last time? There were so many things she had expected to have around her forever. Dresses and shoes and furnishings could be replaced, in time. But what about Mother's good dishes, the silver, those few pieces of nice jewelry, the painting over the mantel in the parlor . . . her herbs.

Gown on and half fastened, boots on but untied, Juliet collected her small valise and then grabbed Isadora's hand once again and raced for the kitchen. Again, the soldiers gave them a wide berth. It would be tempting simply to run, but more than one soldier rested a ready hand over a sword or a dagger, and they were all more than willing to make use of those weapons if given the opportunity.

"What are you doing?" Isadora asked. She sat at a kitchen chair and tied her boot strings while Juliet ran to the shelf of herbs and scraped everything she could into her valise. "Do you expect to need all those medications on the trip? Surely you're not going to doctor the *paivanti* soldiers."

"Don't curse," Juliet said almost absently. She wasn't yet ready to tell her sister that the soldiers planned to burn their home. Heaven above, she could already smell the smoke, the acrid burning of their furniture and clothes and even the soldier's body that would be left in the hallway. "You never know what we might need."

"Warm cloaks, I imagine," Bors said as he walked into the kitchen, brushing past the guard who remained close to Isadora—but not too close. "The nights will only grow colder as we travel to Arthes."

Isadora stood sharply. The guard and Bors both took a step back as she said, "I'll collect our cloaks."

Juliet stared at her sister. "Promise me you won't do anything rash."

Isadora hesitated. She wanted to fight. She would prefer to die fighting than to go peacefully with the soldiers. It was only the threat to her sister and the knowledge that Sophie still needed them that kept her in control. "Fine," she snapped. "I promise."

Perhaps half a minute after Isadora left the room, Bors said, "Time's up."

Juliet closed her valise and snapped it shut. Soldiers began to pour toward the front door. Light from their torches flickered wildly on walls Juliet knew she would never see again; a cold breeze wafted through the broken kitchen window. Isadora, closely guarded but untouched, emerged from the hallway with her own black cloak and Juliet's good gray cape draped over her arm.

"Time to go," Juliet said as she took the cape from Isadora. When her sister realized what the soldiers planned, she was sure to fight. And die.

The sisters donned their cloaks and stepped into the night, surrounded on all sides by soldiers. Juliet held the valise in her left hand, and she fisted her right hand tightly. Isadora stayed close by her side as they walked away from the cabin. Men bearing torches remained behind. She didn't have much time.

Juliet stopped. Isadora stopped, too, and turned to face her sister.

"I'm sorry," Juliet whispered.

"Sorry for—"

Isadora didn't have the chance to finish her sentence. Juliet lifted her right hand and tossed the fine powder into Isadora's face. The effect was immediate. Isadora was silently outraged for a spilt second, and then she collapsed. Juliet did her best to break her sister's fall, catching the unconscious woman and easing her to the ground.

The first torch was thrown onto the roof of the Fyne cabin. And then another. A cretin of a soldier tossed his blazing torch through the parlor window, and watched with a smile on his face as the flames caught and spread.

"What did you do to her?" Bors asked indifferently as he nodded to an unconscious Isadora.

"I saved her life," Juliet whispered.

Bors was greedy and without scruples, but he was not stupid. He understood what had happened. Juliet wondered if her sister ever would.

After a moment of silence Bors said, in a matter-of-fact voice that was as chilling as the wind, "Use that powder or anything like it on my soldiers, and I'll gladly give them permission to do with you as they wish before they kill you."

The Imperial Palace in Arthes

Liane held her breath, unable to believe that this moment was real. With afternoon light streaming through the recently repaired sunroof above, she and Emperor Sebestyen stood side by side in the grand ballroom. The gathering was small but impressive. Ministers and priests had gathered for the celebration.

A few more words remained to be spoken, and when that was done, Sebestyen would be her husband. Liane would be empress. The child she carried—if it was indeed a boy as the witch Gadhra had seen in her dreams—would be emperor one day. The circumstances had changed dramatically for a woman who just a few months ago had been the emperor's favorite concubine and his most trusted assassin.

With Sebestyen by her side, Liane stood before Father Merryl, the highest-ranking priest in Columbyana. For the occasion she wore not a sheer harlot's frock or a plain crimson robe, but a finely crafted luxurious gown in that regal crimson. A gown befitting a lady. A gown studded with jewels and adorned with golden lace. It was generously cut across the midsection, since her belly had already started to swell. She loved that gentle swell of her stomach, and often found herself simply sitting with her hands resting there as she contemplated her own changing body.

Sebestyen was a handsome groom, more handsome than she had imagined he could be. His dark hair was pulled back in a neat queue, and the crimson robe he wore was his finest. The trim around his collar matched the gold lace on her gown, but was much more masculine. For the special occasion he wore his own crown, a simple gold circlet set with a few flawless scarlet stones. She sometimes thought his features too sharp, but today he looked regal and handsome. He looked like an emperor. Her emperor.

His face was not so pale as it had once been. He had seen the sun of late, since the witch Sophie had brought the old prediction true and there was no more need to hide from the sunshine. What was done, was done.

But in spite of the prophesy of doom, no disaster had followed the touch of the sun on the emperor's face. Sebestyen had seen the sun, and now weeks—months—later, there had been no sign of his downfall. Quite the opposite. With a child on the way and a new bride, his life had never been brighter.

While it was a beautiful day and Liane's circumstances

had taken such a wonderful turn, she was well aware that her life was not yet perfect. Sebestyen had not again said that he loved her. His confession that day had been brought about by Sophie's spell, just as the miracle of their child had been made possible by the witch. But still, she believed his vow had been true. He did love her. It was just difficult for a man like Sebestyen to say the words.

Since he'd learned of the child and insisted that Liane become empress, he had not touched her, not in the way she had come to expect and need. He had been busy with other matters, she reasoned. Columbyana was in an uproar, thanks to the small band of rebels which had been a thorn in Sebestyen's side for nearly seven years.

Liane's own brother Kane was one of those thorns. She'd never told Sebestyen that the man who'd taken Sophie out of the palace while Level One had been in an uproar thanks to her spell was her own younger brother. She had made her choice, and in doing so she had to put her old family, what was left of it, out of her mind and out of her heart. She had made her choice on that day when she'd refused to leave with her brother and his woman. It had been the right choice, for her. She had not known at that moment how right it would be.

The priests openly hated Liane for surpassing her station. They were all gathered here today, of course, twenty or so of them in their crimson robes huddled together with their heads bowed, as if they prayed for Liane to be struck dead before she could further corrupt the emperor. In some of their sour faces—Father Merryl's and the younger Father Breccian's, in particular—she saw the potential for real danger. Father Nelyk looked almost amused by the ceremony, as if he knew something the others did not. Liane did her best to ignore them all. Even though the priests were powerful and she had sensed and felt that hate as if it were a tangible thing, she knew she was safe. She carried the next emperor in her body. They would not dare to harm her.

When the time came, Father Merryl commanded that Liane kneel. She did so gracefully. He placed a small golden crown much like Sebestyen's upon her head. It was not at all heavy; not much heavier than the thin gold ring she wore on the middle finger of her left hand.

Sebestyen took her hand with his cool fingers and she rose to her feet, and the ceremony was done. Immediately he released his hold on her.

She was empress. Empress Liane. She would give Sebestyen the child and heir he had never thought to have, and he would lay the world at her feet. And even if he never again said the words, he *did* love her.

When the ceremony was done, she reached for Sebestyen. He had held her hand so briefly as he'd helped her to her feet, and she wanted more. She wanted to intertwine her fingers through her husband's and hold on tight.

She wanted so very much to lace her fingers and his together, but he subtly stepped aside so their hands did not touch.

Two sentinels, men she recognized and knew well from her years in this palace, flanked her. Ferghus was quiet and tall, and wore his fair hair short. He did occasionally flash a friendly smile, but not today. Tatsl never smiled, that Liane was aware of. He was darker, shorter, older, and wearier than Ferghus, and as was the preferred fashion in the palace, he wore his dark hair long.

Sebestyen walked away, leaving her in the company of the sentinels.

"Wait," she called.

Sebestyen turned. There was a trace of amusement in his blue eyes, and also a trace of impatience. "Yes?"

"I thought perhaps I could accompany you to your quarters this afternoon."

"I have meetings planned for the entire day."

She had seen him this way before, with his previous wives. They had been a duty to him, a requirement. Not a love. Not a joy, as she would be. "It is your wedding day, my lord. Surely . . ."

His blue eyes went hard, and all trace of amusement fled; his jaw tightened. "The rebel forces in the north are growing stronger and larger. They have taken the Northern Palace, in case you have not heard. A band of Tryfyn scum murdered my new Minister of Finance, and my Minister of Defense has apparently gone missing. A band of soldiers assigned the simple task of fetching two women from the Southern Province has been gone far too long." His nostrils flared and his mouth thinned. "I have concerns to attend to, and they will not wait simply because this is my wedding day."

"Of course," Liane said meekly. "I was not thinking, my lord."

"Apparently not," he said under his breath as he turned away.

"Fine." Liane gathered her skirts in her hands and walked toward the door and her quarters on Level Three. But when she and her escort reached the lift, Ferghus pushed the lever that would take them to Level Five. Arguing would be a waste of time. She was empress now, and Level Five would be her home.

On Level Five she exited the lift and walked down the wide hallway toward the empress's quarters, her head high and her stride stately. The rooms that would be her new home would be finer than those she had called her own for so long, she knew. Larger and more finely furnished, with servants available at a call. Lavish meals would be brought to her; singers and poets would entertain her. An artist would paint her image, and if she was not pleased with the result, he would torch the portrait and start again.

She would have maids to cater to her needs and pretend to be her friends, and materials for embroidery and painting and whatever other mindless hobby she might enjoy at her fingertips.

If she craved anything, anything at all, all she had to do was ask and it would be delivered to her.

With one exception, of course. Sebestyen was not to be called. No one dared to summon the emperor. He would send for her when and if he desired. He would request her presence or he would ignore her until she delivered him a child.

Tatsl threw open the doors to her chambers. The sitting room had been filled with bouquets and garlands of flowers not easy to come upon at this time of year. The gesture gave her a moment's hope that perhaps Sebestyen did care more deeply than he had allowed her to see this afternoon.

The room was very pink, with plush furniture and thick rugs and all those blossoms. A tray of sweets had been placed on a small table beside the chair that sat nearest the fireplace, where a small, cozy fire burned.

This suite was larger than the cabin where she'd lived as a child with four brothers, a mother, and a father. The sitting room beyond the foyer was vast and elegantly furnished. Down a short hallway her bedchamber, a smaller servant's room, and a lavatory awaited. Another hallway led to a private dining hall, where she would eat her meals in elegance. Alone. It was a very lovely prison.

"Congratulations, my lady." A maid dressed in a simple brown frock stepped from the bedroom, her smile wide and welcoming. "My name is Mahri, and I am at your service."

Liane took a step into the room, and the doors were closed behind her. Ferghus and Tatsl remained in the hallway, where they would no doubt stay until their replacements came on duty.

"Thank you, Mahri," Liane said softly as she glanced

around the room. She approached a large bouquet and picked one pink bloom. Sebestyen was distracted by matters of state, and yet he had taken the time to see that her new rooms were filled with these rare flowers. She lifted the blossom to her nose and inhaled deeply.

Her husband did tend to be moody. She knew that better than anyone. But he loved her. The flowers he had arranged for her proved that he cared more deeply than he was willing to show. When they were alone once again, then he'd be free to reveal his true feelings.

"I do hope the flowers are to your liking, my lady," Mahri said eagerly. "I saw to them myself, as a way of welcoming you to your new home."

"You saw to the flowers," Liane repeated.

"Yes, my lady." Mahri's voice was decidedly less enthusiastic when she asked, "Are they not to your liking? I can have them taken away."

"No, they're lovely." Liane's voice did not reveal her disappointment, but her stomach flipped and her heart sank. She should've realized and accepted the truth from the moment Sebestyen had told her she would be empress.

Sebestyen had done nothing on her behalf. He'd changed the laws that would have kept her from being empress so his child would be legitimate. The wedding, the marriage, it had nothing to do with her. It was all for the child, and she had been a fool to let that obvious fact slip by her in the name of love.

It had been a lovely day, bright and full of promise, but at the moment Liane was filled with the certainty that she did not belong here. She was Sebestyen's lover, his soldier, his *slave*. Not his wife. She was not meant to be anyone's *wife*.

What had she done?

2

THEY'D BEEN TRAVELING MORE THAN A WEEK, THOUGH Juliet had lost count of the exact number of days. Eight? Nine, perhaps? Whatever the number, the days had seemed endless. Bors led the imperial soldiers unerringly forward, stopping only when necessary. He was more considerate of the needs of the horses than of the men or women in his charge. If not for the animals, Juliet imagined he would have insisted on traveling without stopping at all.

Juliet and Isadora each had their own mount, and the horses were led by soldiers who held the reins and kept a close and wary eye on their charges. The duty of leading the witches was rotated often, and three or four times a day the faces closest to the Fyne women changed. Juliet imagined Bors would have made them walk, if not for the fact that it would delay his arrival in the capital city. They might have each shared a horse with a soldier, but that would put a strain on the mounts. In any case, none of the soldiers wanted to touch the sister they called the dark witch.

Isadora had remained silent throughout. She had never been the forgiving sort, but Juliet had expected her to release some of her anger a few days into the trip. Surely Isadora realized logically that Juliet had saved her life—perhaps both their lives—by rendering her unconscious. The sight of their home burning would have enraged Isadora, and she would have fought. If she had fought, she would have died, no matter what the emperor's wishes might be.

The sight of the cabin burning had not enraged Juliet. Instead it had filled her with an incredibly deep sadness that had dropped her to her knees. Home was gone. Memories were now only memories. The smoke from the fire had touched her as she watched, and in that smoke she saw and felt so many truths she had not known. Her mother had loved deeply, once. She'd loved and walked away, afraid of the curse that had ruined so many lives. Isadora had cried on more nights than she'd allowed her sisters to know, after her husband's passing. Sophie had wandered into her sisters' rooms on many a cold night, to see that they were properly covered against the chill. Pain and joy and laughter and tears were in that smoke, and Juliet knew she would never forget the moments she'd spent on her knees, soaking it all in before Bors had snatched her to her feet and dragged her away.

Isadora did not understand, and she did not forgive. Instead she remained stony-faced and refused to respond to Juliet's attempts at conversation and comfort. She was so angry and defiant and alone, but she had not attempted to fight the soldiers or cast a spell that might cause mischief. It was not easy for Isadora to use her magic without the direction of her hands, but there were some simple spells that would work with words alone. Had she given up? Juliet hoped that was so. In the confines of the Emperor's Palace in Arthes there would surely be a time when they were alone, or at least not so horribly outnumbered. At that time they could choose to fight, if it was right that they should do so.

Juliet still could not see their arrival at the palace and what would follow, and she cursed her ability that failed her now when she needed it most. She normally needed touch in order to harness the full power of her abilities, and of late no one had cared to touch her. The last person to lay a hand on her was her captor. She knew that with every breath Bors took, he moved closer to his death, but she could not see how or when he would die.

As for Isadora and herself . . . she saw nothing.

They rode slowly but steadily along the road to Arthes, even though it was well past dark, and even the soldiers were yawning and whispering complaints about the pace of this return journey. Tonight as the sun had set, the full moon had risen into the sky. Shining brightly now, it allowed them to see the road clearly enough to travel well past sundown. They would likely continue this pace for the next three nights, when the moon was at its brightest and fullest.

From the grumblings she'd heard, the soldiers had had trouble finding the mountain cabin of the Fyne witches, even though Bors had been there before. Isadora's spell, meant to keep all conflict and men away from Fyne Mountain, had protected the sisters and their home for a little while. If only Juliet had done her part and seen what was coming before it was too late, they might've escaped. They could've hidden in the hills for a long time. Perhaps forever.

But she had not seen, and to her mind that signified she had not been meant to see. She and Isadora were fated for this journey. They were meant to be here, in this place at this time. She just didn't know why.

Juliet's eyes were suddenly drawn to the darkness of the forest that lined the road to the north. There was movement there that the soldiers did not see or hear, the movement of a watcher hidden in the depths of the woodland. She knew that someone watched, as surely as she had known that the emperor's men would burn the cabin she'd called home all her days.

She should be afraid, to know that a stranger watched so intently, but she was not at all frightened. Instead a deep sense of calm settled over her, as if a mantle of warmth penetrated her cloak and her gown and seeped into her skin. There was little left to fear. Home had been taken from her. Sophie had been taken from her. Even Isadora, who rode close beside her, had been taken. Juliet Fyne was a woman who had little left to lose.

She was not afraid, but her curiosity was definitely roused. What manner of man would be here in the middle of night, so far from any semblance of civilization? They were days from the last village; days still, she had heard, from the next town to the west. Between here and there were only a few isolated farms and ranches. The land hereabouts was hard and unfriendly. The barren heart of Columbyana, some called it. Farming and ranching in this part of the country were not for the timid. The land was cheap and so men tried. Maybe some succeeded for a while, but most did not. Perhaps the man in the forest was a curious farmer, come to watch the parade from the safety of the darkness.

Juliet's world narrowed until she was in a state that usually required the touch of her hand to accomplish. Everything around her faded. The soldiers, the horses, Bors. Even Isadora disappeared. There was no one in her conscious mind but herself and the watcher.

He was a man, yet not a man. A beast, yet not a beast. There was magic in his blood, as there was magic in hers, and he carried within him a force beyond her comprehension. Strength usually frightened her. At the very least she was wary of it. But this watcher's strength was tempered with gentleness and honor.

And need.

The watcher kept pace with the retinue of soldiers and their captives. His eyes were not on Bors or the armed soldiers, but on Juliet. Without fail, his powerful gaze remained fixed on her. She felt that gaze to her bones, and instead of chilling her again, she felt warmth.

In the depths of the wood she caught a glimpse of those eyes. They were gold, and they shone in the night much like the moon above. The connection she felt with the creature in the forest was unlike any she had ever known. She was not close enough to touch the watcher, and yet she felt as if his mind and hers had merged, somehow.

Why do you follow?

The question was silent, a whisper of her mind, but within her mind there was an answer.

You know.

Juliet shook her head. *I don't. I don't know.* And yet deep within her something stirred. A fear. A knowing.

You are connected to the earth with rivers of knowledge. Do you not know all things?

If I knew all things I would not be here.

Do not be afraid.

"I'm not afraid," Juliet whispered.

"Well, you should be," the young soldier who led her mount said, confidence and arrogance in his voice. "The emperor doesn't care much for women, unless they serve him in some way. I don't know why he sent for you, but he has plenty of cooks and maids. Most of his concubines have got themselves with child, and of late he's been procuring new wenches to serve him and his ministers. You and your sister will likely find yourself living on Level Three."

The mental connection Juliet had found with the creature

of the forest disappeared, as if a ribbon had been cut and the severed ends fell free. She dismissed the unusual event as her own imagination, feeding her an intimate conversation when she had need for contact with someone. Anyone.

"What?" she asked, sounding confused and more than a little sleepy. The experience, imagination or not, had left her feeling dazed and headachy. Maybe she had dozed off in the saddle, and the watcher was just a dream.

The soldier glanced back at her, a trace of annoyance on his pretty face. He did not look to be more than twenty years old. A bit of baby fat made his cheeks full and pink, but there was no hint of the child in his harsh voice. "Level Three, witch. Since most of the concubines are pregnant and will soon be too unattractive and unwieldy to serve the emperor and other favored men in positions of importance, he's been collecting replacements. I hear it's not a bad life for a woman, if she does as she's told."

"Most of the . . . uh, ladies . . . they're with child?" Juliet asked. There were ways to prevent conception. Surely the emperor availed himself of such methods.

"Yes. It's odd, if you ask me." The soldier lowered his voice. "They all got pregnant on the same day. There was quite a to-do on Level One. The emperor was supposed to get married again, but his bride-to-be made the skylight in the grand ballroom explode, and the next thing you know there was all sorts of goings-on . . . going on," he finished quickly, more than a little embarrassed. "When springtime comes, Level Three is going to be quite busy, and not in the usual way." The soldier turned his young face to the front once again.

"What happened to the bride?" Juliet held her breath as she waited for the soldier to answer.

"She ran off while the place was in an uproar."

"So, there was no wedding?"

"No wedding."

Juliet looked toward the forest again, and this time she saw no spark of gold. She felt no tug at her soul. Her mind was on the soldier's words, not on the watcher. If the watcher even existed. It was easy to write off the event to her imagination or a dream, and turn her thoughts to something more solid. Springtime, the soldier said. All those women conceiving at the same time. *Goings-on.* Exploding skylights.

In spite of the forest mystery, angry soldiers, Bors, Isadora's foul mood, and the threat of Level Three, Juliet managed a smile. *Sophie.*

LIANE PACED IN HER QUARTERS, WHILE MAHRI WATCHED with increasing dismay. The maid and companion had offered everything she knew to offer. Food, drink, music, novels, poets, a comic or a dramatic play presented for the empress's pleasure. Liane wanted none of those things, so now the young girl wrung her hands and chewed on her lower lip.

Liane had been empress for seven days, and Sebestyen had not yet sent for her. Not once. She was his wife in name only, and she had not even had the pleasure of his company at a meal, much less the pleasure of his company in his bed or hers. She had been all but locked in this damned suite of rooms with everything any woman might desire. Everything but her husband.

She hated pink. It had never been her favorite color, but since moving into these rooms, she had come to detest the putrid shade. Pink coverlet on her bed, pink chair, pink flowers, pink pillows. The shades varied, but no matter where she turned, she was confronted with the color that literally nauseated her. These days she did not need anything, much less something so insignificant as a color she did not care for, to cause her insides to roil.

It was late in the day. Surely Sebestyen was not absorbed in matters of state at this hour. Perhaps he was asleep, resting after a long and arduous day. The rebellion was growing in strength. The rebels had not approached Arthes, but knowing that they grew stronger was a concern.

As was the fact that Maddox Sulyen, the former Minister of Defense and Sophie's father and a traitor in Sebestyen's eyes, had disappeared. The emperor's days were surely long and taxing, given the current state of affairs in Columbyana.

"Your nightgown is on the bed," Mahri said when Liane made a sharp turn and headed for her bedchamber. "I pressed it myself, this afternoon while you were napping." The girl followed, as if to help her mistress prepare for yet another night alone.

"If I slept well at night, I would have no need for naps in the afternoon," Liane said sharply. Too sharply, perhaps. The situation that was driving Liane mad was not Mahri's fault.

"I will have a sleeping potion prepared . . ."

"No potions," Liane snapped. Never again would she take a witch's elixir into her body. For her sake and for the sake of her child, she would not drug herself for any reason. Not to prevent a child or conceive one, not for pleasure or comfort or sleep. She no longer trusted Gadhra's brews, and preferred suffering from the occasional bout of sickness over taking the medicines that were prepared on Level Seven.

"But you must . . ."

"I must see my husband. Now." Liane threw open the doors to her wardrobe, and instinctively reached for a plain crimson robe, much like the ones she had worn as Sebestyen's concubine. Perhaps if he saw her without the trappings of her new station, he would forget for a while that she was empress and remember only that she was his lover.

The swelling of her body was subtle, and yet undeniable. Did Sebestyen find that roundness unattractive? Is that why he had not sent for her? Did her altered physical appearance disgust him? She would like to believe that her husband would not be so shallow, but she knew that he could be unreasonable about even the smallest infraction. Is that how he saw her pregnancy? As an infraction?

Mahri tried to stop her, even as Liane marched out of her bedroom. "We should send word that you wish to see the emperor," she said quickly. "It would be poor manners to arrive unannounced."

Liane spun on the girl. "Poor manners to visit my husband in his bed?"

The young girl paled. "I hear he is not one to be disturbed lightly," she whispered. "That is what I hear."

"I know Sebestyen better than you or anyone else," Liane said. "He will be glad to see me." Eventually.

Liane threw the door to her suite open, only to find the way blocked by two armed sentinels. Ferghus and Tatsl were not on duty tonight. Too bad. She might've been able to reason with them. Balen and Vance might be more difficult. They were unerringly loyal to their emperor, and on more than one occasion she had caught them studying her with what might be called thinly veiled contempt.

They still thought of her as a whore, and perhaps they always would.

"I wish to be taken to the emperor."

The sentinels looked at one another, and a silent message passed between them. "We will tell the emperor's guards that you—"

"I intend to surprise my husband," she interrupted.

Again, they looked at one another. Had Sebestyen ordered that she not go to him? Is that why everyone was trying to stop her?

Liane was not easily stopped. She surprised the guards

by swinging up her fisted right hand and punching Balen in the throat. He dropped to his knees and raised both hands up to protect the injury while he gasped for breath. Vance instinctively reached for his weapon, and then hesitated. He could not harm the empress, especially not while she carried the emperor's heir. He raised one hand to his throat in way of defense, and Liane kicked him solidly between the legs.

She ran for the lift. With any luck, she'd be on Level One and inside Sebestyen's bedchamber before the sentinels could call for help. They were both on the floor, winded and hurting, and it would take them a few minutes to rouse assistance.

The lift carried her from Level Five to Level One quickly. Liane exited the contraption and turned left, walking down the hallway to find four guards loitering casually around Sebestyen's door. They were surprised to see her, and immediately snapped to attention, even though there was distrust and even hate in the eyes of those sentinels who knew her from the time when she had been a concubine. But they did not dare disobey or disrespect her. Not now.

"I wish to see the emperor," she said almost haughtily.

"He is . . ." The sentinel who spoke almost choked on his words. "Engaged."

No minister should be bothering him with official duties at this hour! Perhaps one or more of the priests were with him, haranguing him about his latest choice in wives.

Liane knew too well that she had not been a choice. Sebestyen had married her because she carried the child he had never thought to have. Still, he would likely welcome the interruption. Most of the priests were sour men without joy, and their company could not be pleasant.

"So you intend to stop me from entering my husband's bedchamber?" Liane managed a slight lift of one eyebrow, to convey her outrage in a subtle manner.

One sentinel opened his mouth to answer, but the more

senior Taneli—a young but ambitious guard who had searched and insulted Liane many times before her station had changed—interrupted. "If the empress wishes to call upon her husband, it is not our duty to hinder her."

Taneli did perform a cursory search, but those quickly moving hands were nothing like the insolent invasions he had offered in the past. A gentle skimming to see that she carried no weapons, that was all he dared.

When he was done, Taneli opened the door quietly and bowed, and if not for the tilt of her head, Liane would not have seen the smile he tried to hide.

When she saw that smile, she knew what she would find in Sebestyen's chamber, and for a moment she considered turning away before it was too late. But she didn't. She walked into her husband's bedchamber with her head held high, and the door closed gently behind her.

Sebestyen was in bed, as she had suspected, and he was not alone. He and the woman who shared that bed were so thoroughly engaged they had not yet heard her entrance. Liane walked toward the bed on silent feet.

She should have suspected this. In fact, she was a fool not to have realized the truth of the matter. Sebestyen was not a man to go for weeks without sex, and since he had not touched *her,* it made sense that he was touching someone else.

The dark-haired girl who had milky skin much paler than that of her emperor rode him quickly and without finesse. The lovers had tossed away the coverlet, and so Liane could see everything. They were both naked, of course, joined and sweating and glowing with the flush of sex. There was no art in this encounter, just raw need and a blinding quest for pleasure. Sebestyen seemed not to care that the woman who rode him was not particularly skilled. His large hands gripped the girl's slim hips; his eyes were closed as he neared completion.

Liane made not a sound as she approached the bed. As part of her training in years past, she had watched others perform a variety of sexual acts. Some were interesting and stimulating to watch. Others were repulsive or simply boring.

Nothing she had ever seen cut to the core the way this did. She should have killed Sebestyen when she'd had the chance. She'd been standing before him alone, the tip of the knife in her hand pressing into his flesh, and she had failed to complete the job. She had allowed his insincere *I love you* to sway her. To stop her. The bastard had ruined everything. Her plans, her life. He had given her the child she craved, and even worse, he had made her love him.

She had been completely quiet, but Sebestyen's eyes flew open and found her as if he instinctively knew that he and his whore were no longer alone. He was surprised, momentarily, but there was no shame on his face. No regret. And after a moment he actually smiled at her. He moved deeper into the woman atop him, thrusting his hips and pulling her down hard.

The whore cried out and shuddered; she came as inelegantly as she fucked.

Sebestyen did not. He continued to move without haste, while the sated woman licked her lips and collapsed atop him.

"Do you care to join us, darling?"

It was the first clue for the dark-haired girl that she and her emperor were not alone. She jumped up, squealed, and rolled off a still-hard Sebestyen. She grabbed the coverlet and tried to shield herself.

"You must forgive Wisla's rudeness," Sebestyen said calmly. "She's new, and still cursed with a bit of modesty."

"So I see," Liane said calmly. "You wasted no time replenishing Level Three."

"So many of the concubines are with child." Sebestyen's

lips thinned slightly. "They're all getting fat and misshapen, and more than one of them has a nasty habit of retching without warning."

"You find pregnant women disgusting?"

"Of course," he answered without hesitation. "Doesn't everyone?"

For a moment Liane stood there, studying Sebestyen as if he were a complete stranger. No, she knew this man well. It was the man she had fallen in love with who was a complete stranger. A myth. A fantasy of her mind.

"What do you want?" Sebestyen asked without patience. "Wisla and I have business to attend to."

"I thought I might go now." An obviously embarrassed Wisla edged toward the filmy gown that had been tossed to the floor near the foot of the bed.

Sebestyen turned cold eyes to her and spoke in a voice that no man denied. "You will go when I tell you to go."

The girl stopped in her tracks, wide-eyed and afraid. Not of Sebestyen, not this time, but of the empress who had arrived at such an inopportune moment. Liane vaguely remembered what it was like to be so young and naïve. She remembered what it was like to be dragged away from home and forced into a life she did not want. Had Wisla been kidnapped? Sold by her family? Or was she here because she had no other place to go? Whatever the case, Liane could not hate the girl. She could hate Sebestyen.

"I'm bored," Liane said, her words and the expression on her face revealing none of her pain and anger. "I'd like permission to take a lover."

Sebestyen lifted his eyebrows slightly. "A lover?"

"I could take one without permission, I suppose, but I remember what happened to the last suitor who visited the empress's chambers without your authorization. Since I am already carrying your child and you're obviously not intrigued by this body, there's no reason for me not to take a man into my bed."

Sebestyen's blue eyes hardened, just enough for her to know what the answer would be. "True enough," he said in a lowered voice.

"So I have your permission?"

Sebestyen lifted his hand and summoned Wisla back to the bed. When the girl was near, he sat up and yanked away the coverlet she so modestly held before her body. He pulled her onto the bed, spread her thighs, and rolled atop her. The girl was uncertain at first, since apparently having an audience was a new experience for her.

And then Sebestyen touched her. He placed a hand between her legs and stroked. "Just close your eyes and pretend she's not here," he instructed.

"I don't think I . . ." Wisla began breathlessly.

Sebestyen leaned down to take one nipple into his mouth. He drew that nipple deep and continued to move the hand that rested between the girl's legs. Wisla closed her eyes and her body arched toward his. She'd had some rudimentary training, to respond so quickly. That, or she'd been primed with one of Gadhra's stimulating potions. If that were the case, she might very well be here all night, always wanting, never entirely satisfied.

"Well?" Liane snapped.

Sebestyen lifted up slightly and looked Liane in the eye as he pushed into the girl on the bed. "No," he whispered.

"Why not? It's obvious that you don't consider the vows we took to be binding in any way. Why should I?"

"I have never taken marriage vows seriously, as you well know." He moved in and out of the woman beneath him, but he looked at Liane. She did not turn away or blink or flinch.

"And yet you expect me to—" she began hotly.

"I expect you to protect my child from the pokings of a strange man's cock. I *expect* you to behave as an empress should. You are no longer a concubine, Liane, and it wouldn't be proper for you to behave as if you were. Try to remember that small fact." As he spoke, he moved faster, harder. And he stared at her with eyes so cold she could not see any life in them. No life at all.

And still she wondered . . . Did he care for her a little? Is that why he was so determined that she not lie with another man?

"I won't allow you to make a fool of me," he said, as if he had read her thoughts and decided to dash her last hope. Maybe he had seen a touch of tenderness in her eyes, or in the set of her mouth. Tenderness. Weakness. Whatever it might've been, it was now gone. Everything was gone.

She had once been the woman on the bed, the woman Sebestyen shared his passion with. Even when she had hated him, even when she had plotted to kill him, she'd taken her own pleasure in this bed and laughed at the empresses who resided on Level Five. She'd laughed at their powerlessness and their coldness and their loneliness. And now she had become one of them.

Sebestyen's body stiffened, he climaxed into another woman's body, and Liane turned away. She did not wish or need to see more. She was anxious to make her escape, in fact had her hand on the door handle, when Sebestyen's words stopped her.

"If I hear of any man entering your chambers, I will have him killed without question."

She did not turn to face him. "And what of the poets and singers who provide entertainment?"

"There are surely female entertainers available."

"Surely," Liane whispered as she opened the door.

"Liane," Sebestyen snapped. She turned to face him, fully aware that the sentinels now watched the end of this scene unfold. Taneli was amused, though he would not dare to laugh aloud in her presence. Like it or not, she had too much power for him to laugh in her face.

But he would talk behind her back, and word of this encounter would travel. Palace gossip quickly spread from Level to Level.

So Liane kept her eyes dry, her head high, and her heart cold. Wisla had once again covered herself in the deep blue coverlet from Sebestyen's bed. The modesty would not last. The girl would not last. Sebestyen expected more from his lovers than compliance. He expected passion and skill. Wisla would soon be passed down, and another woman would take her place. There would always be another woman to take her place.

"Yes, my lord?" Liane said, not so much as a waver in her voice.

"Take care with that child you carry. He's the future of Columbyana."

"I'm well aware of that, my lord."

Again Wisla tried to slip from the bed, but Sebestyen snatched her back. The girl fell onto his bare body with another squeal. Sebestyen hated weakness, girlish shrieks, and lovers who lacked skill. And yet it was Wisla who shared his bed. Wisla who would be in the imperial chamber for yet a while longer.

Liane closed the door knowing there was no reason for her to see or converse with Sebestyen ever again. She was a womb for his child and nothing more.

And after the baby was born? She would serve no purpose then, no purpose at all. Her life would be worth nothing, and she would live the rest of her days locked in a fine suite of rooms on Level Five. Perhaps she would be paraded about now and then, when a ceremony took place. If she kept her mouth shut and did not annoy her husband, perhaps he wouldn't kill her or banish her to Level Thirteen, as he had done with his previous wives. If she made this farce of a marriage easy for him, perhaps he would be content with his concubines and his unobtrusive wife and his child.

There could never be another baby. Not for her; not for Sebestyen. This child she carried was a miracle.

No, not a miracle, though the priests were calling it just that and taking credit, as if their prayers had been answered and Liane was nothing more than a poorly chosen vessel. It was magic that had got her this child, as much as Sebestyen's seed and her ill-placed love. Witch's magic.

She should have killed Sebestyen when she'd had the chance.

3

Sunrise turned the sky gray before Bors ordered the soldiers and their prisoners to dismount for a few hours' rest. There was water close by for the horses, and again it was for their sakes that he halted in his relentless journey.

Juliet slept for a while. Her weary body demanded it. Isadora slept, too, or at least it appeared that way. Lying on a coarse blanket, covered with her own cloak to protect her from the morning chill, the eldest Fyne sister remained motionless and silent. She had been that way for most of the journey, as if she had withdrawn into herself completely.

Coming awake with a start, Juliet lifted her head from the rough blanket that lay between her and the rocky ground. Like her sister, her only covering was the cloak she'd worn for this journey. Bors might not want them to die, but he cared nothing for their comfort. He had made that clear.

They were camped on a bit of a hill, where it was possible

to study much of the land that surrounded them. In every direction, the scenery was dramatically different. The thick forest where Juliet had sensed the watcher had been left behind a short while back, and to the north a mountain range such as she had never seen stretched forever, starting with low hills and growing to massive heights as far as her eye could see. The magnificence of the mountain chain made Fyne Mountain seem an anthill. To the south the land was flatter. A few hills turning gold and red rolled across the land, but they looked friendly and warm. If there were farmers and ranchers on this border of the barren heart of Columbyana, they likely lived in that direction.

To the west the barren heart spread for as far as the eye could see. The ground was hard, hilly in some places and completely flat in others. A few scrubby trees grew here and there, but for the most part the landscape was an unwelcoming and harsh brownish gray. Even the few trees that grew there looked dull and faded.

Juliet studied it all with eyes that had never traveled away from the very small part of the Southern Province she called home. The landscape she studied as the sun rose was austere and daunting, but beautiful in its own way. To the south the land was at least similar to home, but to the north and the west . . . she had not known such a land existed. The harshly cold gray of the mountains to the north didn't look at all welcoming, and yet her eyes were drawn there, much as they had been drawn to the forest last night.

As Juliet shifted her body, a tangle of red hair fell past her shoulder. If she had had a mirror in her possession, she would probably have broken it so she could not see her reflection. There had been no time for bathing and primping on this journey, not that she had ever been one to spend more time than necessary in front of a mirror. Sophie was the pretty sister, and Isadora possessed her own elegance. Juliet had never needed the constant reminder of a mirror to know that she was the plainer of the three Fyne sisters.

But she did like to be clean, and it took some time and effort to keep her red curls manageable. Her curly copper hair was always well restrained, pinned back and up, or braided as neatly as possible, though even in a braid her hair was never sleek like Isadora's and Sophie's. Her hair was a tangle now, the braid untidy after too many nights of sleeping on the ground and too many days without the special shampoo she made herself and the combs that were now burned to ashes. When she'd been gathering her herbs to take with her, such things as combs and hairpins had not crossed her mind. Right now she'd gladly trade a few of her medicines for both.

"Are you happy?"

Juliet jerked her head around to see Isadora shift awkwardly into a sitting position. The cloak that had covered her body while she slept fell, draping around her lap. It was not easy for the eldest Fyne sister to manage even that simple move. Her hands remained tied behind her back, a precaution Juliet had not been able to persuade the soldiers to abandon.

"Of course not."

"Your decisions, your actions, brought us to this place." Like Juliet, Isadora was rumpled and travel weary, and strands of dark hair had come loose from her braid. Still, the fire in her eyes had not dimmed.

"Your actions would've killed us both."

"I'd rather be dead than here," Isadora snapped.

"I wouldn't."

As long as they were alive, there was hope. Isadora had left hope behind a long time ago, but Juliet had not. She didn't know what the future held for her or for Isadora, but she did know that whatever came would be preferable to death. It was too soon; they had things to do before they moved into the land of the dead.

Around them soldiers wakened, and those who had
been keeping watch bedded down for what would surely be
a brief sleep. The man nearest the prisoners yawned and
gave them a cursory glance. He was not concerned. After
all, there had been no trouble from the witches since they'd
left the cabin. Another delved into the food supply and
came up with small rations of hard bread he passed around.
When the soldiers had been served, he tossed two small
pieces toward Juliet. She grabbed them both and moved toward Isadora.

"I don't want—" Isadora began.

"You need to eat."

"Why?"

Isadora protested, but when Juliet held a piece of the
hard bread to her mouth, she took a small bite.

The back of Juliet's neck prickled, much as it had on
that night the cabin had been raided. Was Bors watching?
Was it his angry gaze she felt upon her? She shook off the
sensation and concentrated on getting Isadora to eat. When
that was done, she'd consume her own meager breakfast.

The camp came alive slowly, as sleep-deprived soldiers
ate and cared for the horses and moved beyond a large
boulder to empty their bladders. She'd soon need to take
care of such business herself, but she did not look forward
to seeing to the matter while trying to maintain some semblance of privacy. Bors insisted that at least one guard keep
an eye on the women at all times. Most of them were gentlemen who would turn their heads, at least for a few moments. Others were not gentlemen at all.

Juliet watched a soldier round the rock. A few minutes
later, another man followed. Then another. All was quiet.
She heard no banter, no laughter, as was usual. None of the
soldiers returned. Usually they did their business quickly
and returned immediately to their posts or their duties.

Juliet concentrated on the rock, hoping for a flash of

knowing like the one she'd experienced last night with the watcher, or on that night when she'd realized too late that men were coming, but she felt nothing out of the ordinary. If only she could touch that rock, just for one moment, she might be able to have a sense of what was happening beyond.

But she experienced no sense of knowing, and she was too far away to touch the rock. Moving in that direction would only raise suspicions. How could she tap into that rock and the men beyond without alerting the other soldiers to the fact that something might be wrong?

Last night the watcher, if he had indeed been real and not a dream or a fantasy, had told her she was connected to the earth with rivers of knowing. She had never thought of her gift in that way, but it did make some sense. Instinct directed her to place her palm upon the ground. If she could link her mind to another's from such a distance, even for a few minutes, perhaps she could reach for the men on the other side of that boulder. It wouldn't hurt to try.

Palm pressed into dirt and small pebbles, she imagined that a river flowed through the ground. That river traveled swiftly from her hand to the boulder and farther. For a moment there was nothing. No connection, no flash of knowledge. She was too far away, and even concentrating so hard that a sharp headache began to take shape at the back of her neck brought no answers.

And then a jolt of enlightenment shot through her. Her body jerked slightly, but she did not lift her hand from the ground. The men on the other side of the rock were unconscious. All but one. One who was not a soldier; one who did not serve Bors. She did not know whence their rescue came, or if indeed it was rescue. But the man behind the boulder was not a friend to Bors and the soldiers.

Juliet lifted her hooded cape and draped it over her shoulders, fastening the top button while she scooted closer to Isadora. "You look cold," she said for the benefit of any who might be listening. She lifted Isadora's cape and placed it over the obstinate woman's shoulders.

"I am *not* cold," Isadora snapped. "And even if I were—"

"Something's happening," Juliet whispered. No one was watching them closely. They did receive a casual glance now and then, as she worked the braided fastening at Isadora's throat, but nothing she did raised the soldiers' suspicions.

Isadora became very still. "Juliet, what's wrong?" she whispered.

"I'm not sure." Juliet reached around her sister, keeping her hand hidden in the folds of the cloak as she fumbled with the rope that bound Isadora's wrists. Just because the man behind the boulder was an enemy of the soldiers did not mean that he was their friend. Isadora would need her hands to fight, and they might yet need to do so. The rope was tightly snarled, but Juliet was able to loosen the knot. When that was done, she grabbed a loop and slowly pulled it from the tangled twine. Isadora was not yet free, but she was almost there . . .

"Where's Evyn?" The soldier who had earlier tossed Juliet bread glanced about the campsite. "And Orn?" He took a step toward the boulder. "If those slackers have wandered off to the pond to—"

He never got the chance to finish his sentence. A blur of golden hair and bronzed flesh leaped from the rock and seized him; a large hand carried something green to the soldier's nose. He dropped to the ground, inert like the men on the other side of the boulder. The assailant turned his eyes to Juliet, and for a moment she could not breathe. Her heart pounded so hard she could feel it thudding against her chest.

The man who had rendered the soldiers unconscious

was very large, larger than any man she had ever seen. His hair was longer than her own, and it hung in a tangle of golden blond over his shoulders and down his back and across a portion of his face. He wore nothing but a kilt of animal skin that covered his privates and not much more. Even though the morning was chilly, there was no sign of the cold air on his skin. The sun-kissed flesh that stretched over hard muscle was free of goose bumps, and in fact seemed to radiate heat. She could almost feel that heat on her own skin, even though he stood several feet away.

Surprised soldiers reached for their weapons, Isadora struggled with the ropes at her wrists, and the intruder moved. Toward Juliet. He advanced smoothly and with incredible strength, leaping to her in an instant and lifting her from the ground with ease, tossing her over his shoulder as if she weighed no more than a sack of flour.

A brave soldier with his sword drawn moved threateningly toward the large man who held Juliet. The intruder moved, leaping away from the swords that swung in his direction, holding on to his captive and protecting her from the blades that swung so wildly. He ran quickly, making his escape with Juliet perched precariously on his broad, bare shoulder.

Perhaps he was not a man at all, she thought in a panic, but a creature who only assumed the shape of a man. Her body was jostled unmercifully, her breath stolen by the way she bounced across a hard shoulder as her captor ran. She struggled with the fabric from her cape, doing her best to push it from her face so she could see what was happening.

Free of the gray fabric that had shielded her eyes, Juliet lifted her head to look back at the camp. They were already so far away! Impossibly far away. Surely a mere man could not run so fast, especially not while carrying a heavy burden—the weight of another person. She could still see the activities of the frenetic camp, even though she was a fair distance away. Some soldiers scrambled to saddle the horses and give chase, while others foolishly continued to pursue the kidnapper on foot.

Behind Juliet, too far behind, Isadora shook off her bonds and leapt to her feet. One soldier was close enough to notice that the prisoner was loose, but he did not notice soon enough. Isadora reached out and slapped her hand to his forehead. Juliet could not hear the words that were spoken, but she saw Isadora's mouth move. The soldier dropped and Isadora ran. Not toward Juliet, but away. The kidnapper carried Juliet north; Isadora ran south.

"Isadora!" Juliet screamed. The name echoed, hollow and mournful.

The man who had grabbed her turned sharply into an outcropping of gray rocks that slanted upward. He climbed the craggy hill, moving quickly and easily as if the load he carried weighed nothing at all. No horse could follow them here. Juliet had a feeling that even on foot the soldiers would have no chance. In a matter of minutes her situation had changed, but she did not feel it was any less dire.

She had gone from being the emperor's prisoner to being kidnapped by a barely dressed wild creature who had the strength to carry her without discernible effort. Was she better off? Or worse? The way the kidnapper carried Juliet made her head swim and ache. "Stop," she commanded breathlessly.

He did not respond, not with a word or a falter in his step. Bare feet gripped the rock as if he had climbed these very stones a thousand times.

"We must go back for my sister. She ran in the other direction." A leap made her head jerk and wobble, and in a purely instinctive move she wrapped her hands around the man's neck and held on. He was overly warm, considering his state of dress. Or undress. Was he ill? Feverish and crazed? "Please," she added.

Still, the creature did not respond. Was he deaf? Did he not hear her pleas? Or did he simply not care? She laid the palm of one hand on his bare neck, and for no more than a split second she had a sensation of a deep abiding warmth and power. She saw a cave of gray stone and a serene pond. Nothing more. Not a tremor, not a whisper.

Not for the first time, Juliet's abilities failed her. Her glimpse into the man who'd snatched her away from the soldiers did her no good at all. She wanted to know where this creature was taking her, if he planned to harm her, if he was a rescuer or a kidnapper. No matter how she tried, she saw only vague glimpses of the past. There was no hint as to what the future held for her, or for the man who had taken her from the emperor's soldiers. And then, with an abruptness that startled her, she felt nothing at all from her kidnapper. Nothing! She closed her eyes and concentrated, but nothing happened.

He was blocking her.

HOW HAD HE MISTAKEN THE OTHER WITCH—THE ONE called Sophie—for *her?* Days before her arrival, Ryn had realized with every shred of his body and his soul that this woman was his and that she was coming to him. His heart had beat differently as she approached, and her scent had invaded his nose and his lungs until he could think of nothing else.

The red-haired woman had a gift which the other witch had not possessed. She could see pieces of his spirit and his mind. She had even reached into his thoughts last night and asked, *Why do you follow?* He had answered, as best he could, but now, as he carried her away from the soldiers, he did not wish the joining of minds. He had shut down the link between them, and it would remain deadened until the proper time. A man's thoughts were private and not to be shared with abandon. Not even with her. He had never expected his woman to have such a gift, even though he knew her to be a witch.

The woman . . . the witch . . . she was called Juliet. While he'd been watching, he'd heard the darker one call her by that name. At least he now had a name to put to his wife, as well as a face other than the vague visage of his dreams.

He was pleased that Juliet was pretty, though in truth her beauty did not matter overmuch. It was more important that she be brave in mind and body, that she bear him strong sons and embrace the way of the Anwyn and become a proper and competent mate.

As they climbed to a place on the rocky hillside where the soldiers could not follow, she continued to insist that he put her down. He did not. He wanted to put more distance between them and the soldiers before he stopped, and there was a long way to travel before they reached the place he had chosen to camp for the night. The soldiers would not follow far into the hills. The path was harsh and steep and there were too many twists and turns. The soldiers would try but they would turn back soon, if they had not already done so.

Before darkness fell, he could be assured that he and his wife would not be disturbed.

JULIET EVENTUALLY QUIT ASKING THE CREATURE WHO had abducted her to turn back or to put her down. Maybe he really was deaf, or else he spoke a language other than the Emperor's Columbyanan. Or he really was crazed. Time and time again she placed her hands on his neck and reached for answers . . . and got none. There had been many times in her life when she'd wished not to see into others with a touch, and now, when she wished to see, her gift failed her.

She did not even dare to imagine that the soldiers might've followed them this far. The large man ran upon steep ground no human should be able to walk upon, much less race across. The horses could not possibly handle such a terrain, and neither could foot soldiers.

Since she could not see into the captor who carried her to gain a clue as to what might wait ahead, Juliet closed her eyes and concentrated on Isadora. There were no mountains to the south of the road they had been traveling upon, just those gentle hills. The soldiers could have very easily followed Isadora in that direction. Why had she run away from Juliet and not toward her? They should be together now, not separated.

Juliet had always had Isadora and Sophie; she'd never been alone. They were sisters who had planned to be a part of one another's lives forever. Now they were separated by distance and anger and betrayal. She'd never even imagined that she might find herself in such a situation.

No matter how she tried, she couldn't see where her sister was, or if the soldiers had caught up with her, or if she was in immediate danger. As her captor carried her ever upward, she tried to reach out to her sister. Juliet focused her mind on Isadora until she was exhausted from the effort and her head was aching. And still, all she could be certain of was that Isadora was alive. For now, that would have to be enough.

For a while Juliet remained compliant. There was even a moment when she almost dozed off, incredibly. Her attempt to reach Isadora had exhausted her, and she hadn't been sleeping much of late. The nightmare had plagued her, even as she'd slept in snatches on the hard, cold ground.

Now she needed to pee. The creature who carried her had refused to listen to her other pleas. He hadn't even slowed down as she'd all but begged him to stop. Why should this be any different? Like it or not, she had to try.

"We need to stop for a few moments so that I might attend to personal needs," she said primly.

Did she imagine it, or did the large man grunt?

"I realize there are no proper facilities anywhere near." She lifted her head and looked down the rocky terrain they'd just covered. Her head spun and she closed her eyes tightly against the light-headedness that assaulted her. No, she would not find so much as a chamber pot here, much less a proper lavatory facility or an outhouse. "But if I could just have a few moments alone behind a boulder, or if you would simply turn your back like a gentleman . . ."

Unexpectedly, her kidnapper stopped and all but whipped Juliet around and onto her feet. She gripped his massive arms as she regained her balance, and a long strand of red hair whipped across her face. It almost seemed that he made an effort to steady her as she shook the hair out of her face and glanced around. They had reached a narrow plateau of sorts.

He had stopped finally. Maybe the cretin did understand at least some of what she'd said. "I need to . . . to . . ." Oh, this was so embarrassing!

"Piss," he finished for her.

She would have been mortified, if she hadn't had more immediate concerns at the moment. "Yes."

He shook his head, sending golden tangles swaying. "It will do no good for you to leave signs to tell the soldiers in which direction we travel. They are far behind us. They will never reach this place." His voice was deep and velvety, matching the large body. She got her first good look at his face, which was as hard and smooth as the granite he ran across so effortlessly. She did try very hard not to look anywhere else, since all he wore was that slip of an animal skin that barely covered his hips and upper thighs. A bulging pouch made from a similar skin hung from his waist. A knife in a leather sheath also hung there, untouched and yet still threatening.

There had been moments when she'd considered her kidnapper more creature than man, but looking into his face . . . he was definitely a man.

"You speak," she said.

"Of course I speak."

"Then why did you ignore me all morning?" she snapped, her face tilted back to look up into that harsh face and the golden eyes that sparkled there.

"If you do not need to piss, we will continue. We have yet a long way to travel today." He reached for her, but Juliet stepped back and away. Since the plateau was narrow and she was still dizzy, she placed a hand against the rock wall behind her for balance.

"No. I . . . do. Need to, that is." She searched for some shelter, and found it in a large rock that sat behind her.

"If you run, I will catch you," he said as she eased herself in that direction.

"I have no doubt," Juliet muttered as she stepped well behind the boulder.

When she was finished with her personal business, the crude man actually had the gall to walk around the rock and examine the area. Juliet walked away from him, head high. Even Bors and his soldiers had not been so illmannered.

She did her best to ignore the impudence of the wild man and glanced up, which was the direction in which they'd been traveling. All she could see was jagged rock that went almost straight up. Where was he taking her?

He came around the boulder with a small smile on his face. "You are better behaved than your sister," he said.

"Is that why you kidnapped me instead of her?" she asked sharply. "Are you afraid of Isadora?"

For a moment he looked almost confused, and then he nodded. "Not the dark sister, the fair one. Sophie."

Juliet took a step toward the big man, her fears about the journey ahead dismissed for the moment. "You've seen Sophie?"

"Four full moons ago."

"She was well when you saw her?" She had such a sense of peace when she thought of her younger sister, and she trusted her instincts where family was concerned. The soldier's tales of exploding skylights and goings-on and escape provided a small part of the story. Still, it would be nice to have her feelings confirmed by someone who had actually seen Sophie in the flesh.

He shrugged those wide, bare shoulders. "Well enough. I took her because I thought she was you, but I realized my mistake when I tasted her skin."

There was more information than she could handle in that odd sentence. One concern at a time. "You tasted her skin?" All of a sudden Juliet had an image like the one from her nightmare, of claws and blood and pain.

"I did not hurt her," the man insisted, and he sounded insulted by the horror that was no doubt evident in Juliet's voice and on her face.

"I'm glad to hear it." Juliet made a futile attempt to straighten her braid. It was beyond hope. "What do you mean, you thought she was me?" No one in their right mind would ever confuse her with her beautiful sister.

"She smelled of you. In her blood, in the clothes she wore and the things she carried, she smelled of you. I should have known she was not the one. She lied to me. She told me she had to piss and then she left signs for the father of her child to follow."

"I don't understand," Juliet said softly.

"We were further to the south at that time, where the

land was flat in many places and easier for a horse to follow. No horse will follow us here."

Juliet examined the face of her abductor, her rescuer, more carefully. She had not known many men well. Willym, Isadora's late husband, was the only man she had ever called friend. She had never known her father, or Isadora's father, or Sophie's father. And yet this large man insisted he knew how she *smelled*. "Have we met?" Surely not. Surely she would remember such a man.

"In dreams," he answered softly, that velvety voice washing over her.

Dreams. Her heart hitched. Was he talking about that nightmare she had never shared with anyone? "I don't understand." By the stars and the moon in the night sky, there were so many things she did not understand.

He, on the other hand, seemed to be quite well informed. "Juliet, my wife, I have been aware of you all my days. I have *known* you for years." He thumped his chest. "Here."

"Did you say . . ." She took a step back. Surely she had misunderstood. "Wife?"

"Wife. I have been waiting for you." His step forward more than matched her step back.

A ruffle of panic washed through her body. "Obviously you are not well acquainted with the language. I am not your wife." The expression on his face did not change; he was not at all perturbed. "I don't even know your name!"

"Rynfyston Ditteri de Younsterfyn of the Dairgol Clan." He bowed, sharp and shallow, and offered his right hand, palm up. It was an oddly courtly gesture for a man hardly dressed. "At your service, wife."

"I am not your wife!"

He smiled, but only a little. "You may call me Ryn."

She would run, but there was no place to go. She could

jump to her death or she could remain with this Ryn creature until an opportunity for escape arose.

He hefted her gently over his shoulder, and began to climb again. They had gone a good way up the seemingly impossible mountain before he spoke again.

"You are pretty, and soft."

Juliet supposed the words were meant as a compliment, but they scared her. She was not pretty, not like Sophie and Isadora. She was ordinary. She worked very hard to be ordinary, and it would not do for this man to see anything else.

"You are ugly and hard," she responded sharply.

"That is as it should be," he said without rancor. "You will be the softness of home, and I will protect you from the harshness of the world. You will offer comfort and I will offer safekeeping." He climbed, he carried her, but he didn't sound at all winded. "That is the way of a proper mating."

"But this is not . . . I just . . ." Juliet sputtered. She never lost her temper or said unkind words. Ryn was obviously mistaken about many things, and she needed to find a way to reason with him. "I will never *comfort* you. Where I come from, marriage is a sacred ceremony performed in a church before a man of God. It is a solemn covenant undertaken by a man and a woman who are in love and who have decided to spend their lives together. It is a commitment which some women willingly make. It is certainly not a command by an uncivilized abductor who makes a woman his unwilling prisoner."

"You will be willing," he said confidently.

"I will *not*."

Ryn hauled them both onto another plateau. He set Juliet on her feet and looked her squarely in the eye. So, she had been lying when she'd said he was ugly. He was fierce, and sharp-featured and brutish. But he was not ugly.

"You talk too much," he said softly. "In that way you and Sophie are much alike."

"If you don't like the conversation, take me home."

As soon as the words were out of her mouth, tears came to her eyes. Home was gone, burned by the soldiers. A single tear fell down her cheek, and it was cold. The wind here was cold. When Ryn, who was surprisingly warm, wasn't carrying her, she was chilled to the bone.

The big man reached out and wiped the tear away. "Don't cry."

"I just want to go home, but . . ." Home was no more and the Fyne sisters were scattered to the far corners of the land.

Ryn continued to stroke her cheek with surprisingly gentle fingers, even though the tear she'd shed was long gone.

"That's where I'm taking you, wife. Home."

4

IN THE CAMP THAT AWAITED THEM NEAR THE TOP OF this rise, there was a crevice in the rock wall to keep the wind from Juliet. Ryn had prepared her a soft bed of bearskin for tonight. Nothing grew in this place, nothing with which he could build a fire to keep her warm.

Her flesh was cool to the touch, and she shivered as the afternoon breeze that felt pleasant to his skin whipped her skirts and tendrils of her red hair. He knew those who were not Anwyn felt the cold more than the people of the mountain, but he had not known how chilled her skin would become. He had never touched a woman's skin, other than Sophie's. The air had been mild when he'd snatched Juliet's sister from her lover, warm even, and she had not shivered as Juliet did now.

Tomorrow night they would camp in the forest on the trail that led to home, and he would build her a fire before night fell. It was his duty to keep Juliet warm until she became ac-climated to the mountain winters or obtained clothing that was sufficient to keep a woman accustomed to milder climes comfortable.

She had not said much since he'd told her he was taking her home. He should be grateful for the respite. Much of his life was spent in silence, either in his duty as guard in the Palace of the Anwyn Queen, or in the hills surrounding The City when duty did not call him. Some days the sound of another's voice was welcomed, but for that voice to be so strident and endless was not pleasant.

The unpleasantness would not last. Juliet would learn to accept that she was his wife, as all Anwyn captives did. She would be happy, once he proved to her what a good husband and father he could be. He had a fine house waiting for her and the sons they would make. If there were babies right away, then Juliet would be busy at home, and she'd have no time for complaining.

Ryn had never wanted much from life. A wife who would be partner and friend; many sons; a solid home awaiting him at the end of every day. Juliet's ramblings about love and sacred commitment were a woman's fantasies, and she would soon come to see that marriage was a practical concern. The fact that she was meant to be his was a function of the blood that ran through their veins, not the frivolous notion of a destined love. Soon enough, she would see.

They reached the camping site near the top of the hill, and Ryn carefully placed Juliet on her feet. She was dizzy from traveling in an awkward position all day, but he'd had no choice. She could not climb these hills on her own, and he could not afford to take his time getting her to The City. Here, in a high and rocky place where no ordinary man would dare to follow, they were safe for the night.

When her footing was solid, Juliet glanced around to examine her surroundings. Her gaze soon fell on the bearskin beneath the overhang, and for a moment she stared. Her eyes widened and her face paled, and then she said softly, "Home?"

"No," he replied. "Home is still some distance from this place. We will stay here until morning."

Juliet glanced to him with a question in her eyes, and he knew what she was thinking. They had an hour or so until full dark. It did not make sense to stop now, when they could be so much closer to their destination in that amount of time. She wondered why he had stopped here and what he had planned for the night. She wondered what he had planned for her.

His wife was afraid of him.

He really should stop calling her his wife, even though in his mind it was done and had been for all his life. There were words to be said before the Queen. The Anwyn did not marry as lowlanders did, but they did take a vow before their Queen and the inhabitants of The City, pledging themselves to one another before friends and family and neighbors. By the time they reached The City, Juliet would already be his wife in every way, and the vow would be a formality. She would comfort him; she would be willing. He was anxious for her willingness, but he knew it would not happen tonight.

"You will wish to sit," he said, gesturing to the bearskin. It lay not in a cave, but rock walls on two sides sheltered the bed from wind and there was an overhang, in case rain should fall. There would be no rain during the night; he knew that. But he had not known when he'd chosen this place for his wife's first night in the mountains.

Juliet clasped her hands tightly. "No, thank you. I'm fine."

"Surely you are tired and wish to rest."

"No, not really," she insisted. "You did all the work, after all, carrying me and climbing. I'm not at all tired."

"There is fruit and dried meat in a sack beneath the bearskin. You must be hungry."

"Not really."

She was a stubborn woman. Of course, he had known all along that she would be. "You would prefer to stand all night in the wind, hungry and cold, when you could rest in warmth on an animal skin I laid out for you and eat the food I prepared for you?"

"Yes."

Ryn realized that the shiver of his wife's body was not caused entirely by the wind. His instincts were finely honed, and he understood this woman who was meant to be his in a way he had never understood another. She was not only stubborn; she was frightened to the depths of her soul.

"Juliet," he said. He would stop calling her wife for the moment, since it obviously disturbed her to face the truth. "You will rest upon that bed tonight. I will not allow you to become ill through your own stubbornness."

"If I become ill, it will be because you abducted me, not because I refuse to take orders from a man who is obviously crazed."

He took a step toward her, and she took a step back. Her movement took her toward the shelter. "I am not crazed," he said calmly.

"I beg to differ." A flush of bright pink rose to her cheeks.

"Do you fear I will hurt you?" He knew the answer.

Again, she took another step back. "Yes."

"I won't."

"Perhaps you don't intend—"

"I would die before I hurt you."

Her eyes went wide and she looked at him with wonder and awe. Did she recognize the truth when she heard it with her own ears? "But—"

"You are mine to protect. No man will ever hurt you."

Juliet kept moving backward, until she was almost upon the bed he had prepared. She stumbled on the edge of the bearskin, but righted herself quickly.

"Sit," Ryn ordered.

She did, with agility and grace, her gaze never wavering from his face. "See? I'm sitting. You can go away now."

He shook his head. "Not yet. One taste, Juliet. That's all I ask. One taste."

ISADORA CROUCHED BEHIND A WOODPILE AND GATH-ered her cloak around her. Night would be here soon, and then she would be safe. The night was hers. She would be able to travel without being seen, once it was fully dark. She could see in the darkness of midnight when no one else could.

As she'd fled from the camp, she'd cast a quick spell by the side of the road to bewilder the soldiers. For a few precious moments they had been unsure as to which direction they should take. Instead of dividing their ranks and pursuing both sisters, they were confused about which one they should chase. The confusion had not lasted long, and they would not even be aware that a spell had caused the chaos. But it had done the trick.

The spell had been a weak one, but she could not muster anything more at this point in time. Since leaving the cabin, her powers had been dimmed. It was as if the magic within her was a bright flame at the center of her being, and on that night the flame had been weakened. What had been a fire was now no more than a weak flicker that might die with her next breath.

She did not know if it was leaving the mountain she had always called home that had weakened her, or if in killing the soldier who had invaded her home she had dishonored the Fyne House in such a way that her strength had been taken from her. The Fyne witches had not been given special gifts in order to kill.

Now that she'd lost the soldiers, Isadora's plan was to

backtrack and follow Juliet. She would find her sister and rescue her, and together they would search for Sophie. When the three sisters were separated, terrible things happened. Terrible things. Together they could face anything, but apart . . . apart they were weakened and vulnerable. Juliet would know how Isadora's strength could be restored, and together they would make things be as they once were.

Soon it would be dark enough to travel, but for now Isadora remained motionless and silent. She looked across the healthy autumn fields of this isolated farm and tried to make her heart stop pounding so hard.

Will would have loved to have such a place as this to call his own, and he'd had the money to begin such an enterprise. But she'd insisted on remaining on Fyne Mountain with her sisters, at least until Juliet and Sophie were older. Will, thinking only of his wife and the younger girls, had agreed that it was best. In insisting on having her way, she'd robbed him of his chance at realizing his simple dream. He'd been content to farm on the small plot of Fyne land that was suited to farming, while married to Isadora. Would he have lived longer if he'd seen his dream realized, if he'd lived on a place like this one? No. The curse she had challenged in taking a husband and loving him still would have ripped him from her.

Until the day Will died, Isadora had insisted to herself and to her sisters that the curse was a myth which had ruled the Fyne women for too long. No ancient tale would frighten her into not grabbing what she wanted from life; no whispered legend would make her afraid of love. And yet, in the end, she'd learned that she would've been better off if she'd been afraid.

She needed her husband, and she whispered the words she often spoke at midnight to bring him to her. In the months following his death, his spirit had always come to her when she called, but as the years passed, he became more resistant, his image hazier and the visits briefer. He had moved so far beyond her that the day would soon come when she wouldn't be able to rouse his spirit at all. Will did not come to her now, as she called again and again. She called, she begged, she commanded. She was weak, and he did not come.

In the hour in which she needed him most, he had abandoned her. He had deserted her, just as he had when he'd died. She shouldn't be angry with Will for dying; it wasn't at all logical. But there were times when she couldn't help herself. Tears welled up in her eyes, but she refused to let them fall.

Warriors did not cry, and in order to rescue Juliet, she would have to be a warrior.

JULIET SCOOTED BACK AS FAR AS SHE COULD, UNTIL HER spine touched the cold stone wall. Soft fur cushioned the hard rock beneath her. A lump to one side was no doubt the sack of food. Her captor had planned her abduction very well.

Ryn dropped to his knees on the edge of the bearskin. A taste. A taste of what? Oh, she knew very well what, and heaven above she was not ready.

"You said you wouldn't hurt me," she said as he leaned toward her.

"I won't."

He tilted his head, and a tangle of blond strands fell to the side, covering a portion of his face and touching his bare body. Could she fight him? She could try, but unless she was very clever, fighting wouldn't do much good. Ryn was large and muscular, and he could overpower her with one hand, if he chose to. He moved toward her slowly, and when he reached out his hand and caressed her cheek, he was warm. So warm.

"You shake," he whispered as he slanted his face toward hers.

"Of course I shake!" She tried to be stern, but she sounded terrified.

She reached out a hand to halt his progress, but of course her small hand on that massive chest did nothing to slow him down. Isadora had the power to stop a man in his tracks with a few words and a touch of her hand, but Juliet had never possessed such strength. She was a healer, a seer, and a gardener. Nothing in her life had ever prepared her to fight for her life or her virtue.

With the hand at her cheek, Ryn tilted her head to one side, and then he laid his mouth on her throat. It was not a kiss exactly. At least, she didn't think so. She'd never been kissed, but she had caught Willym kissing Isadora more than once. This was definitely not a kiss, it was . . .

It was a taste.

Ryn's heat surrounded her and took away all the chill as he moved his mouth gently over her neck. He sucked, he licked, he moved strands of red windblown hair out of his way so he had before and beneath him a wide expanse of unobstructed skin. Juliet did not stop shivering, but the tremble changed as the tasting continued on and on. Ryn used his tongue, his lips, and even his teeth, in a gentle way. Physical sensations she had never even imagined danced through her body. After a moment she no longer attempted to pull away or fight, but instead found herself leaning toward the mouth that tasted her. She swayed into Ryn, encouraging him, drinking in the warmth as he tasted her. In the back of her mind she wondered what might come next. When he'd mentioned taking a taste, she'd had no idea that *this* was what he intended.

He shifted loosened strands of untidy red hair with a warm, gentle hand, and moved his head to the other side of her neck. Somehow he'd unfastened the buttons of her cloak without her knowledge, because the heavy outer garment fell away and he pushed it aside so he could lay his warm lips on the place where neck curved into shoulder. His tongue rasped over that flesh; his mouth danced until Juliet forgot where she was and who he was and why she was here.

She rested her hand on his shoulder, needing something solid to keep her steady. When she laid her hand on his skin, she saw no unwanted images; she felt no emotions that were not her own. Maybe it was a good thing that Ryn wasn't an easy man to read. That fact had been quite annoying when she'd been trying to get a sense of what her future held at his hand, but at the moment she was glad she couldn't see beyond her own mind.

No blinding flashes, no headaches, no disturbing notions or secrets or knowledge of pains to come. Just an odd and wonderful warmth that traveled from Ryn's mouth through her entire body. Eyes closed, heart beating too fast, Juliet forgot everything but the way Ryn's mouth felt against her skin.

He pulled away slowly, giving that sensitive curve of her neck one last lick. In his eyes she saw something new and frightening. Lust.

Juliet was innocent in the ways of love and intended to remain that way, but she did have knowledge of the mechanics of a man's body. She did not look down to see if Ryn was truly aroused, but kept her eyes pinned to his. Her heart beat too fast, and she remained overly warm. Not because of the rocks that sheltered her from the wind, not because of the bearskin beneath her. It was Ryn's touch that kept her warm.

Ryn lifted his own hair from one side of his neck, and arched his eyebrows slightly in question, presenting his own skin for tasting. That offered neck was massive. Corded and muscled and surely warm. While she was momentarily and insanely tempted, Juliet shook her head quickly. Ryn dropped his hand and the hair without argument.

"You will be safe here tonight," he said as he stood and backed away.

Her heart continued to thud. Safe? She was anything but safe here.

"I will return in the morning."

Her head snapped up sharply. "Return? Where are you going?"

Ryn smiled. He did have a nice smile, she conceded. For a wild, possibly crazy man, that is. "You will miss me," he said.

"I will not," she countered.

He turned and walked away, leaving her alone. Already her senses had begun to return, and she questioned why she had been so moved by his strange actions. Tasting, indeed.

She didn't like being left here alone, in a harsh place so far from civilization. Maybe Ryn's departure was a trick of some kind, and if she moved from this spot, he'd spring out from behind a rock to surprise her. It was a test to see if she'd attempt to escape. Not at all interested in having a large man jump out and surprise her, she stayed put.

All was quiet as night fell, as gray sky turned to black and only the light from a full moon lit the austere landscape. Juliet delved beneath the bedroll and found the animal-skin sack filled with apples and bunting fruit and dried meat. She ate just a little, even though her stomach was quite empty. If she was careful, the food here might last three or four days.

After Juliet had eaten, she crept from her shelter and glanced around, standing and shaking off what little remained of the odd heat and sensations ignited by her captor's tasting. She couldn't see Ryn anywhere, but it was dark and there were plenty of large stones and dark shadows where he might be hiding. She glanced up. He could even be up there, watching and waiting.

Juliet walked to the precipice and looked down. Ryn had carried her up that steep path, and for the life of her she could not understand how he had managed it. The footholds were widely spaced and treacherous, and yet he had not once stopped to catch his breath or question his way. If she tried to climb back down the way they'd come, she'd end up killing herself; of that she had no doubt. She needed no special powers to see that truth.

The terrain was treacherous, and she did not know this part of the country at all. She didn't know what waited around the next bend in the path, or if she'd be able to survive on her own for even a few days. There would be dangers in a place like this one. And still, something inside her screamed *run.* Since Ryn was carrying her north, they moved farther from civilization with every step. If she had any chance at all of finding the road that would take her home, she'd have to make her escape now. To run might be foolhardy and risky, but the alternative was to blithely accept Ryn's insistence that she was his *wife.*

Juliet studied her surroundings in search of an escape route. The clearing had three sides, and three distinct routes of exit. Steeply up, treacherously down, and over a crop of boulders that led north. She did not want to travel north, but if that was what it took to find a way down the mountain, that's what she'd do.

She collected the small sack of food and rolled up the bearskin, preparing herself for travel. Unfortunately the skin was too heavy for her to carry far, so she left it behind. She hugged her cloak to her cold body and lifted her face to the full moon, thankful that she would not be forced to travel in complete darkness to make her escape. The moon was so big here, so close. It seemed as if it hung almost upon her, walking closely with her as she fled.

She climbed up a short ways and rounded the largest boulder to see before her a path of sorts. It was narrow and uneven, but wound more across than up or down. If she was very careful with her footing, she'd be well away from this place before morning and Ryn's return. She would think of him kindly, she decided as she picked her way across the path, since he had inadvertently saved her from Bors and the emperor's soldiers. He would find himself another wife, she was sure. One who wouldn't mind spending her life with a man who wore practically nothing and who lived in caves and who insisted on tasting the women he rescued. Kidnapped, she meant to say. Kidnapped.

After only a few minutes, the path took a decidedly upward turn. Juliet studied the way before her for only a moment before continuing on. If Ryn was so bold as to lick her tonight, then what did he have planned for tomorrow night? And the next night and the next? The thoughts of what might come spurred her upward, though the short climb was not an easy one and she was soon breathing heavily.

The path ended abruptly, and once again she was faced with three choices. Up. Down. Back. Since the "up" this time was a rock face of no more than six or seven feet, she grabbed on to cold stone and hauled herself up a few inches. At least the exertion kept her warm. At the moment she didn't feel the cold so much, except for the chill of the rock seeping into her fingers. She continued upward, hoping that once she'd reached the top of this ledge, she'd find another relatively easy path awaiting her.

She grabbed on and pulled herself up again, so that she could indeed see what appeared to be a path before her.

Movement out of the corner of her eye grabbed her attention and she went very still, standing precariously on a bit of stone so that only half her face cleared the top of the rock face. She thought of Ryn, of course, and then of the bearskin and the very large bear that had once been attached to it. What of other creatures that might live in these mountains? Creatures that would no doubt do more than lick her if she ran across them.

It was not a bear that slithered into her line of vision, but a wolf. A huge, flaxen wolf with blazing golden eyes that were not fooled by her stillness. It came directly to her, walking majestically and with undeniable strength in its haunches.

A man who is not a man. A beast who is not a beast. The words popped into her head, much as they had last night. It was rare for her to sense anything at all without touching, but whoever this unseen man was, he could slip into her mind with ease, or so it appeared.

She jerked her head to the side, hoping to see that man on the edge of the forest. He was the wolf's owner, perhaps, or more likely its companion, since she could not imagine such a creature deigning to be owned by anyone. Would that man who had followed her when she'd been in the control of the soldiers lead her toward safety and what was left of home, or would he declare her his wife in a ridiculous manner and toss her over his shoulder as if she had no say whatsoever in the matter?

But apparently there was no man in the forest. She could not see or sense him. There was just the wolf, and after that initial connection that had struck her like the flat of a palm, her mind had gone quiet and still. Powerless. When Ryn had touched her, she'd felt very little. And now, the message she'd received made no sense to her. She had originally thought that Ryn possessed the ability to block her invasion in some way, but that might not be the case. No one had ever been able to do such a thing, and Sophie and Isadora had both tried on more than one occasion. Perhaps her abilities were failing. Did being so far away from civilization weaken her? If she moved far enough into the mountains, would she be free of her gift entirely? If she had thought that was possible, she would've moved into the wilderness years ago.

The wolf lowered its head and sniffed at her. It made no aggressive moves, but seemed simply curious. That encouraged Juliet. "Nice wolfie," she said softly. "Would you like to be my friend? I could use a friend right about now. You can help me get out of here. What do you say?"

The animal placed its nose close to Juliet's and she held her breath. Stars above, it was huge! Much larger than she had imagined a wolf could be. A growl began deep in its throat and the wolf showed her its teeth. Large, sharp teeth. Lots of them. Juliet made her decision. Down.

She moved downward quickly. Too quickly. Her foot missed a hold. She scrambled frantically for a moment, and then she lost her grip entirely. After falling for a brief and breathless moment, she landed hard upon the ground and the wind was knocked from her body. The wolf leapt down to land gracefully and powerfully beside her. Juliet closed her eyes as she waited for the wild animal to attack her. Eaten alive; it was not the way she had expected to die.

But the animal did not attack. It stood there, studying her with those odd glowing eyes, and waited. Waited for what?

Moving cautiously, so as not to alarm the animal, Juliet sat up and then rose to her feet. "Did you decide to be my friend after all?" She studied the rock face. She hated the prospect of making that climb again, but there was nothing to be done for it. She'd be sore in a few hours, thanks to the fall, but nothing was broken or twisted so there was no need to lie here and moan. She took a single step toward the rock face, and the wolf growled. She looked down at the animal as it moved to stand between her and the route of escape. After a moment, it nudged her with its nose. When she didn't move, it nudged again. A huge paw lifted to prod her thigh more forcefully.

"What do you want?" she asked. Using its nose and its paws, the wolf made her turn about. Juliet faced the way she had come. "Surely you're not—"

A nudge to her backside sent her forward with a squeal. "Hey!" She glanced around. She didn't know where Ryn was tonight, but it wouldn't do for him to hear her yell. Especially since she was not where he had left her. "That's very rude," she whispered.

It seemed almost as if the wolf was trying to force her back to the camp, but surely that was impossible. It was an animal, acting on instinct and instinct alone. When she turned toward the rock face, the animal growled and blocked her progress. When she turned toward camp, it remained silent and calm. To test her theory, she began to walk purposefully back toward the campsite she'd left behind. The wolf followed, but it did not growl or push. When she tried to turn back toward freedom, the wolf placed itself in her path and snarled a warning.

"You're Ryn's wolf, aren't you?" she said as she stared at the animal, who herded her back to camp. "He didn't leave me unguarded after all. You have been on sentinel duty all along." Of course he had left a guard. Had Ryn not said it was his place to protect her? To keep her safe? And all she had to do in return was agree to be his wife and comfort him. Never.

As she walked back to camp, the wolf at her heels, Juliet formulated a plan. Maybe escape would not be as easy as she'd initially thought, but there would come a time when Ryn would trust her enough to leave her unguarded. Not tonight, and perhaps not tomorrow night, but eventually. They would not stay high on this mountain forever. He spoke of a home far away, and surely somewhere between here and there the opportunity for freedom awaited her.

Isadora would try to fight her way out of such a situation, and likely be killed in the process. Sophie would get her way by using her charm and beauty. She might cry a little, or try to wheedle until she got her way. If that failed, she would attempt to run. And when Ryn caught her, she'd run again, as soon as the opportunity presented itself. In truth, if Sophie hadn't fallen in love with Kane Varden, she'd probably consider being kidnapped by a wild man who professed to be her mate exciting.

Isadora would fight; Sophie would run. But Juliet possessed one trait her sisters did not. Patience.

She kicked the bearskin and rolled it out once again, and sat upon it. Moments later, the cold seeped through her cape and her dress, and she began to shiver. It was much colder here, high in the mountains, than it had been on the road to Arthes. She was exhausted, but how could she possibly sleep? As she lay on the bearskin bedroll, still at last, the cold crept beneath her gown and to her skin.

Patience would get her through the next few days, until a route of escape presented itself to her. All she had to do was convince Ryn that she could not offer him comfort of any kind. He seemed determined not to harm her, and had even promised in a most convincing voice that he would never allow any other man to hurt her, either. Maybe she would eventually find a way to reason with him.

She laid her eyes on the wolf, who stood just a few feet away. "Is Ryn a reasonable man? Will he listen with any concern to the wishes of a woman? Maybe if he wants to convince me that we're fated to be together, he'll be wary of making me angry or upset. I can use that, I think. I can pretend to accept my lot as his wife and twist him around my little finger." Sophie could very easily do such a thing, but Juliet? She relied on practicality, and practicality would likely not help her now.

Juliet rubbed her hands along her cold arms and shook off the chill that seeped into her bones. When that didn't work, she lay down and wrapped herself in the bearskin, as if it were a cocoon. Still she shivered. The wolf moved closer, striding slowly forward with its golden eyes on Juliet. It stood very close for a moment, and then moved nearer. Had the wild animal just been waiting for her to be in a completely helpless position before attacking?

"Ryn will be very unhappy if you eat me," she said softly.

But the wolf didn't so much as bare its teeth. It lay down beside Juliet, so close its fur was pressed to the bearskin Juliet had wrapped herself within. Immediately the animal's heat seeped through the bedroll and warmed her. The wolf rested its head on the ground and readjusted its legs so it was comfortable.

The wolf smelled like an animal, which was to be expected. It was musky but clean, not at all unpleasant. Its fur was long and golden and beautiful, and if she could bear to move her hands from the warmth of the bearskin, she might be tempted to reach out and touch that fur, to stroke and discover if it felt as silky as it looked. The wolf's heat soothed her, cradled her. The animal's very presence calmed her.

Juliet worked one hand free of her cocoon, and very slowly reached out to touch the wolf's fur. The animal did not seem alarmed by the gesture, so she worked her fingers into the soft, silky hair and stroked gently. The golden fur was as warm and soft as it looked, and was much more welcoming than she had imagined it might be. While she stroked, the wolf closed its eyes and made a low sound of contentment, something between a growl and a purr.

Juliet closed her eyes, too, and in a matter of moments she drifted to sleep with her fingers buried in the golden fur of the wolf who warmed her.

5

IT WAS THE WOLF'S ABSENCE THAT WOKE HER, THE HOWL of a gust of cold wind and a deep sense of being alone. Juliet sat up, drawing her cloak close and shivering as her eyes were drawn to the empty path that had led her to the animal last night.

The sun was rising, but it had not been visible on the horizon for more than a few minutes and hadn't yet had a chance to warm the air. The night's chill remained. That's why she wished for the wolf, a little. It was the heat she craved—nothing more. How long had the animal been gone? Would it return? How silly of her to get sentimental over a wild animal that had bared its teeth at her and nudged her toward captivity.

Juliet was more than a little surprised that she'd slept so well. She had not even dreamed, that she remembered. It was nice to have a night pass without the disturbance of the nightmare that plagued her or dreams that were more than dreams. It was sheer exhaustion, she reasoned. Even though she'd slept deeply at times, she'd awakened several times in the night to find the wolf snuggled up against her, offering warmth and companionship.

This morning there was no sign of the wolf or Ryn. For a moment, a fleeting moment that passed almost before she was aware of it, Juliet was frightened to be here all alone. She quickly chastised herself for being too timid in a situation that called for bravery. Isadora would never sit around and wait for a man to rescue her, and neither would Sophie. Juliet's thoughts turned to escape once again. Would she find one animal or another—Ryn or the wolf—awaiting her on the path if she tried once more to make her own way down the mountain? She rolled up the bearskin, determined to find a way to carry it with her, and snatched up the sack of food. She wouldn't eat just yet. She didn't know how long the supplies she had would have to last her.

"You slept well." The deep voice was so out of place on this mountain morning that Juliet actually jumped a little. Ryn gracefully rounded the boulder that hid the path from her. Not only had he been silent on his approach, but she'd had no internal warning that she was not alone. "The bearskin is too heavy for you." He took the heavy bedroll from her and tossed it over his own shoulder as if it weighed nothing at all.

He made a move toward her, as if he intended to toss her over his shoulder along with the bedroll.

"I will walk," she said sharply. "Being carried all day yesterday was quite unpleasant."

His smile was brilliant as he backed away from her. In the morning light Ryn was all sun-bronzed skin, hard muscle, and golden hair. And that smile. "Perhaps you will enjoy today's journey."

"Perhaps," she answered suspiciously.

"We must hurry."

She followed him down the same path she'd walked alone last night. Her view of his back was from an entirely different perspective than it had been yesterday, when she'd been dangling there. Ryn's stride was long and powerful, and she had to move quickly to keep up with him. The muscles in his legs and his back and his shoulders worked together in a way that was fascinating. The basics of anatomy were the same for Ryn and any other man, and yet he seemed different, as if he were of another species altogether.

He was taller and stronger, sleeker and more lithe and most definitely bigger, than the average man. The way he moved, with an innate confidence and dexterity, was entirely new to her. Perhaps he truly was of another species. Surely he had not shaved before rejoining her this morning, not here in the wilderness, and yet there was no stubble on his face.

When they reached the rock wall, he climbed it easily, as if his bare feet had never known a misstep or a stumble. When she started to follow, he tossed the bearskin to the ground and reached down one long arm to assist her. She hesitated, and then clasped his hand tightly.

Yesterday she had sensed very little from the man when she'd touched him, and then her abilities had shut down entirely. But today was another matter entirely. While Ryn hauled her slowly and steadily upward, vivid images flashed through her mind.

The forest in shades of gray, flying past as if she flew low across the ground, zigging and zagging to avoid rocks and trees and thick brush.

The full moon bright and clear in an autumn sky, its rays shining down and lighting the night so that there were no secrets, no hidden shadows.

Her, sleeping on the bearskin.

Her, peeking over this very rock face.

Her, riding toward Arthes with the emperor's soldiers all around.

A man who is not a man. A beast who is not a beast.

Ryn placed her on her feet, and she glared up at him. She really did have to look sharply up in order to gaze fully at his face. He did not turn away or present his back on her, but stared down at her intently. There were such magnificent and powerful flashes of gold in his eyes, she could not look away even if she wanted to. Heaven above, she knew those eyes.

"You are the wolf," she said plainly.

He nodded. Once.

"You should have told me."

"I believe I just did." With that, he scooped up the bearskin bedroll and turned. He walked away from her, those strides again long and purposeful.

After a moment's hesitation, Juliet followed. The creature who claimed to be her husband was a shape-shifter. She had heard of such creatures, in tales meant to frighten and even in old witches' texts, but she had never known that they were real. According to legend, on the three nights in each cycle when the moon was at its zenith, such creatures changed. Ryn became a wolf. He became the large, blond wolf who had slept with her last night. A wolf by night, a man by day. A creature of nightmares and campfire tales, not a man. Not a man at all.

Juliet had been frightened of her captor, and she'd been angry. Last night she had been willing to risk her very life to get away from him, but at the moment she found him more fascinating than frightening. A *shape-shifter.*

She rushed to catch up with him, and at the sound of her footsteps he slowed his stride so she could join him. They had a short way to travel in which there were no rock faces or ledges to climb up or down. "I am quite talented with herbs and spells and such. Perhaps I can concoct a cure for you."

He did not slow his stride, but he did look down at her. "A cure? For what?"

"Your affliction. With time and patience I believe I can construct a medicine which will keep the wolf at bay." In her mind she compiled a list of possibly necessary ingredients. Oh, if only she had grabbed her satchel when Ryn had kidnapped her! Some of the herbs she needed were in that very bag.

"Why?"

It was a struggle to keep up with him, and she began to think that being carried wasn't so bad after all. "Why?" The question was unexpected. "Well, so you can be a normal man. So you can rid yourself of the wolf. If I can come up with a cure, you'll be in control at all times."

"No," he said softly.

"But . . ."

"I don't want a cure."

"Of course you want a cure," she insisted breathlessly. "Any man who was cursed with such an affliction would want—"

"The wolf is not a curse," he snapped. Before she could argue with him, he continued, his stride increasing in length and speed. "The wolf is the essence of the Anwyn," he said as he walked away from her. "It is wild and powerful and connected to the core of the earth in a way a man can never be. You should understand this, since you are connected to the earth in your own way."

"I'm not actually connected to the earth," Juliet argued. "I just have the ability to occasionally see what I should not."

"All animals are connected to the earth, some more strongly than others. You have a rare ability, but you have not honed your skill. You fight it."

"First of all, I'm not an animal," Juliet said, almost indignantly.

"You are," Ryn said, "as I am. As all creatures are."

"And second," she said, unwilling to continue that part of the conversation, "I do not fight my gift."

"You fight. I see what you do not."

"You don't see anything where I'm concerned," she said sharply, rushing to catch up with him. "And don't change the subject. I simply offered to try to find a cure for your ailment."

"If you take away the wolf, you take away my soul."

She wanted to argue the point with him awhile longer, but he moved too far away too quickly. She'd have to shout to be heard, and since he was obviously in no mood to listen, she'd be wasting her breath, in any case.

Later, perhaps.

The Northern Palace of the Empire of Columbyana

The Northern Province was too cold for Sophie's liking, but her rooms in the palace were warm enough, and her infant daughter Ariana was happy to sit on a rug near the fire in the parlor and play with the doll her grandfather had given her.

Her husband Kane was in his element, once again at Arik's side. The rebel leader had been surprised but pleased to find that Kane Varden was not dead, as he had believed for such a long time. Kane had been worried about explaining to Arik how he'd lost more than a year of his life, but the man who claimed to be the rightful emperor of Columbyana simply listened and nodded his head and welcomed Kane back into the fold.

The rebels could have killed the occupants of the palace when they'd taken it, but they had not. The lady of the

Northern Palace was Emperor Sebestyen's eldest sister—
and the rebel leader Arik's half sister. Even though they were
brother and sister, Lady Raye and Arik had never met. She
was a legitimate offspring of the late Emperor Nechtyn and
his empress, and Arik was the bastard son of the old emperor's tryst with a favored concubine. Raye and her husband occupied the Northern Palace, collecting taxes and
recruiting soldiers in this cold province. The lord and lady of
this palace were presently under arrest, but Arik had allowed
them to remain in their quarters, unlike the soldiers who had
been killed in battle or tossed into the dungeon prison.

Sophie laid a hand over her slightly swollen belly. There
were months still to carry this child before she was born,
and she savored every day. Kane had missed her pregnancy
with Ariana. He would not miss anything this time.

The knowledge of the curse that could ruin everything
kept her from complete happiness. Kane's thirtieth birthday would arrive with the end of summer. Sophie had not
yet tried to break the curse that would likely take her husband from her shortly before that birthday arrived, but she
had spent many hours researching and planning. Most days
she was confident that she would be able to break the curse
that had plagued the Fyne women and their men for three
hundred years. Other days, she was gripped with the fear
of burying the man she loved as Isadora had buried her
husband, as countless Fyne witches had done in years past.

Maybe Kane would not die, but instead would desert
her, disappearing like the morning dew without warning or
explanation as some husbands and lovers of Fyne women
had done in the past. Such a terrible happening would hurt,
and she would forever wonder if he was coming back—but
it would be preferable to his death. Unfortunately, she did
not think the outcome was hers to choose.

Her father, Maddox Sulyen, sat with her on this cold afternoon, sharing the parlor in this suite of rooms that had

been assigned to Kane and his family. While Kane had been welcomed with open arms, the Emperor Sebestyen's Minister of Defense . . . *former* minister, she imagined . . . had been greeted with suspicion. He would be a great ally to the revolution, when the rebels finally embraced his defection.

Sophie had had only days in which to come to know her father, but her instincts told her that he was a good man. Not because he was powerful and intelligent and handsome, but because he had a good heart.

"I can't believe how much you look like your mother," he said softly.

Ariana glanced up at her grandfather and cooed, smiling widely. She had taken to him from the first moment she laid eyes upon him, and that was one of the reasons Sophie had no problems trusting her father. Ariana had good instincts where men were concerned.

"She always told me I looked like you."

Maddox shrugged broad shoulders. "In coloring, yes. But the shape of your face is hers. When I look at you, the years roll back and . . ." He hesitated, and she understood why. His union with her mother had not been a romantic one, but one of sexual pleasure that had lasted just one night. He had been very young at that time . . . barely eighteen years old, by her figuring. Lucinda Fyne had gone to Sulyen knowing he would leave her with a child. He had known nothing, of course, but that a beautiful older woman offered herself to him.

It must've been an extraordinary night, for him to remember her so clearly after all these years.

"You have no other children?" Sophie asked.

He shook his head slowly. "None. I usually take great care to see that there are no . . ." Again, he stumbled.

"Consequences," Sophie said as she rubbed her slightly rounded tummy.

"Yes."

But that night with Lucinda Fyne had been different. She had not only seduced him, she'd charmed him into forgetting his usual caution. He had never even suspected that the woman who'd come to him had been a witch.

A grimace crossed his face momentarily. "I can't believe I'm a grandfather. I'm not old enough to have a granddaughter."

"Apparently you are," Sophie said with a smile.

"I didn't even get to be a father before . . . and now there's not one but two." He waved a large hand at Sophie's stomach. "Or soon will be. You're sure it will be another girl?"

"Positive. There hasn't been a baby boy born to the Fyne line in . . . well, I don't know how long."

"This is the Varden line now, correct?" he said.

Such a decidedly male way of thinking. "No matter what I call myself, my daughters will be Fyne women. Fyne witches."

Maddox wrinkled his nose. He had a lot more trouble accepting that Sophie was a witch than he had accepting that she was his child.

The door to the suite opened, and Sophie caught a glimpse of the guard that had been posted at the door. Kane stepped into the room. Her husband warmed her heart and her soul, and simply looking at him fed her spirit.

Like the other rebels, Kane wore a cloak embroidered with the shield of Arik, a sword he knew how to wield, and a sharp dagger. His long hair, that unique shade of brown with the liberal blond striations, was pulled back today, against the wind that howled beyond the palace walls. Heaven above, she hated the north. She wanted to go home to warmer climes and wildflowers.

And her sisters. They had not parted on the best of terms, but now that things with Kane were settled, she wanted to see them again. She needed to hug her sisters, tell them she forgave them, ask them to forgive her, tell them all was well, and then . . .

Isadora would help her sister find a way to break the curse. Juliet, too, but Isadora had always been the one to study and practice her craft. She had never been afraid of magic, and if she had truly believed that the curse would take her husband, she would have done something years ago. She might not have succeeded, but she certainly would have tried. Perhaps there were clues of some sort in the letters they had found after Willym's death, letters from Fyne witches who had buried the men they loved over the years.

Sophie's powers were at greater heights than she had imagined possible. With her sisters beside her, surely they could break the curse that had always robbed the Fyne women of love and lasting happiness. Once that was done, she would fight alongside Kane. Not with a sword, but with the talents she had discovered in the past year. Sophie Maddox Fyne Varden was a witch, and Arik took her counsel very much to heart. She was a lover of peace, and she did not want to see anyone harmed. But heaven above, the Emperor Sebestyen had to be ousted from his seat of power. He was not a nice man; he was not a just ruler.

Sophie had proven most useful thus far in advising Arik and his generals about the layout of the upper levels of the Palace in Arthes, as they planned for the future. She had been in the lift, seen the guards at the emperor's door, noted the security measures that an invading force would need to be aware of. She would have more uses in the days to come; of that she was certain.

Kane did not yet completely trust Maddox Sulyen, even though it had been his sister Liane who sent them north to warn the minister not to return to the palace in Arthes. He took Sophie's arm as she rose to greet him, kissed her soundly, and then steered her into the hallway that led to the private bedchambers. Sophie asked her father to keep an eye on the baby as her husband pulled her away from the main parlor.

When they had traveled a few feet down the dim hallway, Kane spun Sophie around and pressed her against the wall, giving her a proper kiss. That done, he laid his hand on her belly and leaned in close. "Tomorrow we travel."

"Where?" She held her breath as she awaited his answer. "South."

Sophie didn't know whether to smile or cry. She wanted to go home, but Arik's journey south meant war would finally visit her home province. "My father will travel with us?"

"Yes. We can't afford to let him go, he's too dangerous to leave behind, and Arik doesn't want to kill him."

The "yet" was unspoken, but hung in the air between them. "He could be a fine ally," Sophie said.

"Or a dangerous enemy."

"He only wants what is best for Columbyana," she argued.

Kane brushed a strand of loose hair away from her face. "I do not want to talk about war tonight."

"Neither do I."

"We'll put your father and the baby to bed early. This might be our last night on a soft mattress for weeks to come."

"I don't think anyone has put Maddox Sulyen to bed in a very long time," she teased.

"We'll give it a try."

There was no way to tell what they'd find on their journey. Maybe there would be sympathizers along the way who would share their homes and their beds. Then again, the rebels might be sleeping on the ground every night for the next month. Or more.

She laid a hand on Kane's cheek. "I'm going home," she whispered.

"You're going home."

JULIET HAD BEGUN TO WISH TO BE CARRIED HOURS AGO, though she didn't dare say such a thing to Ryn. Her legs ached, her feet were sore, and she'd torn her cape on sharp rock so many times it was beginning to look more like a rag than a fine garment. The ache from the fall was sharper than it had been upon rising, but she didn't dare complain. Ryn would only tell her that it was her own fault for trying to run away from him.

The good news was that in the near distance she saw trees again. She and Ryn had climbed up and down and around, always moving northward. She had begun to think she'd never see a tree again, or a creature other than Ryn and the occasional bird that passed overhead.

Directly ahead she saw evergreen trees that did not turn gold and yellow and blue like the trees at home, but maintained their green even in the dead of winter. This place would be beautiful when snow came, she imagined. Judging by the chill in the air, that snow would come soon.

Ryn had taken offense at her suggestion that she cure him. He'd barely spoken three words to her all day. He led her onward and upward and across, occasionally slowing his pace in order to accommodate her, but there was no conversation to speak of. She had intended to gain his trust, and suggesting that the wolf which lived within him was an affliction was apparently not the best way to do that.

"How far?" she asked. If she'd had the strength, she would have hurried to catch up with Ryn, but she could barely walk and hurrying was out of the question.

"We will stop before dark."

"I wasn't asking about tonight," she said. "How far is it to your home?"

He stopped and turned, waiting for her. His brow wrinkled as he watched her limp toward him. "Why did you not tell me that you hurt?"

"Don't you hurt?"

"No."

"For your information, those who are not of Anwyn blood are not accustomed to climbing mountains all day with barely a break to rest their sore legs. For goodness' sakes, Ryn. Bors treated the horses better than you treat me!"

He stood there until she reached him, and then without a word he lifted her off her feet.

Juliet's head swam; her stomach roiled. But she did not tell Ryn to put her down.

"You had only to ask for assistance," he said softly.

"I didn't want to ask for assistance." Juliet wrapped her arms around his neck, just to steady herself, and for a moment she held her breath. When she realized that she would not be assaulted with images of Ryn's past and future, she relaxed.

"Because you are disgusted by my affliction," he said, his deep voice all but rumbling.

"No!" Juliet shifted slightly. Even though Ryn now carried her, her feet and legs were still sore. The shoulders, too, she realized as she tried to find a comfortable position.

"Then why would you not ask for my help when you hurt?"

He carried her and the bedroll without so much as a hitch. Of course she could've asked for help. Ryn would've carried her all day without a word of complaint. "I am accustomed to doing for myself," she said softly. "I don't wish to be beholden to anyone."

"A wife need not feel beholden to her husband just because he . . ." Ryn changed his course of direction. "A woman is naturally weaker than a man. She should not hesitate to ask for a man's strength when it is needed."

"I'm sure that comment is meant to be sweet and gallant, but instead it sounds simply overbearing. Women are not necessarily weaker than men."

"You wish to walk."

"No," she answered quickly.

After a few steps she muttered beneath her breath. "But if you ever meet my sister, you've got a surprise coming."

"The dark one," he said almost reverently.

"Isadora."

He climbed a steep rise as if he still strode easily across flat ground. "I'm glad she's not the one," he said as he crested the rise.

"I wish I could see her again," Juliet said softly, not expecting a response. "I want to know that she's safe, and let her know that I'm alive and unharmed."

"You can, if you try," Ryn said in his deep, matter-of-fact voice.

"That's easy for you to say."

Ryn came to a stop and placed Juliet on her feet. For a moment she was light-headed from the sudden change in movement, and he steadied her with his large, capable hands.

"The mountains, they are powerful. There's magic in the rock, in the trees and the soil, in the air. If you listen to the earth and let it feed you, your affliction will grow to new heights."

"Affliction?" She placed her hands on her hips and glared. "I'll have you know . . ." The corners of Ryn's mouth turned up just slightly, and Juliet knew she'd been teased. "Very funny."

"There is magic here," he said seriously. "All you have to do is reach out for it. Grab it. Make it your own. Do not be afraid of what you will find within yourself."

"For your information, my *affliction* has not grown stronger in these mountains. It doesn't seem to be working at all. I see almost nothing of you."

"That is my doing, not a failing of your abilities."

"I don't understand," she whispered. "You can actually keep me out?"

"Yes."

"How?"

"I don't know how," he replied, unconcerned. "It just is. Your powers are not dampened here. Quite the opposite. I cannot explain well, but I can show you." Ryn took her hand in his, and together they dropped to their knees. It was an awkward move, since Juliet had not been expecting to drop down, but he did not let her fall. "All animals are connected to the earth, wife. You are more connected than others." He forced her hand to the ground and held it there. "You are connected to everything and everyone that shares this land with you. Find the streak of power that binds you to your sisters. Tap into it, drink from it, and you will see."

A surge of something unknown flashed and fluttered through Juliet's body. It was bright, and painful, and frightening. Afraid of the power, she snatched her hand from Ryn's and clutched it to her chest.

"I'm not an animal," she argued, not for the first time today.

"You are not ready," he said kindly, and then he stood and much too easily tossed her over his shoulder.

Ready? Juliet shuddered as Ryn began to run. She could barely stand to touch a person's hand and know secrets of their future; she would never be ready to embrace a power that tied her to everyone and everything.

ISADORA CREPT TOWARD THE SOLDIERS' CAMP, WHICH WAS situated outside a small village. Earlier in the afternoon she'd stolen a man's worn brown cape to cover her black dress. She didn't know how quickly word would spread among the soldiers, but she did know that they would be looking for a dark-haired woman dressed entirely in black. When the opportunity arose, she'd steal a frock, too, but for now the cape was enough.

The soldiers' camp was a small one. No surprise, since the village so far from the main road consisted of no more than ten houses. There were a few small farms in the area, as well, but they were spread far apart. The soldiers had put up tents on the outskirts of the village. They'd been here awhile, judging by the campsite. Maybe from these headquarters the soldiers collected taxes, or perhaps there had been a rebel uprising in the area and they were here to squash any further trouble before it had a chance to start. Whatever the reason for their presence, they were well established.

A long, well-used table sat near a stone circle where a fire burned low and steady. Supper, a pot of something that smelled heavenly to a woman who hadn't had a decent meal in well more than a week, simmered above that fire. Outside one of the tents, on yet another table, loaves of bread had been laid out, ready to be sliced and served to the soldiers.

Isadora was hungry, and she'd need supplies before she headed into the mountains. She glanced north. The mountains looked so far away. She'd been circling around the most direct routes, steering clear of soldiers . . . steering clear of all people . . . and making her way cautiously toward Juliet.

The soldiers had congregated in two groups. One bunch gathered around a tent at the far edge of the camp, drinking deeply from tankards and laughing at words she could not hear from this distance. A smaller band of soldiers assembled not far from the fire. The cook and two friends, she supposed. Friends or assistants. In any case, they looked chummy enough.

These soldiers were not looking for her or any other problem to come along to stir up their cozy existence. They had been here long enough to get comfortable, and apparently saw the villagers as no threat.

Good. Their laziness would make getting to the bread that much easier.

Isadora kept to the edge of the camp, hiding behind the tents and keeping an eye on the larger group of soldiers. The table where the bread sat was just a few feet away, and she hurried quietly toward it intent on one full loaf. Maybe two. She'd need more provisions and a sturdy sack before much longer, before she entered the mountain range to search for her sister. She kept the tents that were arranged in a half-circle around the camp between her and the soldiers. With any luck, they wouldn't realize anyone had been there until they sat down to eat supper and found a loaf missing. Even then—they would likely blame one of their own.

She stopped at one end of the table where the bread was stored, and grabbed one loaf. One only. Then she stepped into the forest behind the camp, breathing deeply and with great relief as she left the camp behind her. A low wind and the whisper of many small animals kept the forest from being completely silent, so she felt confident that no one would hear her step.

Isadora hadn't gone far when she rounded a tree and came face to face with a soldier. He had not seen her and crept around to catch her. She surprised him, as he had surprised her. He'd been urinating against a tree and hadn't even yet righted his trousers. She turned and ran, but he gave chase and quickly caught her, grabbing her arm and yanking her about to face him.

"And just what do you think you're doing?" a gruff

voice asked. The soldier was not very old and not very young, but somewhere in between, and he had the beefy look of a man who could be fat with little effort. He wore an emerald green uniform, a short knife, and a sword, and he was in bad need of soap and water.

The bread she had stolen fell to the ground, and the soldier pinned her arms at her sides. Her power was still weakened, and words alone would do her no good. She could make him drop into unconsciousness, if she could lay her hand on his head while she said the proper incantation, but he was physically stronger than she and his grip was firm.

"I'm very hungry," she said softly, wondering if the soldier had a heart beneath that green uniform. "I haven't eaten all day."

"That's not my problem. Stealing from the emperor's men is as heinous as stealing from the emperor himself."

Would they hang her for taking a loaf of bread? Maybe. Nothing any man would do surprised her, not anymore.

"I haven't seen you around the village," the soldier said as he squeezed her wrists tightly. "Are you traveling through?" His brow furrowed slightly, as if he had only now thought to question her presence in the woods. His eyes widened slightly, and he looked past her brown cloak to the black frock beneath, then raised his gaze to her dark eyes. "Ah, you're the witch they're looking for. There's a nice reward for you. Dead or alive. They say you're a dangerous one, and dead is preferred."

The soldier pressed her against a tree and unsheathed his knife. Isadora closed her eyes. He was going to kill her, here and now. She hadn't found Juliet, and Sophie still needed them. If Juliet said that was true, then it was true. It was too soon, and she didn't want to die. Not yet, not until her duty to her sisters was done.

"If I do the deed without calling for help, I'll have the

reward to myself," the soldier said thoughtfully. The tip of the knife touched her throat. "You don't look particularly dangerous, but I suppose that's a chance I shouldn't take."

Isadora hadn't fought to this point, so her burst of resistance surprised the soldier. She reached not for him but for the immediate threat—the knife. She grabbed his wrist and pushed the blade away from her throat, turning the sharp tip toward his chest. They struggled for a moment, no more than a moment, and then they fell, entangled and wrestling for the knife.

They hit the ground. The soldier grunted and went still. Isadora's weight plunged the knife into his heart and he died almost instantly. There was no shout of alarm and very little blood, just a whoosh of air from his lungs and a surprised expression on his hideous face. His hands fell away and Isadora scrambled up and away from his body.

She leaned down and, with a burst of strength, pulled the knife from his chest and wiped the blood from the blade onto his uniform. The forest around them remained quiet; apparently no one had missed him just yet, and when they did, it would take them a few moments to become alarmed enough to search for him.

With her heart beating so hard it threatened to drown out everything else, she took the time to unfasten the weapons belt that held his sword and the sheath for the knife that had killed him. If he was wearing anything but an imperial uniform, she'd take that, too. There would be less conspicuous clothing to steal down the road. She buckled the weapons belt to her own waist, tying the soft leather instead of fastening the buckle, since the belt was much too large for her. It hung low on her waist and was covered by the cloak.

The other soldiers would find the dead soldier eventually, but there was nothing here to indicate anything other than a simple robbery. The man had been emptying his bladder in privacy when someone had surprised him, killed him, and stolen his weapons. A rebel, perhaps. Not a woman. Not a witch. There was nothing to point Bors or the soldiers in this direction, in their search for her.

Isadora grabbed the bread from the ground and turned away from the body, unexpected tears burning her eyes. The flicker of magic at her core dimmed once more, fluttering and threatening to go dark. It was death that stole her powers from her; she knew that now.

She had been meant for protection, not destruction, and as she turned from her destined path, her magic decayed. Even though this soldier's death had been an accident, it had come at her hand . . . and she was not sorry that he was dead. He would have killed her without a qualm, if she hadn't fought back.

"Help me," she whispered as she hurried away from the camp. "Please, Will, help me." There had been a time when she'd thought Will to be perfect, a loving husband, a kind man. But he'd left her alone. He'd died and abandoned her, and now when she needed him most, he refused to come to her. Was it her own loss of power that kept him from her, or was he punishing her?

"You're no better than the rest of them," she muttered as she moved more deeply into the forest. Was she trying to goad his spirit into appearing? If so, it didn't work. She remained utterly alone. Isadora kept moving away from the soldiers' camp, determined and angry and empty with loneliness. Occasionally tears tried to fill her eyes but she pushed them back, knowing that weakness of any kind could only hurt her and her chances to reach Juliet.

It was almost nightfall before she gasped with the knife-sharp realization that she'd killed a man for a loaf of bread.

6

CAMP WAS MADE BEYOND A STAND OF TREES THAT blocked the wind. Perhaps tonight would not be quite so cold. The trees made this site feel less harsh—less unwelcoming and more like home. A shallow cave offered shelter, in case the snow Juliet continued to feel in the air came during the night, and Ryn gathered wood and built a fire not far from the cave entrance, to offer real warmth and to cook the animal he'd caught and killed for supper. He called the animal a *tilsi,* and it looked and tasted like a large rabbit of some sort Juliet had never encountered.

She did not doubt that all things in these mountains were different, in some way. In many ways.

Ryn glanced to the western sky often, waiting for sundown, and when the darkness of night was near, he walked into the woods. Alone.

Juliet expected that he would join her, once the transformation from man to wolf had taken place, but he did not. She huddled by the fire as the night grew colder, and her eyes searched the wooded area beyond camp for signs of life. Like it or not, she missed Ryn. The wolf, not the man. The man had kidnapped her and dragged her away from her sister and insisted that she was his wife. But the wolf had comforted her. The wolf had become her friend. She missed his company, his warmth, his very presence. Now and then she caught sight of a small flash of gold in the darkness of the forest. Ryn's eyes.

In spite of her mixed feelings, she never forgot that man and wolf were the same being. They shared the same soul, the same mind. The same determination to keep her.

"There's no reason to be angry," she said, her voice soft, but loud enough to carry in the deep silence. "I didn't mean to hurt your feelings. I was just trying to help."

There was no response. Not even a growl or a yip.

Ryn said she was connected to the earth and all things that shared it, which meant she was connected to him. His ability to keep her out of his mind had begun to annoy her. She wanted to know what the future held and how she might escape, but that was impossible as long as Ryn maintained the barrier between them.

Juliet gingerly placed her hand upon the ground, much as she had when she'd first sensed Ryn behind the rock, back at the soldiers' camp. She imagined a river running from her hand to Ryn, lost in darkness and in the commanding form of a wolf. She reached out to him, in a way she had never before reached for anyone but her sisters.

You want to kill me.

Even though she had been attempting to reach Ryn, she was startled by the sudden return of her ability. "I do not want to kill you," she argued.

You want to kill the wolf in me.

She was actually communicating with that wolf, so she considered her response carefully. Did the animal act independently of the man? Or were they always one?

"Can you read my mind as I can read yours?" she asked.

Sometimes.

She watched the forest for a flash of that gold again, but all was dark and quiet. *Then you know I would never knowingly hurt another living soul. It is not my way.*

You do not yet know your way, wife.

I do.

Stay close to the fire tonight.

The connection was severed with a suddenness that startled her, and all was dead once more. She no longer knew what Ryn was thinking. If he believed her to be a danger to himself, would the wolf consider himself justified in doing away with her? Perhaps he had kept her warm last night, but he was a wild beast with powerful claws and sharp teeth, and if he decided to attack her, she would not have a chance against him.

Were the claws in her nightmares his? It was certainly possible, and yet nothing in her sense of Ryn, nothing in the glimpses she had seen in his heart and soul, led her to believe that he would ever hurt her. Not the wolf or the man. Of course, she had seen very little of him, so not sensing violence within was hardly comforting.

Pondering on the thoughts of the animal that paced not so far away only frustrated her, so Juliet turned her thoughts to Sophie and Isadora. Sophie had Kane to take care of her, and her own newly discovered abilities would also keep her safe. Isadora had always been strong, and since she'd escaped to the south, she was likely safe by now.

But they were separated, and Juliet hated that. She stood and shook off her worries, walking toward the edge of the forest searching for the flash of gold to indicate that Ryn watched. She saw nothing.

"What would it take to convince you to escort me back down the mountain?" she asked softly. "There are many women who would be overjoyed to be taken and made wife to an Anwyn such as yourself. You do have many good qualities." And he wasn't at all bad looking, once you got past the fact that he had such long tangled hair and didn't seem to care much for clothing. "But I am not that woman, Ryn. I need my sisters, and you're taking me away from them. With every step, I'm further away from my family. I just want to go home." The cabin was gone, but the land remained. They could build another cabin. Maybe it wouldn't be so nice as the old one, at least in the beginning, but it would be home because her blood, her very essence, flowed through Fyne Mountain.

Without sensing or hearing or seeing anything, she knew that Ryn considered himself as a viable replacement for her sisters. He was family, now. *His* mountain was home.

She glimpsed a flash of something small and bright in the forest, and for a moment she thought it was Ryn's eyes that once again caught her attention.

But the glowing eyes were not gold, they were green. Emerald green and bright as fire. Those bits of light moved quickly and silently closer. Juliet stood motionless, her feet rooted to the ground as those eyes in the darkness came closer and closer. Fallen leaves rustled, and a new sound was added to the quiet of the night.

A low growl.

The black cat leaped toward her, leaving the shadows of the forest and emerging into the firelight. For a moment the animal seemed to be suspended in the air as it pounced. The mountain cat was huge, almost as large as Ryn, and it bared its teeth as it descended toward Juliet.

She tried to scurry away, but tripped over a small rock and fell, landing on her backside vulnerable and exposed and fully aware that it was too late to try to escape again. She waited for the teeth and claws to descend; a scream caught in her throat. But before the cat's body landed upon hers, a blond blur flew across the space between them and knocked the black cat away. The animals fell to the ground several feet away from Juliet.

As Juliet struggled to her feet, the animals fought, rolling across the campsite entangled, their teeth and claws bared. They snarled, snapped, and fought with those deadly talons. Ryn growled; the large cat screamed, a primal shriek that split the night and Juliet's heart. She backed away, moving toward the flame and the cave. Neither the fire nor the cave would save her if the cat won this fight, but instinct drove her to shelter and light.

There had been such pure hatred in the cat's eyes as it had pounced at her. For one terrifying moment she had been sure she would die here, far away from Isadora and Sophie and Fyne Mountain. But Ryn had been watching over her. Even if he was still angry with her for offering to rid him of the wolf that claimed a portion of his soul, he considered it his duty to protect her.

The animals rolled across the ground, both of them bloody and tiring quickly. They snarled and wielded sharp claws like the deadly weapons they were, and wrestled with beastly muscles that rippled in the firelight. They would not stop until one of them was dead.

Or both. As much as she wanted to escape this so-called marriage Ryn insisted was fated, she didn't want to see him die this way. Logically, the death of both animals would be best for her, so why was she terrified that Ryn would not survive?

When her back met the cave wall, she sank to the ground and watched the fight in growing horror. The wolf and the cat rolled near the fire but not into it, and their bodies were too clearly illuminated. Was the blood tinting Ryn's golden fur his own or the cat's? Could she actually feel his energy fading, draining from her as it drained from him, or was that her imagination?

Like it or not, they were connected, just as Ryn had

explained. Through the earth, through the mountain, through the soul. She did not understand how, but she knew it was truth. He said she did not trust her power, that she denied it—that she fought it. If ever she needed to embrace her abilities, it was now. Ryn needed her.

Sitting with her back against the wall and her heart in her throat, Juliet called upon every ounce of magic she possessed. She gathered that strength—that power—pressed her palms to the ground, and reached out to Ryn.

The wolf was infused with a burst of energy that was the advantage he needed, and the tables turned quickly. The cat was tired; Ryn was not. The wolf overpowered the tiring cat, pinning it down. This was no longer an evenly matched fight. With a mighty swipe, the wolf tore away the cat's throat.

The cat fell back, dead, and Ryn limped toward the darkness of the woods. He moved away from Juliet, as if he intended to lick his wounds in the forest. Alone.

She stood shakily and walked toward the fire. Before her eyes the black cat lying on the ground was transformed from a wild animal intent on killing her into a pale, naked man with long black hair around his face. The process was a painfully slow one, as hair receded and paws turned into hands and legs grew longer and paler. Fur became skin; talons became fingers. The wounds Ryn had inflicted remained, uglier and more stark against flesh than they had been when lost in the black fur of a mountain cat. The man's throat, what was left of it, was bloody and torn, and less serious wounds were scattered along his slender body.

Which meant Ryn's wounds would remain, even when morning came and he was man again.

"Stop," she called, turning her back on the dead man and running toward the fair wolf that had reached the edge of the forest. He turned to look at her, and in that instant she could see the Ryn she knew in those eyes. The man, the wolf. Both. How had she not seen it last night? "Let me take care of you." He didn't move, not into the forest or back to her. "I'm a healer," she said.

There was no melding of their minds, as there had been in the past. Ryn was physically and emotionally drained, and yet he maintained the shield between them.

Juliet gathered her own strength, concentrating on the light in her soul and the goodness in her heart and the magic that had surrounded and infused her all her life. She could allow Ryn to go into the forest and die, and in the morning she would be free to move down the mountain. Escape was what she wanted and needed most of all. She could not be married to his man; she could not turn her back on her sisters when she knew they needed her.

And yet, Ryn had saved her. He had been willing to sacrifice his own life in order to protect hers.

She dropped down, pressed her hand against the ground, and delved into his mind as best she could. She felt the change, the shift in the energy between them, as he allowed her in. *Let me care for you, Ryn. Let me bind your wounds and keep you safe as you kept me safe.*

After a moment's hesitation he turned and limped to her. The closer he came to the fire, the more starkly horrible his wounds appeared. She had doctored many women who were ill, and she had cared for her own sisters. But she had never treated a man—or an animal—with such deep, bloody wounds.

It would take all her knowledge and will to keep Ryn alive through the night.

LIANE WOKE KNOWING INSTINCTIVELY THAT SHE WAS not alone, but she took care not to move or make a sound. She opened her eyes very slightly; not even halfway.

The tall, dark figure of a man leaned over her bed, a

hood covering his head and shading his face. How had he gotten past the sentinels at the door? She was always well guarded, and while the empress's sentinels might not like her or her change in station, they would die to protect her. It was their calling.

The *how* didn't matter. The intruder was here, in her room, by her bed. Did he plan a kidnapping for ransom? Or an assassination? She moved her hand slowly and steadily toward the pillow, as if shifting her body in sleep. Even Mahri did not know that her mistress slept with a blade beneath the pillow. No one knew. Old habits were hard to break.

The man leaning over her bed moved quickly, clamping his hand around Liane's wrist before she could reach the weapon. That touch was so familiar, she ached to her core.

"Now, now, sweetling," he whispered. "Is that any way to treat your husband?"

Liane rolled up slowly, genuinely surprised. "What are you doing here?"

Sebestyen did not release or even loosen his grip on her wrist. "Why does a man normally call upon his wife in the middle of the night?"

She tried to jerk her hand away, but he held tight. There had been a time when her heart and body cried out for him to come to her, but that time had passed. "What's the matter?" she asked sharply. "Have you already grown bored with your new concubines?"

"Yes," he whispered.

"So soon?"

"Before I ever saw them."

She wore a plain nightgown that had not been constructed for seduction. It was roomy around the middle, in order to accommodate her growing belly, and warm enough to ward off the night's chill. The gown had been made for warmth and comfort, and yet she felt naked as she sat before Sebestyen.

He had betrayed her by taking another woman—no, *women*—into his bed. He had turned her into one of the foolish, powerless empresses she had always detested. How dare he come to her in the night and assume that she would willingly lie with him?

Liane stretched past Sebestyen, reaching for the lamp on her bedside table. She wanted to see the face that was lost in the darkness of that hood; she wanted the bastard to look her in the eye and try to explain away his transgressions.

"No light," he said softly, easing her away from the table. "Your maid might see the flame and become curious."

"And what if she does?" Liane snapped. "It isn't as though you don't have a right to be here, if you insist upon it."

Sebestyen shook his head, and when he did so, his features were even more lost in the darkness of the hood. "No one can know I came to you," he said. "No one."

"But—"

"Do you trust me, Liane?"

Trust? She had loved Sebestyen, hated him, wanted him, needed him . . . sometimes all at once. But she had never, ever made the mistake of trusting him.

"No," she answered.

"Just a little, perhaps?"

She thought of the way she'd found him in bed with another woman, the way he had continued to entertain the concubine even though she watched while what was left of her heart broke into a million tiny pieces that could never be repaired. "No."

He did not become angry, but he did utter a low, thoughtful, "I see."

Liane almost expected her husband to grab her hair and

push her back onto the bed and spread her legs, the way he'd done a hundred, a *thousand* times before. He was not a man to take no for an answer, and if he wanted her, he would have her. It was his way.

But he didn't push her. Instead he laid his hand upon her belly and left it there, the touch gentle. For several long, silent moments they sat in the dark, one of his large hands resting over their child, her wrist caught in the grip of his other hand.

"What do you want?" Liane finally whispered.

He answered with a harsh laugh, and then he said, "What difference does it make what I want? What difference has it ever made?"

Liane tried to see into the darkness the hood cast over Sebestyen's face. "Everything you have ever wanted has been laid at your feet. By your father, your mother, the priests, your ministers." She swallowed hard. Heaven above, her mouth was dry. "Even by me."

Sebestyen let his hand rest on her stomach. She was very quickly getting fat and misshapen, and he'd made it clear that he didn't care for the changing shape and needs of expectant women. And yet that hand remained in place, steady and strong.

"What do you want, Liane?" he asked. "What do you desire above all else?"

She did not even have to think. "Freedom."

For a moment all was deeply, darkly silent. Sebestyen had likely expected her to confess that *he* was what she wanted more than anything, and if she were smart, that's the answer she would have given. But she was tired of the lies that had colored and filled her life. Just this once, she wanted to speak the truth to her husband.

"What makes you think I'm so different from you?" Sebestyen whispered, ending the uncomfortable silence. One finger moved gently against her stomach. "My cage might have better trappings than those on Level Twelve, but it's still a cage."

"Are you asking me to feel sorry for you?" she asked, incredulous.

"No."

"Then why are you here?"

For a moment there was only the darkness of the night and the feel of his hands on her wrist and her belly. Nothing else mattered.

"I am here to look upon my wife and child."

Suddenly she knew that on those nights when she'd awakened feeling as if she were being spied upon, Sebestyen had been here. Not so close, perhaps, but here. Watching. "How did you get into this room without being seen?"

"I have my ways."

Secret corridors, hooded cloaks, hidden stairs. Liane was one of the few who knew of the passageways behind these walls, narrow corridors and stairs that wound from one level to another. She had used those routes most often in her years as Sebestyen's assassin. Apparently she had not been advised of all the secrets of the palace, because she had not known that it was possible for Sebestyen to leave his quarters without even the sentinels being aware of his departure, or that there was a private way to enter the empress's chamber. Sebestyen knew, and he had used that knowledge to come to her in the night.

A part of her wanted nothing more than to reach up and touch her lips to his. To lie here beside him, beneath him, and pretend that nothing had changed.

But another part remembered watching him make love to his whore, and she did not think she could ever forgive him.

Not that Sebestyen ever asked for forgiveness.

"You wasted your time," she said, as if she did not care. "I won't lie with you ever again."

"You're my wife and I'm emperor. You can't refuse me." She could almost hear the smile in his voice, and again she wished for the light of her bedside lamp.

"I just did."

The shuffle of feet in the hallway that led to Mahri's room distracted an angry Liane, and a moment later a sleepy voice called, "My lady, are you all right?"

"If you ever trusted me . . . if you ever loved me, don't tell," Sebestyen commanded quickly as he left Liane's bed and faded into the shadows of the dark bedchamber.

Mahri arrived a moment later, carrying a candle that cast flickering light around the room. Liane glanced over her shoulder, in the direction of Sebestyen's disappearance, but she saw nothing. No sign of Sebestyen or his exit. No tapestry or curtain stirred as if it had been recently disturbed.

"I heard voices." The young girl stopped just inside the doorway and yawned.

Liane took a deep breath and lay down upon her soft bed, pulling the coverlet to her chin. Sebestyen didn't want anyone to know he'd come here, which meant she should shout the news at the top of her lungs. "I had a bad dream. Perhaps I was talking in my sleep."

"Would you like some tea?" Mahri offered.

"No."

"I can sit with you if you'd like."

"Don't be ridiculous," Liane said sharply. "You need your sleep and so do I."

"You're truly all right?"

"Of course." With her heart pounding and her mind spinning, Liane closed her eyes. "I'm sure I'll drift off to sleep quickly, if you'll get that candlelight out of my eyes."

"I'm sorry, my lady." Mahri backed away quickly. "Call if you need me."

"I will."

Liane listened as Mahri returned to her own small room, and then she waited a moment more. Her ears were keen, and yet she heard not even the faintest sound. "Sebestyen?" she whispered when a few silent moments had lapsed.

There was no response, and before she fell asleep again, she wondered if his appearance at her bedside had been a dream.

JULIET USED STRIPS OF THE NIGHTGOWN SHE WORE BE-neath her frock for bandages to bind the wolf's wounds. The lacerations were deep, where the cat's claws and teeth had ripped at Ryn. It might've been her flesh so horribly ripped. Would've been, if not for Ryn.

"I'll make sure you're on the mend, and then I'm going to head down the mountain," she said as she wrapped one dam-aged hind leg snugly. She ignored the body on the other side of the fire. Were the cats a warring clan of the Anwyn? Or another species altogether? Would she run into more of them as she made her escape? Were they all violent, or was this particular cat an unusually barbarous member of his species? She would probably never know. Ryn would likely not be able to speak, come morning. He had several weeks of healing ahead of him.

She'd see that he was in good shape before she left, of course. There were surely edible roots and fruits in the woods. She'd gather a supply and leave it nearby. She'd also leave a few fresh bandages, so he could change his own dressings. It was a good plan. Ryn was so badly wounded he would not possibly be able to chase after her for at least sev-eral days. By then she'd be far away from this mountain and the wolf creature, if luck was with her.

Luck. She hadn't experienced much of that lately. Not of the good variety.

When the sky turned gray, she left the wolf resting in

the cave and forced herself to study the body that lay close to the dying fire. She could not simply leave it here to decay while Ryn healed. When she screwed up her courage to touch the creature, she took him by the wrists and dragged him, a few inches at a time, into the woods. The going was easier there, since it sloped downhill and there was a bed of needles from the evergreen trees to make their progress quicker. Still, it took all her muscle to handle the chore. She dragged him to the edge of a gorge, and using every bit of the strength she possessed, she rolled the body over the edge, flinching as it dropped.

She returned to camp to find not a wolf but a man. The ugly wounds remained, more devastating on flesh than they had been while lost in fur. Ryn's transformation had left the bandages she'd bound so neatly in disarray.

Where had he left his discarded kilt and knife last night, when he'd transformed into a wolf? The man on the bearskin bedroll was completely naked. While Juliet knew what a naked man was supposed to look like, she had never actually seen one. She really should be genteel and cover Ryn's long body with whatever she could find at hand, but in truth he was beautiful. Wounded, unconscious, naked, and beautiful. She did finally turn the bearskin up and over in order to cover his midsection, though he did not seem to need the warmth.

As she did so, he opened his eyes and looked squarely and strongly at her. "The Caradon is dead?"

"If you mean the mountain cat that turned into a man after you killed him, then yes."

Ryn nodded and closed his eyes briefly in sheer relief. "I smelled him yesterday, but the Caradon do not usually wander so far to the east and I was hoping he'd turn toward home before he came upon us."

"You knew *yesterday* that thing was coming? Why didn't you warn me?"

"I did not wish to frighten you."

"Too late," she muttered as she gathered the bandages to rebind the wounds.

He allowed her to tend to him without moving, without a word of complaint even though she knew her gentlest touch must be painful.

"Will there be more?" she asked softly. "Will his . . . friends or family or comrades come to us to avenge his death?"

"No. The Caradon almost always travel and hunt alone. They are loners. They do not work together well as the Anwyn do."

"Good." Juliet gently pushed a section of tangled hair away from Ryn's face.

"You're leaving," he whispered as she wrapped linen tightly across a long scratch on his forearm.

There was no reason to lie. "Yes. As soon as I'm sure you'll be able to care for yourself, I'm heading back the way we came."

"You are meant to be here," he said weakly. "Why do you fight that truth so hard?"

She sighed in pure distress. "It is your truth, not mine. I can't blithely accept your insistence that we are meant to be together, not when I don't feel that connection myself." She squirmed slightly. There were times when she did feel that connection; she just didn't trust what she felt at the moment. "My sisters need me, and I won't abandon them. By the time you're physically able to follow, I'll be far, far away from this mountain."

"You won't leave. You can't, Juliet."

At least he didn't call her *wife* this time.

"I can and I will," she insisted. In frustration, she tied one bandage a bit too tight. "For goodness' sakes, Ryn, why me? Why can't you just choose another woman?"

"I did not *choose*," he answered. "You did not choose.

What is between us simply is. If you search your mind, you'll know it's true. You have dreamed of me all your life, Juliet, as I have dreamed of you."

Her heart jumped at the mention of her dream.

"I have dreamed of you," he said again. "You had no face in the dream, not that I could ever recall when morning came, but it was you. I knew it the moment I tasted your skin, and when you taste my skin, you will know, as I do, that this is not a choice we make but a destiny over which we have no control."

He should have had no strength, but he found enough to take her hand in his and hold it tight. "I have tried to tell you, Juliet. I have even tried to show you, but you will not listen." He swallowed hard. "Listen to this, wife."

He dropped the mental shield he maintained between them, letting it fall with a suddenness that took her breath away. The world faded, and there was nothing in the world but the beat of his heart and the beat of hers. Those two hearts thudded in time; they pounded together in a rhythm she could not explain. Their blood rushed as one, as if a loud, harmonious chorus began to sing, their fine voices so loud and crystalline the sound deafened her. She felt the wounds on Ryn's skin as if they were on her own, fire on her untouched flesh and pain that cut to the bone.

"You think your gift is weak and beyond your control," he said weakly, "but that is not so. You fight the power, but on this mountain you will discover the depths of your gifts—if you stop fighting what you know to be true."

"You don't know anything about me and my gifts," she protested.

"All your life you have been searching for me, but I was too far away and you did not understand and you have the blood of the witch to give you a strength that most women do not have. You touched others while your soul and your mind reached for me."

"Ryn, that's not—"

His voice grew sharper and more precise, as if he knew he would not be able to talk much longer. "You no longer need to reach for me because I am here. I am here, wife." His mind touched hers, and she knew the depth of his determination, the fervor of his belief that she was the one. The only one. In his mind and his heart, she was already his. *Mine.*

"I am not yours," she argued.

You are. He no longer had the strength to speak, but she heard his thoughts in her mind. She felt his considerable strength ebbing from his body. Soon he would be unconscious.

Mine.

The moment he passed out, the connection ended. She no longer felt even a twinge of discomfort, where only moments ago her skin had burned as if it had been sliced by the Caradon's claws.

"I will leave," she told the unconscious man. "Perhaps not this morning, but as soon as I determine that you're on the mend and will be all right without me, I will make my way down this mountain."

The dreams he spoke of . . . surely she had misunderstood. He did not mean *that* dream, the nightmare that had caused her to swear that no man would ever touch her. That dream always began pleasantly enough, very much like the moment when Ryn had pressed his mouth against her throat for a taste. But it never ended so agreeably. In the end there was always pain and blood and . . . She held her breath for a moment, unable to move or breathe or make a sound.

Claws.

Had the claws that ripped her apart in the dream been Ryn's? Had the nightmares been warning her of this moment in time? She did not believe that he would knowingly harm her, but how well did she know this Anwyn male who claimed she was his wife? His vow that he'd follow her wherever she went might seem romantic to some women, but Juliet had shared too many of the man's thoughts to suffer that delusion. He was determined to have her, and his insistence that they were meant to be together was adamant. He truly believed that she was the only woman for him, that she was meant in some soul-deep way to be his wife. There was no doubt that he did indeed believe she belonged to him, and that the root of her gift of sight was in her lifelong quest for him. Her man, her mate.

He was stubborn, and determined, and noble in his own primitive way. He did care for her, in the way a man might care for a family member or a close friend, and he certainly felt obligated to ensure that she remained safe. He wanted her, but he would never push or force himself upon her, even though his strength and size were formidable.

She'd felt a host of potent emotions when she'd linked with Ryn, emotions that lurked beneath the pain and the determination.

Love was not one of them.

7

CLOUDS MOVED IN AND SNOW DUSTED THE TREES BEFORE
Juliet could begin her trek down the mountain. Just as well.
Ryn wasn't ready to be left alone, not just yet. His skin was
warm to the touch, but then, he was always so warm she
didn't know if that spike in temperature was a sign that he
was getting worse or not.

The shallow cave offered them shelter from the snow,
and when she'd gone into the woods to gather food, she'd
stocked up on kindling and a few larger tree limbs that
had fallen to the ground, most likely in a storm that had
rushed through weeks or even months ago. Hauling these
things from the forest to their camp took all morning, but at
least the activity kept her from feeling the cold.

She was not a hunter, so even if she had known where
Ryn left his knife last night, she wouldn't have been able to
provide meat. The roots and nuts she'd gathered would
have to do for now.

When she sat beside Ryn to examine his wounds once again, she began to feel the chill that cut through her cloak and her frock and what was left of the nightgown she wore beneath them both. She absorbed some of Ryn's warmth while watching the light snow fall.

His wounds were deep but not life threatening, unless some unseen complications arose. She had a feeling he wouldn't tolerate complications of any kind. He was too obstinate to give in to anything so common as skin lacerations or fever. She had even pressed her palms to his skin to reach for some vision of his future. As was usual where Ryn was concerned, she did not see details, which was frustrating to her. But the shield was not complete, and she knew without doubt that he had a life to live. He would not die here.

Was it her imagination or were his wounds already healing? They didn't seem quite as ugly or deep as they had this morning. The laceration on his thigh had definitely healed to some extent. Did the Anwyn people possess the ability to recover from injuries faster than man or wolf? In any case, it appeared that in a couple of days Ryn would be able to move on. At a slower pace than he was accustomed to, perhaps, but he would live. He would survive and heal and thrive. And that meant she could leave him here without guilt.

She didn't know exactly which direction to travel, and being lost in these mountains would be perilous, at best. There were magical creatures here that she could not fight. Treacherous—and now icy—footing. If it grew much colder, she could very likely freeze to death. But what choice did she have? She couldn't simply give in to Ryn's insistence that she belonged here with him, simply because the idea of trekking down this mountain alone was daunting and more than a little frightening. The alternative was surrender to a man and a life that she had not chosen, and she wasn't yet ready to take that step—no matter what dangers would follow her decision to escape.

Juliet Fyne had never been one for taking chances, and no matter what she decided to do—stay with Ryn for the time being or head out on her own—she was taking a chance with her very life.

Ryn stirred, but didn't awaken. He tossed aside the section of bearskin that she'd draped across his midsection, and lay there in the cold without so much as a stitch of clothing covering him. A naked man who turned into a wolf three nights out of the moon's cycle had decided that she was his wife and they were meant to be together. He knew about her dreams . . . or *a* dream, at least. With every step, he took her farther away from the ones she loved—her sisters. If he had his way, she'd never see them again. What choice did she have but to run?

Late in the afternoon, Juliet walked away from a sleeping Ryn and the fire and the safety of camp, snowdrops stinging her face as the wind buffeted her and tossed her cloak and skirts about. The first part of the journey was an easy one. She retraced the steps that had led them to this place, heading toward the unforgiving stone mountain that stood between her and home.

She thought about her sisters as she made her escape. Had Isadora already shaken the soldiers and headed for Fyne Mountain? How could they get word to Sophie that the cabin had burned and that the emperor's men had tried to kidnap them? Even though Sophie had Kane Varden to protect her, she should know that there were evil forces out there who wished to do the Fyne women harm.

Sunset approached when Juliet came upon a ledge that looked down over the mountain she would have to descend on her own. The task would be daunting, but not impossible. It would take Ryn several more days to heal, and by the time he was well enough to chase after her, she'd be gone.

Standing on the precipice, she looked to the horizon and took a deep breath. Ryn said she had the power to touch anything, everything. He said she fought her abilities, that deep inside she denied the depths of her power. Perhaps he was right. Being connected to the earth as he said she could be was a powerful possibility that frightened her. She'd always believed that if she kept her hands to herself, she could be spared seeing that which she should not see, but if her gifts went beyond what she had always known, could she touch her sisters now, even from this distance?

She concentrated, but nothing happened. No sense of peace or danger filled her; no visions of her sisters filled her mind. Frustrated, she dropped down to her haunches and laid her hand—one hand only—upon the cold rock. She imagined a silver river that connected the Fyne sisters to one another, now and always. No longer shielding herself from what might be, she opened her very soul and reached for her sisters.

Suddenly Juliet was blinded to reality. She did not see the mountain or the blue skies or the landscape below her. She was transported to another place, as if her spirit moved through the air quickly and without effort.

Isadora moved closer to this mountain with every step, and she was distraught but unharmed. She was determined as always, angry and worried. Her anger was mighty and almost out of control, but there was a sadness in Isadora, too, a sadness that tore at her heart.

Sophie was well, too, surrounded by her family and beginning her own travels once again. Heaven above, she was strong! That kind of power in Sophie's hands was a frightening prospect, but at least Juliet had the solace of knowing that whatever Sophie accomplished would be colored with love.

Sophie carried her own sadness, worried about what would happen to her husband if she was unable to end the

Fyne Curse. Juliet tried to see if it was possible for Sophie to save her husband, but she saw no answer because that question was yet undecided. Certain events would have to unfold just so before that outcome would be clear. Everything would change for Sophie and her sisters and her daughter, and for all the Fyne women yet to be born, if that curse could be broken.

Ryn had insisted that when Juliet used her powers, she was unconsciously reaching for him. She very purposely did not reach for him now.

As if she had invited Ryn in merely by thinking of him, he intruded on her thoughts.

You can't run from me.

I can and I am. Don't follow me, please.

I won't.

Juliet breathed a deep sigh of relief.

You'll come back to me of your own will, wife. And I'll be waiting.

"CAN YOU DO IT?"

From the saddle of her own mount, a white mare to which she had immediately bonded, Sophie turned to look up at Arik, the rebel leader and rightful heir to the throne of Columbyana. He did look some like his half brother, but was heartier in build and had a touch of curl in his dark hair. Just a touch. They both had the sharp features of their father, as well as his height. No one who had seen them both could contest the fact that they shared blood.

Arik's concern was etched in worry lines and a slight frown, so she smiled at him. "Of course I can do it."

The sloping pathway ahead was slippery with a thin sheet of ice, and Arik's traveling party consisted not only of sure-footed horses but also of pack mules and wagons loaded with food and weaponry. This road had been built for spring and summer and fall, when crops were moved from village to village. During wintertime, the merchants and farmers who made up the majority of the residents of this section of the Northern Province stayed in their homes and villages, and the road was rarely used.

Arik was not a merchant or a farmer, and that was evident to anyone who looked at him. He had the bearing and determination of an emperor. The eye of a hawk and the heart of a lion.

Sophie rode cautiously ahead, Arik on her left, Kane on her right. Ariana was being carried in a sling which was presently draped across her grandfather's massive chest, and she slept soundly in spite of being jostled so horribly during the first leg of the journey. If only Kane would accept his daughter's intuition as proof that Maddox Sulyen was trustworthy, all would be well. But that was a matter for another day. Today's concerns were simpler.

"Wait here," she said, dismounting on a level section of the road and tossing her reins to Kane.

"But . . ." her husband began.

Sophie smiled at him. "I'm not going far."

She walked just a few feet ahead of the men who waited, until her feet were barely touching an upward turn in the road. The ice chilled her toes, even through her boots and socks. Tossing her cloak back over her shoulders, she lifted her arms and turned her face to the cold sky, where clouds that threatened snow dimmed the setting sun.

Sophie filled her heart with spring, with the coming of warmth and growth and a welcoming green. She filled her heart with love. For her husband, her children, her father, and her sisters. That love powered the strength of the sun and chased away the gray.

The change began at her feet, not in a flash but with a seedling of warmth. Her toes were not so cold, and she glanced down to see the ice beneath her boots melting away. The melting continued around her, growing in a circle that changed winter to spring. She felt herself rise slightly so that her feet no longer touched the road but hovered a few inches above it. The sensation of floating was almost exhilarating.

Dead, brown grass beside the road sprung green and new; trees beyond the grassy hills budded at a miraculous rate; the ice before the rebels' caravan, on the long road south, melted away, and amidst the winter cold of a particularly nasty day in the Northern Province came the spring of the Southern Province.

Sophie drifted down gently, then turned to her husband and to Arik. They smiled slightly and shook their heads, believing what they saw only because they had witnessed it with their own eyes. Sophie tried not to pay an undue amount of attention to the soldiers behind them, who watched her with open suspicion.

Her father looked at her with a mixture of pride and awe and perhaps even a touch of fear on his face. And then he shook his head and smiled, and she knew pride was more powerful than the other emotions he experienced. She knew that smile well; she'd seen it in her own mirror more than a few times, over the years.

"We should stop just past that second hill and pick some tiki fruits," she said as she hefted herself into the saddle.

"There are tiki fruits?" Arik asked, a touch of the little boy he had once been in this normally staid voice.

"Of course," she said, riding forward. "And quite a few redberry bushes, as well. We might as well pick the fruits for the journey ahead. The cold will return once the sun sets, and they will be ruined by morning."

Her gift for making things grow was greatest when she was carrying a child. She took special care to stay away from any place where women might gather. In her current condition she had a powerful effect on women of child-bearing years. The men seemed to be fine, as long as their loved ones were not around. She did make an effort to rein in her power when she was around Arik's soldiers. Just to be safe, of course.

"I haven't had a tiki fruit in . . ." Arik shook his head and spurred his horse gently forward. "Years."

"I don't suppose soldiers often stop to enjoy such things." Sophie and Kane rode alongside Arik; the others followed.

"No," Arik answered.

"They should."

Even though she had committed herself to Arik and his cause, Sophie was not a soldier. She never would be. But her husband and her father were warriors, soldiers now and always, and she would do what she could to make their lives fuller and sweeter.

JULIET LAY ON THE BEARSKIN RUG, HER EYES STUDYING the crisp clear blue of the sky above while Ryn tasted her throat. She was always surprised by the intensity of the sensations he aroused with that simple touch. Heaven above, she felt the heat of his mouth all through her body. That warmth made her anxious and tranquil at the same time. She wanted it to go on forever; she needed it to stop.

Ryn still didn't wear any clothes, and she tried not to look. She really did *try*. But he had such an interesting and fine and large body, she couldn't help but look. Since the moment she'd discovered the truth about the workings of a man's body to his wife's, she'd been frightened. Of the invasion, of the pain, of the possibilities.

Touch me.

I'm afraid.

You must never be afraid of me, wife.

The truth came to her in a flash, like lightning across the night sky. *I'm not afraid of you. I'm afraid of myself.*

Ryn rolled atop her and continued to taste her throat. His long blond hair fell across her face, and he situated himself very nicely between her legs. He was heavy, but she liked that heaviness on her body. It was nice. It was right.

It shouldn't be possible, since he was so large and she was not large at all, but they fit together well. His size did not frighten her, and she did not feel overpowered or unprotected. Her strength matched his, and this lying together was not at all awkward, but deeply right. A shift of his body and hers, a realignment of her clothing, a push, and then they would truly fit. She arched toward him, aching and hungry.

Ryn lifted his heavy body and rose up slightly, offering his throat to her.

Taste me, wife.

That throat was so fine, so warm and tempting. She knew how it would taste, as if she had been here before. She craved the saltiness of his sweat, the warm smoothness of his skin, the beat of his pulse on her tongue. Juliet tilted her face back and lifted her mouth. Her mouth watered, her body throbbed. But when she was so close she could feel the heat of Ryn's skin on her lips, she hesitated.

I'm afraid.

Taste me.

I'm afraid.

And then he disappeared. Cold wind whipped across her face and her damp throat, and whipped her skirts about. Clouds moved across the once clear sky.

With Ryn gone, she was more afraid than ever. And the pain remained. It bubbled inside her, a living thing she could not control. The pain changed with a sudden fierceness as claws ripped into her flesh. She saw no wolf; she saw no

Ryn. She saw nothing but the claws that had haunted her for years.

They were coming for her.

Juliet came awake with a start, gulping in a breath of cold air and jumping up off the rock. Her entire body trembled. Ryn had caused the dream somehow; of that she had no doubt. He had invaded her mind and forced the dream upon her.

Stop it! she ordered. There was no response, no feeling of connection at all.

The dream had been so intense, so real. Familiar, and yet different. She tried to chase the memory away, but instead she suddenly recalled that this was a part of the dream she'd been having on those restless nights before Bors had kidnapped her and Isadora and burned the cabin. *This* was the dream that had shaken her to the core.

That fact did not mean that Ryn was right about their destined lifelong bond. It was always possible that the dream had changed to include Ryn only after she'd met him, and that she'd inserted him into the old dream somehow. The memory of a disturbing nightmare could not send her back up this cursed mountain in search of answers. Where claws were concerned, she needed no answers. She was perfectly content to live in the dark.

Juliet chewed on a tasteless root and started moving. The small fire she'd built before going to sleep had died out hours ago, and it was too cold to sit for long. Besides, she had no time to waste. She'd been walking for a day and a half, she'd spent two nights sleeping on the hard, cold ground, and still the mountain stretched before her as if it would go on forever.

She walked quickly, only vaguely wondering exactly what it was she was running from. Ryn, of course, but it wasn't as if he'd ever hurt her. He just had a few mistaken ideas about her. About *them.* Maybe she was trying to run from the dream, which had come to her in some form during both nights she'd slept alone. She'd tried to convince herself that she was not running from Ryn but toward her sisters, but now that she could sense all was well with them, that argument didn't hold together.

Winded and agitated, she stopped on the side of a rock ledge to reach outward. This time she did not even have to touch the ground. The river was with her, in her. And in this place it was stronger than she had imagined was possible. Ryn was right; there was magic in this mountain, a power no one would ever be able to harness, but which many would be able to share. She drank from the mountain; she tapped into the magic that enhanced her own.

When she concentrated, she saw well beyond the mountain. Her sisters did not need her. Not now. Their destinies stretched before them, set in some ways, still to be decided in others. But no matter what happened in the coming days and weeks and months, they did not need her. Not yet. She could not change what was to come for them, good or bad. Right or wrong. She would see Isadora and Sophie again when the time was right, but that reunion would not come soon, no matter how she wished otherwise.

For a while Juliet stubbornly continued downward, and as she found her feet upon a more stable path, memories of last night's dream returned to her. She knew deep down that she wasn't running away from Ryn but from herself. She tried to dismiss that realization as ridiculous, a fantasy brought about by hunger and fear and loneliness. She knew who she was, and there was nothing unknown within her to be afraid of.

The path she'd been taking seemed to wind down safely, but all of a sudden she found herself standing on a ledge. The mountain dropped straight down for such a distance that there was no way for her to safely traverse it. If she tried to shimmy down, she'd surely fall to her death. There was not even a question. She was going to have to turn back, at least for a ways.

"Why?" she asked, her voice echoing. "I can see some things that no woman should be able to know, I can touch Ryn's mind, I can reach out and know that my sisters are safe. But I cannot know the right path down the mountain? How is that fair?" She lifted her head and looked up. If God had gone to all the trouble to give her this gift, why did He make it so unreliable?

She saw little of her own future; she knew little of what was to come to her and her loved ones. But standing on the ledge, slowing her heartbeat to join in the web that connected her to the earth, she knew to the depths of her soul that she was not meant to leave this mountain. Not yet.

"He scares me," she whispered. "In a way no man or beast ever has, the man who calls me *wife* scares me." When she allowed herself to listen to the part of her mind that had always spoken to her in times of darkness, she knew that Ryn had been right all along. She did belong here. With him. For now.

So she turned back, climbing with difficulty and—for the first time in her life—cursing. Out loud, at the top of her lungs, in the two languages in which she was fluent, she cursed. She hadn't even realized she knew such words, but they poured out of her. And as she climbed and cursed, her skin grew warm, her heart pounded too fast, her breath came shallow and quick.

She reached a flat portion of rock and stopped to rest. Her chest heaved, and for the first time she realized that her hair had come completely loose from the braid. Red curls fell past her face, untamed and as tangled as Ryn's blond tresses. Her cloak was torn, her boots were all but ruined, and her frock had been ripped in so many places she could not count the tears in the once-fine fabric.

Since the moment she'd been captured, she'd thought of

and planned for escape. If her abilities were at all reliable, she could now be sure that there was no escape. She would return to Ryn, as he had said she would, or she would die trying to get away from him.

She would go to Ryn, but there would be no marriage of any kind. Perhaps they were meant to be together for a while, but that didn't mean she had no say in the manner in which they behaved. They could be friends, perhaps. Friends only. Eventually he would take her home, whether he liked the idea or not. She would know when the time was right. When that time came, he would carry her down the cursed mountain and forget his foolish ideas about destiny and primitive mating and a wife's soft comfort. She was her own woman, not to be kidnapped and forced into marriage, but that did not mean she wanted to die in order to get home.

Her heart beat too fast, and a pool of something hot welled up inside her. That heat was anger, an emotion all but unknown to her. In truth it was more than anger, but she did not stop to reflect on what it might be. She had one thought on her mind as she climbed. Ryn would take her home, one day.

As she climbed upward, an unwanted vision filled her mind. Ryn's throat. The manly shape of it, the intense heat, the salty scent of her dream. Ryn said she would know the truth when she tasted his throat. She had never had the urge to so much as touch a man much less taste him, but the higher she climbed, the more desperately she wanted to lay her lips on his flesh.

Claws or no claws.

THE MOUNTAIN RANGE JULIET HAD BEEN CARRIED INTO was huge, long and high and austere. Unless Isadora found a way to perfect the location spell she'd been working on for the past two days, she'd never find her sister. They could both get lost in those mountains forever and never even come close to one another. Still, what choice did she have but to try?

Maybe she should not have run south when the chance for escape had come, but it had been the only way she'd known to draw some of the soldiers away from her sister. It had worked . . . but now they were so far apart.

Isadora had not completely forgiven her sister for rendering her unconscious just before the soldiers had set fire to their home, but at least she was now able to accept the why of it. Juliet had saved her life. If she'd had to stand there and watch her home burn, she would have killed soldiers until they killed her.

The forest they'd passed before Juliet had been taken was thick, but there was a path of sorts that led toward the mountain. Isadora pulled her stolen brown cloak close and headed north, staying away from the road. Juliet knew which roots and leaves were safe to eat, but Isadora was not as knowledgeable about plants. She recognized a few edible plants along the way, and gathered what she could.

The bread was gone, and she'd have to steal more food soon in order to survive the trip. Her stomach roiled at the thought. The death of the soldier in the woods had been an accident, but she had been the one to drive the knife into his chest. She didn't want to kill anyone else, not ever again. The souls of the two men she'd killed seemed to follow her wherever she went, and the seat of her magic was still dimmed by the destruction that had come at her hand. They were horrible men, soldiers who would have gladly murdered her given the chance, but that did not mean their deaths didn't weigh on her.

Did foolish women somewhere mourn the soldiers who had threatened her life? Did they cry for their lost loved ones the way she had cried for Will?

If one of the soldiers had killed her, she would have gone to the land of the dead to be with Will, which was where she wanted to be. But as long as her sisters needed her, she couldn't acquiesce. She couldn't simply offer herself up for an easy death. Sophie and Juliet needed her, and besides . . . Will would not allow it. She had thought of death often in the days after his passing, and he had always known. It was then that his spirit had come to her and comforted her, telling her that she must be strong.

She didn't want to be strong anymore. She was so damned tired of being strong.

A rustle of leaves behind Isadora alerted her to the fact that she was no longer alone, and for a brief, shining moment she believed that Will had come to her again. He had come to comfort her, maybe even to take her with him. She stopped and turned to face the sound, and saw three things.

A grinning Bors; a frightened young soldier in green; and a hefty stick swinging toward her head.

ISADORA WAKENED WITH A SPLITTING HEADACHE. ALL
was dark and she could barely move. Her feet were bound
together, her wrists were tied behind her back, and a hood
had been tied over her head. The way she bounced lightly,
together with the sound of creaking wheels and horse's
hooves, told her she was being transported in the back of a
wagon. The wagon was surrounded on all sides by horses—
soldiers, no doubt, guarding her closely even though she
was bound so securely she could barely move.

Bors was taking no chances this time.

"She's moving," an uncertain male voice whispered.
"I think she's awake."

"Is she, now?" Bors asked, a jovial lilt in his voice. "I
had begun to think perhaps the blow had killed her."

Isadora muttered a word not fit for her sisters' ears, but
Bors just laughed.

"Enjoy the ride, witch. As soon as the emperor gets

whatever it is he wants from you, I'll see you hang for killing two of his soldiers."

Her heart hitched and her stomach tightened. When she'd escaped from Bors's party, after Juliet's kidnapping, she hadn't killed the soldier who'd tried to stop her. She'd incapacitated him; she'd made him drop away from her. But when she'd run, he'd been alive and healthy. Which meant Bors knew about the other soldier . . .

"I detected your handiwork when I ran across the murdered man in the forest. That was you, wasn't it?"

Isadora didn't respond. What good would it do to tell Bors that the soldier's death had been an accident? He would never believe her.

"A poor man with his trousers undone and his williker hanging out was stabbed in the heart, and nothing but a loaf of bread and his weapons were stolen. Sounded like the work of a desperate woman to me, so you came to mind long before we found those same weapons on your person. What did you do to the poor man—promise him a taste of something sweet and then stab him while his mind was elsewhere?"

"No," Isadora croaked, so low no one would hear.

"From the camp you were easy to track," Bors continued. "You left a trail a mile wide, witch. I thought about following from a distance for a while, in case you might lead us to your sister, but since she is in all likelihood dead, I decided to save myself the trouble."

It had all been for nothing. Running, killing, stealing . . . and here she was, once again being taken to the emperor. At least Bors didn't have Juliet. It was worth anything, everything, if his pursuit of her gave Juliet more time to get away.

"That last murder of yours was a costly crime," Bors said indifferently. "Before I arrived to set them straight, the soldiers in that camp assumed someone from the village nearby had murdered their comrade. Have you ever seen a soldier set on vengeance, Miss Fyne? It isn't a pretty sight, if you're on the wrong side of that madness."

Isadora was glad the hood covered her face. She didn't want to look at Bors, and she certainly didn't want him to see the tears that stung her eyes. What had the soldiers done? She didn't want to know. She *did not* want to know . . .

"First they hung a couple of local boys who had never taken kindly to the soldiers camping so close by, thinking that they might've done the deed. But one of the brighter men suggested that, considering the poor dead fellow's exposed and vulnerable state, it was likely a woman had killed him. So they visited the homes of a few likely suspects, entertained themselves with the women who protested their innocence until the end, and killed anyone who tried to get in their way or fought back too hard."

Isadora choked back a sob.

"All in all, I'd say your loaf of bread cost three innocent lives, and the weapons cost five. And then there's the one girl who might not live much longer. They left her in mighty terrible shape. She was still screaming—"

"Stop it," Isadora ordered.

"What's this? Do I hear tears in the witch's voice? Surely not. I thought you'd be right proud of yourself, killing the poor soldier and slipping away into the woods as you did to let someone else pay for your crime. Then again," Bors said more softly. "Maybe not. I did run across that lovely spot by the stream, where you retched up your bread. Wasn't it tasty enough for you, sweetness?"

Her stomach roiled and threatened to revolt, as it had on that afternoon. It had never occurred to her that the soldiers might make others pay for their comrade's death. She should've known . . . she should've found a way . . .

She heard Bors yawn. "You behave yourself, witch," he

said when his expression of complete and utter boredom was done. "And maybe no one else will have to die. Except you, of course."

RYN STOOD NEAR THE FIRE AND WATCHED THE PATH. She was coming. Soon.

Juliet had been gone four days, but he had never doubted that she would return. He could've gone after her and carried her back, using one of the tanni leaves he carried in his pouch to render her unconscious if she protested overmuch. But he didn't want to do that, not if there was another way. He didn't want her to fight him at every turn. It was time for his wife to accept what was meant to be.

As he had known she would, Juliet was returning to him on her own. Her scent teased him, and had for the past two days. He did not possess his wife's gift for reaching through the web of life and touching many others, but he did have the ability to reach through that web for her. It was not easy to touch Juliet in that way, but as he concentrated on his wife, she was there, inside his head, mingled with his very spirit.

All Anwyn shared a special bond with their mates, but thanks to Juliet's abilities, their link was special. It was deeper than most. It was extraordinary. When she became his wife in every way, when they were linked in body as well as in spirit, they would know the full power of the bond.

As Juliet returned to him, she experienced a flood of anger, and that fury was a new experience for her. She was also afraid, but she hid the fear behind the anger and did not understand what roused her fears. He knew. She wanted him the way a wife wants her husband, but had not yet come to accept that wanting. She would. Soon. She dreamed of him, and perhaps those dreams were like his. He'd been dreaming of his wife for the past five winters. In the beginning they had come no more than twice in each cycle of the moon, and the face of the woman beneath him had been indistinct. But in the past few months the dream came more often, and gradually the face of the woman who shared those dreams had come into focus. Were they torture for Juliet as they were for him? Did she wake from those dreams with her body shaking and her mind reeling?

He was waiting for her, very near to where she'd left him, when she came around the turn in the path. Unheeded, a smile broke across his face.

She tossed her head and glared at him. "Don't you dare grin at me!"

He forced the smile to leave.

"The only reason I'm here is because I can't find my way off this cursed mountain on my own, and I'm not quite ready to die for a principle."

She looked very different, after a few days on her own. The fear and the anger showed on her, in many ways. Her hair was loose and wild; her dress was torn; her face was smudged with dirt. Her cheeks had taken on a new, pink flush, and her eyes sparkled. She was filled with life. He liked it. This was how she'd looked in his dream last night, as wild a creature as he himself could be, a woman touched with anger and passion and wonder.

This woman was his wife.

"You are here because you are meant to be here," he said calmly. "With me."

She walked directly toward him, strides long and determined. Without so much as slowing her step, she all but ran into him and slapped him soundly on the chest. "If you say another word about us being married or if you call me your wife, or if you utter one more word about how we were meant to be together, I swear, I will walk down this mountain if it takes me all my life to get to the bottom."

He lowered his voice because she was so close. There

was no need to shout as she did. "You do not know what to
do with the fire that burns inside you—that's why you feel
such rage."

She hit him again; he barely felt it. "I do not feel rage. I
never feel rage! I don't lose my temper, and I don't get angry because it never serves any constructive purpose. It is
an entirely worthless emotion." Juliet hit him three times
while she told him how she never lost her temper.

Suddenly she stopped, and the anger in her eyes turned
to wonder. "Your wounds," she whispered. The palm that
had struck him rested over his chest, where a few days ago
a nasty gash had opened his flesh. "They're gone."

"I am healed," he said simply.

"But . . . how?"

"Anwyn heal quickly."

"Apparently so," she whispered as she dropped her
hand. She turned accusing eyes up to him. "You could have
come after me days ago."

"Yes."

"Why didn't you?"

"I knew you would come back to me." He didn't say
more, since his assurances would only enrage her.

"I'm only here because I can't make my way down the
mountain alone. It's that simple."

"It is not that simple."

She glanced toward the fire, avoiding his gaze.

"You have come back because you know you belong
here, and because there is nothing to be done for your sisters. You have come back because the dream plagues and
taunts you."

Her cheeks blushed bright pink, and her lips hardened a
little. "Do not speak to me of dreams."

"You need not make excuses for me, Juliet. I do not see
things as you do, but we share a link you cannot deny.
There are times when I see your heart and mind clearly.

I can sever the link when I wish, but I cannot destroy it."

"Sever it now," she commanded.

He gladly did as she asked. In time, their bond would be complete and unbreakable, but for now he was no more comfortable with a undiminished link than she was. Not only did he feel disturbed by allowing this woman he barely knew to share his innermost thoughts, but he no longer wished to taste her anger.

He took comfort in knowing that the anger would not last. By the time they reached The City, she would be happy. Juliet would declare herself to be his mate long before they took their vows before the Queen.

THEY TRAVELED AS THEY HAD BEFORE, RYN LEADING THE way, Juliet struggling to keep up with him. Over the days the journey had become less of a struggle. Her legs adapted to the hiking; her feet became more sure on the rocks. It helped that at least some of the journey took them over tree-covered hills that were not too steep for her to traverse without getting winded.

Ryn did not call her "wife," and he certainly didn't taste her again. If not for the dreams that persisted, she might consider this journey almost pleasant. On some nights the claws appeared to turn the dream into a nightmare, but on other nights it did not end in such a violent way.

On some nights, the dream ended when her mouth was almost touching Ryn's throat, and his hands were on her body, and he lifted her skirt and touched her where no man had ever touched her before . . . where she had sworn no man would ever touch her . . .

The mountains were undeniably beautiful, crisp and cool and pristine. She felt as if no other woman had ever walked upon this land or seen these fabulous skies. The sky was the blue of her dream, bright and clear, a crisp shade of blue she had never before seen.

The dream was affecting her more than she cared to allow. Just this morning she had awakened to find herself much too close to Ryn. She had fallen against him in the night and found comfort in his warmth. She had opened her eyes and found herself presented with a sight very much like the one in her dreams, and for a moment . . . for one insane moment . . . her mind had taken a definite turn.

He was lovely, she admitted, in a completely untamed and masculine way. Sometimes when he turned his face to her or moved just so, her stomach flipped in an entirely unexpected and not altogether unpleasant way. As they walked down a narrow path past dead trees and sharp rock and the occasional green shrub, she tried to imagine what he'd look like if she cut his hair or pulled it back and restrained it, and bought him ordinary clothes. He would still be handsome. He would also still be wild. Oddly enough, she preferred him this way. The wildness suited him. It was who he was.

She wasn't so sure who she was anymore. There had been a time when there had been no question as to her identity or her plans for the future. But now . . . she just didn't know.

They reached a steep rise, and Ryn turned to wait for her. He offered his hand; she took it. It was a strong hand, steady and sure, and she had no doubts about holding on as he helped her to the top of the hill. The shimmer that went through her was as unexpected as the occasional trick of her stomach.

No, not entirely unexpected, she decided as he released her. Her physical response to him plagued her more and more. He looked at her or touched her and she was affected. She found her mind wandering to fantasies best left unexplored. It was the dream, she reasoned, that forced her mind into this new and disturbing direction. Reality would probably not be so pleasant.

She looked him squarely in the eye while she took a deep, revitalizing breath. "I can never love any man," she said quickly, the words pouring out of her too quickly.

"I did not ask for love," he responded without anger or disappointment.

It was true that she had not felt love from Ryn, and he had certainly never spoken of love. But he continued to insist that she was the one for him, the only one who would do. Was that not love?

"We will have friendship and companionship and lust, when you stop resisting me," he said. "It is the way of the Anwyn."

"The Anwyn don't believe in love?"

"It exists for some," Ryn said. "It is not necessary."

She had always believed love was necessary for a proper marriage, which is one of the reasons she had known she could never marry.

They resumed their journey after that short rest. There was no sign of another living creature along the way, but for the small critters Ryn caught and killed for their supper when they tired of eating roots. The animals he hunted were *tilsis* primarily, moderately sized rabbit-like animals that were timid and tasty and quick. Not quick enough to escape Ryn, but still . . . they moved fast.

She did not ask how far they had to travel before they reached his home, and Ryn offered no detailed information about their journey.

Ryn did not chat needlessly. He was a quiet man, sure of himself and perfectly capable of speaking well if he had something to say. He just usually didn't have much to say. If she was going to be so annoyingly attracted to the man, the least she could do was to get to know him better.

Not that he cared about getting better acquainted. He hadn't even asked her why she couldn't love.

"Does every Anwyn travel so far to fetch his alleged wife?"

"Yes." Ryn moved steadily onward. "When the time comes, we are called, and the quest for the destined mate begins."

"And what happens if you don't find your mate?"

"We don't return to The City until the quest is done, no matter how far the journey takes us."

It wasn't that she needed to know any specifics about their destination, since she didn't plan to stay, but she was a little curious. And Ryn wasn't being at all helpful. He answered her questions, but he did not elaborate.

"Has any woman ever asked to be taken home before?"

"No."

"I find that difficult to believe," she said beneath her breath. Did all the Anwyn look like Ryn? Were they all so quiet and strong and stubborn? She knew many women who wouldn't mind at all being kidnapped by such a man.

The trees they marched past were completely bare, without a single red or yellow or blue leaf to color the landscape. It turned colder here much sooner than in the Southern Province, and they had left behind the evergreen trees they'd once camped beneath. She smelled snow again, even though the skies remained blue and clear. Oddly enough, she had become acclimated to the cold more easily than she'd imagined she would. The icy air no longer cut to the bone through her clothing, but instead lay upon her exposed skin in a perfectly natural way.

"I guess you don't see many of the emperor's soldiers up this way," she said, actually hungry for more talk after the days of walking and sleeping and eating and carrying on only the simplest of conversations.

Ryn glanced over his shoulder and lifted his eyebrows

slightly. "No soldiers here. We crossed the border of Columbyana and entered the land of the Anwyn two days ago."

THEY STOPPED TO REST ON HER ACCOUNT, BUT RYN DID not complain that she was slowing him down, and he did not offer to carry her. He would if she asked, she knew that, but they had moved beyond that stage. In a way she had not expected, she was no longer a captive. She'd finally accepted that this was where she was supposed to be, for now. The acceptance was unexpected and even unwanted, but it was also right, in a soul-deep way. This journey had become an adventure, an adventure she had never expected to have. She felt connected to the mountain just as she felt connected to Ryn.

But it was an adventure, not a change in her life's plan. This brief time in her life was a detour, an escapade she would talk about when she was old and gray.

Well, she would talk about some of it. No one could ever know about the dreams, or the strange desire she had to lay her mouth on Ryn's neck.

"Is your city as beautiful as this?" she asked. From this vantage point she could look over a vast and splendid area of untouched land, mountains and forests, hills and valleys. It seemed she stood at the top of the world, though to the north the mountains grew even higher.

"The City is beautiful in a different way."

"Do all Anwyn live in The City?"

"No. Some choose to live in the mountains, or on farms beyond The City walls."

She turned to look squarely at Ryn. "But you live in The City?"

He nodded. Even that small gesture was made with strength and a touch of wildness. Her eyes were drawn to his neck, massive and corded and attached to fine broad shoulders, and immediately she averted her eyes. "I leave The City to hunt, and to run when the wolf calls."

There were times when she almost forgot that he was a shape-shifter, that the spirit of a beast lived in his heart. That wildness was such an integral part of him, he was never entirely without the wolf.

"I will not hurt you," he said softly.

"I know you won't," she said, trying to sound stern and detached.

"You should not be afraid because you want me. It is natural and right, and when the times comes, it will be a good thing."

Juliet forced a laugh. "I do not want you, Ryn. For goodness' sakes, I—"

"I do not have your gift," he interrupted. "I can keep you out, and I cannot touch your mind unless you invite me in."

Thank the heavens! She certainly didn't want him to know the direction her thoughts had taken in the days since she'd returned to him. "I will not invite you into my mind, of that you can be assured."

"What of your body?"

She shivered. He was so plainspoken at times! There was no artifice in his words, no polished attempts at seduction. "We are not married, I am not your wife. I can't—"

"You can," he said, assurance in his voice. He took a step toward her. "You called me an animal once, and I reminded you that you, too, are an animal."

"I am not an animal," Juliet insisted primly.

Ryn's head cocked to one side. "We are all animals, wife. I smell the desire you deny on your flesh, in your very breath. You call to me the way any animal calls to its mate."

"I am *not* calling to you."

"Let me touch my mind to yours and prove it, wife."

"No." Ryn could not know what directions her thoughts had been taking of late. He could not know that he was right. "I will travel to your city. Perhaps I will even stay there for a few weeks or months. But it is not home, and you are not mine."

"I knew you would be stubborn," he said, not at all bothered by her arguments.

"I am not stubborn." That argument caused Ryn to smile, and Juliet's heart fluttered strangely.

"I will not touch you as a husband touches his wife until you come to me," he said as he approached. "I will wait."

"You're in for a long wait," she said, not as sharply as she'd intended. He was too close, too unrestrained . . . too big. But as in the dream, she did not feel overpowered. Ryn would never use his strength against her; she knew that to the depths of her soul.

"I don't think so," he whispered as he stopped before her, touched her cheek with one long finger, and looked into her eyes. He tipped her head back and laid his lips against her throat. He did not lick and suck and tease, as he had before. His mouth simply rested there. A large tanned hand rose up to brush against her breast, but instead of caressing her there, he pressed his hand beneath, as if to feel her heartbeat.

She could push him away—she *should* push him away. But instead she closed her eyes and drank him in, not with her mind but with her body. Her insides began to pulse; her heart rate quickened. She reached out to touch him, but before she could do that, she let her hands fall away. The fingers flexed and clenched. She wanted to touch him. She wanted to feel the heat of his flesh against her hands.

Ryn let his hand fall, long brown fingers brushing against her frock as it dropped. He took his mouth from her throat, and she came to her senses and took a step back.

"You always kiss my throat," she said, her voice just short of shaking. Why didn't he lay his lips on hers, or kiss her cheek? Even in her dreams, it was the throat that tempted her.

"The offering of the throat is the ultimate sign of trust." Ryn reached out and brushed one long finger down the column of her neck. "Here you are most vulnerable. One bite, and your life's blood drains from the body. And yet the right touch in that vulnerable place is undeniably sexual. It is life and death. Commitment and pleasure."

"That sounds very primitive." The finger at her throat stirred all kinds of sensations inside her, and she couldn't make them cease. She didn't want them to cease.

"Don't deny the animal, wife," Ryn said as he turned away and started down the path once again. "It is a good thing."

Juliet would've argued with him, but as she followed with quick steps, she couldn't find her breath.

SOMETHING IN JULIET HAD CHANGED, AND SHE DID NOT know it yet. Ryn saw as much as felt the transformation in her. This change was on her face and in her body, as well as in the spirit she tried to hide from him. He tried to explain away what he saw with his own eyes, but this could not be explained away.

They sat by the fire in silence, supper done. This afternoon's conversation remained between them, awkward and unfinished.

It was past time for Juliet to come to him in the way a wife should, and yet she remained distant and frightened. He had realized days ago that she was afraid not of him, but of herself. She was frightened of the passion that coursed through her.

He leaned in close to study her eyes by the light of the fire. When they'd stopped on the trail this afternoon and he'd touched her, he had been almost certain he saw something different, something unexpected. Flecks of gold had begun to appear amidst the warm brown of her eyes. Those flecks had not been there when he'd first taken her; of that he was certain. Neither had the flush of her skin been evident. She had been paler when he'd taken her, and now her skin was healthy and pink. If he laid his hand to her chest again, would he feel that her heart beat faster? Had it only raced earlier today because she fought what she wanted? He wondered if she had begun hearing sounds from a distance she had not known possible before she came here, or if she saw farther into the darkness than she had on that first night.

She was his mate and he should know everything about her, but this . . . this was a surprise.

Ryn hated surprises.

Perhaps he was mistaken, and the changes in her were caused by the angle of the firelight or the exertion of walking. He would know soon enough.

They shared the bearskin bedroll, sitting close to the fire but not too close. Juliet did not shiver as she had on those first nights, even though the air had grown considerably colder in days past. That was yet another clue that something had changed, or was in the process of changing.

"Anwyn do not feel the cold the way lowlanders do," he said, his eyes turning to the fire for a moment.

"I judged that by your attire," she said. "Or rather by the lack of it," she added, actually smiling a little.

"It's the blood of the wolf."

She nodded and turned her head toward him, and there it was, that flash of gold in her brown eyes. Maybe it was the fire and he only imagined the gold. Maybe the flecks had been there all along and he had not noticed. His stomach sank a little. No. He had paid very close attention to everything about her. He had missed nothing.

"I'm sorry that I offered to cure you," she said, desperate to change the subject to something safe. "It wasn't my place to suggest that there's anything wrong with who you are."

He nodded his head slightly.

"It's just . . ." She let the sentence die, but he heard the reservations in her voice, the uncertainty. Maybe she would not fight what she felt for him so strenuously if he didn't have the wolf inside him.

"If I wish to deny the wolf, I need only travel far away from The City and The Heart."

"The heart?" she repeated.

"The Heart of the Anwyn. It's a sacred stone which is kept in the Queen's palace, closely guarded by her most favored and trusted soldiers. I am one of those soldiers."

She smiled. "Then you don't spend your entire life running about the mountains kidnapping women?"

"Only when you call, wife."

Her smile faded; she still was not pleased when he called her *wife*. "So, the Heart of the Anwyn? What is that, exactly?"

"The Heart of the Anwyn is a precious stone the color of the eyes of the Queen. The magic of our people is protected by and energized by The Heart. When the new Queen comes, she will be crowned while the power of the stone surrounds her. When young Anwyn reach the proper age, they take a vow upon The Heart and embrace the animal within."

"So, Anwyn children don't change into little wolves?"

"No."

"And if you wished, you could move away from The City and The Heart and become an ordinary man?"

Is that what she wanted of him? Now that she was plagued by sexual feelings she tried to dismiss, did she truly wish that he was an ordinary man?

"Yes," he answered. He did not tell her that denying the

wolf would be like cutting off his own arm. He did not tell her that he would rather die than be an ordinary man. "The further away from The Heart I travel, the weaker the power and pull of it become."

"Pull. Does it draw you home?"

"Yes."

Juliet struggled with the fact that she wanted him. That's why she remained awake when she should be sleeping. She knew the dream would come to her, more real tonight than it had been last night. Tomorrow night it would be yet even more real, and it would come to her every night until they became man and wife in the most basic way. She knew that, but refused to accept it. She would accept, though. Soon. The scent of a woman calling for her man radiated from her so strongly he could almost touch and see it.

Ryn reached out his hand and touched her face. He had to know if what he'd felt this afternoon was real or imagination. Yes, her skin was warmer than it had been when he'd taken her. She did not draw away from the touch, as he'd thought she might, so he lifted his other hand to her heart. She did flinch a little, more in surprise than displeasure, but she didn't back away. His thumb brushed against the softness of her breast as he pressed his palm to her. Again her heart was beating too fast. Anticipation and excitement caused her heart to race, but there was more. Much more.

Juliet licked her lips, and her eyes dropped to his throat. She was drawn to him, no matter how determined she might be to maintain her distance. He hadn't told her that her battle was a hopeless one, that she would know no peace until she gave herself over to the need that had been sleeping within her for so long. She could not stop the flow of desire that surged between them, no matter how she tried.

After a few moments she stopped trying. He felt the

release, in a torrent of heat and a wave of energy. The river of hunger between them was so strong the flame of their campfire grew higher and brighter. Juliet's eyes remained fixed on his throat, and her lips parted and grew soft.

"You want to taste me."

She shook her head no, but answered in a whisper, "Yes. More than anything, I want that."

Very slowly, he moved closer to her. She shifted her body toward his, and he leaned his head to one side so she could lay her mouth on his throat. She was very hesitant at first, but Ryn did not weave his fingers into her tangled hair and pull her closer. He let her taste him in her own way, in her own time.

Soft lips danced upon his throat. Ryn closed his eyes. This real touching was much better than any dream. He felt the caress of those lips throughout his body, and his instinct was to pull Juliet's body to his and make her give him more. But he didn't. He remained very still, allowing her to take her own time. A hesitant brushing of her tongue against his throat made his mind spin and his body roar, and a moment later Juliet let loose a gentle moan as she fully pressed her mouth to the flesh he offered her. There was still a small fragment of doubt within her.

"It's all right," he whispered, his voice husky and near shaking as he rested his hand in her hair.

Once Juliet had sampled his flesh, she did not stop and gently pull away. She tasted him fully; she drew him into her mouth, breathed him in through her nose, tasted him with her tongue. One soft hand grabbed a tangle of hair and held on, as she moved her mouth to the other side of his neck. Her body trembled, but not with fear. Not this time.

He not only felt and saw her need for him, he smelled it growing stronger on her flesh. That need was everywhere. In her hair, on her face, in the mouth that tasted him, in the hands that held him.

"You taste good," she whispered, barely taking her mouth from his neck. "So good. Oh, heavens, I could sit here all night and just . . . just . . ." She moved her entire body closer until she was sitting in his lap, her arms draped around him while she lost control at a fast rate.

Her skin was hot; her heart raced. And while she lavished her attentions on his neck, she pressed her body to his and held on as if for her very life. She moaned and laughed and sucked his flesh into her mouth.

"You were right," she whispered, and then she touched the tip of her tongue to a sensitive place on his throat. "When I taste you, I know I am meant to be here. It's familiar, as if I have always known the flavor of you."

"You have," Ryn rumbled. He was ready for her, had been ready for days. Weeks. Months. A shift of his clothing and hers, and he could be inside her. He was tempted, his body was tempted, but when they joined, it would be her first time. Hers and his, but he knew the pain would be hers.

It was getting harder and harder to think at all. Juliet's mouth was relentlessly hungry, and she did not satisfy herself with a simple taste. Her soft lips moved from one side of his throat to the other. Her tongue flicked out and teased him. One hand fisted in his hair. Her body quivered. Her hands raked over his bare skin, as if she sought to learn the shape of him in all ways. Her fingers were bold and arousing.

And then she bit him.

Not hard. It was a little nip that barely drew blood. Yet another clue that he had not known all about his wife when he had captured her.

He had to know if there was any truth to his suspicions. He carried a number of tanni leaves in the pouch at his waist, and that weapon—which he had used to disable the soldiers when he had taken Juliet—would tell him all he needed to know. But there were other ways to determine if he was right or not. Better ways.

Ryn wrapped his arms around Juliet, flipped her onto her back, and covered her body with his. She gasped and lost her breath for a moment, but almost without pause she wrapped her arms around him. He laid his mouth on her throat and suckled, and she threaded her fingers through his hair and held on tight. She did what he had not; she pulled him closer.

A trace of her fear remained, but it had been replaced by something stronger. Need. She was almost overcome with the need for him.

The flavor of her skin had changed a little, as he had detected this afternoon. If he had not tasted her on that first night, he might not realize, but he remembered very well the sweet taste of her flesh. It was different now. No less sweet, but . . . different. She pressed her body to his and tilted her head back to offer him all of her throat. It was the ultimate offering, to lie beneath a man in this most vulnerable position, head back and thighs parted, throat and body unprotected.

He took full advantage of the offer, kissing Juliet from her chin to her shoulder, sucking against the skin beneath her ear while his hand delved beneath her skirt. The flesh of her thighs was soft and tender, warm and slightly trembling. While his hand caressed her there, he nipped lightly at the side of her neck, just barely drawing blood.

Juliet didn't cry out or try to push him away. Instead she moaned and lifted one leg to drape it over his. He was so close to being inside her. So close. And it was what she wanted, as much as he did. When that was done, she would be his wife in every way that counted. There would be no more talk of escape, no more threats about going back down the mountain.

He licked away a drop of the blood he had drawn and let it lie on his tongue. One taste was all he needed to know the truth. Juliet truly was changing, as they traveled closer to The City and the sacred Heart. She felt the draw of the stone as he did, but did not yet realize that it called to her and that by returning to him she had taken a step not only toward him but also toward that stone and her destiny. The blood of Juliet's father awakened within her, growing stronger with every step they took toward The City.

Ryn watched by the light of the fire as the small cut healed before his eyes until the flesh of her throat was perfect once more.

His woman, his mate, was Anwyn. She was the lost one, the girl child they had been waiting for.

When they reached The City, Juliet would be Queen.

9

JULIET THREADED HER FINGERS THROUGH RYN'S HAIR, hanging on because she felt as if she'd fly out of her body if she didn't hold on to something solid to keep her earthbound. Days of dreams and isolation, of watching Ryn and taking his hand when it was offered, of sleeping beside him, it all caught up with her in a rush and she felt as if she were tumbling down the mountain. The rush wasn't frightening, as it should've been. Instead she felt exhilarated and oddly free. Laying her mouth on his throat had started a reaction that she could not stop, that she did not want to stop. He was in her blood now, and she understood. She finally understood so many things.

Sophie had often encouraged her sister to take a lover, since Juliet had always declared marriage out of the question. In the past she'd been horrified by the suggestion, but now, with Ryn's body over hers and the most wonderful sensations dancing through her body, a lover seemed like a very good idea. It wasn't as if the curse would ruin what they'd discovered here. She didn't love him; he didn't love her. And so no curse would take Ryn's life before his time.

Maybe she didn't love Ryn, but she loved the way he tasted and she loved the feel of his skin against her mouth. As much, maybe more, she loved the way his mouth felt on her. Lightning coursed through her blood, and no matter how good it felt, no matter how good he felt, she wanted more.

There were no claws. This was not a dream, not a nightmare meant to frighten her away from something beautiful and natural.

Destiny had brought her here, to this place and this time. Everything about this moment felt true and good, and to fight what she wanted and needed would be wrong. Juliet felt as if she hadn't come alive until she'd stepped foot on this mountain. She'd been sleeping until Ryn had found her, and when she'd tried to escape, she'd been running not from him but from this part of herself. The animal. The beast. Every inch of her was alive, and for the first time in her life she wanted something for herself. She wanted what the pleasurable parts of the dream had only teased her with—Ryn's body joined with hers.

It would be easy to be lost in physical sensation, but a nagging doubt in the back of her mind plagued her as Ryn lowered his head to kiss her throat again. She was undeniably connected to this man. When he was inside her, would she be overcome with his essence until she lost her own? And what of babies?

That thought made her flinch a little. How could she even consider lying with this man as a wife lies with her husband, when such an action might very well lead to a child? An Anwyn child, who would one day turn with the full moon if she didn't take him far, far away from this mountain and his father. And if she could not take the child from his father? No matter how she tried, she couldn't imagine living in an isolated, primitive city far from everything she had ever known, with a man who didn't love her, a man she could never love.

A child would bind her to Ryn in a way one night of sex would not. If they created a family and stayed together, would she eventually love him? It would be easy, she suspected. Much too easy. And with love came disaster.

She fisted her hand in his hair. "Ryn . . . I can't."

He growled, deep in his throat. "There will be no babies," he whispered. "Not tonight."

She didn't even question how he knew what she'd been thinking. He was in her mind; she was in his. "You can't be sure."

"It isn't time."

Juliet relaxed a little. While Ryn had often infuriated her, he had not lied to her once. As far as she knew, the Anwyn were a completely different species and it was certainly possible that they were able to make babies only at a certain time of the year or of the cycle of the moon. And in truth, she doubted she would conceive easily, without Sophie's help. Her cycle had never been regular. She usually bled for three days out of every four months or so, instead of the usual once a month like her sisters and most other women.

Between that and Ryn's assurance that it wasn't time, she allowed herself to relax, certain she didn't have to worry about tonight leading to a child she was not yet ready to have.

There was still the psychic connection to deal with. Right now the sensations she drank in were pleasant and warm, but how much of Ryn would she take into herself while he was in her body? How deep would the connection become? It was her greatest fear, to know that it was even possible for another to be forever linked with her.

"You wish the physical joining without the joining of

spirits." He rose up slightly to look down at her. Firelight flickered over half his face, and it almost seemed that he was hurt, or disappointed.

"Yes," she whispered.

"Why?"

I'm afraid.

You have the power to keep me out. You know how.

"I don't think I can," she said. "Not like this. Can you?"

"If it is what you wish, wife." Ryn laid his mouth on her throat again and she got wonderfully lost in that physical sensation. And that was all she felt: physical sensation.

It was hot, so close to the fire. Almost too hot. The night's chill didn't cut through her clothes the way it had in her early days on the mountain. Maybe she had acclimated quickly. Then again, maybe it was Ryn and the way he touched her and the promise of what was to come that took the night's chill away.

He unclasped her cloak and let it fall, then began to unfasten the buttons of her dress. With his hand on her back, he lifted her into a sitting position, and there he worked the sleeves of her heavy green dress down and off. Juliet expected the cold to assault her bare skin, but it didn't. Ryn's closeness and her desire for him kept her warm.

She suffered a moment's uncertainty—a virgin's uncertainty. No man had ever seen her unclothed, and it was a daunting prospect to lay oneself beneath a man completely vulnerable and exposed. What if he didn't find her desirable? She didn't have Sophie's curves or Isadora's angles, but was ordinary. And when it came to matters of physical love, she had no training, no experience. Ryn might find her boring, or—heaven forbid—what if she did something wrong?

As Ryn undressed her, it was clear that he didn't find her ordinary or boring. He raked the tips of trembling fingers against her skin, arousing and studying her. He looked at her with longing and anticipation, his golden eyes warm with passion. The last of Juliet's uncertainty left her. She did not need their unearthly connection to know that he found her desirable.

Ryn lifted her onto his lap and worked the tattered dress down over her hips. When she was naked, he raked his large hand over her body, touching her throat and her breasts and her soft belly, and then delving gently between her legs in a way that made her arch and moan. Her wanting increased in a way she had not expected. It was fine, this wanting, this promise of more.

He caressed her as if she were the finest treasure, delicate and precious. She had never felt precious, not once in her twenty-six years.

"I've never done this before," she whispered shakily.

"I know. Neither have I."

She swallowed hard. "Never?" She would've expected a man who looked like this one, a man who was obviously virile, a man who knew how and where to touch her, to be experienced in the ways of love. She had heard from many of her female patients about husbands who were unfaithful, or who had availed themselves of every obtainable woman before marriage.

"I have been waiting for you," Ryn said.

Juliet licked her lips. He had been waiting for her, all this time. It was as frightening as the possibility of taking him into her completely, not only with her body but with her mind and soul.

He looked her in the eye as if he were waiting for her to change her mind.

She didn't. Some primal part of her had taken over, at least for tonight, and she wanted Ryn more than she wanted her own freedom, her own life.

"You are sure?" he asked softly, giving her this one last chance to tell him to stop.

"Yes."

His clothing was much easier to remove than hers had been. The kilt was laced up one side, and it was simple enough to untie the leather string and loosen it, then push the kilt down and away. She didn't have to ask if Ryn was sure about what was to come. His skin was hot to the touch, and without the kilt to cover him, she could see that he was most definitely certain about what he wanted. She stared shamelessly, studying the length and breadth of his arousal, reaching down to stroke him to feel the heat and the hardness. He was like stone and velvet, long and hot and so hard she was amazed. Touching him, stroking him, she felt an answering call deep in her own body. A quiver. A clenching.

Ryn touched her, much as she touched him, his fingers finding the nub at her entrance and caressing it lightly, with little circles that incited a new and stronger fire in her belly. Her folds grew damp and ready for what was to come. Instinctively she swayed very slightly against his hand, her body taking charge and moving as it wished. A small moan escaped from her throat as a new and more powerful ribbon of pleasure shot through her.

He laid her on her back once again, and she spread her legs so he could fit himself between them. Her body quivered, with uncertainty and desire and anticipation. Ryn was so big, so strong and hard. And yet she felt as if the control in this moment was as much hers as his. There was one more thing she needed to make this moment perfect. While Ryn hovered above her, she took his face in her hands and drew it down.

Juliet pressed her lips to his for her first true kiss. Naked and trembling, she took her first kiss from the man who would soon be inside her. The kiss was soft at first, almost tentative, and then Ryn began to move his mouth over hers.

Maybe it was his first kiss, too. She didn't know. It was very nice that she didn't know. This kiss, this night, was of the body and the body alone.

She flicked the tip of her tongue against Ryn's lips, and he answered in kind. Her hips rocked gently against his, and the tip of his erection barely brushed against her. That pressure was enough to make her shudder; it was enough to make her lower belly lurch and clench. She deepened the kiss, and threaded her fingers through his hair once again to hold on tight.

Juliet knew she was not the woman who had begun this journey; she was not the woman who had been taken against her will. She'd changed. Her shyness and her gentleness were gone. No, not gone, but faded. Put away, here in this land where such attributes were not called for. It was as if a savageness she had never known she possessed had been sleeping inside her, and it awakened with Ryn's touch. With Ryn's taste.

She *was* an animal, every bit as much as the man above her.

He guided himself into her, slowly, gradually. She held her breath while he became a part of her. There was pain and pleasure as her body accepted his, wonder and dread all wrapped into one moment she knew she would never forget. Her heart pounded, her breath caught in her chest while Ryn pushed and they became one.

Instinct told her she wanted more, while common sense told her *more* was impossible. For tonight, instinct ruled over common sense.

Ryn's hips began to rock. He withdrew and then plunged deeper. Juliet gasped, not with pain but with gratification and surprise. Every thrust took him deeper, and with each plunge her body shuddered and reached for his. They moved together in a silent rhythm, as if they danced without music. They generated a heat that belied the cold of a winter night. They moved toward something beautiful and powerful.

For tonight, Ryn was hers, as he had always claimed to be. And she was his. In body, they were mated. They were one being, searching for pleasure and perfection. This went beyond magic.

Ryn moved faster, deeper, and Juliet arched her back and lifted into him. She could not breathe; she could do nothing but meet Ryn's body with her own in search of something not yet tasted. She began to sweat, and so did he. She could feel her heart hasten, beating faster and faster.

With a shift of her hips he pushed deeper than before, and ribbons of intense pleasure began to unfurl. Ryn plunged to the limit and she shattered, her body splintering in release and physical delight that made her clench and shudder around him. The release stole her breath and her heartbeat, shocking her with its force. Ryn shuddered, too, and in every way he shared this moment where everything Juliet had ever believed about physical love changed.

The act of love was wonderful; it was beautiful. How had she lived without this for so long? How had she lived without Ryn?

As he drifted down to cover her body with his, she expected the cold to return. It didn't, not completely. She remained warm, covered by Ryn's body and shaking with the power of her climax. No wonder Sophie had suggested that she take a lover.

"I think you will make a good wife," Ryn said breathlessly.

Juliet laughed. "Let's save that discussion for tomorrow."

"If that is what you wish, it is done."

"It is," she whispered.

"Tonight I can deny you nothing," Ryn whispered

against her throat. He lifted his head and touched his mouth to hers, and again they kissed. Slow and intimate and powerful, they kissed. Juliet felt happy and strong and content with where life had taken her. She did not think of the events that had brought her to this place, the troubles she'd left behind, or where tomorrow might find her.

There was no tomorrow, not at this moment.

LAST NIGHT LIANE HAD DREAMED OF THE BABY'S CRY drifting up from the dungeon of Level Thirteen, as she had so often in the past few months. When Sebestyen had thrown his fourth wife, Rikka, into that dark pit in the ground, Liane had been at his side—at his insistence. No one else, not Sebestyen or the prison guards or a drugged Rikka, had seemed to hear that cry that continued to haunt Liane. No matter how often or how strenuously she tried to tell herself that sound had been a product of her own imagination, the memory persisted.

The more real her own child became, the more real that cry became. She could no longer push the recollection aside as fantasy. Maybe it had been a figment of her imagination, but if it had not been . . . she had to know the truth.

Sebestyen's infidelity and his nighttime visit confused her. They also made her angry. Just because she had been relegated to Level Five like the previous empresses did not mean she had to remain powerless. Did her husband care for her or not? Something had to be done, and she was sick with waiting around in this pretty prison for someone to save her. She had been to hell and back, and she did not wait for any man to rescue her.

She would rescue herself.

The priests might hate her and wish her ill, but they did not dare to hurt her while she carried the next emperor in her belly. That safety gave her some confidence that she could do as she wished, for now.

"Mahri," she said brightly as the girl laid out a fancy gown of royal crimson, a gown befitting the mother of the next emperor. "I am going on an excursion today."

The girl paled. "An excursion?"

"Yes. I'm leaving my rooms this morning. I'll need my boots rather than my slippers."

"But, my lady, that surely is not wise. Whatever you desire can be brought to you here."

Liane spun on the girl. "Who do you serve, Mahri?"

Mahri's face went even paler, turning almost entirely white. "You, my lady. Only you."

"Then do as I say." Liane looked the trembling girl up and down. "Don't worry, I don't plan to ask you to accompany me." Mahri was exceptionally skittish, and Liane would not dare to expose her to Level Thirteen, not even in the smallest way.

"You cannot wander the palace alone, my lady!"

"I will take a sentinel with me." Ferghus, who was quiet and who could be trusted.

Liane dressed in the too-fancy gown, with Mahri's help, then pulled on stockings and boots. Her hair was twisted into a tight knot. "I do have an assignment for you," Liane said as she patted the crimson fabric that covered her increasing belly.

"Anything you wish, my lady."

"I wish for you to redecorate my apartment."

"What is it you wish changed?" Mahri asked sweetly.

"Everything," Liane said beneath her breath. In a louder voice, she said, "I am tired of pink. Have the sitting room done in blue, the bedroom in green, the dining room in gold."

"May I leave my room pink?" Mahri asked sheepishly. "It's my favorite color."

"Your bedchamber can be any color you wish," Liane said sharply. "But I don't want a scrap of pink fabric to remain in my living quarters."

While Mahri wrung her hands like an old woman and nodded her head in assent, Liane opened the door to exit her bedchamber. The sentinels stood in the corridor, awaiting her orders. Liane ignored Tatsl and looked at Ferghus. "I wish to go to Level Seven to speak with Gadhra."

"We will have her brought to you, my lady," Ferghus offered.

"No," Liane said strongly. "I wish to go to her. Now."

Since Tatsl was openly afraid of magic of any kind, and he remembered Sophie's momentous visit too well, she knew he would offer to stay behind and guard the empress's quarters, while the less senior Ferghus escorted Liane to Level Seven.

Ferghus nodded cordially and obediently, and followed as Liane led the way to the lift. When she reached past him and pressed the lever that would take them all the way down, he protested.

"I cannot allow you to leave the palace."

"I'm not leaving."

"Then why—"

"You're going to escort me to Level Thirteen."

The sentinel paled and took a step back.

"Don't worry," Liane snapped. "I'm not planning to toss you down." She would need his help, and so he had to know why she traveled to the pit of the palace. "I think I might've heard a baby down there," she said softly. "Do you remember when we took Empress Rikka to Level Thirteen?" Months ago, before Sophie Fyne had arrived and changed everything.

"Yes, my lady," he answered softly.

"You and Taneli waited in the stairwell, but I was with Sebestyen when the portal was opened. While I was standing over the opening to the pit, I heard a baby's cry. At least, I think I did. I have tried to convince myself that the sound was my own imagination, but what if it wasn't?"

"Surely it was your imagination, my lady. Even Emperor Sebestyen . . ." Ferghus choked on his words when Liane gave him a regal glare. "I'm sure the emperor would not be so cruel."

"I need to be sure."

They made their way to Level Ten, which was as far down as the lift would carry them. Narrow winding stairs led from Level Ten to the noisy technological Level Eleven and then to the bleak prison on Level Twelve.

Beneath Level Twelve was the pit where Sebestyen sent his enemies and discarded empresses. Level Thirteen. It was a horrible place, worse than death.

Four guards stood in the hallway, near enough to the hatch in the ground to hear anything that went on once it was opened. Liane asked, in a lowered voice. "Who among them can you trust?"

Ferghus answered just as softly. "Only Gant, the sentinel with the dark beard. We come from the same village in the Northern Province."

Liane nodded subtly. The guards noticed that their visitors were of the special sort, and their posture improved in an instant. Liane lifted her chin. "All but Gant are to leave us. Now. I will summon you when it's time for you to return."

"But, my lady . . ." one older guard began.

"Wait in the stairwell," she ordered.

After a moment's hesitation, they did as she commanded. Poor Gant. The young sentinel's lips actually quivered. "Never fear," Liane said softly. "I do not plan to banish you or anyone else into Level Thirteen today."

It took both men to lift the hatch, and it would take both

to raise the child out of there, if it turned out that she was right.

Ferghus and Gant lifted the heavy hatchway with a heave. Three or four men made the job easier, but two could manage. When the hatch had been tossed back, Gant held a torch over the opening and the three of them glanced down. The torch didn't offer much illumination, but it was more than enough for Liane to see the gaunt faces that gathered below.

"Since no one has yet joined them, they think they will be fed," Gant said softly.

The hapless souls, all of them addicted to the drug Panwyr, most of them starving and delusional, stared up at her with wide, desperate eyes. The light from the torch showed Liane those eyes too well. The prisoners murmured lowly, enough to drown out any sounds from beyond the opening.

"Quiet," she ordered.

Her command only made some of the prisoners howl. A few clapped hands over their mouths, trying to force themselves to comply. One lifted his head and screamed.

"Be quiet, and I will have extra food tossed down when I am finished here." Liane shouted to be heard over the din. Some of the men grew quiet; a few did not. "And more Panwyr," she added.

The offer of food and drug silenced them, and Liane strained to listen. For a moment all was silent. There was a deep dank silence in this place, something beyond a normal quietness. It was ominous. It was *bad*. She wasn't afraid of much, but she was afraid of ending up in this place. The sounds and smells and sensations of death and suffering were powerful here.

All remained silent. She almost breathed a sigh of relief. Maybe the baby's cry had been her imagination after all. If not then the child had died, which was surely a blessing. Still, she preferred to believe that she'd never heard a baby at all. She'd heard one of those pathetic men below howling or crying, and her fantasies had provided the rest.

Just as Liane was about to order the hatch closed, a faint sound stopped her. A cry, soft and weak and very, very real. Ferghus heard it, too; she knew by the swearing beneath his breath.

Liane leaned closer to the opening in the floor. "Bring me the baby," she shouted, hoping that whoever cared for the child was still sane enough to know that it needed to be rescued. The men beneath her scattered, as if expecting a monster to arrive along with the baby. "I don't want to hurt the child," she cried. "It doesn't belong here. I want to help."

She waited a moment, and then a few moments more. In frustration she knelt on the floor, took the torch from Gant, and thrust it into the hole as far as she could reach. What she saw illuminated beneath her almost made her retch into the opening in the earth. A few bodies lay in the dirt, pushed out of the way by the others, unceremoniously dumped against a muddy wall. The smell, as always, made her stomach roil, but she ignored the gut reaction and did not empty her breakfast onto those below. The living who had moved away from the light didn't look much better than the dead. Gaunt and pale and ragged, they were barely living at all. A child did not belong down there.

A soft, female voice called from beyond the light. "Have you come to kill her? I swear by all that is holy, I will not let you murder my daughter."

That voice was vaguely familiar to Liane, but she couldn't quite place it. "Come into the light."

"I won't let you—"

"I have come to save your child, not harm it."

"Why?" the soft voice asked.

"Because no child belongs down there. I can't save you, but I can take your daughter to a safe place."

A woman wearing the ragged remains of a pale-colored dress stepped into the edge of the light cast by Liane's torch. Blond hair, tangled and dirty, covered the woman's face. She held in her arms a child wrapped in rags. When the woman—the mother of the child—lifted her face, Liane's heart skipped a beat.

"Ryona?"

Ryona could barely be called a woman. She was little more than a child herself. She'd spent a few months on Level Three, as a servant who would one day—when she was old enough—take training to become a concubine. When she'd disappeared, one of the crones told Liane she'd been sent home to her father, who'd apparently had a change of heart about selling his daughter.

Liane lifted her face to Ferghus. "We're going to get them both out of there."

He shook his head. "I can't—"

"You will," she snapped. Prisoners were never removed from Level Thirteen, but Liane knew to the depths of her soul that Ryona did not belong down there. "I command it."

He swallowed hard and looked at his friend. "Is there a way to lift them up?"

"We can use the basket we employ to collect the dead bodies now and then, I suppose."

Liane turned her attention to Gant. "Do it."

He fetched the basket from a storage unit at the end of the hallway. Poor Ryona—some of the gaunt men who had initially gathered at the opening had begun to paw at her ragged skirts, and she was rightfully frightened of them.

"Keep your hands off of her," Liane ordered. "Or I will not throw down the food and Panwyr I promised." They backed away, some of them sending desperate and hate-filled glances her way. Some of them were beyond emotion of any kind, and they simply did as they were told, like frightened animals.

The basket was attached to a pulley that extended from the wall, and then it was lowered with the turn of a crank. "Hurry," Liane said as the basket reached the bottom of the pit. Ryona, clutching her baby to her chest, climbed into the basket. She had to push back a few bony hands of men who wanted to join her in her escape, but they were not strong enough to force their way past her resistance. As soon as she was in the basket, Ferghus and Gant turned the crank to lift Ryona and her child up.

The light hurt her eyes—that much was clear as the basket rose—but Ryona looked remarkably well as she left the darkness of Level Thirteen behind. She was filthy and frightened and her clothes were in tatters, but she was not gaunt like the others, and there was still life in her eyes.

When the girl and her baby were on solid ground, Liane gave her orders to Gant. "Send down the Panwyr and food I promised as soon as we're well away from here."

"Yes, my lady."

"And for God's sake, when the other sentinels return, send down that basket again and collect the dead bodies."

"It's not time—" He began to argue, but did not get far.

"They're dead," Liane said sharply. "Removing their bodies will not in any way commute their sentences!"

"Yes, my lady."

Ryona shuddered. She was malnourished, anxious, and possibly permanently damaged by the Panwyr, which was always administered to the prisoners before their descent into Level Thirteen. The baby, while small and dirty, looked to be healthy enough.

They left Gant behind. Ferghus helped the girl along the hallway, his arm around her in needed support. Liane would've carried the baby, but Ryona refused to release the hold on her child. Liane opened the door to the stairwell to find three surprised sentinels staring at her and the rest of her party.

"Speak of this to anyone, and I will know," she promised. "It'll be the last secret you spill."

They nodded, obedient and frightened. Were they frightened of her because she was empress, or had whispers that she'd once been Sebestyen's assassin drifted through the palace? In either case, their fear would keep them silent.

Climbing the stairs with a depleted woman and a child was difficult, but soon Liane and Ferghus were in the lift once again, this time with Ryona and a baby who couldn't be more than six months old along for the ride.

With his hand on the lever, Ferghus asked, "Where shall we take her, my lady?"

"Level Three."

Ryona flinched and held her baby tight.

"You'll be safe there," Liane promised.

As they began moving upward, Liane turned to an obviously shaken Ferghus. "I ask you for one favor," she said softly. "If Sebestyen ever decides to throw me into Level Thirteen, kill me."

"My lady," the sentinel said, obviously shocked by her request. "I could never do such a horrible thing."

Ferghus was fully grown, a man perhaps somewhere between twenty-five and thirty. He was a few years younger than she, but eons more naïve.

Liane turned her gaze to a shaking Ryona. Was the child Sebestyen's? Is that why the girl had been tossed into Level Thirteen? No. For years, he'd been desperate for a child. If this baby girl was Sebestyen's daughter, Ryona would likely be empress instead of Liane. She had believed for many years that she was the only woman Sebestyen called to his bed at night, other than the empresses which were his duty. But then again, she had been proved wrong about Sebestyen of late, so anything was possible.

Had the inexperienced girl been thrown away for some small slight, and the child she clutched to her chest conceived down there in that wretched place? It was a terrible thought.

"Did you look into the pit?"

"Yes, my lady," Ferghus answered.

"Would you let me suffer there?"

He swallowed hard. "No, my lady."

"Promise me," she said softly.

Before they reached Level Three, Ferghus muttered a very soft, very uncertain, "I swear, my lady."

MOST MORNINGS THEY WOKE WITH THE SUN AND BEGAN their journey quickly, but not today. Today was different. Juliet knew she would forever remember *today*.

She had always been the one of the three Fyne sisters to most easily accept what was meant to be. For so many days and nights she'd been fighting what Ryn swore was destined, but now she could accept that he had been right all along, to some extent. She could not see herself living forever among the Anwyn, a willing slave and wife to a man who wanted her body and her soul.

But this—the wanting and the lying together—was very nice. She would have missed this moment if not for Ryn, for she could not see herself lying with any other man in this way.

She had not bothered to dress last night after she and Ryn had finished coming together on this bearskin bed. He and the fire kept the chill from her body. She still felt no psychic connection with him; the break in the tendril that connected them remained. In an odd sort of way, she missed it. She missed him. But she could not risk the power of joining with him in body *and* in mind.

He slept still, long after the sun had risen in the sky.

Juliet found she was in no hurry to rush to an unknown city filled with strangers and a destiny she had not yet accepted and might never accept. But this moment was a good one. It was warm and alive and special.

She laid her hand on Ryn's chest. His body was lovely and hard and not quite as warm as she had thought in those first days. She traced a muscle with her thumb. Yes, he was a fine specimen of manhood, and at the moment he was hers. She raked her hand upward and touched his throat with the back of her hand, and his eyes fluttered open slowly. She didn't move her hand away, but traced her fingers over his jaw. She didn't have to worry about abrasive morning stubble, since no hair grew on his cheeks or his jaw. It was smooth and hard and finely shaped. He was beautiful in the morning light.

"We slept late," he said simply.

"Yes, we did."

"Our laziness will delay our arrival in The City."

"Is that a problem?"

For a moment he was quiet, and then he said, "No. It is not a problem at all."

Since he did not seem to mind the way her hand explored his face and neck, she allowed the other hand to caress one hip. He watched her as she learned his curves and found the tender places on his body where the softest touch aroused him.

Her hand looked pale against his sun-bronzed skin. It looked soft and dainty against the muscles that rippled through his body. She remembered what he said about her being soft and him being hard. She had not known that gentleness combined with harshness could create something so wonderful.

Ryn shuddered when her fingers brushed against his inner thigh; he quivered when she raked her palm along his lower belly, her fingers just out of reach of his erection.

With a growl, he rolled her onto her back. They fit very nicely this way, with her legs spread and his body cradled there, so close to being inside her again.

Ryn tilted his head slightly and offered her his throat, his beautiful, soft, hard, tasty throat, and with the blue sky above them and the energy flowing between them, the dream came to life. The good part of the dream, not the nightmare that had frightened her for so many years. There were no claws awaiting at the end of this journey, no pain, no blood. Only pleasure.

Last night there had been a little pain and a little blood, but her virgin's blood had been drops, not the river of her dreams, and the pain had been so quickly replaced with pleasure that it had already been forgotten.

The claws were nothing more than the remnants of a nightmare. They were not a sad omen, not a portent of something violent to come. Perhaps those claws had only been a warning that the man she'd give herself to would be different. Ryn did have claws, on the three nights out of the cycle of the moon when the moon was full, but they would never harm her. She believed as strongly as she had ever believed anything that he would not hurt her.

She had misinterpreted the dream; she had made the glimpse of her future into a nightmare all on her own. There was nothing within Ryn to incite fear.

She lifted her head to gently touch his throat with her tongue, and as soon as she tasted him, her body responded with a wild and uncontrollable need that only he could satisfy. He responded, too, with a deep shudder that whipped through his fine, naked body.

When she took her mouth from Ryn's throat, he kissed her. His lips moved over hers, his tongue danced and fluttered, and her lips parted to urge and accept a deepening of the kiss. Like the tasting of her throat, the kiss touched her everywhere, more deeply than she had imagined possible.

His fingers teased her—her sensitive breasts, her tender stomach, the folds that grew wet when he touched them—and within minutes of waking he plunged inside her with a fierceness unlike last night's gentle joining. They were one, in body and in this quest for release and pleasure. The mental barrier Ryn had constructed remained strong. She did not touch his mind; he did not invade her soul.

Today they were just a man and a woman, with no magic between them.

IO

LIANE ESCORTED RYONA TO A GUEST SUITE ON LEVEL Three. There were moments when she did not completely trust Mahri, even though the girl seemed loyal enough. Her years in this palace had taught her not to trust anyone completely, and that had not changed. She would likely always feel more at home on Level Three, where pleasure was more meaningful than politics, and love never entered the equation.

Ferghus was as loyal as anyone else around her, more loyal than most, and together they would keep Ryona's rescue and whereabouts a secret for as long as possible. Until Liane was sure that Ryona and her child were strong enough to travel, she couldn't allow them to leave. And until she knew why the girl had been thrown into Level Thirteen, she couldn't allow anyone to know that she'd been rescued.

Ryona perched on the edge of a fine blue and green striped chair in this small guest suite that was reserved for visiting dignitaries intent on sampling the emperor's greatest delights. Liane had taken care not to be seen by the crone who had wrongly informed her that Ryona had gone home months ago. The old woman might've been told by someone else that Ryona had gone home, in order to cover up the girl's disappearance, but that wasn't a chance Liane cared to take. Only two concubines, women Liane could trust because she had once been in their shoes, knew this room was now occupied. They would keep her secret, because they knew they'd pay a high price if they did not.

The young mother shook. She sat, trembling and watching Liane with open suspicion, as if she expected a knife to appear at any moment to end her suffering. The luxurious surroundings only made the girl's skin seem dirtier, her eyes wilder, her dress more ragged. Ferghus was discretely fetching food, while the women who knew Ryona was here were getting clean clothing for mother and child, along with warm water and soap for both. It would take a while to accomplish such things in true secrecy.

"Why were you down there?" Liane asked.

Ryona's head snapped to the side, and she stared out the window, squinting against the sun. "You know," she whispered.

"I don't," she said gently.

"You know everything that goes on here, so you must . . . This is a trick," the girl said beneath her breath. "He said it was a trick. You'll make me think I'm rescued and then you'll put me back down there with the demons and the monsters, and the screaming and the death. Or else you'll make me lie with him again." She shuddered. "Bastard. I'd rather go back down there. I'd rather face a demon than let that horrible man touch me again." She lifted her head and looked Liane in the eye. "Just don't make Dorie go back."

"Dorie is your daughter's name?" Liane asked.

"It's short for Dorantha."

Liane made an effort to remain calm, to keep her voice low and even so she wouldn't frighten Ryona. Poor girl, talking irrationally about demons. Maybe the Panwyr had caused her to suffer delusions, or else those sad prisoners in Level Thirteen seemed like demons to her. They were certainly no longer men.

As for the bastard she spoke of . . . He was likely very real, and more a demon that any imagined monsters in the dark.

"Dorantha. That's a very pretty name."

Ryona glanced up suspiciously. "Thank you."

Liane reached out and very gently touched the baby's soft head. "Who told you the rescue was a trick?" she asked. Obviously someone in Level Thirteen had been protecting the girl. She was healthier than the prisoners who'd gathered beneath the portal, and the way they'd grabbed at her . . . yes, someone had been looking after Ryona in the depths of Level Thirteen.

Ryona just shook her head. "I won't tell. You can send me back down there, but I won't—"

"It's all right, "Liane said calmly. "You don't have to tell anything you don't want to. But I would like to know who put you in that place, and what you did for such a thing to happen."

"I didn't do anything," Ryona said with a frantic shake of her head. "It wasn't my fault."

"I'm sure that's true. But I would like to know so I can help you."

Ryona glared at Liane. "Why?" she asked caustically. "I don't recall you helping when I was sold onto Level Three. You didn't feel obligated to help when I begged that awful man not to touch me. I wasn't ready. I hadn't had any training at all and I hadn't started taking the medications to make sure I didn't get with child. I told him, I was just supposed to fetch towels and lotions and things for the concubines, not become one. Not yet. But he said he didn't want a trained whore, he wanted a nice girl to warm his bed." Her lower lip trembled slightly. "And then he said he could love me and take care of me, that he could give me a good life if I would only do as he asked."

Ryona had been seduced or raped. Before training, before she'd started taking the drug that was supposed to prevent unwanted babies like Dorie. Such a thing wasn't supposed to happen.

"You didn't help when I told him I was carrying his child and he hit me." Ryona's voice got louder and fiercer. "You didn't *help* when he said he was taking me home, but instead he threw me into that awful place and left me and my unborn child there to die."

"I didn't know," Liane said softly. "I swear, I didn't know. Tell me who did this to you, and I'll kill him." And if Ryona told her Sebestyen had done these things? Would she kill him? Yes. Of course she would. But he wouldn't have done such a thing. Even if he had known the child Ryona carried was a daughter and not a son, he would've welcomed it. And as Ferghus said, *Even Emperor Sebestyen . . .*

Even Sebestyen wouldn't toss a pregnant child into Level Thirteen.

"Tell me."

"Will you really kill him?"

"Yes."

Ryona shuffled her feet and cut her eyes to the floor. She held her baby close and whispered a few bars of a lullaby. And then she said, "It was Nelyk."

Liane almost jumped out of her skin. "Father Nelyk?"

"Yes." The expression on Ryona's face as she finally looked Liane in the eye convinced her the girl was telling the truth.

Liane and the young priest Nelyk had never been on the best of terms, and she was quite sure that he despised her for the part she played in Sebestyen's life. But she'd never imagined that he could do such a thing.

She doubted Ryona was an isolated case. "Are there others?" she asked.

"Other what?"

"Girls in Level Thirteen. Girls that Father Nelyk put there."

Ryona shrugged her shoulders. "Not anymore," she said softly. "There have been a few over the years, but he said they all died. The babies, too. They died down there in that awful place."

He again. This time Liane didn't bother to ask who. "We're going to keep you here until you're strong enough to travel, and then you and the baby are getting out of the palace once and for all."

Ryona's eyes went wide, and she was impossibly beautiful. "I can go home?"

Liane's heart sank. The girl's father had sold her to Sebestyen to be a sexual slave to him and his ministers and guests, and still she wanted to go home. "That might not be such a good idea, not at first. After Nelyk is dead, then if you still want to, you can go home. Until then, you'll have to stay out of sight."

Ryona nodded.

After Ferghus delivered food, Liane returned to her rooms. She was tired of waiting around for things to change. She would make things change. Nelyk would die, though that would take some time to plan and execute. The priests were almost as heavily guarded as Sebestyen.

More immediately, she would no longer spend all day every day trapped in her pretty prison. If she was to be empress, she would do something with her days besides rest and try to learn to master the boring pastimes of embroidery and painting flowers.

And she would find out, one way or another, if her husband cared for her in even the smallest way. She had been pushed out of his life and his bed, and she had allowed the situation to go on for too long. Liane was not a meek girl who would cower in her rooms, and she never had been. She was not a sexless woman content to sleep alone. Her marriage would be consummated.

Tonight.

JULIET SMILED AS SHE WALKED QUICKLY AND SURELY along the path. She had an easier time keeping up with Ryn today. There was a lightness of spirit within her that had not been there before, and that lightness spurred her forward. She was no longer achy and tired, but full of life as she followed Ryn along the narrow path that led upward.

When she'd dressed this morning, she'd left off the nightshift, though she had saved it in case she needed bandages or rags along the way. She had rolled her cloak and the remains of the nightgown in the bearskin bedroll, since the air seemed milder today and she didn't have need of the layers of clothing.

She did not suffer visions of any sort. Not only did Ryn maintain the break with her, but she had gone deep into her mind and found the silver tendril that connected her to all other living things, and she'd mentally tied a knot in the thread. She didn't know if such an attempt would be successful for very long or not, but if it was . . .

She could have what she'd always wanted. Isadora loved her magic, and Sophie had accepted hers well enough. Juliet had always acknowledged her own witchcraft, but she had never embraced it. She had never loved that part of herself.

Her hopes for a normal existence were hers and hers alone; she had never shared them with anyone. Not even her sisters. Deep in her heart Juliet Fyne, witch and seer, wanted nothing more than a small house somewhere. A place where she could make herbal remedies and help people with their problems without magic of any kind. She wanted to spend her days in her own mind, not peeking into the minds and hearts of others. She wanted to touch a neighbor's hand without seeing their jealousy or bitterness or pain. Most of all, she wanted not to know what tomorrow would bring to those around her.

Maybe it was selfish to wish her gifts away, but she didn't feel at all selfish for wishing to be ordinary. After all, her power of sight hadn't helped her when Ariana had been kidnapped or when she and Isadora had been taken and the cabin burned to the ground, so what good was such a gift? It had been a plague to her, nothing more.

A small house. An herbal kitchen. A few patients. Babies.

She watched Ryn's back, and in spite of herself she wanted him again. Again and again and again. He stirred something unknown in her, something wanton and wild. And he certainly had the physical attributes any woman would find attractive. But did she want daughters who would be not only witches but shape-shifters who grew into women who would become wolves for three nights out of each month?

Ryn said he did not believe in or want love, and that suited Juliet well. Maybe if they approached their relationship as he suggested, as friends and companions and sexually compatible mates who never cluttered their hearts and minds with romantic love, the curse would not be effective. There was nothing in the Fyne Curse that she knew of to keep her from *liking* a man.

Since she was keeping pace better today, it didn't take long to catch up with Ryn once the rocky path widened a bit. "How can you be sure I won't get pregnant?" she asked as she pulled up alongside him.

"I just know."

"But—"

"Anwyn are different." He looked down at her as they continued to walk along the trail. "You do not want babies?"

"Someday. Maybe."

"You just do not want my babies."

"That's not what I meant."

"That is what you said."

The view from this path was breathtaking. A little farther to the north, a pristine snow covered the mountaintops. It seemed that from here she could see forever. "It's just . . . it's a little frightening to think of giving birth to children who will turn into wolves with the full moon."

"As I explained, our sons will not take on the change until they come of age and take the vow."

"What about our daughters?"

His head snapped around, and after a moment he actually smiled. "Anwyn men make Anwyn men. That is why we must travel so far to fetch our wives."

"Well then, we have a problem, because Fyne women make Fyne women."

"That will change," he said confidently.

"I don't think so."

After a few thoughtful moments, Ryn said, "Anwyn females are rare creatures. They are more than Anwyn, more than woman."

"So if we have a few daughters, they'll be extra special," Juliet teased.

Ryn glanced at her briefly. "Anwyn females come into the world once every fifty years or so, and when they are of age, they become Queen."

"So, it's the Queen who gives birth to these rare creatures of yours? Is that how the royal line is carried on?"

"No. Any Anwyn male can sire this rare daughter. She becomes Queen simply because she is female. Anwyn daughters, Anwyn Queens, are more powerful than the males of our species or any other."

"So, the Anwyn Queen that awaits us is this rare, powerful woman?"

For a moment, Ryn was silent. "Queen Etaina is old, and the new Queen has not yet arrived. It is past time for her coming, and the people wait anxiously. If Etaina dies before the new Queen comes, there will be war among those who believe they should rule in the absence of the Queen."

"Maybe it's time for things to change in The City."

"Anwyn do not like change."

No, Anwyn were stubborn men who insisted on having things their own way at all times. But if they were at all like Ryn, they made up for that annoying trait in other ways. "Your male-dominant bloodline aside, I will have daughters," Juliet said confidently.

"I will have sons," Ryn answered with matching conviction.

It was a few minutes before Juliet realized that she and Ryn had talked about their future children, and she hadn't once had a second thought or a shimmer of doubt.

HE SHOULD HAVE KNOWN, BUT HOW COULD HE HAVE smelled the Anwyn blood in Juliet before it began to dominate? The Anwyn scent was his own, and so he had not caught even a hint of it when he'd first come across his mate.

Maybe he was wrong. She was different from other women. Perhaps her gift for connecting to the earth caused her to absorb Anwyn traits from him, or even from the mountain itself. Maybe she embraced him so completely she took on his Anwyn qualities.

If not for the prophesy, he might allow himself to believe that, for a while.

Since long before his birth, there had been whispered tales of the red-haired Queen who would bring a time of peace and prosperity to the Anwyn. She would have the gift of sight, this Queen, a gift so powerful people would kneel before her in awe. Prophets had spoken of this Queen for such a long time, no one doubted that one day she would come.

The Anwyn were a peaceful people. Only their continuing conflict with the Caradon kept them from an existence free of conflict. The Caradon were not organized, not even in warfare. They fought among themselves and attacked only in small groups, as was their nature. They did not trust even one another, and so they had never been a serious threat to The City.

They had killed, though. They had killed many Anwyn over the years. Ryn's own father had fallen in battle with a Caradon. His mother had died two moons later, heartbroken. Ryn had been only fifteen at the time, but he still remembered the pain and the hate. Pain at losing his parents; hate for the animal who had killed them both. Four years later he had tracked that Caradon down, the scent from his father's body too well remembered, and killed it.

The peace the red-haired Queen was supposed to bring, the end to a conflict with the Caradon . . . according to the prophesy it came from her union with a Caradon male, a lover she would bring into her bed, the beast who would father her child, the first offspring of Anwyn and Caradon.

If his instincts were right, Juliet was that red-haired Queen.

He could not imagine allowing a Caradon to touch his wife in any way, but if she were Queen, he'd have no say in the matter. Queen's consorts were useless, powerless males, called upon only when the Queen was in heat and a child was required. There would be no marriage. Her only vow would be to the Anwyn people she ruled. The Anwyn Queen was not like the captives who made such compliant, devoted wives. They ruled the Anwyn people, The City, their own lives, and their own bodies.

From the tales he had heard, there was nothing quite so spectacular as an Anwyn Queen in heat. She could call any man to her bed to satisfy her, if she chose. And if she chose to turn her back on the Anwyn way and take a Caradon lover, her mate would be powerless to stop her.

No. He would not be powerless. Peace or no peace, he would not allow a Caradon . . . or any other male . . . near Juliet. He did not care that she was Queen, that she was superior, that she would be his ruler in every way. She was still his woman, and in some ways he could not bow to her.

He heard her running to catch up with him. While he'd been thinking, his stride had increased and had taken him too far away. He slowed his step until she came alongside him.

"I cannot walk as fast as you," Juliet said breathlessly.

He stopped and swung her up into his arms, and she squealed and then laughed as he carried her up the trail at a quick pace. She was not tossed over his shoulder, as she had been when he'd first taken her, but caught in his arms so he could see her face and feel her heart beating against his. Her arms snaked easily around his neck, and she held on tight.

"What are you thinking of that makes you look so fierce?" she asked softly as he carried her toward home.

"Do I look fierce?" he asked.

"Yes."

He took a few more long steps before answering. "I was thinking of the Caradon."

"The one you killed?"

"All of them."

She stiffened slightly. "Do you sense others nearby?"

"No. Like Anwyn, they change with the full moon, and all Caradon are more dangerous when in their cat form. As men they are cowardly and devious, and do not attack those who are stronger than they."

She relaxed. "You don't care for the Caradon at all."

He looked into her eyes, studying the gold flecks that grew brighter and more dominant with each step toward The City. "I do not, and neither should you. The Caradon cannot be trusted, Juliet. They are dangerous, and dishonest, and if you let them come too near, they will rip out your throat and devour your eyes."

"Ew." She shivered lightly.

"I did not wish to frighten you," he said in a softer voice.

"Well, you did."

"My deepest apologies."

She leaned against him, relaxing and hiding her eyes from him. "Apology accepted."

"I will take care of you, Juliet," he promised. "I will protect you from the Caradon."

"For now," she said softly.

"Always."

For once, she did not argue with him.

IT HAD BEEN A LONG TIME SINCE LIANE HAD PREPARED herself for an evening with Sebestyen, but she had not forgotten how. Sitting before her vanity, she let her hair down and brushed it out until it shone. Sebestyen loved the gold and pale brown streaks that made her hair unique. When that was done, she dabbed a touch of perfume behind her ears. Not a flowery cologne, but a musk that screamed of sex. She hadn't used face paint at all since becoming empress, but tonight she lined her eyes in black and put a touch of rose color on her lips.

She was tempted to send for one of her old frocks, a sheer gown that would tell Sebestyen without doubt why she'd come to him, but that was not wise. She would have to learn to walk the line between being empress and lover. To Mahri and the sentinels and anyone else she saw in the hallways on her way to Sebestyen tonight, she had to be regal, empress and mother to the future ruler of Columbyana. To Sebestyen, she would be wife and lover.

If she thought she could navigate her way through the secret passageways to his chambers, she would. But try as she might, she had not been able to find the hidden entrance Sebestyen had used, nor did she know the route to his chambers. Access to the emperor's private rooms would be disguised well, and there might even be dangerous traps along the way. Besides, she did not wish to sneak her way into her husband's bed. She would go to him as a wife should, head held high. And if she found him with another woman tonight? Her heart hitched and her mouth went dry. The other woman would go this time, and the wife would stay.

Ferghus did not approve of her insistence that she be taken to her husband once again. He did not dare to suggest that she stay in her suite for the remainder of the evening, but cynicism narrowed his eyes and the set of his mouth. Everyone knew what a disaster her unannounced visit to Sebestyen had had been last time. But Liane insisted, and Ferghus grudgingly escorted her to Level One. They did not speak of Ryona, who—bathed and well fed for the first time in almost a year—rested in a soft bed on Level Three with her baby nestled at her side.

Once again the sentinels were surprised to see her, and Taneli—the insolent sentinel who had been so happy to open the door on Sebestyen's infidelity last time—actually snickered. Liane looked him in the eye. "Open the door."

"If you insist, my lady."

He knocked briefly, then opened the double doors with a flourish. Liane held her breath, until she saw that Sebestyen rested in his bed all alone.

Her husband was surprised to see her. He sat up quickly. "What do you want?" he asked, as if her appearance was the greatest annoyance.

Liane stood in the doorway. Tonight she was unafraid and she knew what she wanted. "I want many things, my lord. First of all, I would ask that you post this heathen in the furthest regions of the Northern Province." She turned and smiled at the gloating Taneli. "He has insulted me for the last time."

"Done," Sebestyen said, no warmth in his voice. "What else do you want? I'm expecting a woman to be delivered within the hour, and your presence will surely put a damper on our evening."

She didn't flinch but looked him in the eye. And saw the lie.

Liane turned to Ferghus. "If another woman dares to come to my husband's room at such an inappropriate hour, kill her."

"Yes, my lady," Ferghus answered with a twinkle in his eye.

Liane turned away from the sentinels, stepped into her husband's bedchamber, and slammed the doors shut.

Sebestyen lifted his eyebrows slightly. "*Kill* her?"

Liane smiled as she walked purposefully toward her husband. "It is a wife's right, is it not?"

"Not to my knowledge."

She stood by the side of the bed and stared down at Sebestyen. His long dark hair was loose and his features seemed sharper than ever, as if he'd lost weight. His eyes were tired.

"From this night forward, if you want a woman beneath you or atop you or wrapped around you, it will be me."

"Liane, don't embarrass yourself this way."

She held her left hand up for him to see, and she waggled the middle finger where a simple gold band glittered. "This ring says that if you fuck anyone at all, it will be me."

"That's hardly proper language for an empress, Liane." Sebestyen tossed back the covers and sat on the edge of the mattress. He wore a crimson robe suited for the cool nights. Another clue that he was not expecting a visitor from Level Three. When she'd come to him in the past, he had almost always been waiting for her naked. Saved precious minutes, or so he said. "Haven't I made myself clear where this matter is concerned?"

"No," she said honestly. "You have not."

Sebestyen could, she supposed, take her by the arm and forcibly remove her from his presence. He possessed the physical strength she did not. He could toss her out of his bedchamber, and everyone in the palace would know that he truly and deeply did not want her.

"For a while I believed that I understood you perfectly." She unfastened the top two buttons of her gown, a robe-like frock that was much too adorned to be called a robe. "I bore you, I disgust you, you no longer want me in the way a man wants a woman. I thought I understood too well. And then you crept to my room in the middle of the night just to look at me."

"You're mistaken," he snapped. "I did no such thing."

Her fingers continued to work the buttons. "You sat there in the dark and all but told me that you cared for me and for our child."

"It was a dream."

"It was no dream."

This time he did not argue with her.

Liane dropped her unfastened frock to the floor. Beneath it she wore nothing, and the swell of her belly was undeniable, but she was not ashamed of the change in her body. It was a miracle; it was magic. She would not be embarrassed by the physical signs of that magic. She sat beside Sebestyen and began to unfasten his robe, as she had on so many nights before they'd become man and wife.

"You are no longer a concubine, Liane."

"No, but I am still a woman."

"I have told you—"

"You don't want me. My pregnancy disgusts you. There are a hundred women or more available to fill the place I once kept in your bed and you would rather have any one of them instead of me."

"Yes."

She slipped her hand inside his robe and grasped his erection. "Liar."

He had a way of catching her eyes with his and holding them, and he did that now. Blue eyes hooded and piercing, he did his best to stare her down. Down and out of his room and out of his life. It was a stare that sent many men running, but Liane didn't run. She stroked. Sebestyen's words and his eyes could lie, but his body could not. "I'm not going away."

"This is not proper behavior for my empress and the mother of my—"

Liane pushed Sebestyen back onto the bed before he could finish his sentence. She straddled him quickly so that her legs and her body held him in place. He could push her off and away to be rid of her, but he didn't. "If you expect me to behave like one of the women who preceded me on Level Five, then think again, my lord. They might've been your empresses, they might've lain beneath you when you commanded it in quest of a child, but they were not true wives to you."

"And you are?" he asked coldly.

"Yes, my lord."

"What if I don't want a true wife?" Sebestyen would not

push her away physically, for fear of hurting the child she carried, but he had no problem with trying to push her away with harsh words.

"How do you know what you want when you won't even try?"

He wanted her. He had always wanted her. For more than half her life, she had belonged to this man in one way or another. A slave, a lover, a soldier. A wife. She continued to undress him, while he lay inflexible and uncooperative beneath her. The robe unfastened and parted, and she tossed the folds back and away from his body.

His face had seen the sun on occasion in recent weeks, but not his body. It remained pale and solid, and she ran her hands over the muscles there, more delighted than she had imagined she would be to touch him again. He was beautiful, in his own way.

"We should make love on the balcony, by the light of day," she said as she raked her nails over his skin. "I would like to see your body turned golden by the sun."

She did not intend to jump on her husband and have her way as if she were no more talented than the girl she'd caught him with not so long ago. Her hands caressed and teased, and she leaned forward to lay her lips on his shoulder and leave them there. Her belly rested against his, her soft breasts pressed to his hard chest. She breathed him in, closing her eyes and reveling in the familiar scent of his skin as her fingers and her tongue aroused.

A large hand settled in her hair, gentler than she had imagined it could be. With words he tried to push her away, but with his body he drew her in.

After resting against him for a moment, glad for the relief of his skin against hers, she rose up slowly. "If I ever catch another woman in your bed, I will kill her."

His eyebrows lifted slightly.

"I'll do it, Sebestyen. Like it or not, you are my husband, and my place is here."

"Liane . . ."

She brushed her damp folds along his length but did not take him into her body. A fire of desire she knew well burned in his eyes.

"I'm not asking you to treat me like an empress, or to love me, or to behave as a normal husband might. You and I, we don't even know what normal is, do we?"

"I suppose not."

"I am asking you to fulfill my physical desires and let me fulfill yours. I am asking you to be faithful to me sexually." She bent down and laid her lips over his as she fisted her hand in his hair. "I am asking you to be a proper husband and make me scream."

She placed the tip of his erection to her center, but before she could plunge down and take him in, he rolled her onto her back. He was still right there, touching her, but he did not push inside. Instead, he slipped his hand between their bodies and rested it over her belly.

"The priests already fear your influence," he whispered. "They cannot know."

"They cannot know what?" That he loved her? That theirs was a real and true marriage?

"They cannot know," he said again, his voice even softer than before.

"They need know nothing," she said, "but that I come to you for the same pleasure we have shared for years. If anything between us is changed, they need not be aware of it."

He did not say that he loved her; he didn't even whisper that he cared. But he must. Why else hide what he felt from the priests?

His hand stroked her belly. "I do need you here, I want

you more than I dare to confess. But I don't want to hurt the baby. He is . . . very important to me."

She saw something new amidst the lust. Fear.

"He is very small yet." She grinned widely. "And, my lord, you flatter yourself and all other men."

For the first time in a very long time—a *very* long time—he returned her smile. "Are you sure?"

"Of course I'm sure. I would not risk this child for anything in the—"

She did not get to finish her assurances. Sebestyen filled her achingly empty body, and there were no more words.

II

SINCE RYN HAD WARNED HER OF THE VICIOUSNESS OF the Caradon, she had slept as closely as possible to him through the night, a situation which very often led to gloriously bright and interesting mornings. It was a lovely way to start the day, invigorated and glowing and happy. Until she'd come here, she had not realized that so few of her days had been spent in true happiness.

There were moments, hours, days, when she actually considered turning her back on her sisters and the life she had once led, and giving herself fully and completely to Ryn. She could be his wife, and live quite happily among the Anwyn. She could sleep with him at night, give him sons—or daughters—and she could give him comfort.

But she could not turn her back on her sisters. She would find her way back to them, and when she was sure that their conflicts were settled, then she would decide where and how to spend the rest of her life.

It even occurred to her, on occasion, that maybe Ryn could come home with her. The life waiting for him far away from these mountains would be as foreign to him as this place was to her, but she thought that they might make it work somehow.

There would be worse fates than to be married to a shape-shifter, mated to a man who became wolf, linked forever to a man who understood her abilities better than she did . . . and accepted them without so much as a blink of an eye. She could be married to a man who would protect her from the linking she had feared all her adult life. They could enjoy physical pleasure without the mental link, because he knew how to keep himself separate from her even when they touched intimately, even when he was a part of her.

Today they raced across rocks that revealed no true path, and yet the way seemed very natural. Very easy. Juliet's feet fell upon the rock with precision, and she did not feel even a moment's trepidation when she walked quickly across a narrow precipice that looked down over a steep, rocky gorge. The new lightness in her heart, a joy that almost bubbled within her, made her want to sing as she came to the end of the narrow precipice. She did not know much music, but her mother had sung a few children's songs to her, once upon a time. She and Sophie had sung this particular song together, many times, first as children and then as a way to soothe Ariana.

The tune was simple, the rhyming words silly. The song was nonsense, about sunshine, cows, wildflowers, and the moon. Before she finished the first verse, Ryn turned to watch her, and to listen. Juliet left the precipice and stepped upon more solid ground, and she walked to Ryn and sang even louder. He wrinkled his nose as she sang the final chorus.

"That was quite bad," he said seriously. "I did not know you were unable to sing."

"I am able to sing," she argued. "Badly, perhaps, but I *can* sing." Ryn waited for her, and when she reached him, she wrapped her arms around his neck and leaned into him. "Does my poor singing ability make you think less of me?" she asked. "Does it make me a poor mate?"

"You have other qualities to make up for your disturbing singing voice," he said.

"Such as?" She lifted her eyebrows slightly and awaited an answer.

"A fine and willing body," he said.

"I suspected that was the first thing you'd think of," she teased.

"It is difficult not to think of such things when you're touching me."

"Does anything else come to you, or are my only attributes physical in nature?"

He pushed away a strand of red hair that had fallen across her face. "You have courage, which is a virtue until it causes you to head down the mountain alone. Willfulness, which makes you deny what you know to be true but which also makes you strong. And you have the heart of a wolf. You have a fearless heart that opens for the world and all the people in it, but which sometimes denies that which you need yourself. No man could ask for more from a wife than that which you have to give."

The teasing had quickly turned serious. "Do you mean that?"

"Yes, *vidara*."

"*Vidara*. Is that an Anwyn word?"

"Yes."

"What does it mean?"

He hesitated, but not for long. "It means wife, only more. There is no word in your language to compare."

"It's an endearment."

"Yes."

"What is the word for husband, only . . . more?"

"*Vanir.*"

"A lovely word," Juliet said softly. She traced his jaw with her finger. There were so many ways she could respond to Ryn's words. He had many fine qualities himself. Bravery and gentleness. Stubbornness and courage of his own. And as for heart . . . she had never known a man with a bigger heart.

Something welled up inside her, and she did her best to push it away. She could not love Ryn; she could not let what she felt for him turn into anything more. She was already dancing too close to the edge of a danger she was not prepared to face.

HE SHOULD TELL HER THE TRUTH. ALL OF IT. JULIET WAS Queen, or soon would be, and to keep that knowledge from her . . .

It was wrong perhaps, but also necessary. Juliet was beginning to accept that she was his mate. She was not ready to accept the fact that she also had Anwyn blood, that when they reached The City, she would become ruler by virtue of her blood, that once she took the vow that would make her Queen, she would also become wolf under a full moon.

She had not said so, not in many days, but a part of her hated the wolf.

There was also the legend to consider. Did he dare take to heart an old story told for hundreds of years? Could there be any truth to the fable? If Juliet was fated to be mated to a Caradon . . .

That was a fate he would change, no matter if it robbed the Anwyn of peace. No matter if it meant a hundred years of war. He would guard her, protect her. He would kill for her, and no Caradon would ever get close enough to her to fulfill the prophesy.

He could not prevent the displeasure that kept this time from perfection. It was the way of the Anwyn that households were ruled by the men. Women were important figures in the family, and in many cases they were held equal. But males were dominant, and that was a given, indisputable fact.

With the exception of the household of the Queen.

In all of Anwyn history, they had been ruled by women. By Queens. There was much power in the palace of the Anwyn, and the Queen's word and wishes were indisputable. Even her mate bowed to her. He was bound by tradition to do as she asked, as were all others.

Juliet's word would be law, and even he would be obligated to obey.

There was no traditional marriage for the Queen of the Anwyn. Her mate became consort, an unimportant figure set aside until the fertile time came upon her. It was important that the Queen bear sons. They held places of importance in the palace, until another girl child was born and came of age. Queens were rare creatures, and they were duty-bound to rule until another Anwyn female came to take the throne.

There was more to worry about than the prophesy of a Caradon lover. The pure-blooded sons of the Queen—those extraordinary men who were the offspring of an Anwyn father *and* an Anywn mother—displayed the strength and virility of the Anwyn. If a Queen's chosen mate did not get her with child quickly, she was not only allowed to call another to her bed, but was obligated to do so. And if her consort did not satisfy the need of the heat that came upon her when she was fertile, she had the right to take any Anwyn male into her bed until she was satisfied. No man would refuse her if she asked. Even though it meant breaking the lifelong vow to a mate, it was not only acceptable—it was an honor.

The prophesy teased his mind. A red-haired Queen with powers beyond those of any other known to the Anwyn would guide her people into a greater, more peaceful time. She would bring prosperity. And through her union with a Caradon, she would bring an end to the long conflict between the two species.

Whenever the Caradon attacked, which had not been often during the past several years, the story was told to assure the people that this war would not continue forever. There would be peace when the red-haired Queen and her Caradon came to the palace.

Juliet was his, and he would kill any Caradon who came near her. Even if it meant conflict with the Caradon would continue forever, he would fight for his mate.

As they traveled and his anger grew, he tried to turn his mind to more agreeable thoughts. In Juliet's body he had found pleasures much greater than those of a dream, and during the day there were times when all he had to do was look upon her and he wanted to be inside her again. She wanted him, too, more than she cared to admit. If he had given in to his passions and taken her in the middle of the day, on the path that led them toward The City, she would not have protested. When he had captured her, he had not known that she would be so passionate, but he was glad of it. She would make a good mate in all ways.

If only she were not Queen.

When they came upon the mountain lake, the sun hung low in the western sky. Juliet gasped. Not in fear, but in delight. Ryn looked at the body of water and tried to see it through her eyes. Such a sight was commonplace to him, and he had long taken for granted the beauty of mountains beyond his home.

But to Juliet, such majestic beauty was new and exciting. She stood by the lake and smiled as she focused her eyes out across the still waters. A breeze caught her hair and lifted it, pushing the copper red curls back and away from her face. Gone was the prim woman he had taken from the soldiers. In her place there stood a woman as powerful and wild as he, a beauty to rival any other.

A Queen.

"I suppose it's too cold to swim," she said, a touch of longing in her voice.

Juliet hadn't yet realized that as they drew near The City, she instinctively awakened the Anwyn within herself, and that if she were to touch the water that would feel icy to human skin, she'd simply detect a refreshing coolness.

"It is not so cold."

She laughed. "Not for you, perhaps." But to test the waters, she squatted down and reached out to trail her fingers through the water. Her eyes widened, as she was pleasantly surprised that the lake did not feel like ice against her fingers. "You're right! It feels very pleasant." She lifted her face to the sun. "I thought it would be much colder as we climbed higher, but it's actually quite mild for this time of year."

"Yes, it is. Do you wish to make camp here for the night?"

She smiled, at him this time instead of at the lake she found so enticing. "Can we?"

"If you wish it."

She began to eagerly strip off her clothes, unbuttoning the tattered dress with nimble fingers, pushing it down and off when that was done. Naked, as she had been as she lay beneath him last night, she stepped cautiously into the lake.

Ryn placed the bearskin bedroll on a flat portion of ground well away from the lake, then dropped his knife and kilt beside the bed he would share with his woman again tonight. By the time he had joined Juliet in the lake, she was standing in waist-high water, twirling about and creating ripples on the still water with her hands. Her smile dimmed when he joined her, but not in a bad way. The heat of passion flushed her cheeks pink and made the gold flecks in her brown eyes sparkle as she watched him walk into the lake.

She reached up and touched his face, when he was close enough for touching. "There's something about me and my family that I haven't told you," she said. "I don't want to tell you, because I don't want anything to spoil this moment. But you need to know." She took a moment to gather her courage. "No matter what happens between us, no matter how wonderful it is at times, I can't love you."

"I never asked for love."

She flinched at that, a little, and he realized that even though she fought it, she wanted love, very much. "I'm afraid that if we continue as we have, I will love you, and that can't happen."

"Why not?" Ryn was not disappointed. From what he had seen of his eldest brother's marriage, romantic love was untidy and complicated, and he was a man who had always longed for an uncomplicated life. But he was curious as to why a woman who so obviously wanted love denied the very possibility.

Juliet licked her lips, and for the first time in days she looked nervous. "There is a curse, a very old and powerful curse. No Fyne witch shall know a true and lasting love. For the past three hundred years, many of the men who were loved by Fyne women have died before their thirtieth birthday." She raked the back of her hand along his throat. "Others just . . . walked away. How old are you?"

"I was born on the same day that you were born," he answered.

Juliet blinked twice, very quickly. "How can you be sure?"

"We were sent into this world to be together, two halves of a whole, male and female, neither complete without the other. We came into the world when the leaves were new and the chill of spring filled the air. Next spring, it will be twenty-seven years."

She shook her head in silent denial, and red curls danced around her shoulder. "Ryn, you must promise that you will never love me."

"If that is what you wish."

"It is. I'm afraid I don't have the strength not to fall in love. Love is not complete if it's not returned. Maybe that will protect you."

"In many instances love seems to be a complication. What we have is better."

"What do we have?" she asked softly.

He would prefer to be inside her again, but if she insisted on talking, he supposed he could comply. For a short while. "We have a bond that ties us to the earth and to one another, a shared desire to build a family and a home. And we have lust."

"Lust is not a very pretty word," she said softly.

"Many good things are not very pretty, *vidara*." He could call her wife now. Once they reached the city and she learned of the ways of the Queen, everything would change. But for now she was his wife.

Juliet leaned forward and rested her head against his chest. The ends of her long hair were damp, and her skin almost matched his in heat. "Isadora, my sister you call the dark one, she loved her husband very much. When he died, it almost destroyed her. I'm not altogether sure it won't still, someday. She's never recovered."

Ryn rested his hand in Juliet's curls.

"Sophie found love with a man she did not expect to love, and so far things seem to be going well for them, but . . ."

"But?" Ryn prodded.

"This love of hers has caused all sorts of complications,

and who knows what the years will bring? It will destroy her if she has to bury him."

"What we have is better," he insisted again.

"Yes, I suppose it is." She did not sound entirely convinced. "But . . ."

Again she hesitated. Instead of prodding her on this time, Ryn placed his hands on her bare backside and pulled her closer to him. "Enough talk." He bent down and placed his mouth on her bare shoulder.

She laughed. "So, sex is your answer to everything?"

"Yes," he said, barely taking his mouth from her flesh.

"Will we never be able to conduct a serious conversation?"

"I hope not."

Again she laughed, but she also offered her mouth to him, and he took it.

When they reached The City, everything would change. As Queen, she would have duties that took her away from him. There would be no simple home, no quiet nights in the house he had built for her. These days of travel would be the only days of his life in which he had his wife all to himself. Ryn wished, deep in his heart, that Juliet was not Anwyn, that she was not Queen.

But no matter who she was or what the future held, he did want her.

Lust was much more beneficial than love.

IT WAS AN ODDLY WARM DAY, PLEASANT AND REFRESHING. And Ryn felt not so hot as he had in the beginning days. His flesh against hers was merely warm. Maybe it was the lust he spoke of that warmed her, not the sun or his skin or the oddly warm waters of the lake.

Ryn lifted Juliet easily and carried her from the lake. While he walked toward shore, leaving a rippling wake behind him, she laid her mouth on his neck, kissing, tasting, and growing warmer. Did she want love in spite of the curse that had plagued her family, or could she be satisfied with this? The physical connection was spectacular, and she could not deny that she liked Ryn well enough. But romantic love . . . was that what she'd been afraid of all her adult life? It had destroyed Isadora, and it had made fools of many of the women she'd treated for unwanted pregnancy or a broken heart. It had destroyed many a Fyne witch in the past three hundred years.

Maybe love was the claws that always ruined her dreams. Maybe Ryn was right, and what they had was better.

He kicked the bedroll open and laid her upon it. There was still light in the sky, but not much. Just enough for her to see the man who called himself her husband as he lowered himself to hover just slightly above her. She had seen the wildness in him first, before she'd seen the man. The wildness remained, in his hair and his method of dress and in the way he moved, but it was the man she had come to like so well.

"I never realized that skin against skin could feel so good," she said as she raked her hand along his side.

"Neither did I," Ryn growled.

She wrapped her legs around him and pulled him closer, just a little bit. "You said that you'd been waiting for me. What if we'd never met?"

"We did meet."

"But what if the soldiers hadn't taken Isadora and me along that road, or if we'd defeated them at the cabin, or . . ." She didn't want to ask what would've happened if the soldiers had killed her. "Would you have found your connection to another woman and taken her instead?"

Ryn laid one hand on her breast, and she closed her eyes and let the sensations ripple through her body as he tenderly caressed her. "Do you not yet know, wife?"

Tonight she would not tell him not to call her wife. She felt very much like his wife at the moment, though she still wasn't sure what tomorrow would bring. With Ryn touching her, tomorrow seemed very far away. "All I know is that I want you."

He touched her where she throbbed for him, and stroked his fingers there. "That is as it should be."

He filled her, not slowly as he had last night but with a thrust that quickly took him deep inside. Her body arched and shuddered, and she gasped. She fisted his hair in her hand and moaned, and there were no more words. The lust Ryn spoke of ruled their bodies, and they mated in a way that was primal, without gentleness or beauty or sweet words. Everything else faded, but the way he felt inside her. It was primitive sex and nothing more, a fast and furious mating that brought new sensations to life in the body she had protected for so long.

Not because she was afraid of men, after all, but because she had been waiting for Ryn, just as he had waited for her.

Juliet arched her back and he drove deep, and she climaxed with a cry that echoed around them. Ryn came with her, with a growl instead of a scream. When the lust he declared better than love had been sated, he lowered himself to cover her body with his. She trembled from head to toe, her heart beat much too fast, and her mouth had gone dry. They remained joined, and she did not let go—not of his hair, not of his body.

"There can never be another," Ryn said as he rose up slightly. "If you had not come along that road, I would have followed your scent and my instincts until I found you."

"But if something were to happen to me . . ."

"Nothing will happen," he said in a raspy voice. "You are my woman, my wife. I will protect you from all harm until the end of our days."

"But . . ."

"You have spoken too many buts today," Ryn protested. "You have too many questions. You are my woman and always will be." They were still joined, and she didn't want to let him go. Not yet. He placed his hand beneath her head and lifted her slightly, threading his fingers in her tangled curls and bringing her face closer to his. "Anwyn mate for life."

ISADORA HAD LOST COUNT OF THE DAYS. WINTER HAD come at last, and it was bitterly cold. She wished for the comfort of Will's spirit, but he had deserted her once again. She wished for death, so she could join him, but that wish did not come true, either.

Bors was very cautious with her, assigning one expendable soldier or another to touch her when it was necessary that she be fed or allowed to see to her personal needs. It was an unnecessary precaution. Even if she could rouse the power to do so, she didn't intend to kill again, not when taking the life of one soldier or even two would not save her or her sisters. Destruction had dampened her magic, and she didn't know if it would ever grow strong again. She remained compliant, and her captor became quite bold at his success.

It was dawn when Bors woke her, prodding her into a sitting position with the end of a stout stick, and then pointing westward with that same stick. "By the light of day you can see the palace from here," he said in a voice that grated like coarse sand on flesh.

Sure enough, the towering structure that had been unseen last night when they'd stopped to rest was now visible in the morning gray.

"Ugly, isn't it?" Bors observed. "On the outside, at least. Some of the Levels are quite nice on the inside. Silks and furs of the finest quality, food such as you have never tasted, jewels everywhere you turn, the most comfortable

furnishings that exist in this or any land. And the women . . .
I hear the women on Level Three are trained in all ways of
pleasuring a man."

The palace was ugly, from this vantage point. The massive, gray-stone structure climbed high, sloping slightly in-
ward toward the top. Sophie had gone there to save her
child, and now Bors was taking Isadora there to die.

"Have you given any thought as to how you wish to be
executed, once the emperor has finished with you?" Bors
asked casually. "Fire, hanging, beheading, poison. All have
been utilized in the prison on Level Twelve."

"I don't care," she said, a deadness in her voice. There
had been times when she'd wished for death, so she could
join Will in the land of the dead. But now she wondered if
she would join him after all. He had been such a good and
kind and tender man, he had surely found a place in para-
dise. She had killed, and caused others to be killed and tor-
tured. The odds that her spirit would join that of her
husband were small.

But she was not afraid. She'd lost everything. Her husband, her magic, her home, even her sisters. She had nothing of value for Bors to take from her.

JULIET TIED HER SKIRT UP TO HER KNEES, TO MAKE LONG
strides easier and to let the cool air whip under her skirts.
She ran up the slope, not behind Ryn this time, but ahead of
him. There was something about the air in these mountains
that invigorated her, that filled her with life and joy in a
way nothing else ever had. Even Ryn, with his talk of mating for life, couldn't dampen her newfound enchantment.

"How far?" she asked as she crested the rise and sur-
veyed the land below.

"Four days," Ryn answered in a soft, strong voice.

"Is it pretty?"

"The City?"

"Yes, The City." She turned and grinned at him. "Will I like it there?"

"It is very pretty, in some places, and you will most certainly like it there."

"What about your house, what's it like?" She leaned against a rock that was barely taller than she was and rested for a moment. Ryn was anxious to keep moving, but he would stop on occasion on her account.

"Our house," he corrected.

"Our house," she repeated softly. "What's it like?"

He hesitated for a moment, and his eyes turned toward home. "I built it myself, when I began to feel that the time for finding you was near."

There was something very touching about the fact that Ryn had built a home for her. For them.

"It's of a moderate size, and constructed of gray and pink stone. There is a family parlor and a small parlor for visitors, a kitchen, and three bedrooms. The parlors and the kitchen are at the front of the house, and they have many windows, but the bedrooms are set in the deep stone of the mountain. You might find it too plain to suit you."

"There's nothing wrong with plain," Juliet said.

"It has been a long time since the Caradon have gotten past the walls of The City, but if that ever happens again, my family will be protected on all sides. We will be well inside the rock, where no man or beast can touch us."

No one would ever burn that home down, Juliet realized.

"Furniture?" she asked.

"Some. You will choose your own furnishings and the best artisans in The City will build them for you. Again, they will be plain, but sturdy and comfortable."

Oddly enough she could see the house in her mind's eye, even though the connection to Ryn remained severed and she could see nothing through his eyes.

"And if I decide not to stay?" she asked softly.

"You will stay."

He sounded so confident. She was happy; she was excited. But she was not confident that she would be content to remain in Ryn's city forever. She could not settle down, not even in a pretty place with a beautiful man, until she knew her sisters were safe and well. Once that was done, then . . . perhaps.

Judging by the look in his golden eyes, Ryn was no longer thinking of the home that awaited them in four days, but of how it would feel to take her up against this rock, quick and hard. She had been thinking of that, too. She wanted him with the sun on her face and the warm air on her legs.

"We've been all but running toward your city," she said, offering him a hand.

"Yes, we have." He took her hand and dropped the bedroll to the ground.

"Would five days not be soon enough?"

"Soon enough." He lifted her skirt and his and picked her up as if she weighed nothing at all. She wrapped her legs around him and held on tight.

JULIET DID NOT KNOW WHAT AWAITED HER, AND HE DID not know how to tell her. He would have to tell her soon. Otherwise, she would not understand.

She asked often about babies, not because she wanted them but because she did not. That alone told him she was not yet sure about her future. He was sure, though. He wished he could be less sure.

Juliet would be fertile three times a year, as those extraordinary Anwyn females through history had been. She would bleed for three or four days, and then she would be caught in a frenzy of desire that would put the past days of passion to shame. She would drag her mate to her bed and they would not leave it for days. In that time she would conceive. Boys, not girls. Anwyn sons.

She lay with her bare body against his, but she did not sleep. The draw of The City that was in her blood called to her, and with each step the Anwyn in her came more to life. She had no mirror to see the change, but he saw. Her eyes were now as much gold as brown.

The color of her eyes was only a small part of the change. She was discovering the life of the mountain within her. Just this afternoon she had discarded her boots as unworthy, and she walked barefoot as he did. Her step was steadier, more sure on the rocks, and she possessed a strength and speed she had not yet tested.

She placed her hand upon his chest. "If I decide I cannot live so far away from my sisters, we could always move, right?"

"Move?"

"We could live in a village somewhere in Columbyana, in the lowlands, and I could make money as a healer, and you could hunt and work with stone."

"Why would we move?"

"The City sounds strange to me," she confided. "And it's so far away from home."

"No, it is home." He rested a hand in her hair.

She did not give up easily. "We could cut your hair or pull it back, and buy you some nice clothes, and when we had babies, if they didn't take that vow before the Queen, they wouldn't have to become shape-shifters, right? And you said if you were far enough away from The City, even you . . ."

His entire body reacted to her offer, his muscles tightening and his stomach turning over unpleasantly. "Again, you ask me to deny the wolf."

She rose up slowly and looked down at him. He had

built a small fire with which to cook their dinner, and what remained of that fire illuminated her face for him. The wolf agreed with her. She was more beautiful than ever.

"I was just thinking out loud."

They wanted the same things from life. A small home, a family, a normal life—though what was normal for him and normal for her were not the same. Neither of them would have what they wanted. She would rule. He would be the Queen's consort, available at her command.

"What do you know of your father?" he asked.

She blinked in surprise. "I never knew him."

Ryn nodded, but he did not understand. It was unheard of for an Anwyn to travel to the lowlands to lie with a woman who was not his mate.

"His name was Kei, that's all I know of him."

Ryn's heart thudded in his chest. *Kei.* There were not many rogues among the Anwyn, but Kei Deverin of the Ancikyn Clan was one of them. Years ago, the unthinkable had happened. His mate, the woman who was meant to be his wife, had died shortly after he'd captured her. There had been no children from that very short union, and having his promised happiness ripped away from him had driven Kei from The City. He lived in the hills, the man as wild as the wolf. Apparently he had also traveled far from home and lain with another woman, one who was not his promised mate. Such was not the way of the Anwyn, but neither was it impossible.

"You speak of sisters," he said.

"Half sisters, actually. The three of us have different fathers." She squirmed as if the discussion made her uncomfortable. "My mother was a very sweet woman and she loved her daughters, but she was unconventional where men were concerned. She would have agreed with you that lust is preferable to love. The curse frightened her, so she didn't want to risk loving any man." She fidgeted, obviously uncomfortable with the conversation. "What of your family? Do your parents live in The City?"

"My father died more than ten years ago, during an attack by the Caradon."

"I'm sorry. Your mother?"

"She died in her sleep within two cycles of the moon. Anwyn rarely outlive their mates, but when it happens . . . it shouldn't happen," he finished softly.

"But your mother, she wasn't Anwyn. Right?" Juliet asked, confused.

"She was not born Anwyn, but she became Anwyn."

"Do you have brothers?" she asked, desperately trying to shift the conversation to a happier subject.

"Three."

"Are you close to them?"

"They are family. Calum and Ansgar have mates and sons to keep them occupied so I do not see them every day, but before I was called to fetch you, I visited often. Denton is a soldier in the Queen's palace, as I am, so I see him more frequently."

"Denton has not yet fetched his mate?" she asked.

Ryn shook his head. "He has not been called, but he is still young. The day will come."

He didn't want to tell Juliet what he knew to be true, not now when she had just begun to accept that she was fated to be his wife. But he could not allow her to enter The City unprepared. "Your father is Anwyn," he said softly, not knowing how to tell her the truth in any other way.

"No, that's not possible," she argued sweetly. "You said yourself that Anwyn men make Anwyn men, and besides, I am certainly not a shape-shifter."

"I explained this to you. Every fifty years or so, an Anwyn girl child is born," he explained. "This girl child can be the offspring of any Anwyn male, and she becomes

Queen when she reaches the age where the wolf can come upon her under the full moon."

"I'm not . . ."

Ryn spun Juliet onto her back, not for reasons of pleasure as he had been known to do in the days since she became his wife in every way, but because she would not listen to him and somehow he had to make her understand.

"I built a house for you, but we will not live in it. I planned a life for us, but we will not live it. When we get to The City, I am honor bound to take you directly to the Palace of the Anwyn Queen. We will not be wed. You will place your hand upon the sacred stone and take the vow that will make you Queen. That vow will also make you Anwyn in every way."

She blinked hard and pushed lightly against him. "I would know if such a horrible thing was true."

To be one of his kind was horrible to her. He had known that she despised the wolf within him all along, but he had hoped she would come to accept what he was. What would she say when he told her she was destined to bring about peace by taking a Caradon lover?

"You have cut yourself off from your abilities, in days past."

"Yes."

"Open the tendrils that connect you to the earth and tell me what you feel."

"I don't—"

"If you wish to know the whole of the truth, reach into the heart of the earth and let it come to you. I will be with you, *vidara,* I promise."

Ryn lowered the barrier between them, and skeptically, uneasily, she did as he asked. He felt the release of energy, the jolt of power, the raw force. Juliet's gift of sight had become stronger in past days, not because she had kept it closed but because as she grew nearer The City, her power grew. Touching her, allowing her gifts to wash over them both, he saw some of what she saw. He felt her pain because she shared it with him.

Her eyes changed, grew more gold and then turned almost black. Her back arched, and she cried out in pain. Ryn pinned her wrists to the ground to keep her from pushing him aside and running from the truth. She tried to fight him, but even the strength of an Anwyn Queen was not enough to displace him.

Her body jerked as the truth rushed through her veins and her spirit—and through his. She screamed and tried in vain to push him away. Images flashed through his mind, so quick and disordered he could not decipher them all. Emotion he did not want filled him, broken images made him flinch and gasp, but he did not take his hands or the weight of his body from Juliet.

The images faded and she went slack, exhausted by the experience of her newly enhanced powers.

"It's not possible," Juliet said hoarsely, her eyes drifting closed and the visions abating at last.

"It is," Ryn said gently.

She had seen not only the palace and the crown that awaited her, but the power of the animal that was locked deep within her. The wolf had slept inside Juliet for a long time, but it had always been there. She knew that now. The presence of the wolf was the secret truth that had frightened her from the first moment she saw him. Power, violence, the wild animal hidden beneath the trappings of an ordinary woman.

The blood of the Anwyn ran in her veins, and she could no longer deny it.

"The claws are mine," she whispered, terror in her low voice. "Dear God in Heaven, the claws are mine."

12

BORS AND ONE OF HIS SOLDIERS KEPT ISADORA'S FACE covered as they dragged her up the stairs, and her hands remained tied behind her back. Up and up and up, stumbling since she could not see the steps before her, Isadora walked. Bors kept a tight grip on her arm, and the soldier remained behind the prisoner, occasionally placing a prodding hand on her back when she moved too slowly.

Bors was no longer afraid to touch her; she'd been so meek in days past that he'd apparently forgotten how she'd killed the soldier at the Fyne cabin. That night seemed like a lifetime ago, but in truth it had been a matter of weeks. She had not seen the cabin burn, thanks to Juliet's intervention, so there were moments when she allowed herself to forget that it didn't still stand, as it had stood for more than three hundred years.

There were moments when Isadora didn't care if she lived or died. Bors and his soldiers could kill her, for all she cared, and she knew that if she stopped being so meek and lashed out at them, that would happen quick enough. But Juliet's words rang in her head, and she could not force them out. *Sophie still needs us.* She had failed Will; she had failed her mother. She would not fail her sisters.

Finally, they reached their destination. Isadora was yanked to a stop, her legs aching from the long climb and her heart beating too fast. Bors ordered someone to announce his arrival. It seemed he was expected.

She heard the very faint squeak of a heavy door opening. The air changed, as warmer air mingled with the cool air that had chilled Isadora for more days than she cared to count. In the background she heard the crackle of a fire, and she welcomed the warmth.

"You took your sweet time," a man said crisply.

"There were complications, my lord." There was deference in Bors's voice, and the very formal "my lord." Did he address the emperor himself? Or another high-ranking official?

"Obviously," the man said in a lowered voice.

Bors dragged Isadora forward and snatched the hood from her head. Bright light streamed through the windows and from the skylight above, where thick glass kept out the winter cold but allowed sunshine to pour in. For a moment the flood of light blinded her; she had been wearing the hood over her face for most of a week now, and had become accustomed to the darkness. But eventually her eyes adjusted to the light.

The immense room was furnished sparsely, but no expense had been spared in choosing the furnishings and tapestries and rugs. The chamber was decorated with gold and silk and fine upholstery. There was not one fireplace but two—one on each side of the massive room. Healthy fires burned in both, robbing the room of its winter chill.

Oddest of all were the batons set in the walls. Thick rods had been set into the stone at regular intervals. They all glowed brightly, adding light to the dark corners of the sun-filled room. Isadora blinked as she studied the batons. Was this magic? Or some science that was unknown to her?

The man who sat upon the throne just a few feet away was surely the Emperor Sebestyen. He was tall, slender, and regal, and he quickly commanded her attention. His crimson robe was made of the finest quality fabric and was adorned with a touch of gold filigree. Not enough to make the apparel seem unmanly, but more than enough for any observer to conclude that this was an important man who had money and fine things at this fingertips. He had the coldest blue eyes she had ever seen.

The woman beside him was likely the empress. Her throne was also placed on the dais, but was slightly lower and less ornate than the emperor's chair. Her demeanor was as hostile as the emperor's, and she looked upon their visitors as if they were an annoyance. An unwelcome interruption. She was also dressed in crimson, but her regal outfit was trimmed with jewels as well as gold. Blond and brown spun hair had been twisted up and back, and a jeweled headpiece held the silky strands in place. Isadora had seen hair like that only once in her lifetime. Sophie's Kane had that unusual hair color.

There were others in the large room, priests and sentinels who stood back and waited to be called upon, but the two sitting on the dais commanded Isadora's attention. They were trouble, in a very big way.

The emperor studied her with lazy, contemptuous eyes. "I thought there were two."

Bors actually shuffled his big feet as he answered. "One was taken on the road," he explained.

"Taken? By whom?"

"A man," Bors said awkwardly. "He—"

"*A man?*" the emperor asked incredulously.

"Yes, my lord," Bors answered softly.

"A single man managed to take a prisoner from the Imperial Army?"

"Yes, my lord."

Emperor Sebestyen leaned back in his chair. His pose was casual, but the intensity in his face and his eyes were not. "Please explain to me how this happened."

Bors began to spin a tale, and what a tale it was. The taker who had stolen Juliet away in this tale became larger, quicker, and better armed than the man Isadora had seen. He was not actually a man at all, according to Bors, but a monstrous beast. Once, Isadora opened her mouth to call him a liar, and the grip on her arm tightened in warning.

Emperor Sebestyen leaned forward, slightly more interested by the end of the story. "Details aside, your prisoner was taken and you did not go after her. Why should I not kill you now?"

"Of course we went after her, my lord. The soldiers and I gave chase, but it was no use. And after a while it seemed foolish to continue the pursuit. I'm quite sure the witch was killed as soon as the brutish animal was done with her."

Isadora didn't have Juliet's psychic abilities, and her magic was dampened and unreliable, and still she felt certain that she would know in the pit of her soul if her sister had been killed by her abductor. Will's spirit had found its way to her after death; she felt sure Juliet's would do the same, if the worst happened.

Again the emperor looked squarely at Isadora. She looked right back, unafraid.

"Are you the one with the gift of sight?" he asked.

"No," Isadora answered sharply.

Bors kicked the backs of her legs so that she dropped to her knees. "That's *no, my lord* to you, witch."

Isadora said nothing, and Bors kicked her again.

"That's enough," the emperor said, bored with the game. "If you had to lose one of them, why did it have to be the one with the sight? I have great uses for such a power at this time, as I'm sure you well know."

"A thousand apologies, my—"

"Don't apologize," the emperor snapped. "Fetch her."

"But . . ." Bors began to argue, then thought better of it. Apparently arguing with Emperor Sebestyen was not wise. "I will leave directly and do my best to follow her trail."

"Come back without her and I'll have your head," the emperor said, again seemingly bored. He turned his gaze to Isadora again. "What can you do?"

"At home I tend the animals and help with the garden, my lord," Isadora answered.

For a moment, the emperor was silent. The entire massive room was silent. "I believe you fully understand the nature of my question," he finally said in a slow, deliberate voice. "I'll give you one more opportunity to answer."

Isadora swallowed hard. "I know a few spells, my lord."

"A few spells," he repeated, unimpressed.

"She does seem to be the less useful of the two," Bors said, a hint of good humor in his voice. "And the most dangerous, my lord. She killed two of your soldiers and wounded another."

The emperor looked more amused than offended. "Did she?"

"With just a touch and a few words she killed, in one instance. It would be best to keep your distance from this one, and whatever you do, don't let her lay her hands on you, my lord."

"Is she going to be more trouble than she's worth?" the ruler asked.

Bors nodded. "Yes, my lord. Most definitely."

Isadora struggled to her feet. "If you're going to kill me, make it quick. I can't bear the thought of spending another day in this liar's company."

Bors lifted a hand to strike her, but the emperor stopped him with a raised finger. "Liar?"

"The man who took my sister is just that. A man. Bors is afraid he's outmatched, that's why he spun such a tale for your benefit. My lord," she added belatedly.

"A tale."

"Juliet is not dead," Isadora said hotly, "but Bors is afraid he will be if he goes up against the man who took her."

"How do you know she's not dead?"

Isadora locked her eyes to the emperor's. She did not know what to make of him. The man who sat on the throne of Columbyana was certainly not her friend. He had dispatched the soldiers who'd kidnapped her and Juliet and burned the cabin. But he was not her enemy in the way Bors was. Not yet, at least. "I know, my lord."

"You know?"

Isadora nodded.

"Perhaps this witch is more useful than you allowed me to believe," the man on the dais said thoughtfully.

"She's lying," Bors responded.

"And if she's not? What if she possesses a magical way of reaching her sister across long distances? If she can communicate with her sister, perhaps she can do the same with others. Do you not think such a gift would be useful to me?"

After a moment of thought, Bors managed an uneasy grin. "She has no useful gifts that I have discovered, my lord, other than her ability to kill without weapons. She's much too unstable to be of any real use. I suggest we toss her into Level Thirteen. It's suitable punishment for her crimes, and if it turns out that she and her sister can communicate across long distances, this one's misery will call to the other one and bring her to us. If she's not dead," he added quickly, "as I suspect she is."

Level Thirteen? Isadora didn't know what Bors was referring to, but whatever it was, it couldn't be good.

"Perhaps," the emperor responded.

The empress moved, for the first time. She laid a gentle hand on her husband's arm and leaned toward him. He moved also, tilting his head toward her as she began to whisper into his ear. From this vantage point, Isadora could see that the empress was with child. Her stomach was definitely rounded.

Her discussion with the emperor finished, the pregnant woman returned to her staunch position.

The emperor addressed Bors. "You will fetch the other one, this Juliet that you allowed to be taken. This one . . ." He turned pale eyes to Bors's captive. "What is your given name?"

"Isadora, my lord." She tried to sound compliant. She knew Bors wanted her dead; she wasn't yet sure about the emperor.

"Isadora will serve the empress for now."

"My lord, that is not—" Bors began.

"My wife wishes to have her own witch," the emperor interrupted. "What the Empress Liane wants, she shall have."

Isadora's gaze shot to the empress. The woman's eyes caught Isadora's, and in spite of the apathy and the determination there, Isadora knew this woman had just saved her from Level Thirteen.

Once again, the emperor laid his cold gaze on Isadora. "You will keep your hands to yourself, and there will always be someone nearby to cut them off if you forget that edict."

Isadora's stomach flipped. "I have no intention of harming the empress or anyone else, my lord."

"I'm glad to hear it."

The emperor issued curt, irrefutable orders. Isadora was to be taken away, bathed, and prepared for her new job as the empress's personal witch. Bors was to collect a handful of men and go after Juliet.

Bors didn't care for either edict, but he was not in a position to argue.

A PART OF JULIET WANTED TO TURN BACK AND RUN TOward home. Ryn could chase her and he could catch her, but he could not hold her forever.

But another part of her, an undeniably strong part that she had only recently discovered, was drawn toward The City and the sacred stone that waited there. The Heart of the Anwyn, Ryn had called it.

She had not lain with Ryn in the days since he'd told her she was Queen, since he'd instructed her to connect to the earth as he had told her she could and she'd seen the truth. No wonder the sex and the claws always came together in her nightmares. Ryn brought them both to her. Pleasure and pain, wonder and savagery.

Since seeing the truth for herself, Juliet had not been able to completely sever her ties to the earth. Perhaps she would never be able to do so again. Ryn had erected that barrier between them once again, but there was so much more. She saw and felt those who had come along this road before. Couples, some already in love, others intrigued with one another, still others uncertain of their future, had all traveled this same road. Caradon, watching and waiting, had hidden here. She did her best to push those thoughts out . . . they were ugly and filled with hate, and she did not want that bitterness to take root inside her.

Her days in the mountains, traveling with Ryn and lying with him and even thinking of falling in love, might be the only days of her life spent in absolute peace. She certainly knew no peace now, and she might never again. With all her heart and soul, she wished not to become a wolf; she did not want to be Queen. She didn't want the claws which she now knew slept inside her to be set free, any more than she wanted to know that an Anwyn male, a slender man with dark hair, had made love for the first time to his newly captured wife, who already cherished him to distraction, on the road she now walked upon.

Ryn said love was not necessary for an Anwyn and his mate, but she knew that for some there was love. She felt it here, in the earth and in the air.

She didn't turn back and run away from the destiny Ryn had shown her, even though she found it frightening and even repulsive. Her father lived. Her *father!* Ryn had explained that Kei didn't live within The City's walls, but he visited several times a year. Seeing him and confronting her Anwyn blood didn't mean that she had to take the vow that would transform her fully to Anwyn. She would meet her father, decline the place of power that Ryn swore was meant for her, and decline to take the vow that would awaken the wolf in her. When her business there was done, she would leave The City without Ryn, and without ever seeing or feeling the claws that lay hidden inside her. It was the only plan she could contemplate at this time.

They would soon reach The City. She knew this not because Ryn told her, but because she felt it. Since she was unable to close off her connection to all things, The Heart called to her. It drew her into its embrace as if it were yet another lover. There was power in The Heart, just as there was power in these mountains, and they both fed Juliet in a way she did not wish to be fed.

None of it mattered, overmuch. In the end she would leave The Heart and The City, just as she would leave Ryn.

"I wish you would speak," her captor said in a lowered and distinctly unhappy voice.

"I have nothing to say to you."

"You have much to say to me, you simply choose not to."

"Perhaps I should sing," she threatened.

"Please do so."

She scoffed as she climbed a rugged rock that blocked their path. "As I remember, you had unkind words about my singing voice."

"Yes, but you were happy then, and I miss the happiness."

She stopped on the path and turned to face Ryn. "So do I, but that's over."

"Why?"

Ryn understood why; and she knew without touching him how deeply and truly he understood. "I can't disconnect the ties anymore," she said.

"You can, when you shake free the anger and regain control."

It sounded so simple. "When I leave here, will I be able to shut down my ability whenever I want?"

"I don't know," he answered. And though he didn't say so aloud, she knew he didn't think she'd ever have the opportunity to find out. He didn't think she'd ever leave these mountains. He was wrong.

"Do you wish to disengage from that ability now?" Ryn asked.

More than anything, but going home. "Yes."

Ryn indicated a rock ledge behind her. "Sit."

Juliet shook her head. "I can't sit. We don't have time . . ."

"We have all the time we need. Sit," he said again, his voice soft and strong.

Juliet clambered up the steep rock and sat, and when Ryn walked to her, they were face-to-face. She had tried very hard not to look at him too often in the past few days. She felt betrayed, and like it or not, she still had feelings for him. He'd lied to her, he'd seduced her . . . he was a part of the destiny she did not want.

"Your link to me is strongest," he said. "Break that link first, and the rest will follow."

"You've already broken it."

"No, I have built a wall. Only you have the power to undo it." He took her hand, the wall came down, and she knew that he would never harm her . . .

She yanked her hand away. "I can't."

"Your mind is going in too many directions at once," he said calmly. "The City, The Heart, your father, your sisters . . ."

"So you're psychic, too, now?" she snapped.

"No. I only feel you. Close your eyes."

"What does that—"

"Close. Your. Eyes."

She did, but only because she didn't want to look at Ryn's face any longer. Looking at him hurt her heart in a way she had never expected.

"Remember the lake where we camped?" he asked in an insanely calm voice.

"Yes, of course I do."

"It was beautiful."

"Yes."

"See it now, Juliet. See the still waters, and the trees on the far bank. Feel the water against your skin and the sun on your face."

Amazingly, she did. Her heart seemed to beat more steadily, and she was able to breathe deeper.

"Are you there?" Ryn whispered.

"Yes."

"Good. Breathe in the scent of the water."

She took a deep breath, and the scent of the lake filled her.

"Run your fingers through the water and watch the ripples you create."

She lifted her hand and made the motion.

"Take another deep breath."

It was a breath that cleared her head and her soul.

"Find the tendril that connects your spirit to mine."

The link was there, fatter and stronger and deeper than any other. It pulsed with life. It fed her spirit.

"It is not meant to be cut, it is never to be severed, but you can close it, for a time."

"It's too strong."

"You are stronger."

Juliet concentrated on the pulsing, on the rush of life . . . and she made it slow just as her heartbeat had slowed. She tied off that cord, that link to Ryn, and when she did, it stopped pulsing altogether.

And he knew. The moment it happened, he *knew*. "Now, the others should be easy. Close them, shut them down. The power is yours, Juliet. You control the link; it does not control you."

Even though her powers were stronger, more acute than ever before, she was able to shut them down. One link at a time.

Juliet opened her eyes and found Ryn standing close. He lifted his hand and reached out to touch the tip of her nose. She felt nothing but the warmth of his finger. Nothing at all. "Thank you," she said as his hand fell away. It would be dangerous to sit here and talk to Ryn and let him touch her, so she jumped down with a newly found grace and started walking toward The City once again. Ryn remained behind her, silent and separate.

One aspect of the Anwyn blood that she did not mind was the warmth. She'd left her boots behind days ago, and had pulled her skirt up and bundled it so that her legs were free. She was not as near-naked as Ryn, but even if she were, she wouldn't feel the winter cold. The strength was nice, too. She could move more quickly and surely, and she did not tire as she had in the early days.

Since she was no longer fighting the connection to all

things, other abilities became sharper to her. Scents teased her nose, and in an intuitive way she knew those smells. Plants, Anwyn, small animals . . . Ryn. None of the smells were unpleasant. Instead they all seemed very natural to her. Very right.

When she left The City, would she leave all her new-found abilities behind? Probably so, but it was a fair enough trade. The heat and the strength and the other enhanced abilities came with the claws.

Not long after Juliet began to experience the invigorated power of her Anwyn senses, Ryn reached down and took her hand. Together they crested a sharp rise. Instead of letting go and moving on when she reached the top of the rise, he held her hand and pointed with the other. "It is there."

Juliet followed the direction of his finger, but she saw nothing but more mountain. There was a valley of sorts, but it was all jagged stone. Maybe that was all that awaited her in The City. Maybe it wasn't a city at all, but a collection of caves that would be easy enough to leave behind when the time came.

"I don't see . . ." she began, but then Ryn tugged on her hand and pulled her forward, a single step, and the valley changed. A rock wall surrounded buildings, all made of stone. Some of the buildings beyond the wall were tall and impressive; others were no bigger or finer than the cabin she had called home for so long. In the rock face that climbed high behind the city, doors had been carved in the rock. The City was made of pink and gray and pale green stones, beautiful in a way wood could never be. Puzzled, she stepped back. Once again, The City disappeared from view, and it seemed that she was looking down into a barren valley.

"I don't understand."

"Anwyn have a magic of their own, wife."

She looked at Ryn, her eyes sharp and her heart hardened. "I am not your wife, Ryn, and I won't ever be."

"I know," he said in a lowered voice. He dropped her hand and loped ahead before she could answer, anxious to get home. She followed more slowly, not quite so anxious to face what awaited her in The City.

As they drew closer, The City became more real. It did not disappear, as it had at the top of the rise, but took shape and form. When they reached the lowest part of the road, they could no longer see beyond the wall that surrounded The City, but they could clearly see the wall itself. Even more, they could hear and smell the sounds of life beyond the wall. There were many happy sounds. Laughter, lively conversation, the soft cry of a small child that was quickly soothed. There was safety inside those walls. The people there were safe and warm and beautiful. She knew this as if she had been here before, as if she had lived here for a hundred years.

They were close. So close. She could actually hear the distant sounds of city life . . . sounds she should not have been able to hear from this distance, and yet they were clear to her. Laughter. Voices. The clink of metal on metal, and metal on stone. The path she and Ryn walked upon was wide and flat. There was nothing between them and their destination.

She stopped and Ryn, who walked before her, stopped a heartbeat later. Perhaps he heard her. Perhaps he just knew . . .

"What's wrong?" he asked, turning to face her.

"Will they know?" she asked softly. "When I walk through those gates and they see me . . . will everyone know that I'm like them?"

Ryn studied her critically for a moment before answering, "Yes."

Her heart sank, and her anger began to grow all over

again. "You knew all along, didn't you? And you didn't tell me until we were almost here and it was too late to turn back . . ."

"No. I did not realize that you were anything more than my mate until you began to change."

"I have not changed!" she argued, even though she knew Ryn spoke the truth.

He stepped toward her, laid a hand on her face, and looked into her eyes. "You have had no looking glass to study the changes, but I see them well. You can let down your skirts and pretend to feel the chill like the other women who have been taken, and you can alter your step so that no one sees your strength. You can pretend that you don't hear or smell what a human woman should not, and no one will get close enough to know that your heart beats too quickly. But you cannot hide your eyes."

"What's wrong with my eyes?" she whispered.

"Nothing," he said sharply. "They are beautiful and intelligent and tender. But they are now more gold than brown. They won't become completely gold until you take the vow, but—"

"I'm not taking any vow," she said, reiterating the promises she had made in days past.

Ryn was not deterred. "You have Anwyn eyes, Juliet."

She could do as he'd suggested and let down her skirts. Put her cloak over her shoulders and pretend to feel the cold. If she were very careful, she could walk slightly behind Ryn with her eyes downcast, and maybe no one would see that she had begun to change.

Or she could walk into The City with her head high and take what came.

In the end, it was no decision at all. She had been meek in the past, yes, but she did not hide from anything or anyone.

The gates to The City stood open, and the two guards who manned it were relaxed. They nodded to Ryn, but barely looked at Juliet. Ryn said it had been years since there had been any kind of major conflict here, that the Caradon were much more likely to attack those Anwyn who lived well beyond The City. Apparently the guards had become complacent. Or confident. If the men beyond that gate were anything like Ryn, only a fool would dare to attack.

Juliet walked into The City with Ryn beside her, her head high and her eyes on the wonders spread before her. From a distance, The City was beautiful, in a crude sort of way. The buildings were constructed of the most exquisite stone she had ever seen, many of them constructed in part of the mountain itself. The people who walked about on the stone streets were not dressed in primitive kilts, like Ryn. The women wore long, flowing frocks and furs to ward off the chill, and the men were dressed in snugly fitting trousers and loose shirts and fine boots. There was much laughter and many little boys who were dressed as miniatures of their fathers and ran and laughed and played.

There was a collection of lively shops spread along two main thoroughfares that met at a massive town square. Like the homes carved into the mountain, they were made of stone, and were plain and solid. People shopped and laughed and visited, many of them carrying large baskets filled with their purchases.

Juliet wanted to take Ryn's hand as she walked down the street, but she didn't want him or anyone else to think that she would easily accept what he called her destiny. So she did not reach for him, even though she very much wanted to.

Eventually a friend of Ryn's spotted him and came their way to say hello and meet the woman Ryn had been gone so long to collect. The man's hair was long, like Ryn's, but was much darker and more well restrained. His smile remained wide until he came close enough to get a good look at Juliet. The man stopped on the street, several feet away, and stared at Juliet. He swallowed hard and took a step back, and then he dropped to his knees and leaned forward, laying himself prostrate before her.

"Please get up," Juliet insisted.

The man lifted his head and glanced upward, but did not rise.

"This is Kerymi," Ryn said, gesturing to his friend. "Your very presence seems to have stolen his normally quick tongue."

"Ryn," Kerymi said beneath his breath. "She is . . . it is *her*."

"Yes, I know."

Again, the dark-haired man glanced suspiciously at Juliet. "You say you are going to fetch your mate, and you come home with a Queen. Not just any queen, mind you, but a red-haired queen."

"I believe she instructed you to stand," Ryn said with a tight smile.

Kerymi scrambled to his feet. Like Ryn, he was tall and well built. The golden eyes looked rather odd, since his coloring was so dark, but the combination was more striking than bizarre. She imagined when the moon was full he made a fine, black wolf.

He was also terrified of her. Perhaps awed was a better word. She thought it odd that he'd commented on her hair color. Perhaps there weren't many red-haired Anwyn.

"You are to be the Queen's consort," Kerymi said with a half-smile. "Many men will envy you, Ryn." Ryn's answer was a low, unhappy grunt, and after a moment Kerymi's smile faded.

"Oh, I had forgotten that," he said in a soft voice. "Maybe that part of the legend is wrong." He did not sound convinced.

"Forgotten what?" Juliet asked. "And what legend does he speak of?"

"It is unimportant," Ryn answered.

There was no time or opportunity to press the matter. Others had seen Kerymi bow to Juliet, and they came. One at a time, cautiously and curiously, they came. When they saw her eyes, a flash of realization crossed their faces, and like Kerymi they dropped down and pressed their foreheads to the ground. The men were Anwyn, but the woman—captives from Columbyana and perhaps beyond—came, too. Like their husbands, they recognized that the Queen they had been waiting for had come, and they fell to their knees and pressed their foreheads to the ground in a gesture of respect and honor. For every person Juliet ordered to stand, another came and fell to the ground, until she and Ryn were surrounded on all sides by people who considered themselves her subjects. Over and over again she heard "the red-haired Queen" whispered in hushed tones.

At first Ryn had seemed to be almost amused, but as the crowd grew, his smile faded and his eyes grew stormy. Juliet did not dare to unleash her powers, not even to learn what Ryn was feeling and thinking at this moment. Then again, after a moment of studying his face, she did not need to tap into her powers to understand.

She did not wish to be Queen.

Just as strongly, perhaps more so, Ryn did not wish to be the Queen's consort.

13

ISADORA FIDDLED NERVOUSLY WITH THE SKIRT OF THE blue gown that had been given to her when she'd finished bathing in a large, marble pool. She'd asked for black, but the girl who'd been assigned to help had merely laughed as she'd informed Isadora that there was no black on Level Three. Isadora requested that her own gown be returned, but again the servant had laughed. That rag had been disposed of as Isadora had been stepping into the pool. It was already gone. Apparently the laughing girl didn't know that she was supposed to be afraid of the witch.

Damp hair hanging loose, blue frock clinging to a frame that had seen only black in more than five years, Isadora stood in the empress's chambers on Level Five. Isadora did wonder why the level that had been devoted to the empress was two floors lower than the level where the concubines were housed, but she did not ask. In fact, she said nothing at all, as the empress examined her from the comfort of a fat blue chair a few feet away. A young twittering girl dressed in brown stood behind the empress, and so did one staunch sentinel. The sentinel was obviously devoted to his charge. He was a large, blond man with big hands and dark blue eyes. Intelligent eyes, unlike so many of the soldiers she had come to know in the past weeks.

"Don't be afraid," Empress Liane said in a voice that was soft and unforgiving at the same time.

"I'm not afraid," Isadora said. The sentinel glared at her, and she added deferentially, "my lady."

"I came to know your sister well," the empress continued. "Are you very much like her?"

"Those who know us say not, my lady," Isadora answered.

Empress Liane smiled. She had the look of a woman who did not smile easily or often. The empress was beautiful, there was no denying that, but she also looked like a woman who'd led a hard life to this point. "Yes, I can see that the two of you are very different. You lack her sweetness."

Isadora did not respond.

"However, she no longer lacks your strength."

Isadora very much wanted to ask about Sophie and what had happened here, but she kept her questions to herself for the moment. Could she trust Empress Liane? The woman was in a position of great power, and her husband had ordered the kidnapping that had led to this moment . . . and to Juliet's abduction. And yet, the woman had saved Isadora by requesting that she become her personal witch.

The empress studied Isadora with great interest, silent and thoughtful. After a moment, she lifted her hand in a dismissive gesture that seemed to come naturally. "I'd like a word with the witch. Alone."

The girl in brown scurried away, gratefully leaving her post at her mistress's side and skirting around Isadora to make her way into a narrow hallway.

The sentinel was not so anxious to escape. "My lady,"

he said in a respectful but strong voice. "You cannot be alone with her."

"She won't hurt me, Ferghus," Empress Liane insisted confidently. "She knows that if she dares to try, not only will she pay with her life, so will her sisters." The empress looked Isadora in the eye as she delivered the promise. "And when that is done, every person who lives in the village near her home will pay the price. Shandley, I believe it's called."

Isadora's heart lurched as she remembered how the soldiers had made innocents from the village near their camp pay for the death of the man who had threatened to kill her for a promised reward. She didn't doubt that Empress Liane, with those cold eyes and that regal air, would do the same.

"The emperor commanded—"

"You are my sentinel, Ferghus," the empress said confidently. "You obey my commands, not those of my husband."

An uneasy Ferghus leaned down and whispered something insistent into Empress Liane's ear, and the woman dismissed him once again, with a sharp word and another wave of her hand. In frustration, he handed the empress the short sword that hung from his belt. She took the weapon as if she were quite familiar with it.

When the sentinel had stepped into the hallway and the two women were alone, the empress propped the sword at her side, where it was no longer a threat but was close enough at hand for someone familiar with such weapons to make use of in the blink of an eye. "I do not know that I can save you," she said in a lowered voice.

Isadora bowed her head. "You already have, by my way of thinking."

"It might not last. My husband is . . ." She searched for the right word.

Isadora came up with a few of her own. Cruel. Powerful. Unpredictable. Demented.

"Hotheaded," the empress finally finished. "He has been known to make hasty decisions and regret them later, and I can't guarantee that he won't wake up tomorrow and decide you're simply not worth the trouble it will be to keep you alive." She laid a hand over her belly. "But he does listen to me, on occasion." She leaned slightly forward. "Come closer, Isadora Fyne."

Isadora took a step forward, and in a flash the sword was firmly seated in the empress's hand, blade up and ready. She stopped abruptly. "I'm only doing as you asked."

The sword did not drop. "I'm aware of that. I need you close enough that we might share words that are sure to be private, but one can't be too careful where witchcraft is concerned. I'm not yet certain that you care so much about your sisters and the residents of your village that you'll behave as you should."

"I care nothing for the people of Shandley," Isadora said bluntly, "but I would never do anything to endanger my sisters in any way."

The blade lowered, a little, and it seemed that the empress almost smiled. "You're honest. I should warn you, that's not always considered an admirable trait in this palace."

Isadora did not immediately respond. She and the empress were alone when they should not be; the lady of this cursed palace had mentioned private words still to be spoken; and the woman with the sword studied her as if she could not decide whether she should hug or skewer her. After a few moments of strained silence, Isadora asked, "What do you want from me?"

The empress relaxed a little. "Kane Varden is my brother."

Surprised, Isadora took a short step back. The hair, the eyes. There was definitely a resemblance. The empress's brother was a relation . . . and a rebel. No wonder this conversation had to be private.

"Does anyone else know?"

"No one in this palace is aware of the kinship, not even my husband."

Of course no one was aware! Rebels and witches did not make fine and regal relations. "And yet you've trusted me with this secret, even though you still hold a sword on me while we speak."

Empress Liane set the sword aside once again, but it was not too far away to call upon, if necessary. "I came to care for Sophie very much while she was here. She hugged me before she made her escape, and she called me sister. For her sake, I could not allow Sebestyen to kill you, or worse. I can't promise that I can keep you safe, but I am going to try. I wanted you to know why."

It was hard to imagine Sophie embracing this cold woman and calling her sister. Perhaps the youngest Fyne sister had seen something in Empress Liane that Isadora missed. "Were Sophie and Kane truly well when they left this place?"

"Madly in love, together, and expecting another child," the empress said with a minimum of emotion. "Yes, I'd say they were well."

Relief rushed through Isadora, leaving her light-headed. "I'm glad to hear that. Even though I did not approve of the match in the beginning, I'm glad Sophie has Kane with her now."

"So am I," Empress Liane said almost grudgingly. She squirmed slightly. "What am I to do with you? I told Sebestyen that I fancied having my own witch, but it'll take more than that to satisfy him for more than a few days. Mahri is a good, compliant maid, and I'd rather not replace her. If I release her, she has nowhere to go but down, and she is a sweet enough girl." The empress's lips twisted as if she were thinking of smiling. "Besides, the Fyne women don't strike me as being at all compliant."

Empress Liane stood and took a few steps to move close to Isadora. Was the woman brave, confident, or stupid?

Not stupid; of that Isadora was certain.

When they were very close, Liane said in a lowered voice, "I have few friends in this palace, Isadora. I trust a handful of the people closest to me, and even then . . ." She shrugged. "I can't be sure of them." Her eyes met and held Isadora's. "I can't be entirely sure about you, either, but we do have a bond that no one else knows of. Kane and Sophie. My brother, your sister. And I sense that we are the same in many ways. We are not entirely like other women. So you see, I have no choice but to trust you, to some degree."

Isadora nodded.

"You need to be here. It's very likely that Bors will find your sister Juliet and bring her to Sebestyen, and it would be best if you're not only here but well established in the palace before that happens. Do you understand?"

"Juliet is more likely to survive if I am here and in a position to help her," Isadora said.

"Exactly," Empress Liane said with a soft sigh. "I have selfish reasons of my own for wanting you here. In a few months I will give birth to the next emperor of Columbyana. I need a strong woman to stand beside me, someone I can trust, a companion who will deliver my baby and keep him out of the hands of the priests. Help me, Isadora. Deliver my child and keep us both safe and someday, as soon as it is possible, I will see you free from here."

THE ANWYN PALACE WAS THREE STORIES HIGH, MASSIVE in length and breadth and constructed of the beautiful stones Juliet had seen throughout The City. Even if there had been no columns lining the portico, no armed and uniformed guards, no silk flags in gold and bright blue, it would still be the most magnificent place she'd ever seen.

The Palace of the Anwyn Queen was undeniably regal, and yet it also looked primitive, as if it had stood just so for a thousand years, as if it were a part of the mountain and always would be.

The guards wore blue uniforms and carried spears instead of swords. The tips of those spears were sharp, and the arms of those who carried them were muscular. All of the soldiers had long hair, dark and pale and even red, and in each case it had been pulled back and fashioned into a long, thick braid that fell down a muscled back. She had to remind herself, again and again—these men were like Ryn; they changed with the moon.

Word of her arrival preceded her, and all along the road people had halted their daily chores to bow. After a while she stopped telling people to stand; eventually they'd learn that she did not wish to be Queen, and the bowing would cease.

As they stepped into the palace, she sensed Ryn's reluctance. She could reach out to him, find that connection they shared and take comfort from it. But she was afraid. Afraid she would not be able to stop the sensations that were bound to assault her, here in this place where her abilities could grow to unknown heights.

Guards lined the long hallway. The corridor was as wide as the parlor of the Fyne cabin, and the tapestries on the walls were fine and richly colored. The stone beneath her feet was cool and uncarpeted, but shone with its own rugged beauty. The guards did not bow as she passed, but their stance did change. They dropped their heads and extended the spears to the side, in a straight-arm salute of sorts. All of them appeared to be young; many were younger than Ryn, she would guess, perhaps by a few years.

It was as if she were being pulled toward the center of the palace, tugged unerringly toward the destiny Ryn told her awaited. He thought it was the sacred stone that called her, but she could not believe that an object had power over her in any way. Yes, she believed wholeheartedly in magic. But a sacred stone? Magic was in the heart and the soul, not encased in an inanimate object.

Before them, a massive set of double doors was well guarded by more spear-carrying guards. The guards dropped their heads in salute, and then opened those doors.

Columns of varying widths and shapes and stone were scattered throughout the massive room, holding up the ornate ceiling above and adding elegance to a room that was so large it could easily be called stark. The ceiling was so high above, Juliet lifted her head in amazement.

There was much here to amaze. Silk draperies, tapestries, finely crafted chairs and chests and tables. The chamber was a mixture of fine and crudely crafted things, all blending together into a fashion that was, well, Anwyn. Ryn was this way—crude and refined, wild and civilized.

She could very well imagine that at times this massive room was filled with revelers or friends or family. The most powerful of the Anwyn would meet here when necessary. Even though there was an ancient aspect to this palace, it was far from the crude cave she had expected when Ryn had first told her he was taking her to his home.

At the far end of the room, a throne awaited. It was an impressive but lonely-looking chair of power. The chair-back was high, the wood of that back and the legs carved ornately, the armrests wide. A gold cushion covered the seat, awaiting Queen Etaina. At the moment the throne was empty, but it was guarded on either side by more armed guards.

As Juliet and Ryn walked toward the vacant throne, an old woman appeared from a door to the side. Her back was slightly bent, her hair as white as the snow that had fallen on the journey. Still, she moved with a kind of gentle grace. She wore a gold silk frock that danced around her thin frame as she took her throne and the silk settled around her body.

There was no welcoming smile, and suddenly Juliet was more uncertain about this journey than she had ever been.

She wished she'd taken the time to bathe and dress properly. The white-haired woman was a Queen, after all, while she herself was road weary and dirty, her clothes torn and her hair wildly tangled. When they stood before the throne, Juliet took her cue from Ryn. When he dropped down, she did the same. When he placed his forehead on the floor, so did she.

"Oh, get up," the Queen commanded brusquely. "I have no time for this."

They rose, and Juliet took her first good look at the Queen of the Anwyn. The old woman looked no more happy to see Juliet than Juliet was at the thought of taking her place. If the Queen was unhappy because she thought Juliet wanted her throne, perhaps they could come to an agreement that would make everyone happy.

"It certainly took you long enough to get here," the old woman said sharply. "Do you have any idea how long I've been waiting for you?"

"No, ma'am," Juliet answered, her voice soft and confused.

"My mate passed on eight winters ago."

"I'm very sorry."

"Very sorry," the Queen muttered. "I would have joined him within three cycles of the moon if you had been here to take my place, as you should have been."

"Juliet did not know of her duty," Ryn said, his welcome voice deep and warm and comforting.

The Queen turned her old, golden eyes to the man who had spoken. "I did not ask for your opinion." Again, she looked pointedly at Juliet. "You truly did not know of your place here? How could you not know?" Her eyes narrowed. "The red-haired Queen is said to have the gift of sight."

No wonder so many of the people on the street had whispered about the color of her hair. Her coming had been foretold in some way. "I have that gift, but it has never worked well in regards to my own life," Juliet explained. "Sometimes I see, other times I do not."

The old woman relaxed. "You have much explaining to do. I don't understand why you were not born and raised here in The City, as you should have been. In all of recorded Anwyn history, the Queen has come to us as an infant and been reared in the palace with the knowledge that she would be Queen when the time came. Did your father hide you away to keep you from us?"

"I never knew my father," Juliet said softly.

The Queen's eyebrows lifted slightly. "Unusual. I will want to hear all the details, perhaps over the evening meal. For now I will only say that I am grateful that you have come to us at last. I and all of your subjects have been waiting for you for a very long time."

Even though Ryn had warned her of this days ago, the concept of being Queen was too much to comprehend. Subjects? She did not want or need subjects. She did not wish to sit on that throne. All she wanted was to go home. If she were very lucky, she could keep this newly found ability to turn her psychic powers down and even off. It was all she wanted. Home and peace. Best to start by telling the old Queen the truth.

"Queen Etaina, I have no desire to take your place. I don't understand what has happened here, but there must be some kind of misunderstanding. A mistake. I am not meant to be Queen."

"You are Anwyn female; you are Queen. Your desire is not important. The throne is your obligation. The Anwyn people are your subjects."

"But—"

"Your consort is dismissed," Queen Etaina said with a wave of her hand. "You and I need to talk, just the two of us. Apparently you do not understand the full magnitude of this matter."

They did need to have a talk. Somehow Juliet had to convince the Queen that she didn't plan to stay and claim the throne. Even so, she would not allow Ryn to be dismissed in such an offhanded way.

"Ryn is not my consort," she said.

"Of course he is," the Queen said impatiently. "He is your partner, your lover. Before he was called to retrieve his mate, he was a fine palace guard. It was a noble and honorable station, but his station has improved considerably. He is your first and closest servant. He is your subordinate, put on this earth to answer your every command, to pleasure you when you wish it, to give you sons, and to *leave* when he is no longer needed. You are to be Queen and he is here to do your bidding. Tell him he may go."

No wonder Ryn did not want to be the Queen's consort! He wasn't the type to be ordered about, not by a woman or anyone else.

Without saying a word aloud, Ryn turned and walked away. The doors far behind opened and closed, and without turning to look, Juliet knew he was gone. The Queen raised her hand, and the guards on either side of her stepped away. They did not leave the room, but they no longer hovered over Queen Etaina.

"Ryn will take some training, I imagine," the Queen said. "My own mate had years to come to terms with being my consort, since we knew from childhood that we were mated. Ryn is no doubt surprised by this turn of events, but eventually he'll do. He'll make fine, strong sons, I imagine."

"Do you have sons?" Juliet asked.

"Yes." The Queen smiled. "Eleven of them."

Eleven! "Why have you not handed rule of The City and the Anwyn over to one of them?"

"That is not the way of the Anwyn, Juliet." The woman shook her white head. "While my sons and the clan leaders do see to the inconsequential matters of government, it is women who rule. It has been so for many hundreds of years. Our hierarchy is well established. Captive wives are placed lowest in the social stratum, but are ranked well above all other humans. Anwyn males are ranked higher than their wives, which is only natural since they are stronger than any other and have the gift of the wolf. Above them are the purebred Anwyn males, offspring of Anwyn father and those rarely born Anwyn females. Queens, Juliet. Those women, the Queens who come twice in a hundred years, hold the highest station of all. You will be worshipped, thanks to the Anwyn blood that runs in your veins and the womb which will bear purebred sons."

"I do not wish to be worshipped," Juliet said softly.

"It does not matter what you wish." The Queen lost her temper in a flash, then regained it just as quickly. "All that matters is what is. You are very much needed here. No one dares to defy the Queen, but if there is no Queen, the Anwyn will fight among themselves. Clans will battle for power. Rogue Anwyn will move back into the city and disturb our peace. Men fight wars over inconsequential matters. Their pride dictates their decisions, and so they make poor rulers. They are better suited for serving women, and they serve well in many capacities. As consorts, as soldiers, as servants . . ."

"Ryn is none of those things."

"He will be," the Queen said with assurance. "It is his place. Now, we have many other things to discuss. The ceremony to make you ruler will take several days to plan. You may, of course, invite your mate to stay here in the palace during the preparatory period. We will have a smaller chamber prepared for him near your bedroom, so that you may call him if he's needed. I can see that the two of you are already lovers."

"We are . . ." Juliet started to deny the charge, but of course it was not at all false.

"I smell him on you, child, and in you," the Queen said. "Every Anwyn who comes close to you knows that your mate has already claimed you."

"We have taken no vows," she said simply. *And won't.* She did not say those words aloud, but she knew, without question, that the woman on the throne understood.

Queen Etaina smiled. "Of course you have not. Your vow will be to the Anwyn people, not to one man. As Queen, you cannot afford to give yourself over to the whims of a husband as an ordinary woman might."

"There's nothing wrong with being ordinary," Juliet said, her voice near panic.

"For some that is true," Queen Etaina replied calmly. "But you and I, we are not at all ordinary."

"I will be so if I choose," Juliet insisted.

"You have a wide stubborn streak," the Queen observed. "It will serve you well when you take this throne."

"I don't intend to take that throne."

The Queen was not surprised or angered. "Your intentions mean nothing. You will sit on this throne before the next full moon."

The next full moon would come in a matter of days.

"GET BACK."

Sophie heard Kane utter the order that would send Arik and his soldiers away from her. She noted the words in the back of her mind, grasped the reasoning for the warning, and pulled her anger and grief deep within herself.

The Fyne cabin had been burned to the ground, and all that remained of the home where she had been born and raised were ashes and charred wood and unidentifiable lumps of furnishings. Whatever had happened here had happened weeks, perhaps even months, ago. The ground was cold.

Behind her, the soldiers wisely took Kane's direction and headed down the mountain. Sophie's father took Ariana and went with them, but Kane remained. He walked up behind Sophie and placed his arms around her. Her first tear fell, and with it came a cold, gentle rain that dampened the ruins of home. Kane did not tell her to stop, and he did not run for shelter. He was not afraid of this unnatural rain her grief created.

"We did not part on the best of terms," she said softly. "Ariana had been taken, and they'd tricked me into drugging you, and I was so very angry. They never knew that I forgave them, that I loved them . . ."

The rain soaked them both, but Kane kept her warm. "Arik is going to make inquiries in Shandley. Your sisters might be just fine." He planted a kiss on her damp hair.

"If they were fine, they would be here," Sophie said gently. "They would be camping in the barn, or they would have already started to rebuild. Look at this place, Kane. Whatever happened here, it happened a long while ago."

"They might've moved to town after the fire," he suggested.

"They did not move to town." Juliet might, in dire circumstances, but Isadora? Never. If she were able, she'd be here. "We had no trouble finding this place, today," she said.

"You led us," Kane answered sensibly.

"Someone should've stumbled. One man or more should've taken a wrong turn or fallen behind. Getting here was too easy. The protective spell has been broken." Sophie turned in her husband's arms and rested her head on his chest, hiding from the sight that ripped at her heart. The rain turned to snow, the first snow of the winter for the Southern Province.

"I'm scared," she whispered.

He held her head against his chest, protecting her from the snow her grief and her power and the child inside her created. Even though she had learned to rein in her powers so that they did not affect those around her, she had never dealt with an emotion like this one. The pain was too much to control.

"Arik will come back with good news," Kane assured her.

She closed her eyes and prayed with all her heart that he was right.

"When I left here, I told Isadora and Juliet that I had no sisters. I told them I never wanted to see them again." A howling wind made the snow swirl around her and Kane and the cabin. Her long yellow skirt was lifted from the ground, and it swirled and whipped in the wind.

"They know how much you love them."

"Do they? How can I be sure?"

He just held her close, his arms warm and strong around her. Eventually the wind died down, and then the snow stopped falling. Sophie took control of her emotions and tucked them deep inside. She replaced the grief with more constructive emotions. Anger. Determination.

If Juliet and Isadora were alive, she'd find them.

And if they were not alive, she would find the person responsible for this tragedy and she would make them pay.

RYN SAT AT HIS ELDEST BROTHER'S TABLE. CALUM'S WIFE had herded the children outdoors, where they were to play with neighboring friends until called inside for the evening meal.

"I'm sure that everything will be just fine," Becca said

brightly. Calum's wife Becca was pretty enough, but she was also unerringly optimistic. To Ryn's way of thinking, this was not the time for optimism.

"Nothing will be fine," Ryn said in a low, calm voice. "My mate is Queen, which means my only duties are to impregnate her when she so desires. Not only that, she is the red-haired Queen, who will bring peace to the people by taking a Caradon into her bed and giving him a child. How is this fine? How is that in any way *fine?*"

Becca flinched as he shouted and slammed his fist into her dining room table.

"Maybe the legend is wrong?" she offered in a trembling voice.

Calum, who had for the past six years been leader of the Dairgol Clan, laid a hand on his wife's shoulder. "Becca, would you make my brother something to eat? He looks as if he's been living on leaves and overcooked *tilsi* for weeks."

She gladly escaped to the kitchen, and within minutes they heard the rattle of iron pots and spoons from the room beyond.

Ryn pointed to the kitchen door and said, "I can never do that."

Calum sat beside him. Married to Becca for the past seven years, he was not the restless man he had once been. Being a husband and father and clan leader suited him well. "Do what?" he asked.

"I can never ask my wife to prepare a meal, or rub my shoulders after a long day. She will command me. She might very well ask me to fetch her something to eat!"

Calum grinned widely. "You cannot know this. It is too soon."

Ryn leaned toward his older brother. "And what of the Caradon? Am I to sit back meekly and allow a beast to touch my wife? To give her a child?"

Calum's smile faded. "In the name of lasting peace? Perhaps you have no choice."

"Would you allow it if the woman in question was your wife?"

Calum did not answer, and wouldn't. He and his Becca had found the love that Juliet had inquired about on more than one occasion, and it was messy. They argued often, venting their feelings for anyone who might be about to see, and then made up with kisses and apologies. Becca always worried overmuch when the full moon came and her husband took to the hills, and she cried when he came home because she had missed him and worried for his safety. And Calum was no better than his overly emotional wife.

Ansgar and his wife Dona had a more palatable arrangement. They had children, and they liked one another very well. They were friends and partners and lovers, but there was little messy emotion to muddy the waters.

Calum would never allow a Caradon or any other man to touch his Becca, no matter what the benefit to the Anwyn might be. In the name of peace, Ansgar would grudgingly allow his wife to share her body with another.

Ryn refused to admit that it was possible this meant he had fallen in love with Juliet. She was simply his. Emotion would only complicate matters.

"There is no need to worry now. It is possible the day the legend speaks of might not come for many years," Calum offered sensibly.

"After my death," Ryn replied.

"Not necessarily . . ."

"After my death," Ryn said again. He looked his brother in the eye. "I don't care if it means unending war with the Caradon, no other man will touch Juliet while I live."

Calum clapped his steady hand to Ryn's shoulder. "You love her."

Ryn did not immediately confirm or deny the accusation.

"I'm sorry." With that, and another clap of his hand to Ryn's shoulder, Calum left the table.

Love? No, that couldn't be it. Surely what he felt was a possessiveness that was only natural where one's mate was concerned. The feeling would pass. Eventually.

14

It was impossible to sneak anywhere when surrounded by guards who could not only see unnaturally well, but who could *smell* their prey at a moderate distance.

Juliet wanted to see Ryn; she wanted to find her father. But instead of doing those two simple things, she had been relegated to a suite of luxurious rooms where she had more devoted servants than she could ever possibly use. The two times she'd tried to sneak out of the palace, she had found herself being followed by not one but three spear-toting blue-clad guards. They meant well, but still . . . it was an annoyance.

The old Queen had already started planning Juliet's coronation and her own funeral. Apparently once there was a ruler to take her place, she would simply lie down and die, her duty to the Anwyn done, at least for this lifetime. Her mate awaited her in the next life, and only her duty as Queen had kept her living for such a long time. It was a concept Juliet had a hard time accepting. That two people could be born to be together, that they could carry their bond into the next life, that the concept of forever was more than a concept, it was very real.

If that was true, then Ryn was her forever. It was as frightening to her as the idea of a lover who changed into a wolf with the appearance of a full moon. When he touched her and she allowed herself to forget who she was and what she had planned for her life, forever seemed like a fine idea.

Ryn disdained love as unnecessary and overly senti-mental, but Juliet knew that if she embraced the concept of a fated union, she would come to love Ryn, and in doing so she'd condemn him to an early death. Maybe if she kept her distance and focused her mind on other things, she would not fall into that trap.

Sitting blessedly alone before an ornately framed mirror in her bedchamber, Juliet studied the changes in herself. In many ways, she felt as if she were looking at a stranger. The gold striations in her brown eyes were startling, but that was not the only physical change in her appearance. Her cheeks were pink, flushed with the heat of her newly invigorated blood. Instead of being restrained in a knot or a braid, her hair had been left loose. It was as if she could no longer stand to have it bound tightly atop her head.

She had been gifted with a selection of blue gowns, all of them made of the finest silk. The maids who tended Juliet had already told her how magnificent she would look in the fine gold frocks she'd wear as Queen.

Juliet still did not wish to be Queen, but for now she had resigned herself to the fate Ryn and the old Queen and everyone else claimed was inescapable. If denying who she had been born to be would bring war to this peaceful place, how could she walk away?

Perhaps she was destined to be Queen, for a while. That didn't mean she had to remain ruler. Once the old Queen had taken her place in the next life with her mate, Juliet would devise a plan to put one of the old woman's sons on the throne in a peaceful and orderly way. Since there were eleven of them, surely *one* would make an acceptable King.

Two days remained until the next full moon. Like it or not, Juliet felt the tug of her Anwyn blood. What would it be like to take the vow that not only made her Queen, but made her fully Anwyn as well? What would it be like to become a wolf? The nightmare of the claws still terrified her, even though she had not suffered with it in more than a week.

The transformation from woman to wolf would be painful, she knew. How could it not be? Perhaps that was the pain she'd experienced in her dream, the ripping of flesh and the blood and the scream of transformation. A part of her was terrified of the change to come. But another part of her, the Anwyn that had slept for so long, wanted it. She wanted to run sure-footed in the mountains by the light of a full moon. She wanted to embrace the animal that slept inside her, to find and discover the wildness that had been hidden inside a meek woman for such a long time. She wasn't meek anymore.

The door to her suite opened, and four women filed in. All of them had been dressed in pale blue, and all of them entered the chamber with their gaze trained to the floor in deference. The Anwyn Queen must think her incapable of even the smallest chore. Otherwise, why were there always so many servants around?

She doesn't trust you. The answer came to her as clearly as if it had been spoken. Queen Etaina knew that Juliet had doubts about her destiny. She knew there was fear and uncertainty in Juliet's heart. The old woman wouldn't risk losing her replacement, not after all this time. The women who seemed to be everywhere she turned were not only maids; they were guards.

Juliet stood and turned to face the servants. Women who

had been taken and who were wed to palace guards, they were different in many ways. Short, tall, skinny, round, dark, fair. They came from many regions.

They had one thing in common. They were all very happy.

Juliet had resisted commanding Ryn's presence. Distance was best; logically she knew that to be true. But she missed him; she needed to see him. Since she could not sneak out and go to him, what choice did she have but to request his presence here?

"I'd like to see my friend this afternoon."

"Your friend? You have many friends in The City, my lady Juliet," the short blond maid said sweetly. She lifted her pretty face slightly as she spoke. The others didn't say a word.

They were going to make her say it. "Ryn."

Still, the ladies before her didn't react.

"My mate," she said more tersely.

The blond smiled. "Of course, my lady Juliet. He will be ordered here immediately."

"It's a request, not an order," Juliet corrected.

All four girls stood there with unasked questions all too clear on their faces. They did not understand why Ryn wasn't already here, and they certainly wondered why their ruler would make such a humble request when her every word was a command.

"Don't order Ryn to the palace," Juliet explained. "*Ask* him if he would please come to see me at his convenience."

They did not comprehend her reasoning. How long had they been away from the real world that they did not remember that no man took kindly to being ordered about by a woman?

Surely these women had forgotten nothing. Their own husbands were like men everywhere. If anything, the Anwyn males were more dominant than most. But these captive wives saw Juliet not as a woman but as Queen. Her word was law. Two of the women nodded their heads and left; two stayed behind. Guards, Juliet thought once again. They wouldn't stop her if she tried to leave, but she'd soon have soldiers on her heels, and that wasn't the way she wanted to go to Ryn.

How on earth was she going to tell the man that she missed him?

It was mere minutes before the doors to her suite opened and Ryn stepped into the room, flanked by guards on either side. Armed soldiers, not the pretty women who served Juliet in her chambers. Judging by the expression on Ryn's face, he had not been *asked* at all.

Juliet stood and faced him. Heavens he looked good. Different, but very, very good. Gone was the leather kilt and wild hair. His long blond hair had been captured in a neat braid that fell down his broad back. He wore snug trousers made of a soft brown fabric, and a loose-sleeved shirt that remained open at the neck. There were soft leather boots on his feet. She had often thought him beautiful, but until this moment, she had not realized that he was so conventionally handsome.

"You look different," she said softly.

"So do you." He had closed off the strand of the web that bound them together, and she did her best to keep her abilities dampened, so she did not know if he was pleased with the change in her or not.

Juliet dismissed her guards, male and female, with a wave of her hand. They departed silently and quickly, leaving her alone with Ryn.

He walked toward her. "I understand you are to become Queen on the morning of the next full moon. Two days," he said softly.

"I tried to delay the ceremony, but . . ." Juliet took a deep, nervous breath. "Queen Etaina insists." She tried to lift her shoulders casually, but this was not a matter to be shrugged off. "I don't know what happens next," she said softly.

Perhaps she was to be ruler for a time, but she needed Ryn right now. She needed the Ryn who had rescued her. The Ryn who had hauled her an immeasurable distance, insisting all the way that they were meant to be together.

"Of course you know what comes next," he said in an emotionless voice. "You become Queen, and I come running whenever you call."

"It won't be that way," she insisted.

Ryn lifted his hands, palms up. "It is already that way."

"I told them to *ask* you to come," she argued. "I did not issue an order."

"When the Queen asks, the answer is always yes."

"You're angry."

"I'm disappointed."

In her? How could she ask that question? It revealed a neediness in her nature; it made her feel like the meek woman Ryn had rescued. She had a feeling this conversation could be endless, so she abruptly changed the subject. "I would like to meet my father."

"All you need do is ask."

Queen Etaina had been dismayed to discover that Juliet's Anwyn father was a rogue, but it did explain why she hadn't been born here in The City. "I don't want my first meeting with my father to be a public display. I don't want to share that moment with just anyone. Could you bring him to me? Quietly?"

"He lives beyond The City walls. It might take a few days, perhaps even weeks, to locate him."

The idea of being alone here without Ryn caused a shiver that touched Juliet's bones. She had fought him for so long, and now she didn't want him to be too far away. "Can you send someone else out to find him? I'd like you to be here when I . . ." When she became Queen, when she became wolf.

Ryn bowed sharply. "Whatever you command, my lady Juliet."

She'd liked it better when he called her wife and *vidara*.

IT WAS NOT JULIET'S FAULT THAT SHE'D BEEN BORN Queen. Ryn told himself that as he walked through the square, searching for a man he could trust to find and collect Kei Deverin of the Ancikyn Clan, Juliet's father. She didn't want the throne any more than he wanted to be the Queen's consort, unmanned and powerless and always at the beck and call of a woman.

Women ruled The City and the Anwyn, but in families that was not the case. The males ruled their own households. An Anwyn male worked a trade and built a home, and the woman he claimed as his mate came to him when he called. It was the life Ryn had always imagined for himself—ruler not of a people, but of his own home and family. It wasn't Juliet's fault that such a simple wish was now impossible.

The man he wanted to see was always hereabouts. Birk was barely twenty years old, and his mate had not yet called to him. He was an adventurous sort, and instead of becoming an apprentice and mastering a trade or serving in the palace, he hired himself out for odd jobs of any sort. Birk would be able to find Kei, if the rogue had not wandered too far from The City.

He could wander himself, Ryn supposed. When he found life in the palace unbearable, when he found answering to a woman intolerable, when he could no longer bear being an accessory for a woman of power, he could don his kilt and leave The City for cycles at a time. It wouldn't be so very different from the days he spent in the hills hunting.

A man could not be expected to answer if he were not close enough to hear his Queen's call.

Maybe he could even follow Kei's example and travel far to claim other women. It was not the Anwyn way; it was not Ryn's way. But if he found life as the Queen's consort unbearable, perhaps he would be forced to turn his back on the Anwyn way.

His mind turned again and again to the legend that said the red-haired Queen would take a Caradon lover. No matter how he tried, he could not divert his thoughts away from that detested subject. What Anwyn male would allow such a thing to happen? Even in the name of peace, what self-respecting Anwyn would stand back and allow an enemy, or any other man, to take pleasure in his wife's body? No, not his wife. His mate, his woman, his Queen. Not his wife.

Ryn found Birk playing kiva-ball not far from the busy market, wasting his time kicking the small soft ball to his friends . . . most of whom were younger than the adventurer. When Ryn called his name, Birk gave the kiva-ball a mighty kick and loped easily to Ryn.

"I hear you returned with a red-haired queen tucked under your arm," the young man said irreverently.

Ryn was in no mood for banter. "She has requested a task of you."

Birk's eyes widened. "Me?"

"Kei Deverin of the Ancikyn Clan. Do you know him?"

"Yes."

"My lady Juliet wishes to meet with him."

Even Birk knew better than to ask why. No one asked "why" of a queen. They simply obeyed. "I will leave immediately in search of Kei."

"My lady Juliet thanks you, for your service and for your discretion."

Birk nodded, understanding that this mission was to be

a secretive one. Mission accepted, he gave Ryn a wicked smile. "What is she like, this new Queen of ours?"

"Beautiful," Ryn said. "Strong. Kind. Everything any man might want in a woman."

"Will you live in the palace? Are your rooms grand and wonderful?"

Ryn walked away without answering the young man's questions. Of course he could and should reside in the palace, near Juliet. There he would live his life as her consort, her paramour, a man who rushed to her bed when she called and departed when she was done with him.

If he found the demeaning role intolerable, he would break with Anwyn tradition and become a rogue, like Juliet's father.

SINCE THE EMPRESS SPENT HER NIGHTS IN THE EMperor's bed, she'd instructed that Isadora sleep in her old bed, at least for now. The room was too luxurious for Isadora's liking; the mattress too soft and the comforter too warm. She was accustomed to plainer, simpler things.

She would do as Empress Liane wished, at least for now. The health and well-being of the imperial mother and child were now Isadora's responsibility. She needed that— a purpose, a responsibility. The chore of protection might undo what the destruction had done. In time, perhaps her powers would grow strong again.

One day she'd be reunited with Sophie and Juliet and she'd leave this cursed palace forever, but for now it was good to have a purpose beyond survival.

Isadora had cast a simple protection spell around Empress Liane and her unborn son, and had taken to concocting a health potion for consumption each morning. The empress had protested at first. She was afraid of potions, and rightfully so. Isadora explained to her exactly what went into the brew. There was no magic in it, just herbs that would make the blood strong. To ease the mother-to-be's fears, Isadora had taken to drinking the stuff herself. The potion was safe. In fact, it was beneficial for the mother and the child, even though it tasted bitter.

Isadora stayed awake long after she should have gone to sleep, her mind taking her to places it should not go. The people of the small village who had suffered on her behalf, Juliet's uncertain fate, Sophie's whereabouts . . . so much to keep her mind active when she should be asleep. She had once been so in control of her life and now nothing was as it should be. Nothing.

She leaped from the bed and rushed to the window, unable to sleep with her mind spinning as it did every night of late. A thick carpet kept her bare feet from feeling the chill. Winter was fully here, and she felt that winter to her bones. At the window, she tossed back the curtains and stared out at a clear, black sky filled with brilliant stars. She wished upon every one of those stars. With all that had happened, she had much to wish for. Freedom, safety, word of her sisters.

But as always, she wished for what her heart most desired. Will. As she wished, she spoke the words of the spell that sometimes brought him to her and sometimes failed. She closed her hand into a tight fist, crumpling the curtain in her hand as she whispered the spell a second time. And a third. A tear slipped down her cold cheek.

"This has to stop."

At the sound of that deep, familiar voice, Isadora turned to see Will sitting on the side of her bed. Her husband looked more solid, more real, than he had since the day he'd died.

"You can't expect me to stop calling for you." She walked toward the bed, moving cautiously lest she disturb whatever forces had brought him to her. His short brown hair was neat and thick as it had always been; his clothes looked just as they had on that last day. They were a farmer's clothes, simply cut and sturdy and without adornment. Will had not been the most beautiful man in Shandley, but he had been . . . no, he *was* . . . handsome and robust and good-hearted. Isadora had never known that a strong man could be kind and loving, but he had shown her that it was possible.

"I can't come to you anymore, Izzy," he whispered. "I miss you, I wish I hadn't left you when I did. When I came to you in the beginning, I only wanted to comfort you. But I should've stayed away when you called. Your summonses are keeping me stuck between the land of the living and the land of the dead, and—"

Her heart caught in her throat. "I didn't mean to hurt you."

"You didn't."

Will patted the bed beside him, and Isadora cautiously, *very* cautiously, sat. The mattress dipped. He put his arm around her, and she felt the touch. It was almost as if he were real. The weight was slight, the warmth was muted. But she did feel him, in a shimmer of sensation.

"I did hurt you," she said softly. "I killed you."

"You did not."

"By loving you, by ignoring the curse, I caused your death."

"It was worth it, to know your love for a while," he responded.

"No, it wasn't," she whispered.

She wanted to lean against him as she had done in the past, but she knew he wasn't substantial enough to support her weight, and she was terrified that if she fell into him, he'd disappear.

"I have hurt other people." Tears filled her eyes as she confessed. "Some of them deserved what they got," she said angrily. "Others didn't." Those final two words were ripped from her throat, raw and low. "People died. I don't regret the two that deserved it, but the others . . . I don't think I'll ever get the weight of their suffering out of my soul. What I've done, it made my magic weak. Killing those men robbed me of all but my simplest gifts."

She felt his hand in her hair. She *felt* it, like a spring breeze in the midst of winter.

"Your gifts aren't gone, Izzy, they're sleeping while you decide."

"While I decide what?"

Invisible fingers trailed through her hair. "Light or dark. Good or evil."

"Protection or destruction," she whispered.

"You can't have both," Will said. "Your power will grow strong again, once you have decided."

"I don't want darkness," she said. "I never wanted darkness." And yet she knew it rested inside her, and always had. "How do I turn it back?"

"I want to be here to help you, Izzy. I want to protect you and support you and love you and tell you what to do, but I can't. It's time for both of us to move on."

Her heart hitched. "No. I don't want to move on, not without you."

"You can have such a wonderful life," he whispered.

"Not without you."

She could not imagine living the rest of her life without Will in it, but she did understand what he was trying to say to her. This was the last time she'd see him, in this life. He wasn't coming to her ever again. Not when she wished on a star, not when she cast a spell, not when she demanded that he return to her.

"I don't think I can live without you," she whispered.

"You can," he said. "Everything is going to get better for you, I promise."

"Better?" She laughed bitterly. "How?"

"I can't tell you what's to happen, Izzy. Life is a surprise."

Isadora scoffed aloud. She hated surprises. Her mother dying, Will dying, Sophie getting pregnant and running off with that damned rebel, she and Juliet being kidnapped, Juliet getting herself carried off by a wild man, being brought here . . . Tonight . . .

Will tipped her head back and up and kissed her, as he had done a thousand times when he'd been living. The kiss was faint, but it was warm and arousing and real. Oh, it felt so real. Isadora reached out and laid her hand on his chest, and she could feel him. In all the times she'd called him to her since his death, they'd never touched. Not once. Even now he wasn't solid, but there was energy beneath her fingertips, energy like lightning that shimmered in the air before a storm.

"All you have to do to find your magic and your happiness is to trust yourself," he said.

"I don't, not anymore."

"The girl I loved never doubted herself, not for a minute."

"The girl you loved is as dead as you are." Again, it was as if she felt him touching her, kissing her. "Is this a dream?" she whispered against his lips.

"Yes and no," he responded.

"I want it to be real."

"Then it is."

Isadora stood slowly and drew her nightgown over her head, tossing it aside so that she stood before her husband naked. He smiled at her, as he so often had. No other man had ever loved her; no other man ever would. She lay upon the bed that no longer seemed too fine and too soft. Instead it seemed perfect, for tonight. For this.

"Izzy, I can't . . ."

"I touched you," she argued. "I felt you beneath my hand and on my mouth. You're never coming back, I know that. But if I can just love you one more time." She waited. Will would either disappear, or he would lie beside her.

His lips brushed hers, faint, almost warm, filled with lightning. They shared soft, nibbling kisses, and a low heat that she had forgotten grew inside her. She had never thought to experience this again. It was desire and need. It was love.

A winter chill brushed against her flesh, reminding her that the kisses did not come from a mortal man. But there was heat here in this bed. It began inside her and spread, through her midsection, into her limbs, into the mouth that kissed so gently. Instinctively she arched against the warm energy that hovered above her.

She could not hold Will, so she grasped the fine sheet on the empress's bed and arched her back to bring him closer. She needed this, so much. Something beautiful, after years of knowing nothing but pain. Pleasure, to remind her that the world could still be a good place. Love, to prove to her that she did still have that emotion within her, to prove to her that what she'd felt when Will had been alive hadn't been a fantasy. She could see Will's shimmering shape, his face, his body. She had tossed her nightgown away but he remained the same, staunchly dressed in those clothes in which he had died.

"I want you to make love to me," she said softly.

"I can't give you what you want."

"You kissed me," she argued.

"But I am no longer a flesh-and-blood man."

"You feel . . . almost flesh and blood." She said the words, and yet she knew they were wrong. She did not experience the heaviness and the heat of her husband atop her. She did not taste his sweat and feel his muscle and swallow his laughter, because he had none.

But he was here. She felt Will's lips against hers, still. She felt the warmth of his hands on her body.

"I loved you so much," he whispered. "I'll miss you. Be careful, Izzy. Be happy."

"Don't . . ." Before she could say *go,* Will was gone and she lay alone and cold in a bed that was too big for one woman. Her bare body very quickly grew chilled, but that wasn't why she trembled to her bones.

JULIET MISSED RYN, BUT WAS HESITANT TO SEND FOR him again. He had not been pleased yesterday when she'd sent for him and tonight she had no excuse to summon him. He had surely already taken care of sending someone for her father.

Her father. She wondered so much what he looked like, if he knew of her existence, if he would be glad to learn that his union with Lucinda Fyne had led to the birth of a child. A daughter who would be Queen, at least for a while.

It was easy to let her mind wander over a late evening meal at this fine table. Queen Etaina was livelier than she had been when they'd first met. She was not only willing to step down from the throne and join her mate in death, she was looking forward to it.

Her sons, all eleven of them, sat at the long table. They ranged in age from perhaps fifty years to what looked to be no more than twenty-five. Etaina's eleven sons were pure Anwyn, the offspring of the Queen and an Anwyn father. Not the same father, Juliet's finely tuned senses told her. Nine were the children of Queen Etaina and her mate. Two had been fathered by other men, which went against everything Ryn had told her about the way of the Anwyn. Then again, she had already learned that everything was different where the Anwyn Queen was concerned.

All of the Queen's sons had wives, attractive women who wore the finest jewels and gowns and did not contribute anything at all to the conversation. There were an insane number of grandsons and even great-grandsons about the palace, many of them well into adulthood, some of them mere children. They did not sit at the table, not tonight on this special occasion.

These fine men made her wonder . . . if she and Ryn had children, would they all be sons? Would there be so many of them?

The conversation was primarily about tomorrow's ceremony that would make Juliet Queen, and the celebration that would come after. The festival would not take place immediately, but would begin a few weeks after the rites. It was quite a production, this welcoming of a new Queen.

While others planned the celebration of her coming, Juliet poked at a piece of rare meat that dominated her plate. She liked Sophie's chicken and dumplings better, and she would give her right arm for a piece of redberry pie. Of course, as Queen, she could command that the cooks in this palace learn to prepare the dishes she most enjoyed.

She lifted her head when she heard her name called. Everyone was looking at her. Staring. Waiting.

"I'm sorry," she said. "I allowed my mind to wander a bit." Had someone asked her a question?

Queen Etaina saved her. "Understandable, considering all that has happened to you of late. I just asked if you would like to meet the priestesses tonight or if you would prefer to wait until tomorrow morning, before the ceremony."

"There are priestesses?" Juliet asked.

Queen Etaina's youngest son Janys, who sat to Juliet's right, smiled and said, "Thirteen, all of them Anwyn brides who have been blessed by the Goddess Ranon."

"The Goddess Ranon," Juliet repeated.

"The fertility goddess," he explained, a puzzled light in his gold eyes. "Surely you are acquainted—"

"Juliet is acquainted with nothing of the Anwyn traditions, Janys," Etaina interrupted. "She has been cheated out of her rightful heritage by circumstances over which she had no control. A few weeks of intensive instruction and she will know all she needs to know. I expect you boys to see to her instruction, after I'm gone. Language, customs, history, religion. Even prophesies."

While a few of the Queen's sons looked into their laps and cleared their throats in what seemed to be embarrassment, they agreed to a man to instruct Juliet as was necessary. There were no tears or laments over Etaina's impending death. Not because they didn't love their mother and their Queen. They did, very much.

Watching the Queen's sons sitting beside their wives, Juliet longed for Ryn in a way that had nothing to do with the passion they'd shared. He was her friend, and without him she was lonely and lost.

15

Ryn watched Juliet approach the sacred stone. She was anxious and unsure, but also determined and accepting and curious. He knew her well enough to understand it was that curiosity that had gotten her into trouble over the years.

Everyone wanted to watch the coming of the new Queen, so the ceremony was held in the palace courtyard, where there was room for all to attend. The Heart of the Anwyn, the sacred stone that invigorated this mountain and its people with magic, had been placed on an altar at the center of the courtyard and was surrounded on all sides by armed palace guards. If Ryn were not mated to the new Queen, he would be one of those guards.

The morning sun was warm enough on Anwyn skin, but a light snow fell and the women of The City had dressed accordingly, in long woolen skirts and heavy cloaks. Juliet wore a sleeveless gown of shimmering gold that hugged her curves. Her hair fell in a riot of red curls over her shoulders and down her back. A few icy snowflakes nested in her hair and sparkled like tiny jewels. She wore no jewels or gold to detract from her simple beauty. As Queen she would be entitled to wear the royal jewels, but for now, while she was not yet quite Queen, her throat, ears, and fingers were bare.

She had insisted that Ryn stand near the front of the crowd, so that she might reach out to him for comfort if she needed it, and of course since she had insisted, he had obeyed. Her eyes, still as much brown as gold, turned to him time and time again, but he did not see or feel an extraordinary nervousness in her. Her gaze held his and he saw and felt the strength she was discovering within herself.

Tonight she would embrace the wolf. If anything scared her more than becoming Queen, it was the transformation that came with the acceptance of her place here. She feared the claws that would come from within. More than that, she feared the loss of control and the wildness the transformation would bring to her life. She did not yet know that the transformation would also bring joy, and freedom, and power unlike any she had ever known.

Queen Etaina followed Juliet. Ryn had never seen the old woman with such a sense of serenity about her. She was usually quite brusque, even angry. But this morning she exuded a warmth and joy that radiated from her, making her old face seem radiant.

It was no coincidence that this ceremony took place on the morning before the first full moon of this cycle. Beneath the full moon the old Queen would embrace the wild aspect of her Anwyn self one last time. Tonight—perhaps tomorrow morning as the sun rose—she would join her mate in death, as had wished to do for so long. Obligation had kept her alive as she'd awaited Juliet's arrival, but now her obligation was done. Her personal guards would bury her in the hills where she had run as wolf and ruled as Queen.

The stone upon the altar at the center of the courtyard

glowed, amber and brilliant. It grew brighter as Juliet approached, as if it sensed with hope and anxiety and excitement that a new Queen of unimaginable power had come. When she was almost upon it, the light of the stone began to throb as the Heart of the Anwyn beat in time with Juliet's heart.

Ryn did not watch the pulsing, powerful stone that contained the heart and power of his people. He kept his gaze on Juliet. She was magnificently beautiful, lovelier and more striking than he had imagined she could be when he'd taken her from the soldiers. There was a brightness and beauty about her that outshone all others. And he wished with all his heart and soul that she were not Queen. He wished that she was nothing more than his mate, his woman, his wife.

Words were spoken at the altar, by the elder of the thirteen priestesses and then by Queen Etaina. From the crowd there was not so much as a whisper. After all, to see a new Queen take her throne was a rare and sacred moment. When the high priestess nodded, Juliet raised her right hand and repeated the vow in a voice that was strong and tender, unwavering in its strength. Standing before her people, she took a vow to serve the Anwyn until another came to take her place. A vow to dedicate her life to the service of her people. A vow to rule with kindness, intelligence, and fierceness.

When the vow had been spoken in its entirety, Juliet laid her hand on the stone. The Heart glowed so brightly that some of the women in the crowd closed their eyes. The Anwyn did not look away or shield their eyes, but basked in the glorious golden light that flooded The City. The new Queen's delicate fingers did not quite cover the width and breadth of the precious stone, as it infused her with power.

And she infused it.

Juliet's body jerked, but she remained on her feet and her hand did not leave the stone. Her lips parted, but she said nothing. Snow continued to fall, light and sparkling, on the woman who discovered a new part of herself, who embraced an obligation to a people she did not yet know. The stone and Juliet were connected, their power melding as they fed one another and each grew strong.

The glow surrounding the stone and the woman dimmed, Juliet visibly relaxed, and the ceremony was done. The crowd remained silent, in awe of what they had seen here. Juliet turned her head and looked at Ryn the moment her hand left the stone. He could see the power in and all around her. The gown she wore swayed slightly as if a gentle wind caught the folds; her golden eyes glowed with power and vitality.

She was Queen.

LIANE SAT BACK AND WATCHED AS ISADORA PREPARED the tea the two of them had taken to drinking every morning. Something was wrong, but she couldn't quite put her finger on the problem. Isadora was paler than usual, and there was a tightness to her lips and a redness to her puffy eyes.

Something had upset the witch, and whatever it was had happened last night, sometime between supper and an early rising. No one had been in these quarters last night but Isadora; of that Liane was certain. She did trust the witch, to a certain extent, but she wasn't a foolishly trusting empress. A sentinel had been posted outside the door. No one had entered and Isadora had not left the room all night.

Unless she'd somehow found and used the hidden passageway that connected to the bedchamber.

"Are you ill?" Liane asked.

Isadora did not lift her head. "No, my lady."

"Did you sleep well last night?"

"I did not sleep at all," Isadora replied without emotion as she continued to stir.

"Why not?"

The witch pursed her lips and said nothing.

"I demand an answer."

Isadora poured the elixir she'd prepared into two small cups and walked toward Liane with one in each hand. "My husband dropped by for a visit." She held out both cups. Liane would choose one; Isadora would drink from the other.

"I thought you were a widow." Liane chose the cup made of green glass and left Isadora with the clear.

"I am." With that Isadora upended the glass cup and drank the vile but supposedly healthy potion in one swallow.

Liane followed suit, draining her glass quickly. It was easiest that way. "His spirit visited you? Is that why you're upset?"

"I am not upset because the spirit of my late husband paid me a visit last night," Isadora said as she took the empty glasses to a table, where Mahri quickly collected them and rushed from the room. The young girl was not fond of discussions which concerned magic, and she certainly didn't care to hear of spirits in the palace.

"Then what is it?" Liane asked sharply. Between Mahri and Ryona, she had enough of girlish emotions to deal with. Isadora was a woman stronger than Mahri and Ryona combined. Liane expected strength from her witch, not girlish tears and pouting.

"I am upset because he's not coming back."

Sebestyen was meeting with his priests this morning, and though Liane wanted to be there, she had complied when her husband had requested that she stay in her quarters on Level Five this morning. She would prefer to be with him, of course, but she trusted him enough to accede to his request and leave him to his work.

He trusted her enough to take her word that it was not dangerous to be alone with Isadora. She trusted her husband; he trusted her. It was a new and frightening concept.

"Sit with me," Liane commanded, indicating the chair at her side. Isadora sat and clasped her hands in her lap, and it was only then that Liane noticed how the woman trembled. "You loved him very much."

"I did," Isadora replied in a soft voice.

"You miss him."

Isadora's spine stiffened, as if she were drawing on her strength. "I do."

"Men are plentiful and much the same no matter where you go," Liane said confidently. "Choose another."

Isadora's head snapped up and she glared at Liane. At least there was something besides sadness in her dark eyes. Anger was better than sorrow. Stronger and deeper. "I have no wish to choose another."

"Stupid," Liane said beneath her breath, but loudly enough for Isadora to plainly hear.

"If the emperor died, would you blithely replace him?"

Liane's heart gave a small and unexpected leap. Fear? Of losing Sebestyen the way Isadora had lost her husband? "If I so desired."

"It is not so easy," Isadora said softly.

"I imagine not. But neither is it impossible."

Isadora shook her head gently.

"On Level Three there are a number of men trained in the ways of giving pleasure. Any one of them could make you forget a man long dead."

"I don't wish to forget," Isadora whispered.

"Then call them to you in the dark, close your eyes, and pretend the man who pleasures you is your husband."

Isadora looked at Liane, her eyes widening. "Such a thing is not possible."

"Of course it's possible. I've done it myself." Many

times. All before Sebestyen had made her his wife, of course. Before he'd become the only man who touched her; before she had admitted to herself that she loved him.

"I'd rather die."

Liane stood slowly. Her stomach was growing at an alarming rate, and she found it best to move slowly and carefully at all times. She had months yet to go before it would be time for this child to come into the world, and yet he grew larger every day. She had only just begun to worry about the practical problem of pushing this child from her body.

"Foolish," Liane said angrily. "I should send you to Level Three for proper training, whether you want it or not. A day with the Masters and you'll give up these romantic fantasies that hold you from the life you should be living."

"If any man lays a hand on me, it will be the last time he touches a woman."

It was a steadfast promise, a vow Isadora was capable of and likely to keep.

Liane turned to study Isadora, who leaped to her feet as she remembered that she should not remain seated while the empress stood. Such foolishness was not important to Liane. True power transcended such trivialities. She had true power now. Sebestyen listened to her, the ministers respected her, and even the priests no longer dared to insult her in the emperor's presence.

But she had not yet found a way to do away with Nelyk. As empress she was constantly surrounded by sentinels and servants, and she no longer had the luxury of time alone. Time to plan, to execute.

"Bors accused you of murder," Liane said simply.

Isadora flinched, but she did not turn her head and look away.

"Was the accusation just?"

"Yes," the witch answered softly.

"I have killed my share of men who deserved death," Liane confessed. "It isn't pleasant, but in some instances there is no other way."

Isadora glanced toward the window, as if she wished to flee from this conversation by any means available.

"There is a man," Liane said in a lowered voice as she walked toward Isadora. "He has abused his position of power and made a number of young girls suffer at his hand. He cloaks himself in the garments of a priest, and does things no godly man would ever do."

Isadora was already shaking her head. "I will not kill again, if that is what you're asking of me."

"I am your empress," Liane said without heat.

"Punish me if you must, kill me, but I won't do murder again."

Liane cocked her head and studied Isadora's pale face. "You have a great strength about you. Do you not believe it is the duty of those who are strong to protect the weak?"

She flinched a little. "I suppose."

"This man, this priest, he seduced a young girl. Perhaps he even raped her. I could never get her to tell me exactly what happened."

"Perhaps this girl of yours is guilty of poor judgment, and the priest is guilty of nothing more than breaking his vows of chastity."

"This girl of mine, as you call her, might be guilty of many things herself, but that does not mean the priest is innocent. When he found out she was carrying his child, he threw her into a pit in the ground where her child was born amongst filth and drug addicts and death. Level Thirteen," she said. "Perhaps you have heard the place mentioned in fearful whispers."

The witch lifted her head and glared at her empress.

"It was not the first time he had done such a thing," Liane added.

Isadora continued to stare, and Liane allowed her a few moments to contemplate the request. Surely the witch knew, as she did, that sometimes justice wasn't an easy thing. The world needed strong men . . . and women . . . to mete out that justice.

"I don't suppose it matters what I do with what's left of this life," Isadora said passively. "What is it that you wish me to do, my lady?"

HER BODY SANG WITH POWER, AND INSTEAD OF BEING afraid, Juliet was invigorated. She had not been alive until she'd taken the vow that made her fully Anwyn. She had not known what joy was until she'd embraced that once-hidden part of herself.

She looked at Ryn and smiled, but his face remained solemn. No wonder he had been angry when she'd offered to take the wolf from him. Colors were brighter; scents from the gardens of The City were sweeter; she felt more alive than ever before. Ryn's scent teased her, mingled in with all the rest and calling to her in a primal way. She knew that scent to the depths of her soul. He was hers. He had been right all along. She was connected to the earth; she was an integral part of it. She was an animal, just as he was, and it was a good and powerful thing to be.

And love . . . There was so much love in the world, and she felt it within her as she looked at Ryn. No, she did not love him, not yet, but she would.

She was tempted to release her powers, to undo the detachment Ryn had taught her. If she did so, she would finally know the full depths of her abilities. In the past, she had been able to touch people and see into their minds and hearts. Sometimes she'd been able to concentrate on her sisters and know they were safe, or not safe. All her life, she'd had very little control over her gift. It was sure to be enhanced now, to a new and perhaps even frightening level. Could she handle such powers? Or would they be the end of her, as she had often suspected they would be? She didn't want to find out here and now, in front of all these people.

But neither did she want to be alone. While she stood in the palace courtyard surrounded by people who loved and feared her, Juliet saw only Ryn. She lifted her hand, palm upward, inviting him to join her.

He had been right all along; she knew that now. They were meant to be together. It was fated and there was no escaping what was meant to be. She needed no powers beyond her Anwyn senses to know that. Why had she fought him for so long? And she had fought him, risking death to escape from the truth of who she was.

After a moment's hesitation, Ryn walked toward her and took the hand she offered. Everyone watched, and so she did not speak to him of what she had discovered. He knew; he had always known. When they reached her chambers, she would tell him that he'd been right all along.

They had made love on hard ground and standing against cold rock and with no bed but a bearskin. Today she would take him into her soft bed, and after he made love to her, she'd tell him that she accepted his offer. She would be his mate, and for a while she would be Queen as well. Not forever, though. She would find a way to put someone else in power while maintaining the peace of the Anwyn.

She wanted to live in the house Ryn had built for her and fill it with children, and she wanted to run with him when the wolf came upon them both.

He said nothing as they walked into the palace. Guards followed along behind them at a distance. Juliet could not wipe the smile from her face. Why had she been afraid of this? She was where she was meant to be, with the man she was meant to call her own.

The walk from the courtyard to her quarters was a long one. The palace was massive and somewhat of a maze, but she had already learned to navigate the hallways as if she'd lived here all her life. It was home, in a way the Fyne cabin had never been. This palace, this mountain, they were in her blood.

Everyone—she and Ryn, the soldiers who followed— remained silent as they made their way through the maze of stone hallways. Eventually she would take up residence in the Queen's apartment on the third floor, but for now Queen Etaina still called those rooms home. Juliet was in no rush to claim the royal apartment. There would be time enough for that in the days and weeks to come.

She and Ryn stepped into her chamber, and with a wave of her hand she dismissed the soldiers who had escorted her from the courtyard. They would remain close by, she knew, standing guard in the hallway and beyond.

But inside this room, she and Ryn were alone.

She dropped his hand and spun around, coming to a halt facing him, her head tilted back so she could look into his face. "I feel wonderful."

"The Queen feels the rush of the Heart in a way no other Anwyn ever can." He did not smile at her. She missed his smile most of all.

Juliet stepped forward and lifted her hand to touch Ryn's face. "I can share it with you," she whispered. "It's wonderful, bright and heady and exhilarating." Since they were alone, she reached inside herself and loosened the cord that connected her to him. Just that one deeply seated tendril that was more important than all the rest.

As soon as the gates were opened between them, she was sorry she had invited him in. Ryn did not want to be here. He did not want her to touch him; he did not wish to share her newly discovered joy. Her hand dropped, and her smile faded. "You're angry."

"It would be improper of me to be angry, My Queen."

"Juliet," she corrected.

"My Queen Juliet."

Ryn had wanted her in days past, and in truth he still did want her . . . though he fought his desire mightily. Juliet went up on her toes and kissed him, and he did kiss her back. But the kiss was without the passion she had come to expect from him. She knew she could command Ryn to kiss her more thoroughly, and he would. She could command him to make love to her, and he would do his duty well.

While they were kissing, he blocked her as he had on that first day. He threw up that barrier between them. Juliet now had the power to push her way past the barrier, she knew. But she didn't.

"You were right, you know," she said as she took her mouth from his and stepped away. "We are meant to be together."

"Yes."

"You don't sound very happy about that."

He didn't respond, and Juliet made her first command of her mate. "Ryn, I insist that you tell me the truth. What's changed since we came here?"

"You," he said gently. "You have changed. The plans I made for us, the plans I have been making for years, have changed. They changed the moment I learned that you were Anwyn. I never planned to live in this place, surrounded by guards and soldiers, second to the duties of a Queen. I wanted a simpler life."

She could see too much into him, now that she had discovered her full power. It was not even necessary to touch him, though she knew if she did, she'd be inundated with a flood of his emotions. "What you really want is a simpler *wife*."

"Yes," he answered sharply.

"And the Queen doesn't marry," she said.

"It is not the way of the Anwyn."

Juliet turned her back on Ryn, walked to the window, and looked out over The City. Her city. It was magnificent. More magnificent than she had ever imagined a place could be. The City stretched deep into the mountain. It spread across this valley, each stone of every house carved to perfection. And her people . . . her people didn't only live here in this beautiful place. They lived beyond the walls, in simple homes and caves beyond The City.

They would come, now that she had taken her throne. Through their dreams and their Anwyn senses, they would know that a new Queen had arrived in The City. They would want to see her, speak to her. Touch her.

Ryn did not want to touch her; not now.

"You may go," she said, not turning to look at her mate. Her abductor. Her husband. He left so quietly, if she did not have Anwyn ears, she would not have heard the door open and close.

Ryn WALKED QUICKLY THROUGH THE WIDE PALACE hallways, ignoring the soldiers who waited at every turn. He did not know these guards who worked here in the residential section of the palace, and they paid him little mind. As the Queen's consort, he was not considered a threat. As the Queen's consort, he was not considered to be of any importance at all.

It was foolish to walk away from the woman he desperately wanted, especially when she'd finally decided that she wanted him just as much. But she was not the woman he'd captured; she was not the woman he'd dreamed of. She was more.

His choices were limited, but he did have a choice. He could be her lover—or he could leave The City behind to live in the hills, a rogue who had no home, who lived only for the wolf. Tonight Juliet would find the wolf within herself. It would be painful at first, but when the transformation was done, she would know why he'd refused even to consider her offered cure that would rob him of the wolf.

It would likely be easier to live in the hills, embracing the life of the wolf, than to stay here under the rule of a woman.

But he would not leave her to the mercy of strangers just yet. Tonight, when she went through her first transformation, he would be with her. It was true that Juliet had many guards and servants to protect her, but he was her mate and it was his duty to be with her as she came to understand who and what she was.

The palace was large, with echoing walls and high ceilings. For many years he had been assigned to guard the Heart of the Anwyn, and other treasures. He had never ventured into this part of the palace. In his confusion and anger, Ryn took a wrong turn. Or two. He found himself alone in a narrow hallway free of soldiers. There were either personal offices or lesser bedchambers along this corridor that stretched into the mountain itself.

He did not share Juliet's newly enhanced powers, but she had not been closed to him. When she'd taken the vow that made her Queen and Anwyn, she had been overwhelmed and her fear of the unknown had left her for a time. Now that she was alone, the fear had returned. She was not afraid of the duties and wonders that awaited her, but she was afraid of facing them alone.

Ryn turned about sharply. Even though this corridor was unfamiliar to him, he could find his way to Juliet—no matter how far apart they happened to be.

A COMPANY OF GUARDS TRAVELED WITH JULIET AND RYN as they walked beyond the walls of The City. As the sun dipped toward the horizon, many Anwyn—all males, but for Juliet and the old Queen—left their homes and their families and headed into the hills.

Hills, indeed. These were mountains, steep and rocky and cold. But in the distance a green forest waited, inviting and untamed. Juliet's eyes were turned toward that forest, and so were Ryn's.

Ryn had not entirely explained why he'd returned to her this morning, but she knew. He felt responsible for her. There was no love in his heart, no affection that led him to her. She was a responsibility for him, just as The City and the Anwyn had become a responsibility for her.

The guards kept a distance from their new Queen, but they surrounded her on all sides. Instead of wearing their usual blue uniforms, they were dressed as Ryn had been when he'd found her, in short leather kilts that could be quickly and easily shed. They carried spears, with which they would protect her if necessary.

Juliet had donned the shift her maids had presented to her this afternoon. It was more substantial than the male's clothing, but it was much simpler than the blue and gold gowns that had been stored in her apartments in the palace. Made of a soft animal skin, it fit her loosely and was fastened down the front with a small number of large buttons. If she did not wish to unfasten the buttons, the neckline was loose enough that she need only whip the frock over her head.

As sundown approached, she reached out and took Ryn's hand. He didn't want the touch, but he didn't push her away. She'd opened herself to him this afternoon, and she had not yet closed off that connection. Information, knowledge, feelings . . . not from Ryn, but from others around her . . . they had been trickling in all day, at a rate that did not frighten or alarm her.

"Will it hurt?" she asked softly.

"Yes," Ryn replied, his voice as low as hers. "More the first time, because you don't know what to expect."

She shuddered.

"It will be over quickly," he assured her.

"Will you stay with me?"

"If you wish."

"I do." She knew Ryn could not refuse her anything. Her pride directed her to tell him to do as he wished tonight, that she had her guards to comfort her and acquaint her with the ways of the wolf. But she didn't. She wanted Ryn with her, at least for tonight. Tomorrow night he could run free without her at his side, if that's what he desired. For tonight, she needed him beside her.

They climbed downward, arriving at a flat expanse of rock that overlooked a valley unlike any other. Green trees awaited below, and from this vantage point she watched as the Anwyn poured into the forest.

But her guards stopped here. They laid their weapons aside, and some of them began to disrobe. The sun was almost gone. Would the change begin the moment the last sliver of the sun disappeared? Or would they have to wait here in the dark for the proper moment?

"Why do I not know what is to come?" she asked as Ryn laid his hands on her shoulders. "So much knowledge dances in my head, and I see so clearly now. But when I look ahead to tonight, I don't know what's going to happen to me."

"You have told me many times that you do not often see your own future."

"It has always been that way, but I'm stronger now than I have ever been, and I thought maybe that had changed."

The last sliver of the sun disappeared. The sky was not yet dark, but the full moon was out and would soon shine down on them all. As the night came upon them, Ryn reached down and unfastened one button for her. He and the guards had already shed their kilts, and she sensed and saw a restlessness in many of the men who had vowed to protect her. She felt that restlessness within herself.

"Why are you angry with me?" she whispered, so no one else could hear.

"I cannot be angry with you," Ryn replied stoically.

"If I wish, I can reach into your heart and see the truth for myself, but I don't want to do that. I need you to tell me what I can do to make things right."

Something in Ryn changed subtly. She saw it in the softening of his lips, in the new life springing to his gold eyes. Even with all the guards around them, standing on this ledge while the light of day faded was more like the weeks they'd spent on the road. Here they did not have the rules of the palace between them. Here they could be as they once were.

"Have you heard the legend of the red-haired Queen?" he asked.

"The Queen who will bring peace to the Anwyn. I did hear some whispers, though no one has been quick to tell me anything."

"The red-haired Queen with the gift of sight will bring that peace by taking a Caradon lover," Ryn said in a low voice.

"No," Juliet whispered. She could not imagine ever taking another man into her bed or her body. Ryn was her husband as truly as if they'd taken vows in a church in Shandley, conventional and ordinary and enduring. She could not imagine ever allowing another man to touch her. "I would never . . ." Her breath caught in her throat as a new thought came to her. What if she killed Ryn? What if the curse took him from her the way it had taken Willym from Isadora, and she found herself alone? All alone, for years and years . . .

"It's time," Ryn said, changing the uncomfortable subject. "The change will be easier if you do not have to fight your way past clothes that bind."

Juliet unfastened the rest of the buttons herself, and let the leather frock drop to the rocky ground. Her fingers curled and uncurled; the full moon overhead seemed to dip down and touch her bare flesh. Her heartrate increased until it was racing, pounding against her bare chest and calling to the wolf that was coming . . . coming . . . here.

A sharp stab of pain shot through her entire body, and she screamed. The agony shot through her arms, her legs, into her heart, and the scream faded and changed to a low growl that rumbled in her throat. She turned to face Ryn.

The metamorphosis she felt showed on Ryn's face, in the shifting muscles and the golden hair that sprang up all over his body. Muscles realigned and reshaped beneath her skin; red hair grew on her own smooth skin. She fell to her knees, unable to control the transformation. It hurt. She felt as if her body was being torn apart. This was the pain of her dream, the pain she had feared all her life.

She lifted one hand, and before her eyes that hand changed into a large paw, and claws ripped through her skin. Her claws.

The pain stopped as suddenly as it had begun, and Juliet turned her gaze to Ryn. Ryn the wolf, as she was now Juliet the wolf. Her heart continued to race, but everything had changed. Her connection to the earth and the people in it was deeper and more real than it had been before. Smells were sweeter, sounds were sharper, colors had faded to shades of gray. More than all that, the power of muscles she had endured agony to discover called to her. The world awaited her, and she wanted only one thing.

Her eyes locked to Ryn's. *Run with me.*

16

PROTECTION AND DESTRUCTION. IN THE PAST ISADORA had most often called upon her gift for protection, but those who were wary of her had seen the destruction all along. Had Will seen it in her? Was that why he wasn't coming back? In order to restore her magic, she had to devote herself to protection. She'd done just that, with the empress and her unborn child, but what of the task Empress Liane had given her? Would ridding the world of a degenerate priest who had harmed innocents turn her toward the light again, or awaken the dark?

Nothing was as it had once been, and she wondered if it would ever be so again. With every day that passed without word of Juliet, Isadora began to fear that she would live the rest of her life alone. Sophie had her own family, Juliet had been taken—ripped away—in the arms of a monster. Will was gone. She had never even imagined that *alone* was the most frightening word in any language.

Isadora silently navigated the stark hallways of Level

Two. Empress Liane had secreted the rescued girl Ryona and her child out of the palace this afternoon, and now it was Isadora's job to dispatch the priest who had abused the girl. If she was caught here, she would be punished. She would probably be killed. The empress would not save her, and Isadora would not ask to be saved.

Father Nelyk's bedchamber was near the end of the long hallway. At this time of night the hall and the rooms attached to it were silent. The priests slept, as did most of the palace. A few widely scattered bowls of flame burned softly on plain wooden tables along the corridor. The flames lit her way.

Isadora hesitated with her hand on the doorknob. The empress had told her the door would be not be bolted. The foolish priests believed themselves to be safe here. It was true that for anyone outside the palace to reach this room would be near impossible. But Empress Liane had given Isadora directions that had taken her from a hidden stairway on Level Three to a storage room on Level Two.

The door swung open without so much as a squeak. Moonlight shone through an uncovered window, illuminating the man who slept on a massive and soft bed in the center of the room. Even with the door closed behind her and the light from the hallway gone, she could see Father Nelyk well enough.

While the corridor and the dining hall she had passed were plain to the point of austere, this room was as luxurious as the empress's bedchamber. Tapestries covered the walls; gold candlesticks and ornate bowls for oil and flame sat upon finely polished tables. There were a number of chairs, all of them fat and wide and soft. A crimson canopy covered the bed where the priest slept.

Nelyk opened his eyes as she sat on the edge of the bed, and oddly enough he was not at all surprised. "I did not ask for companionship on this night," he said in a sleepy voice.

Since the moonlight shone on her blue frock, he obviously thought she had come to him from Level Three. All the concubines wore blue.

She pulled the thick coverlet back to expose his bare chest, and laid her hand over his heart. The priest slept naked.

"You're new," he said. "Did Rosana send you?"

Rosana. Isadora filed that name away. Liane would want to know who had been sending untrained girls to him. "Yes, I'm very new."

He placed his hand over hers. "Let me light a candle. I wish to see you."

"Let me." Isadora turned her gaze to the bedside table and whispered, *"Seana ildicio."* Two candles and one small bowl of oil leapt to life, illuminating her and the man on the bed. He was younger than she'd expected, and would even be handsome if she didn't know what he had done.

"You're the witch," he said in alarm as he ripped his hand from hers and tried to sit up.

"One word, and you're dead," she whispered as she pressed him back down into his soft mattress. "Call for help or fight me in any way, and you'll meet your maker before your next heartbeat."

He lay beneath her hand, unmoving. "I can be a friend to you, if you give me the chance," he promised, with the ease of a man who is accustomed to lying and charming to get what he wanted.

"How?"

"I can get you out of here. Tonight."

He did not know that she had nowhere to go, even if she did escape. She didn't know where either of her sisters were, or if they even still lived. She no longer trusted her heart's insistence that they lived. Empress Liane and her baby were her only obligations in this world, and Isadora had committed herself to them, at least for now.

"Perhaps I will allow you to save me," she said, "but first I would like to know if what I heard of you is true."

"What did you hear?"

"I heard that in spite of your vow of chastity, you often have women come to this very nice room. If you lie," she added. "I will know."

"I could deny your accusations," he said easily. "But since I assumed aloud that you had been sent here by Rosana, it would be pointless. Do you find me appealing? Is that why you're here?" His voice was touched with a hope she would soon dash.

"You prefer the new girls," Isadora said. "The untrained ones."

"A priest cannot lie with a well-used harlot," he explained. "It wouldn't be appropriate."

Isadora's hand remained steady over his heart. "Is it appropriate to throw young girls who carry your children into a hole in the ground to die?"

Nelyk started to deny the accusation, and then thought better of it. Perhaps he really did believe that she would know a lie when she heard it. "A priest can't have children," he explained. "I would be dismissed from my post, and—"

"And you'd have to leave all this behind," Isadora finished.

"Yes," he whispered.

She pressed her hand more firmly against his chest.

"I can offer you riches and power," he said, for the first time sounding desperate. "Anything you want."

"Anything." She leaned toward him, and she saw the light of hope in his eyes. He really thought he might escape unpunished. "Can you turn back time?"

JULIET SLEPT WELL INTO THE AFTERNOON, EXHAUSTED by her first night as the wolf. Not any wolf, but Queen of the Anwyn. Queen of the wolves that ruled these mountains. Ryn watched her closely, taking in every scent, every sight, as if it would be his last. Her bed was a large bearskin. Not the one she had slept upon during their journey, but one much like it. Others slept on hard rock or dead leaves, but not the Queen.

One of her guards had collected their clothing and placed it close by, but most of the soldiers slept. They would rest in shifts, taking turns keeping watch over Juliet. Ryn often didn't sleep at all on the days and nights of the wolf, and he would not sleep during these three days. The soldiers were bound by duty to protect her. He was bound by blood.

Juliet turned often, murmuring softly as she dreamed. She did not dream of him, not today. Instead her mind relived running through the forest, discovering her new strength, embracing the ecstasy of the wolf in moonlight.

"You should sleep," a familiar voice said.

Ryn, who sat beside Juliet's bed, turned to watch his brother approach. "Sleep will wait."

Denton, who had their mother's dark coloring instead of the fairness of the other brothers, smiled widely. "You will make my job unnecessary, I fear." The youngest of the Ditteri brothers had been a guard in the palace for three years, joining his brother Ryn in that noble duty. This morning he had begun his shift as one of the guardians of the Queen. He looked at Juliet with a mixture of pride and admiration. "Serving her will be much more enjoyable than attending Queen Etaina."

Ryn covered Juliet as best he could by turning the animal skin she slept upon over much of her body.

"I meant no disrespect," Denton said as he dropped to his haunches a short distance away. Like Ryn and the other soldiers on duty, he wore a leather kilt that offered freedom of movement.

"I know," Ryn replied. "The new Queen has not yet become accustomed to our ways. She maintains some unnecessary humility and would not like to learn that men she does not know have seen her sleeping and unclothed."

"How else can we soldiers protect her when the moon is full?" Denton argued.

Most of the soldiers were married and unerringly faithful to their mates, and to see the Queen bare, between the time of wolf and the time of woman, was a natural and inconsequential part of their duties. Denton and a few others were as yet unmated, but they knew the women who were meant to be theirs would soon call to them, and again . . . Juliet's nakedness was as natural as their own.

So why did he wish to hide her from all others? Calum would say he was suffering from the human failing of jealousy.

Ryn looked to his little brother, who was a fine and capable man in his own right. "You must promise to protect her when I am not here."

"Why would you not be—"

"Promise."

"Of course," Denton replied in a low voice. "It is my duty as a soldier."

"And as a brother," Ryn added.

Denton nodded, and twisted strands of dark hair fell across his face.

When Juliet began to stir, Denton stood and walked away, and like the other soldiers, he remained at a respectable distance.

Juliet sat up, tossed aside the bearskin, and stretched her arms over her head. Like him, her long hair was tangled and wild, but she seemed not to notice, or to care. Even her nakedness did not alarm her. She smiled at him, a bright, extraordinary smile. And he responded by making sure the barrier between them remained intact.

"I am so sorry I ever suggested that I take the wolf from you."

He nodded, understanding.

"Last night was . . ." She wrapped her arms around herself and looked to the clear blue sky. "Unlike anything I had ever imagined. When I ran, I felt like I was flying. The very air trembled and made way for us."

"You make a fine wolf," he said.

She cocked her head to one side and looked at him with golden eyes he was not yet accustomed to. They were the true and brilliant gold of a Queen, and they saw too much, barrier or no barrier. "I should rise and dress and eat, I suppose, but I really just want to sleep awhile longer."

"You may do as you wish."

"Would you lie down with me? Just lie beside me," she added quickly. "Maybe put your arms around me."

He made a reluctant move toward her, but did not say a word.

"It's not a command, Ryn," she said as he moved toward her. "It's a request."

Not that it mattered. Her word was law, and he could not refuse her. But that wasn't why he lay down and wrapped his arms around her. He wanted to hold her, here in the forest where he could almost forget that her guardians waited so close by.

She snuggled against him. "Sleep with me, Ryn," she said warmly. "You look tired."

"I'm not—"

"Sleep with me," she said again. "We are safe here. No one will bother us, not today and not tomorrow. For this moment in time, all is well." She closed her eyes and drifted toward sleep again. "All is well, *vanir.*"

Vanir. It was everything he hoped for and would never have. But for now . . . maybe Juliet was right and all was well, for the moment.

After Juliet had fallen slack against him, Ryn closed his own eyes and felt sleep rushing upon him. He protected her body with his, and breathed in her scent as only a mate could. "Dream well, *vidara*," he said in a voice so low no other could hear. "I won't leave you." Not today.

LIANE HAD COME TO ENJOY HER VISITS WITH ISADORA. She had always known that she and Sophie's sister had much in common, but she had never expected the woman to become a friend. The Empress of Columbyana could not afford to have friends.

This afternoon, she sat in her sitting room with Mahri and Isadora close by. Sebestyen was busy with the priests, who were all atwitter over the disappearance of Father Nelyk. Everyone was in shock that such a dedicated man could've deserted his post, and some of them suspected he might've met with foul play—though how that was possible had not yet been discerned.

Liane dismissed Mahri with a list of insignificant chores, and called Isadora to sit beside her. From the looks of the witch, she hadn't slept at all last night. Gadhra would arrive soon, and together the two witches would bless this child Liane carried. Maybe they would tell her that she carried a daughter, not a son, and she would be able to keep this child for herself. For herself and for Sebestyen. She did not care about producing an heir and emperor. She cared only about giving birth to a healthy child.

"Your work is excellent," Liane said softly.

"Thank you, my lady." It seemed that the poor girl was going to choke on her words.

"You probably saved countless innocent lives last night," Liane reminded the witch.

"I hope that is true."

Liane sat back and watched a restless Isadora. "What did you do with him?"

Isadora did not respond.

"You can tell me what happened. Surely you'd like to share the details with someone, and as no one but I knows you did the deed, I am the logical recipient of such details."

Again, the witch remained silent.

Liane thought of pushing, even of ordering compliance, but in the end she did neither. There had been a time when Sebestyen had insisted on details from her, and she had been loath to give them. She'd preferred to spin a tale rather than to relive her unpleasant but necessary work. She would not put Isadora in that position. "Now and again, there are others in the palace who need to be dispatched, for one reason or another."

Isadora lifted her head to look Liane in the eye. "I am not a murderer," she said gently.

"Actually, you are," Liane said without kindness. "Two times, that I am aware of. Three, if Nelyk's body surfaces."

"I'm not—"

Liane silenced Isadora with a lifted hand. "I wish for you to remain my caretaker, at least until the baby is born. But in addition to your duties you could handle other chores from time to time." She smiled. "We are in need of a palace assassin, and I can think of no one better suited to the position."

JULIET WOKE, AS SHE HAD FOR THE PAST THREE AFTERnoons, on a soft bearskin bed with Ryn at her side. He slept beside her and she knew that her guardians were not far away. Some of them rested while others kept watch. She had never been unguarded during these three days and nights, not for even one moment.

Ryn had been right all along, it seemed. The wolf was a

vital and exciting part of herself, and of him. She had never run so fast or felt so strong, and even though it would be weeks before the change came to her again, she felt the power of the wolf waiting inside her, surging even as it slept.

She reached out her hand and touched Ryn's shoulder, and he stirred but did not awake. He had remained with her for these three days, as man and as wolf. As her mate and her friend. He was still angry about their circumstances, but she sensed that the anger had faded somewhat. He could love her, and maybe one day he would.

She already loved him, to the depths of her soul. Had she fallen in love with the wolf before the man? Had she fallen in love, at least a little, on that night when he'd kept her warm and she'd comforted herself with the feel of his fur in her hands?

His eyes drifted open and he rolled toward her. Golden eyes studied her, striking and powerful, and made her breath and her heart catch and lurch. Did her eyes look like this to Ryn? Did they affect him in the same way? Catching a glimpse of herself in a mirror was still a shock. Her eyes were entirely gold now, as were all Anwyn eyes. They were golden like the stone that was the Heart of the Anwyn.

"I suppose we must go home today," she said softly.

"We will return to The City," Ryn said. He still did not think of the palace as home. She was afraid he never would.

She shifted toward Ryn slightly, tipping her face up as if for a kiss. She knew he desired her, and yet he had withdrawn as if they were strangers, not lovers. There was a coolness about him, a stone wall she could not penetrate.

Before she could kiss him, he rolled away. "I hear the others stirring. You should dress."

He handed her the leather frock and she quickly pulled it on. It was silly, perhaps, to feel any modesty when these men had not only seen her naked, but had seen her transform from an unclothed woman into a she-wolf. But as a woman, she did still have some modesty, and she was glad to be dressed as the others came awake. Like Ryn, they had little modesty themselves. Those who had been sleeping took their time coming awake and donning their own clothes.

Ryn's own brother was among those men. He had not been with her on that first night. The faces of the guardians had changed during these three days, so that each man might have at least one night to run without the responsibility of watching over the Queen.

They began to walk toward home, and Juliet had only to train her gaze beyond her immediate area to see that other scantily clad men also walked toward The City. Some of them were tired; others were invigorated. All of them embraced the wolf as Juliet had done.

She tried, more than once, to take Ryn's hand in hers, but he always managed to move away very subtly before she could catch and hold his hand. There were moments when he was completely closed to her, and others when the barrier slipped and she could read his every thought. She did not need to touch him to connect in this small way. One thought came through very clearly.

Ryn did not intend to stay. He did not intend to be the Queen's consort, useless and insignificant, secondary and powerless. As soon as he felt that she was well settled into her position of Queen, he was going to leave. He was going to walk away from The City, his family, and his home. More importantly, he was going to walk away from her.

They entered a city reinvigorated by the returning Anwyn. As Juliet walked down the street in her simple garb, surrounded by half-dressed soldiers and her reluctant mate, people stopped to bow. They smiled at her; they whispered greetings. Juliet's mind was on other things—most specifically Ryn. He was going to get her safely to the palace and then he was going to run. Into the hills, away from her and this life he did not want.

When they reached the palace steps, Ryn stopped. Juliet felt him withdraw moments before he stopped walking. She stopped, too, and turned to face him. She did not want to issue commands, but even more, she did not want him to leave. She hadn't had a chance to tell him how she felt.

"You said you are bound to do anything I ask."

"Yes," he answered in a low voice.

Juliet took a deep breath and lifted her chin. She was Queen; she was Anwyn. And in that moment she felt the full power of her true self.

"Don't go."

LIANE WAS WAITING FOR SEBESTYEN WHEN HE CAME TO their bedchamber, even though it was late. He'd been meeting with his new Minister of Defense, General Hansh Maslin. Liane didn't care for General Maslin. He was pompous, like some of the elder priests, and he always looked at his empress as if he disdained her. At least she had never slept with him during her years as a concubine.

Sebestyen was surprised to find his wife awake, but he smiled at her. When she did not smile back, he came to the bed and sat beside her.

"What's wrong?"

Tears she did not want welled up in her eyes. She would not be a weakling about this; she would not cry. "Isadora and Gadhra examined me this afternoon. They laid me out on a table and said things I don't understand and swung an odd pendulum over my stomach."

"If they've scared you, I will kill them both," Sebestyen said, quite seriously.

"No." She laid her hand over his. "It's just . . . something's not quite right, they said. I am in danger of delivering the child too soon."

She saw the fear she felt in Sebestyen's eyes. They could not lose this baby. There would never be another, not for either of them.

"I am to have no more sex until after the baby is born," she said, lifting her chin slightly so she would appear to be strong. "I am to remain in bed for the majority of each and every day, though I'm allowed a short walk in the morning. No excitement, Isadora said," Liane added in a lowered voice.

"Is that all?" Sebestyen leaned forward and kissed her on the forehead.

"Is that all?" Liane sat up quickly. "Four months, Sebestyen. Four months! You can't go four days without . . ." She stopped speaking. He was amused with her. Outwardly and greatly amused. "I can see to your needs in other ways," she suggested. "If we are cautious and I don't overexert myself and—"

"Don't be ridiculous."

Of course, such a plan did not suit him. Caution and a lack of exertion would certainly not satisfy him. "Fine. Just be discreet," she said. "You have embarrassed me enough for one lifetime. I don't want to see or hear any of the women from Level Three. It will be easy enough to make arrangements for a separate bedchamber to be outfitted either here or on Level Three for your—"

Sebestyen silenced her with a kiss on the mouth. It was a deep kiss, with slightly parted lips and unexpected warmth and a very slight flicker of his tongue. There had been a time when he had not kissed her at all. She had not known how much she would love such a kiss . . .

He pulled away from her slowly. "There will be no separate bedchamber," he said, his eyes narrowing.

She shook off the teasing warmth of his kiss. "If you expect me to waddle down to Level Five and take up residence there like an obedient empress . . ."

"I do not expect you to waddle anywhere," Sebestyen said, resting his hand over her swollen belly. She was too large for five months, she knew that. Isadora had already expressed concern over the matter.

Her husband lay down beside her, his hand resting over their child, his breath against her hair. "There will be no waddling, no separate chamber, no women from Level Three taking your place in my bed. If we must suffer, we will suffer together."

"Do not tease me, Sebestyen," she said sharply.

"Trust me, I will not ever tease you about going four months without sex. It isn't at all funny."

Liane laughed. A few moments ago she'd thought laughter to be impossible, but here she was, resting her hand over Sebestyen's and laughing out loud.

"I thought we agreed it wasn't funny," Sebestyen said dryly.

Liane snuggled against her husband. "I love you," she said impulsively, the words leaving her mouth without thought.

For a moment the bedchamber was ominously silent, and Liane wished she could take the words back. Sebestyen would see them as weakness, and he detested weakness. And then he said, "I suppose I must love you, too, to offer four months of celibacy."

"Five," Liane whispered. "There's a period of weeks after the birth . . ."

"Please, no more."

Liane was tired, so she closed her eyes and held on to her husband. "I'm glad you're going to wait for me," she said softly. "If I were to find you with another woman again, I would likely kill you both."

"I don't doubt it," Sebesyten said thoughtfully. He stroked her hair. "This new witch of yours, is she giving you any trouble at all?"

"No," Liane answered quickly. "I need her. At least until the baby's born, I need her."

"At least until the baby's born," he repeated.

Liane nodded. She would not suggest to Sebestyen that Isadora take her old position as assassin, not tonight. If she did, Sebestyen might realize that Isadora had been responsible for Nelyk's disappearance. He'd always rather liked Nelyk. Besides, it might be nice to have her own assassin close at hand.

Just before she drifted off to sleep, she heard Sebestyen whisper, "If anything happens to this child, Isadora Fyne will be the first one to pay."

JULIET DIDN'T UNDERSTAND WHY SHE WAS SO ANXIOUS and worried about the possibility of Ryn leaving The City. He understood very well.

For three days after their return to the palace she had snapped at her servants, frightened her guards, and cried on many occasions, apparently over nothing at all. She had not complained to him or anyone else, but he had smelled the blood on her and knew there were times when she was in pain. Today she had been quiet and pale, a sign that these difficult days were behind her.

Juliet was coming into her first heat. He smelled her desire, felt it; shared it in a way he should have expected but had not. She'd bled for three days, and now she had begun to feel a burning fervor she could not explain.

It was the reason, unknown to her, that she had ordered him not to leave The City; and it was the reason he'd so willingly obeyed. By the end of the week she'd be carrying his son.

A Queen needed many sons, it was true. The old Queen's purebred sons still held positions of power in the palace, and would continue to serve the Anwyn for many years to come. But in time Juliet would want to be surrounded by her own sons. They would be mediators and teachers, and they would offer guidance in many different areas of expertise. It was not the life he had planned for his sons, but it was the life they would have.

He could refuse to lie with Juliet, if his will was great enough. But it was not. He'd always had a great desire for her, and even if they would live a different life than what he had planned for them, he wanted sons. He wanted to hold them, watch them grow, teach them kiva-ball and how to throw a spear and cut stone and shoot a bow and arrow. They could still know these things, even if they would never follow in their father's footsteps as a soldier.

Perhaps Juliet would not allow him to have such an influence on his sons' lives. It was possible that she would deny him that place, that she would hand their sons over to priestesses and teachers to be trained in the way princes should be trained. Until he knew, how could he lie with her?

Juliet commanded his presence after a fine supper he had not shared with her. He had requested his own quarters when she'd commanded that he remain in the palace, and though she had not approved, she had allowed him to claim those quarters. They were larger and finer than his own house, and the clothes he had been given were much nicer than any a Queen's guard would ever own.

He wanted to escape, but the fate he had told a reluctant Juliet bound them together forever had not changed. Only now, he was the prisoner.

Maybe once she was with child, she would allow him to leave. He could live the life of a rogue, returning to the palace when Juliet had need of him in her bed. He would know when the time came, just as he knew now. If he did not return in time, she would avail herself of another An-wyn male . . . at least until her Caradon lover appeared.

The idea of any other man taking his place did not sit well with Ryn. In fact, it roused an anger that usually came only with the wolf. If he was not willing to allow another to take on his duties as Queen's consort, how could he consider leaving her?

Juliet had not yet claimed the apartment of the old Queen, an apartment which encompassed the entire third floor of the palace. She had become comfortable here, in the rooms she had first been assigned. She met him at the door, dressed in a simple gold satin gown that hugged her curves. Her cheeks were flushed, her lips full and anxious, her hair curling around her face and down her back. Her golden eyes danced, anxious and lively, as she stepped back and invited him to enter.

The window was open, and a cold breeze made the curtains dance and filled the room with a welcome chill. A few months ago, even a few weeks ago, such a chill would have made Juliet shake. Now she welcomed the cold. She needed it.

Without preface, she grabbed the front of his new blue shirt and pulled him toward her. "I have been eager to see you all day," she said softly, not loosening her grip on his shirt.

"Have you?"

"I have." She pressed her body to his and laid her cheek against his chest. "I can't stop thinking about you, and I keep remembering the way I feel when you're inside me. Do you remember?"

"Of course I remember," he answered hoarsely.

"I want that again, Ryn. I want it now." She tilted her head back and looked up at him. "Why have you pulled away from me?"

"You know why."

"Just because I am Queen that doesn't mean I can't be your mate."

"No, it doesn't."

There was an added flush to her cheeks, a wicked sparkle to her golden eyes. "You look so stern, not at all like yourself. That ridiculous prophesy has stolen your smile." Her voice was too bright, too quick. "Whatever seer told of that prophesy was in a drunken stupor. I don't want any man but you to touch me, Ryn. No one but you, ever."

It was what he wanted, too, but he still wasn't convinced it was likely. "You don't see your own future clearly," he said as calmly as he could manage. "We don't know what the years to come will bring."

"I see with great clarity that I love you."

She didn't understand what was happening to her. "What you're feeling right now isn't love."

"If I say it's love, then it's love. I'm Queen, remember?"

He brushed a curl away from her cheek. "You have embraced your right to command very well, for a woman who swore she did not wish to be Queen."

She licked her lips; her gold eyes danced. "I don't want to argue with you, Ryn, I don't, but this must be love. I miss you. I can't stop thinking about you." She fit her body against his and undulated gently. "I want you so much I hurt with it, and I would kill or die to get you into my bed. At this moment, I don't care if a foolish old curse takes your life three years from now, not when I can have you with me until then. Is that not love?"

"No."

"What is it then?"

He pushed the thin strap at her shoulder down and lowered his head to kiss her creamy shoulder. Walking away from her was impossible, as he had known it would be. She wanted him and she would have him. Reasoning with her at this point was a waste of breath. Tonight he would need his energy for other things. "It is need, my Queen."

"A need you will fill?"

"Yes." He had not tasted her for days. It had been too many days and too many nights since he'd raked his tongue across her flesh. He pressed his mouth to her throat and tasted her sweat and her desire while he pushed her golden gown down so that her breasts were bared. He teased the nipples with his fingertips while he sucked gently on her throat, and her answering moan was all he needed to push him over the edge.

The gown ripped as he pushed it off and down. She kicked it aside without a care. When she was naked, she began to unfasten the buttons of his trousers, all the while touching and tasting and demanding. Not content to have this done too soon, Ryn stopped Juliet before her job was done. He laid her over his arm and took a nipple into his mouth, drawing it deep and teasing with his tongue. She shuddered and bucked slightly, and the moan that escaped from her lips was low and sweet and arousing.

He had almost forgotten how beautiful and passionate she could be, how sweet her skin tasted, how he craved the feel of her flesh. A fine soft bed waited in the next room. A few steps, and they would be there. But the bed seemed too far away; the walk to the bedchamber would surely be too long.

Juliet agreed. "Now," she said hoarsely.

He placed her on the edge of the table where they sometimes shared a meal, where she sometimes perused boring papers submitted by her advisors. The desk was almost bare tonight; he had only to push aside one small stack of papers that were surely unimportant. He freed himself, and Juliet wrapped her legs around his hips and guided him to her wet, hot center.

When he was deep inside her, she closed her eyes and

seemed to be satisfied, for a moment. Then she began to move, gyrating against him, urging him deeper. Had he really considered leaving this behind for the sake of his wounded pride? This moment was so fine, so exciting and right and pleasurable, he could not imagine ever walking away from this woman. She grasped his hair in her small, tight fist and moaned. Her hips ground against him and he pushed deep inside her.

She pulsed around him and cried out, her body jerking and shuddering and milking him, when he joined her in completion. For a moment he was blinded, the pleasure was so great, and then he was taken beyond anything resembling normal pleasure.

In her desire, Juliet had forgotten to block herself. For a moment, just a moment, the barrier he had been maintaining between them crumbled. While their bodies shook and found release, he was inside her in a way that went past the physical. Their bodies were joined, but so were their spirits. Their minds. Even their hearts.

Juliet was powerful, more powerful than she had ever imagined she could be. Her connection to the earth and the Anwyn was almost beyond his comprehension. She was more than a Queen like the Anwyn women who had come before her. She was a goddess. The Anwyn would speak of her in hushed, worshipping tones for hundreds of years after she left this life.

And she loved him. Now, when he was inside her and pleasure still filled her world. As they'd walked into The City, afraid and unsure. When she had known that he was uncertain about his place here, when she had known that he was thinking of leaving her here alone. The love had always been there.

He had not wanted love when he'd claimed this woman as his wife. In fact, the emotion seemed to be a great complication. But feeling it now . . . fully inside her in every possible way . . . maybe it was a good thing, this love of hers.

Ryn swept Juliet from the table and carried her to the bedchamber that had, moments earlier, seemed so far away. He laid her on the center of the big bed, shed his clothes, and joined her.

Hovering above her, he brushed a strand of wild red hair away from her face.

"You're smiling," she said.

"I suppose I am."

"I've missed that smile, Ryn. I've missed it so much. Does it mean . . ." She stopped, unable to ask the question.

"*Vidara,* my Queen," he whispered, answering the question she could not ask. "I am yours."

17

Ryn lay down beside her and placed one long, strong arm across her midsection. It took them both a few moments to regain their breath and find a regular heartbeat.

Vidara. Wife, only more, he'd told her on their journey to this place.

"You have not called me wife in a very long time," she whispered.

"Not so that you could hear," he confessed.

"You have not felt that I was truly your wife in a very long time."

"I feel so now."

A few candles burned in the room, casting enough light for her to see Ryn well. He was not the wild man she had first met. His long blond hair was caught in a thick braid, and the clothes he had removed were much more conventional than the leather kilt. And yet the wild man remained, locked inside this long, hard body, released only when the wolf or his mate called.

"Will you feel so when we are no longer naked?" she asked.

"I don't know." He cupped her breast with one large hand and tweaked the nipple, and a spark shot through her body. She had just experienced a pleasure so intense she could barely move, and yet she had already begun to want him again.

"Do you think I'm already carrying a child?" she asked.

"Perhaps. Perhaps not."

"But I could be."

"Perhaps."

"On the journey here you said you knew I would not conceive because Anwyn are different in that respect. I thought you were talking about yourself, but you were talking about me."

"Yes."

"It's time, isn't it?" He gently spread her thighs and touched her intimately, and she quivered to her bones. Was that intense response her answer? "I did not know it was possible to want anyone or anything as much as I want you now," Juliet whispered.

Ryn continued to stroke, to kiss, to arouse. "We need not leave this bed for days. Food will be left in the hallway for us, but no one will dare to interrupt."

"Everyone knows?"

"Yes. The days of a Queen's fertility are celebrated among the Anwyn."

"That's a little bit . . ." She started to say *embarrassing,* and then a particular stroke of a particular finger robbed all thoughts that did not concern Ryn from her mind.

It seemed he cared only for arousing her. He tasted her throat, caressed her breasts, raked his hand along her body as if he were memorizing every curve and swell. Her flesh had never felt so sensitive; no touch had ever felt so sensual. She could think of nothing but where he had just caressed her, and where he would next caress her.

She touched him, found him hard, stroked the length she longed to have inside her. Sparks of anticipation danced through her body, and she found herself arching against his touch and stroking him harder and harder. Nothing else mattered but this room, this bed, these two bodies. Ryn aroused her, and she could no longer think of anything but what was to come.

"Before, while we were traveling to The City, I asked you to maintain the barrier between us when you were inside me," she said.

"I let it fall tonight," Ryn answered. "I'm sorry."

"Don't be," she whispered. "It was very nice."

"Yes," he responded gruffly.

"I felt more of you, as we were truly one in every way. As if we were meant to celebrate our joining in that way. Completely."

Ryn's hands and fingers slowed, but did not stop stimulating her.

Her body arched and quivered. "From the day I learned how a husband and a wife make love, I've been worried that if a man were inside me in all ways, I would never be able to get him out. I had nightmares about taking so much of another into myself that it drove me crazy. I worried ceaselessly that if I ever took a man entirely into myself, I would never again be the same. Do you think that's silly?"

"I don't know."

"If I take all of you, body and mind and spirit, with no barriers and no ties in the tendrils that connect us, will we ever again be separated?"

"I don't know."

"You're not helping," she said with a soft smile.

He rolled atop her, and she wrapped her legs around his hips once more. A push and he was inside her. The barrier he had built remained strong, and she did not attempt to break through it. Another thrust took him deep, and she shattered with a cry. She arched off the bed and clenched around Ryn's length, while she whispered his name and trembled around him. He went very still, as the waves of her completion faded. He did not come with her; he did not give her the seed she needed to give him a son.

She lay boneless beneath him, spent and sated and warm to the pit of her soul. When she could speak, she asked, "Why didn't you—"

Ryn hushed her with a deep kiss. Heaven above, she loved the way his mouth felt on hers. It was intimate and exciting and it made her insides do strange and wonderful things. While his mouth danced over hers, he began to move again, almost idly, kissing her, loving her.

He pushed deep inside her and held himself there as he lifted his lips from hers. "Tonight and tomorrow night and the next night, you will discover a new intensity to your sexuality. You will need me in a way you have never known before, and I want to give you everything I possibly can, Juliet."

She smiled. "You called me Juliet. I'm so glad. I'm tired of being called Queen."

"Tonight you are not Queen," he said as he moved deeply and slowly inside her. "You are my woman, nothing more."

"That's all I want to be," she said hoarsely. Ribbons of pleasure had begun again, but she held back. This part of making love, the just before, was extraordinary. She didn't want to lose it. Not yet. As long as Ryn was moving as he did, languidly and with great control, she knew she could wait and enjoy.

And she did.

"Ryn," she whispered as her body arched into his and completion danced just out of reach. *"Vanir."*

"Yes."

"I want everything from you, no matter what might come after. Let everything that stands between us fall away."

The barrier crumbled, and she opened the tendril that connected her spirit to his. Like the moment when she'd laid her hand upon the Heart of the Anwyn, like the night when she'd run in the form of a wolf, she was overcome with sensation and beauty and wonder. Ryn was a part of her in so many ways. She drank him in, in body and spirit. She tasted him in a thousand ways and found pleasure in him in an entirely new manner.

And she knew him as she had never known another. He was a good man, strong and noble, loyal and honest. He would do anything for her, and for the children they would make together. His incredible strength was tempered with an equally incredible heart.

She saw glimpses of his past, while he moved in and out of her. A fair-haired child playing in the street with a small ball of some sort, laughing with his friends. A young man, dreaming of her, dreaming of this very moment. A determined man, searching for his mate. He was dedicated to her, and while he was not happy to be relegated to Queen's consort, he would not leave her. Not now, when he knew how deeply she cared for him. Not now, when he knew how she needed him.

And he did know, because she was no longer blocking him from her thoughts or her spirit. She not only didn't shield herself from him, she drew him in and offered herself in a way she never had before. It was not frightening to be so united to another in body and spirit. It was beautiful, right, and sacred.

It was more powerful than anything she had ever known.

When he began to move faster, she did the same, her hips rocking in time, her body drawing him deeper. When she shattered beneath him, he pushed harder and deeper than before, and their bodies clenched and quivered together, in their own rhythm and their own time.

The connection did not end, but instead grew to a more intimate level than she had known was possible. This man was a part of her in so many ways, she had been incomplete her entire life and had not realized it. He had known, though. Ryn had known all along that apart they were not whole.

He drifted down to cover her body with his, and she grabbed his braid and held on tight. "I love you," she said breathlessly.

"I know."

Ryn didn't tell her that he loved her, too, but he was smart enough to know that a lie would not get past her. She saw too much, now more than ever. He did love her, but he hadn't yet realized and accepted that love. He would, though. One day.

"You are a remarkable woman and you will be a wonderful Queen."

She sounded a bit wistful when she asked, "Will I make a good mate, as well?"

"I believe so," Ryn whispered. He lifted up his head and grinned at her. "Ask me again in a few days if you want a true answer. I cannot think when I am inside you."

SOPHIE KEPT HER EYES ON THE PATH AS HER HORSE CARRIED her in a roundabout and maddeningly slow route toward Arthes. Rebels could not travel in the open, not without inviting warfare.

Many of the rebels were afraid of her now. Her despair at finding her family cabin burned to the ground had affected many of those around her, even though she did her best to keep her feelings corralled.

What she wouldn't give for Juliet's gift at this moment. She could not sense that her sisters were alive and well, but neither did she know that they were not. What would she do if they were gone? Her last words to them had been spoken in anger. She had told them she'd never forgive them for interfering in her relationship with Kane and that she never wanted to see them again. She would forgive them anything if she could see them now.

In a few days, perhaps a week, they would be in Arthes. The emperor had to be involved in whatever had happened to Isadora and Juliet. She would make him tell her where they were. They had to be alive. Somewhere, somehow.

The rebel army grew stronger every day. Whispers that the emperor had taken a concubine and made her empress had infuriated some of the common people and incited them to join the rebels. That former concubine was Liane, Sophie knew, even though she had not heard the new empress's name spoken. She and Kane should have forced Liane to leave the palace with them, instead of allowing her to walk back into that cursed ballroom.

In addition to the Columbyanans who had joined the rebellion, members of a Tryfyn clan who wanted to see the Emperor Sebestyen unseated had joined Arik, and so his forces grew once again. There were even whispers that the Circle of Bacwyr, legendary Tryfyn warriors who had been silent for many years, would soon join the battle. If they chose to support the rebels, what had started as an annoyance to the emperor would soon become war.

Sophie hated the idea of war. It was not in her nature to accept violence of any kind.

The party stopped for the night in a clearing far from the road. Even though Sophie wanted to ride nonstop to the capital city, she knew she, the baby she carried, Ariana, and even the rebels needed rest. The night was cold, but not horribly so. A fire was built, and a tent was quickly and efficiently constructed for Sophie and her family. Another, smaller tent was assembled for Arik. As leader of the rebels he enjoyed comforts the others did not.

Maddox Sulyen was more prisoner than family at the moment, but at least he had not been harmed. Some of the rebels openly detested the former Minister of Defense, a man who had been their enemy until just a few months ago. Others recognized that he would have great influence over the armies he had once commanded. If he could bring just a few of the emperor's soldiers to Arik's side, it would make a vast difference in the outcome of the rebellion. Perhaps *the* difference.

In the comfort of her tent, with only a sleeping Ariana to keep her company, Sophie turned her mind to other matters. Kane would reach thirty years at the end of summer. The Fyne Curse would take him from her before that date, unless she found a way to break it once and for all. She had planned to have Isadora assist her. With their combined powers, surely they could put an end to the curse that had robbed so many Fyne witches of the men they loved.

She didn't know that she could do it alone, but since she didn't know when she'd find Isadora, or even if either of her sisters were still alive, she had to try.

Sophie closed her eyes, found the bright light at the center of her being, and began to chant in a whisper. She was not as proficient in the ancient language their mother had taught them, not as Isadora and Juliet were, so she chanted in Columbyanan, asking again and again that the curse of the wizard be lifted, that Fyne women be allowed to find lasting happiness again without being punished for a long-ago unrequited love. She whispered the chant seven times, then opened her eyes and looked upon her sleeping daughter. A hand settled over a rounded stomach.

She wanted the curse destroyed not only for herself and for Kane. Her daughters deserved to have love and happiness one day. They should not be punished for something that had happened so long ago.

She had not broken the curse tonight with her simple chant. It continued to weigh upon her, a tangible and bitter thing that felt heavy on her shoulders and her heart.

Kane lifted the tent flap and walked in, and Sophie knew immediately that something was wrong. His mouth was thinned and his eyes were worried.

"We're heading east," he said sharply.

"*Away* from Arthes? Now?" Sophie glanced at her sleeping daughter. "Maybe we can move Ariana without waking her. She's exhausted."

Kane touched Sophie's cheek and made her look at him. "You're not going with us."

"What do you mean—"

"Arik has received word that a band of rebels is in dire need of help. They're fighting superior forces and are barely holding on."

"You're going into battle."

"Yes."

Kane had fought before, and he was a gifted warrior. But Sophie sensed that this battle would be different. The rebels would be outnumbered. No, the rebels were almost always outnumbered. But this time Kane would be among them, and she would know, and she would worry . . .

"And you wish me to stay here?" Alone?

"Six rebels will stay with you, Ariana, and your father. There's a sympathizer on a small farm a two-day ride from here. In the morning you'll be escorted to the farm. You're to wait there."

"I am not very good at waiting," she said softly.

"I know." Kane gave her a small, tense smile. "But I need you to wait for me and take care of our babies."

"I will." She pressed the palm of her hand to Kane's chest so that she might hear the beat of his heart for herself. "I do not have need of six escorts. One will suffice." She wished that one could be her husband, but knew that was impossible. He would not allow others to fight in his place so that he could remain safely with her.

"One would suffice for you and Ariana," Kane replied, "but your father is another matter."

No one in this rebel camp yet trusted Maddox Sulyen. He had been an enemy for too long. "You could leave me in his trust. I don't doubt that he would care for me and Ariana, and you might need those six men you're leaving behind."

Kane refused to budge on the subject of her father. "No."

Sophie nodded gently. If Kane needed to know she was surrounded by armed men in order to keep his mind on the battle to come and his own survival, then she would not argue with him.

A part of her wanted to continue on toward Arthes, even if she had to travel on her own. Her father would help her find her sisters, even if it meant going back into a palace where his life was worth nothing. She knew that.

She also knew that she and Kane needed to do this together.

Her husband kissed her before leaving the tent. Sophie did not walk into the night to watch him ride away. He did not need the distraction of her tears, and she did not particularly want to watch him, armed and ready for battle, ride off to face the dangers he had lived with for so long before they'd met.

As the rebels rode away from the camp, their horses' hooves pounding on the hard-packed ground, Sophie dropped to her knees and began to chant again. This time she asked seven times for the rebels to be protected. And then with tears in her eyes, she prayed for her husband to come back to her, unharmed.

* * *

AFTER A LONG NIGHT OF RIDING HARD, BORS ENTERED the castle with a new and burning anger in his heart. He had left Arthes with ten able soldiers, and he was returning with two. Two! He had found his way into the mountains, for all the good it had done him. Two men had slipped and fallen to their deaths on one particularly icy day. Another had either run away or gotten lost during the night.

The other five had been viciously killed by a huge mountain lion that had long, wicked claws and hungry teeth. Bors himself had barely escaped death.

It was unlikely that the witch the emperor wanted was still alive, and if she were . . . would she be worth saving? If she lived, she had been in the company of that monster for well more than a month now. She'd be worthless.

No man told Emperor Sebestyen that the task he required could not be accomplished. But Bors knew if he told the emperor that he had not found Juliet Fyne, he'd be sent out again, with more soldiers this time. And what of the reward he had worked so hard to earn? So he stood before the emperor in the ballroom, morning sun shining in, and told a lie.

"She's dead," Bors said simply. "The beast who took the redheaded witch tore her to pieces, most likely on the same day she was taken."

"Did you bring me proof? A head, perhaps? A bloody gown? Anything at all?"

"My lord, we did find remains, but they were much too indelicate to present in such a fine palace, and they, uh, they smelled mightily."

The Emperor Sebestyen was in a particularly foul mood today. The empress was not present, as she had been on Bors's last visit to this room, but a sour-looking priest stood close by, stoic and wordless.

"You lost eight of my men looking for a dead woman?" the emperor asked.

"There was a mountain lion, my lord, a very large—"

"Did I ask for an excuse?" The emperor stood slowly. "It was a mistake on my part to trust such a delicate task to you. Fetching two women. How hard could it be?"

"My lord—"

"Do not speak." Emperor Sebestyen stepped down from the dais. Judging by the expression on his face, there would be no reward for getting one of the witches here, no appointment to sheriff, no high position in the palace itself. "You picked a very bad time to disappoint me."

"I should like the pleasure of telling the other one that her sister is dead," Bors said.

"Would you?"

"Yes. She's trouble, that one. I hope you have her locked away in a safe place so she can't harm anyone else."

"Are you offering me advice?" The emperor continued to walk lazily toward Bors.

"I have seen the witch's dangerous side, my lord. I want only what's best for Columbyana. And for you, of course."

"Then perhaps you should have kept the other one alive."

He had never noticed quite how tall Emperor Sebestyen was, but standing almost nose to nose, Bors definitely took notice. The emperor was tall and slender, and those eyes were so cold . . .

Bors didn't realize he was in danger until he felt the sharp blade slip into his belly.

"You incompetent oaf," the emperor said softly. "You are not worth the expense of a vial of Panwyr, or the food I'd feel obligated to feed you if you were locked in a cell on Level Twelve."

"But . . . but . . ." Bors looked down at his belly. The knife the emperor wielded remained buried there, and blood stained the front of his shirt.

His wife had made this shirt. He hadn't seen her in more than a year, hadn't even thought of her for months.

Emperor Sebestyen twisted the blade gently, and Bors screamed as newer, sharper pain sliced through him. He would've fallen to the floor, but the emperor held him up. He was strong, that one, stronger than he appeared to be.

Bors knew he was going to bleed to death, slowly and painfully. There was nothing worse than a wound to the gut. He knew, because he'd delivered more than his share. The emperor leaned in slightly. "I can't abide incompetence," he said softly. "You not only failed me, you did it badly." He twisted the blade once again, harder this time, and again Bors screamed. He screamed and he pleaded. Not for life, it was too late for that. He pleaded for death to come quickly.

The emperor withdrew the knife and let Bors fall to the floor. He leaned down and wiped the blade on a clean portion of the shirt Bors's wife had made for him. Then he turned away. To one soldier, he said, "Dispose of this garbage accordingly." The ashen young soldier nodded once, and the emperor turned his attention to the priest on the dais.

"Father Breccian," the emperor said cordially, the crying man on the floor dismissed from his mind. "I'm going to have a glass of wine while this unpleasant business is completed. Would you care to join me?"

IT HAD BEEN A WEEK SINCE JULIET AND RYN HAD BECOME husband and wife in every way, and still she was not tired of the way they came together. In the past three days she had been learning about her responsibilities as Queen and learning about the Anwyn people and their ways. She met with her advisors, with priestesses and heads of various clans and the old Queen's sons. She had expected there might be animosity among them, since her position would naturally rob them of some of their power. But she felt no anger or resentment from them. They all knew how much moving on meant to their mother, and instead of longing for power, they were relieved to have the new Queen in place.

They wanted what she and Ryn had wanted. A simple home, responsibilities to one's own family . . . something beautiful and ordinary. She hadn't yet told them that she planned to find a new and peaceful way for the Anwyn to be ruled. She hadn't given up on that simple life she and Ryn both craved.

She had asked all of Queen Etaina's sons to stay on to advise her, if they so wished, as her own sons would not be in a position to accept their responsibilities for many, many years.

It was not difficult to rule in a place where there was no conflict other than the occasional battles that took place with the Caradon beyond The City walls. There were disagreements among the clans, but they were trivial. Insignificant differences she was easily able to resolve.

Many of her duties were social in nature. She entertained the heads of clans over fine meals and beautiful music, and made plans for the holidays that would be celebrated in the months to come. There were many holidays among the Anwyn, festivals that celebrated the moon, the gods and goddesses of the Anwyn, and previous Queens who had served well. Now that Queen Etaina was gone, there would be a new holiday to celebrate her lengthy reign, as there would soon be a celebration to welcome Juliet to her throne.

She had endured a long day of meetings and planning for the festival that would take place before the next full moon. There would be dancing and singing in the palace and in the streets, costumes and games, a soirée that would be held in the grand ballroom.

For someone who had lived her life before coming to The City in a simple cabin with little contact with the outside world, it was quite a change.

Juliet paced in her outer chamber, anxiously waiting for Ryn to arrive. For the past three days she had seen to business during the daylight hours, but saved her nights for him. This heat he had explained, it consumed her. She could think of nothing but the moment when Ryn would hold her again. She no longer suffered from the frenzied need of those first four days, when they had not left her chambers, but by the time he came to her at night, she was almost frantic for his touch.

She had never thought herself to be a sensual woman. Until she'd met Ryn, she'd planned to live her life chaste and alone. Now, all she had to do was think of him and it was as if she could actually feel him pushing against and inside her.

The door opened, Ryn walked in, and Juliet rushed to meet him. Grabbing the front of his shirt, she pulled him to her for a kiss. Her lips parted; her tongue danced. If she could, she would consume him, and he felt the same way about her.

I want you.

He responded to her silent communication by flicking the strap of her gold gown aside and pushing the garment down so that her breasts were freed. He caressed one breast with a large, sun-kissed hand. *You are soft and beautiful.*

You are hard and beautiful.

They kissed, and undressed one another as they touched and aroused and even laughed.

"I think of you all day," Juliet said aloud as they walked toward the bedchamber, more undressed than dressed. Her heart beat too quickly, and deep inside she felt the gentle clenching and heat that demanded Ryn.

"And I think of you," he responded. He raked his fingers

along the swell of her breasts, teasing the sensitive nipples and watching the way they peaked. Her insides quivered and clenched, and she was tempted to command that he take her here, now, with no more preparation and no more touching.

But she didn't want to command Ryn, and in truth she didn't want this to be over too quickly. She laid the palm of her hand against his flat belly, felt his own deep quiver. That palm skimmed lower and she studied his length with curious fingers that were quickly becoming talented in the ways of arousal.

She had been so afraid of taking a man inside her in all ways, and now that she had . . . she had never known anything more wonderful. Ryn was with her always, and instead of being frightened, she felt as if she'd needed this attachment all her life.

Still, she did not know every thought that passed through his head, every feeling he experienced. At some moments she wanted everything from him. At others, she was more than satisfied to be allowed the glimmers of his spirit throughout the day. Even if she didn't know his every thought, physically their union was perfection. He said her body was driven by the need to reproduce. Was the same true of him? Was his response to her purely biological?

He tweaked one nipple and she almost came out of her skin.

"I didn't know this heat you told me about would last for such a long time," Juliet said as they continued to ease toward the bed.

Ryn stopped, lifted his head to look down at her, and smiled. "Juliet, you have been out of heat for three days."

She blinked quickly, and then smiled back. "Then this urgency that I feel for you . . ."

"It is nothing more than a woman's call for her mate," he said, lifting her easily off her feet and dropping her on the bed, before finishing the job of undressing himself.

She had been so certain that this intense need was a product of her Anwyn blood and the moon and the awakening of her fertility. As Ryn joined her on the bed and took her into his arms, Juliet closed her eyes and opened herself not only to him but to everything around her. The mountain, the people who lived on it . . . even herself.

Her heart beat differently here; her very soul was brighter. She missed her sisters, she missed the cabin she had always called home, but she belonged here. She belonged with this man, for as long as she was allowed to have him. Three years or thirty or a hundred.

"Ryn," she whispered, drawing slightly away from him but keeping her hands on his body. She did not want to be without that sensation of touch, not now, not ever. "There's something I need to ask you."

His eyebrows arched slightly. Normally there was very little talk after they fell into bed.

"I know that when we came here, you were disturbed by the idea that you would not have the life you'd always planned for us."

"Juliet, don't . . ."

"And I'm sorry. I'm so sorry. I would love to live in the house you built for me, and fill it with sons, and be there waiting for you when you came home at night."

"What is to be is," he said stoically.

She kissed him, for strength. Her own and his. "I want things to be different, and I will find a way. But until that time comes, you will not be the Queen's consort. You will not be relegated to an insignificant position and come when I call as if your only reason for being here is to warm my bed and satisfy the needs of my body and make babies."

"It is not my place to change the way things are done."

"No, it's not," she said. "It's my place." She took his face in her hands and looked him in the eye. "Marry me, *vanir.* Be my King. Stand by my side, run with me when the wolf calls, and help me raise our children." She pressed her bare stomach to his. "The first of those babies is growing now, I think."

He laid the palm of one hand against her side, and his fingers slipped between their bodies to touch her soft belly.

She suffered a moment of indecision. Ryn had not yet said yes to her proposal. Perhaps he cared only for the pleasure he found in her body. Perhaps he did not want to change the way things were done among the Anwyn. Seeing into him was very much like seeing her own life. Some things were clear. Others were maddeningly indistinct. She could not see into his heart now, even though he did not try to hide from her.

Maybe she could not see because he had not yet decided.

"I am asking you not as Queen, but as your mate and the woman who loves you. Ryn, will you marry me?"

"Yes, *vidara*," he answered softly.

She did not want to pry where she was not welcomed, but it was so easy to touch his mind when they were this close. And as he held her, something changed. The future that had been muddy cleared. The last of the barriers that kept her from seeing into his heart fell, and she felt the gleam of something new inside Ryn, something beautiful that he had just this moment accepted for himself.

Love.

18

THE EMPEROR SEBESTYEN HIMSELF HAD TOLD HER THAT Juliet was dead. For one terrible moment, Isadora had felt as if the floor had dropped out from beneath her and she was falling ten stories to the ground. And then he'd informed her that Bors had been the one to tell him of her death, and the oaf had paid for daring to deliver bad news.

Bors was a liar, and would tell any tale in order to save his own skin. Isadora couldn't make herself be sorry he was dead, and she could not believe that he'd been telling the truth about Juliet.

Isadora leaned over a tense and fidgeting Empress Liane, who lay prone on the emperor's bed. Isadora herself had recently been moved from Level Five to a room on this very level, so she'd be closer to the empress. Her new room was smaller than the one on Level Five, plainer and more prison-like. There was only one small window, and the bed was narrow and hard. It was more to her liking than the luxury of Level Five, more like the home that was gone.

Empress Liane had not again suggested that her personal witch take on the position of palace assassin, but Isadora knew if Kane's sister wanted an enemy dead, she would be called upon again. Would she refuse? Did she dare? She could feel the light of her magic coming alive once again, slowly but surely. It was no longer the blazing flame it had once been, but it was no longer a weak flicker, either. It was protection that fed her magic. There were many different methods of protection, as she was discovering.

Some days she wondered if she should tell the empress that the priest Nelyk wasn't dead. He'd just been put away in a place where he couldn't hurt anyone else. He was no longer in a position to do harm, and to Isadora's mind that was good enough.

"Be still," she instructed in a soft voice as the pregnant woman squirmed.

"I can't be still," the empress declared.

"Then do not expect an accurate reporting of your child's condition."

Isadora suspected no one spoke to the empress in such a candid way, but it was certainly long past time someone did so. Besides, there was nothing Empress Liane and her emperor could do to make matters worse for her. Will was gone, home was burned, Juliet was lost, and Sophie no longer needed her sisters, no matter what Juliet had said on the night the Fyne cabin had been destroyed.

The empress went still, and Isadora turned her full attention to her patient. The pendulum swung in an odd pattern as she whispered the spell in the old language Empress Liane would not understand. At first, the peculiar path of the swinging of the enchanted pendulum didn't make any sense.

And then it did.

Isadora stepped back and dropped the pendulum into the pocket of her dark blue gown.

"Is it a boy, as Gadhra said?" the pregnant woman asked. She sat up carefully, one hand on the mattress, the other on her massive belly. She was much too large for a woman who was not set to deliver for another three months.

Isadora now knew why the empress was so large. "You're going to have twins," she said. "You must be especially careful—"

"I cannot have twins!" The empress sat up straight but did not leave the bed. She had gone pale, but suddenly a flood of color rushed into her cheeks. "Unless it is a boy and a girl," she said hopefully. "Sebestyen can have his heir, and I can have a daughter to call my own. The priests and Sebestyen won't care about a girl. She can be mine. My daughter." Empress Liane lifted expectant green eyes to Isadora.

"Two sons," Isadora said gently. "One conceived in shadows, another conceived in the sun."

Empress Liane grabbed a pillow and threw it across the room. "There must be one true and uncontested heir," she insisted. "The country is at war at this moment because Sebestyen's father had two sons who each claim the throne. Twins!" She stood awkwardly and threw another pillow. "I can't have twins. Perhaps you're wrong and this is simply one large child, or if it is twins, one could be a girl. You could be mistaken."

"I am not mistaken," Isadora said calmly. "We need to concentrate on what we must do to keep you and the babies safe. The delivery of two babies can be difficult, and will require—"

"This will require some planning," Empress Liane said, stubbornly walking away from Isadora. "But for now, the important thing is that no one else knows."

"Your husband should be told. There are risks involved."

Empress Liane turned and glared at Isadora. "No one.

Especially not Sebestyen. He will not allow twin sons to be born, don't you understand that? We can't tell him and he can't be with me when the babies are born. No one but you can be with me when these children come into the world."

"I doubt very much that the emperor will allow me to be alone with you when it is time for delivery," Isadora said. "What are you going to do?"

Empress Liane turned away so Isadora could no longer see her face. "I don't know," she said softly. "We will think of something."

Sophie rocked Ariana to sleep. There were hours still until bedtime, but her little girl was tired and needed her rest.

Sophie needed rest herself, but lately sleep did not come easily. The safe house where she had been staying for the past three weeks was comfortable enough, and the widow who farmed here with the help of her two youngest sons had been more than gracious.

As a matter of fact, the widow had become much too friendly with Sophie's father. She tried to turn a blind eye, but they made it impossible. They smiled at one another, and often disappeared simultaneously, returning a few minutes or an hour later looking guilty and much too happy. Maddox Sulyen was old enough to know better than to behave in such an inappropriate manner. The widow was probably fifteen years younger than he! Sophie was very careful to dampen her abilities when the widow and her father were about. The last thing she needed at this point in time was a baby brother or sister. Or a stepmother, heaven forbid.

The soldiers who helped with the farm and guarded Sophie were younger than her father, and a couple of them were also interested in the pretty widow. But she had eyes only for the older man. Sophie realized that she did not know her father. Not at all.

Sophie placed a sleeping Ariana in the small bed they had shared for the past three weeks. She tried not to worry overmuch, but she had expected Kane to return days ago. Weeks ago! In her heart she believed that if something had happened to him, she would know it. If he'd died in battle, his spirit would have found his way to her to say good-bye. But three weeks!

She'd spent her spare hours trying to end the curse that would take Kane from her if she didn't find a way. Incantations, prayers, demands . . . they all went unheeded. She still felt the curse all around her. It weighed on her mind and her heart.

A terrible thought crossed her mind. In years past, some of the men who were loved by Fyne women simply walked away. That was usually the case with older men, those who had come into the circle of the witches after their thirtieth birthdays. But was that what had happened to Kane? Had he fallen out of love with her and abandoned her here? Tears filled her eyes, stinging and unwanted. Maybe it was for the best. If she couldn't end the curse, it would be better this way. Better to have Kane alive and elsewhere than dead because she loved him. Better for him, but just as devastating for her. She would always be looking for him, wouldn't she? She would forever be waiting.

"How is it possible that you're more beautiful than you were when I left?"

Sophie spun around to face her husband, and all her fears fled. "I didn't hear you come in." She rushed to him and threw her arms around his neck, trying to hide her thoughts of abandonment and death. He didn't appear to be hurt, but he did flinch when she hugged him. "You're hurt."

"Only a little." He kissed her, gently and warmly.

"I'll fix you right up," Sophie said, a note of false cheer

in her voice and those tears still caught in her eyes. "You'll soon be as good as new." With a new scar or two to add to his collection.

"Don't cry." Kane wiped away a tear that slipped down her cheek. "There's no reason for tears."

She didn't want to lie to her husband, not ever. "I thought you weren't coming back."

He took her hand and walked with her to the rocking chair, and there he sat and pulled her onto his lap, wrapping his arms around her. "I will always come back to you."

It was a nice promise, but one he might not be able to keep. Always was a long time. "Let me look at those wounds." She tried to pull away, but he held fast.

"They will wait."

"You flinched when I hugged you!"

"Holding you does me much more good than a fresh bandage."

She settled back against him and relaxed. It was good to be here in his arms again, better even than she had imagined.

"Did you lose many men in the battle?" she asked, thinking of all the young and old faces that had surrounded her on the journey from the Northern Palace to Fyne Mountain and beyond.

"A few," Kane said. "Ard and Culain fell."

"I'm sorry to hear that. They were good men." Sophie reached out and touched a strand of Kane's long hair. It needed washing, he needed bathing and bandaging, and yet for now she was content just to hold him.

"They did not fall in vain."

Sophie lifted her head up slightly to look into Kane's eyes. "You won?"

He smiled at her. "You needn't sound so surprised."

"But there are so many more imperial soldiers than rebels. How—"

"That's changing," he said. "The rebel following is growing. A band of soldiers from the Southern Province arrived unexpected, and another clan from Tryfyn has joined us. The Circle of Bacwyr is stirring. Some of them favor defending Sebestyen as the rightful emperor, but others believe Arik's claim is just. Arik stayed behind to coordinate some of the new troops. He's to meet us here in a few weeks."

"Weeks? What about Arthes?" Sophie asked. "What about finding Juliet and Isadora?"

"We will march on Arthes in summer," he said.

"Summer! I cannot wait until summer to find my sisters!"

He comforted her with a hand in her hair. "By summer we will have enough men to defeat the emperor and take the palace. If anyone there knows where Isadora and Juliet are, we'll find them."

Summer. Just after this child she carried was born and mere weeks before Kane's thirtieth birthday. If she didn't find a way to bring an end to the curse, the man she loved would die in Arthes.

THERE HAD NEVER BEEN A ROYAL ANWYN WEDDING, so there were no traditions to follow. Juliet and Ryn made their own traditions. There was a feast at the palace to which the entire city was invited, followed by a three-day celebration with music and games and dancing to celebrate the coming of the first Anwyn King. Tonight's ceremony would conclude the festivities.

Whispers of the red-haired Queen with the power of sight and her Caradon lover did not go unheard. Juliet heard everything, when she so desired. Even with her newly heightened powers she maintained the ability to disengage herself from the earth and all the creatures in it, when her mind and her spirit craved quiet. But her connection with

Ryn was always with her, in one way or another, and that was as it should be. He was a part of her.

Juliet was dressed in her finest gold silk gown, and she wore jewels befitting a Queen. Ryn wore a fine suit of gold and blue, and his hair had been braided so that it fell down his back. Something new had appeared on his person; he wore a small amber stone in one earlobe, and like Juliet, he wore a circlet of gold on his head.

As she said her marriage vows, before an assembly of attentive priestesses and the population of The City, Juliet connected only to Ryn. All else was dismissed for this precious moment in time.

There was no mention of love in the vows. The pledge they took spoke of commitment, duty, and fidelity. It was the Anwyn way. When the ceremony was done, Ryn leaned toward Juliet, took her hands in his, and whispered in her ear, "I love you, *vidara*." Together they placed their hands on the Heart of the Anwyn, and the stone began to glow.

Connected to her husband and the Heart and the earth itself, Juliet felt a rush of knowing that went beyond everything she had experienced to this point. A sensation that was physical and spiritual rushed through her, almost knocking her off her feet. Time seemed to stand still, as information and emotion and knowledge whipped through her. It was everything she had not wanted; it was her greatest fear. And it was dazzling. More than that, it was who she was. Who she had become. It was who she had always been meant to be.

The curse she had feared all her life would soon be ended. She did not know how or why, but she knew it would not take the man she loved from her, and it would not take Sophie's Kane.

Her father was coming. He had not known of her existence until Ryn's friend had found him, and he was angry. Kei was often angry, but he was not a bad man. He would not like Ryn at first, but they would soon join forces.

Isadora had found trouble. She was physically well, but a darkness threatened to envelope her, a darkness Juliet did not understand. It frightened her to the pit of her soul.

Coloring everything she discovered in that instant was the certainty that she and Ryn were indeed joined forever, mated, meant to be.

She and Ryn took their hands from the stone as one, and she looked up at him. "Did you feel that?" she asked in a whisper.

"I felt a rush of energy, an infusion of power that was much like the coming of the wolf."

He had felt the energy but had not seen all that she had seen. The knowledge that had come had been for her alone. Juliet turned to the smiling faces of their wedding guests and stepped forward. Realizing that the Queen was about to speak, the crowd hushed.

"You have all heard the myth of the red-haired Queen who will lead the Anwyn into a time of prosperity and peace," Juliet said in a clear voice that carried throughout the crowd. "The Queen with the gift of sight, the Queen who will bring peace with the Caradon by taking a Caradon lover in this very palace."

"Juliet," Ryn said softly, his hand resting on her shoulder. "We need not explain anything."

"I am not that Queen," Juliet continued. She lifted her hand to lay it over Ryn's.

There were a few murmurs in the crowd, and Juliet turned to face Ryn. "I see so much more now, I see more than I thought possible. The curse I have been afraid of all my life will not kill you, no matter how much I love you. It's going to end somehow. Someday. And I see children, Ryn. Boys and girls who possess so much strength I cannot yet comprehend it. The red-haired Queen who will lead the Anwyn to a time of great prosperity and peace . . . she is not me. She is our firstborn daughter, and she's already growing here." She took his hand and pressed the palm to her still-flat stomach.

"A daughter?" Ryn asked softly.

"The first of many. There will be sons, too, and they will have daughters as well. Anwyn women, witches and shape-shifters who will have more power than I can even imagine." She smiled gently. "We will one day get to live in the house you built for us, when our daughter becomes Queen. She is extraordinary, Ryn. She will be Queen by the time she turns fifteen."

"What else do you see?" Ryn asked.

Those who stood close by were listening in, and word spread quickly through the crowd. Juliet leaned closer to Ryn and whispered, "My sisters need me. I can't stay here and fulfill a token role while they suffer. Queen Etaina's sons and the clan leaders can see to the governing of the An-wyn while we continue the trip I began to Arthes, together."

Ryn nodded. He would be beside her, and a crew of guardians would travel with them. And so would her father. They needed Kei along in order to do what had to be done. She did not see what would happen once they reached the Columbyana capital. Perhaps that outcome was not yet set.

She kissed Ryn on the mouth, and took his hand. They would not begin the journey to Arthes for another two weeks or more. Her father would arrive in a matter of days, but he would take some convincing before he agreed to join forces with them. There would be yet another full moon to lead them into the hills before it was time to leave.

Juliet did not think overmuch on the details of the weeks to come. That could wait until tomorrow. This was her wedding night, and she had plans for her new husband.

As they walked toward their apartment and the bed that waited there, Ryn asked with a start, "Our daughter is to be mated to a *Caradon?*"

Juliet patted her husband's hand and pulled him closer. "Don't worry. We won't have to face that crisis for a very long time. There will be other obstacles and many happy times to keep us busy until then."

In the privacy of a palace hallway Ryn pressed her back against the wall and leaned down to bring his face close to hers. He kissed her, deeply and completely. *What kinds of obstacles?*

Juliet moved her mouth over the lips of her King, joyfully kissing the man who was her mate in all ways. While they kissed, she touched him in a manner that assured him she had the coming happy times on her mind. *Nothing we can't handle together, vanir.*

Lucan Hern, Captain of the Circle of Bacwyr, has known
all his life that he is destined to be Prince of Swords—*if* he
can perform the task required of him and collect the Star of
Bacwyr from the Imperial Palace in Arthes and deliver it to
the Circle. Such a retrieval will mean his ascension into the
position of Prince, and the long-awaited coming of the King
of Tryfyn. The new king will bring an end to the strife that
has torn his country apart. Lucan's only admonition from
the Circle Wizard who foretold his destiny has stayed with
him all these years. Beware the witch.

Isadora's powers have suffered in months past, as she
tries to find and claim her place in the world of magic.
Dark or light? Destruction or protection? She cannot embrace both, and living on the cusp keeps her magic weak.
She uses her powers of protection to care for Empress
Liane and her unborn children, but the call of destruction
still lives within her. As war approaches the palace, she
finds an unexpected ally in Lucan Hern.

Lucan is the only man who has touched Isadora's heart,
since the death of her husband years earlier, but she knows
that if the Fyne Curse doesn't prevent her from loving him,
his hatred of witches will.

Since the publication of her first book in 1994, **Linda Winstead Jones** has published more than forty novels and novellas. She's a three-time finalist for the Romance Writers of America's RITA Award and a winner of the 2004 RITA Award for Best Paranormal Romance. She's also a two-time winner of the Colorado Romance Writers Award of Excellence. A compulsive taker of classes, she has studied Asian cooking, belly dancing, cake decorating, yoga, real estate, candy making, and creative writing. She was a full-time wife and mother for several years, and spent a few months here and there as a Realtor and candy maker. Linda and her husband owned a picture frame shop for several years before she left retail to pursue writing full-time. An active member of the Romance Writers of America, she lives in northern Alabama with her husband of more than thirty years. Visit her website at www.lindawinsteadjones.com.

Praise for *Emma's Secret*

"Readers who loved *A Woman of Substance* will enjoy *Emma's Secret*."
—*Denver Post*

"Promises to tantalize, mesmerize, and titillate readers of all ages. It has all the Bradford touches: strong and swift plot, hints of secrets about to be revealed…spellbinding…destined to fly off booksellers' racks and be passed around many book clubs. It is a darn good read."
—*Roanoke Times*

"It will be…appreciated by those with an irresistible desire to follow the further adventures of the Harte clan."
—*Publishers Weekly*

"You're certain these are living, breathing people."
—*USA Weekend*

"[An] original story with new energy. Emma Harte is one of those characters whom we never want to leave behind, and thank goodness Bradford has brought her back to us with a story worthy of this truly remarkable woman." —*Romantic Times*, "Top Pick"

"Promises to breathe new life into the popular series."
—*Fort Myers News-Press* (Florida)

More praise for Barbara Taylor Bradford and her novels

"Barbara Taylor Bradford is the storyteller of substance."
—*The Times* (London)

"An extravagant, absorbing novel of love, courage, ambition, war, death and passion."
—*The New York Times* on *A Woman of Substance*

"Pure gold." —*Cosmopolitan* on *Act of Will*

"Legions of readers will be satisfied by the romantic fortunes of the cultured, wealthy, and powerful people she evokes."
—*Publishers Weekly* on *The Women in His Life*

"Few novelists are as consummate as Barbara Taylor Bradford at keeping the reader turning the page. She is one of the world's best at spinning yarns." —*The Guardian* (UK) on *Dangerous to Know*

BOOKS BY BARBARA TAYLOR BRADFORD

SERIES
THE EMMA HARTE SAGA

A Woman of Substance

Hold the Dream

To Be the Best

Emma's Secret

OTHERS

Voice of the Heart

Act of Will

The Women in His Life

Remember

Angel

Everything to Gain

Dangerous to Know

Love in Another Town

Her Own Rules

A Secret Affair

Power of a Woman

A Sudden Change of Heart

Where You Belong

The Triumph of Katie Byrne

Three Weeks in Paris